Love in a Dead Language

Love
in a
Dead
Language

a romance by

Lee Siegel

being the Kamasutra *of*
Guru Vatsyayana Mallanaga
as translated and interpreted by
Professor Leopold Roth
with a foreword and annotation by
Anang Saighal
following the commentary of
Pandit Pralayananga Lilaraja

The University of Chicago Press • Chicago and London

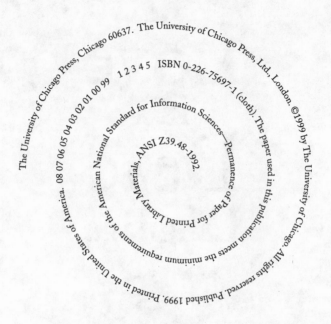

The University of Chicago Press, Chicago 60637. The University of Chicago Press, Ltd., London. ©1999 by The University of Chicago. All rights reserved. Published 1999. Printed in the United States of America. 08 07 06 05 04 03 02 01 00 99 1 2 3 4 5 ISBN 0-226-75697-1 (cloth). The paper used in this publication meets the minimum requirements of the American National Standard for Information Sciences—Permanence of Paper for Printed Library Materials, ANSI Z39.48-1992.

Lee Siegel is professor of Indian religions at the University of Hawaii. He is the author of five books, including *Net of Magic: Wonder and Deceptions in India* and *City of Dreadful Night: A Tale of Horror and the Macabre in India.*

Library of Congress Cataloging-in-Publication Data

Siegel, Lee, 1945–
Love in a dead language
Lee Siegel
p.   cm.
Includes bibliographical references (p.   ) and index.
ISBN 0-226-75697-1 (alk. paper)
I. Title.
PS3569.I377L68   1999
813´.54—dc21   98-31296
CIP

Illustration credits
Pages 284 and 319: *Lalita Weeps (as Radha),* 1998 (detail),
painting by Frank Gaard. ©Frank Gaard.
Page 320: *Client Trouble,* 1998 (detail), painting by
Frank Gaard. ©Frank Gaard.

to Bridget,

the actress and snake
charmer, who taught me
how not to be Leopold Roth
in love

—*Lee Siegel*

to Auddalaki,

the pedagogue of the
erotic arts and sciences, who
taught me the customs and conventions,
the mores and manners,
of love

—*Vatsyayana Mallanaga*

to Lalita,

the student, who taught
me the reality of the illusions
and the illusion of the realities that
are India, and her, and me,
and love

—*Leopold Roth*

to Mayavati,
the courtesan of Varanasi,
who taught me the terror of
beauty and the possibility of a
redemption in death
through love

—*Pralayananga Lilaraja*

to the professors,
ancient—Vatsyayana and
Pralayananga—and modern—
Leopold Roth and Lee Siegel—who taught
me about the *Kamasutra*, the
persistent textbook on love

—*Anang Saighal*

Contents

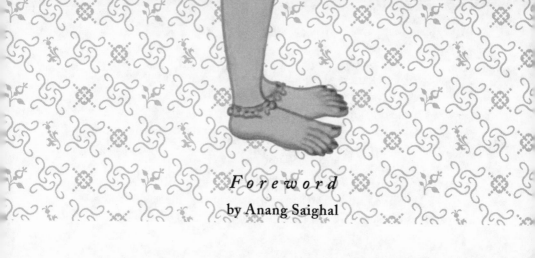

Foreword
by Anang Saighal

My dear Anang:

   I can appreciate your interest in the *Kamasutra*, but not your concern with Roth's perversion of that text. While I might concede that it is perhaps unfortunate that scholars lack substantial biographical information on Vatsyayana Mallanaga, I think it would be just as well if we are spared this incriminating evidence of the existence of Leopold Roth. Let him enjoy the very anonymity that has protected Vatsyayana from castigation. Roth's so-called "commentary" is no more than the intellectual jetsam of a troubled mind and the emotional flotsam of a wrecked heart. His gloss is as unfaithful to life as his translation is to text. I would never permit my name to be associated with a book such as this.

                                                    —Lee Siegel, personal communication

This is a book about love. It is a conglomeration of sundry understandings and misunderstandings, Eastern and Western, of love as a philosophical ideal and literary sentiment, an exhilarating transport and humiliating affliction, a promise of redemption and a threat of perdition.

   This is a translation from Sanskrit of the *Kāmasūtra* of Vātsyāyana, an Indian anatomy of love and grammar of sexual behavior. Spiraling around that ancient textual epicenter is the modern autobiographical commentary of the translator, Leopold Roth, which amounts to an intimate account of his liaison with a college student, Lalita Gupta, an East Indian girl born in the United States.

   The book is a love story, a true confession, and a murder mystery; it is a western (but there are no cowboys) and science fiction (and the science is sexology); there's philology and apology, travelogue and travesty. The text plays out as a rhetorical game in which the author struggles against the odds to win at love.

The words are spoken by many mouths and written by many hands. The two principal narrators are Pandit Vātsyāyana Mallanāga, Indian philosopher, pedagogue, and author of the *Kāmasūtra;* and the late Professor Leopold Roth, my former teacher, American Indologist, linguist, and translator-interpreter of the *Kāmasūtra.* Pralayānanga Līlārāja, literary dilettante and Hindu intellectual ornament to the Moghul court, and Anang Saighal (me), Indian-American doctoral candidate, annotator, and editor, provide supplementary commentary. These prolocutors, as players in the game, demand introduction.

VĀTSYĀYANA MALLANĀGA

We know very little about the Brahmin moralist who composed the *Kāmasūtra* by gathering and digesting a vast corpus of ancient, orally transmitted erotological data and dicta. Although the sober sexual savant may have lived any time between the fifth century B.C.E. and the fifth century C.E., the least frivolous of the tenuous biographical arguments place him in the robust and prosperous Gupta period (third century C.E.). We cannot be any more certain of where Vātsyāyana lived than of when; some historians maintain that he resided in Patna, others that he studied and taught in Varanasi, still others that his home was in Orissa. A few have said he never lived at all.

We do know that Vātsyāyana's academic imperative was to codify, and thus preserve, a body of traditional knowledge. He catalogued all aspects of love and types of lovers, their sexual proclivities and activities, as the sages who had come before him had objectified and evaluated them. This taxonomic act reflects a pervasive and persistent Indian intellectual impulse. All domains of life—erotic as well as linguistic, political, economic, and religious—all phases of experience were categorized, subcategorized, and sub-subcategorized compulsively and obsessively in the *śāstra*s, the learned compendiums and normative treatises that have regulated life in India throughout the history of that civilization. The implicit assumption behind the composition of this vast body of literature is that to catalogue and classify, to name and systematize, is to know and understand. The *Kāmasūtra* is the fun-

damentally representative text of a larger *śāstra* that details the traditional Indian perception of love, a scientific literature in which universal human passions and urges are ordered in accordance with
specific norms and official values. The *Kāmasūtra* was articulated in a
conventionally aphoristic style for a sophisticated audience of aristo-
crats and wealthy merchants, urbane gentlemen and sprightly ladies. It
was required reading for scholars, poets, physicians, litterateurs, aes-
thetes, artists, courtiers, courtesans, dandies, newlyweds, and anyone
else who aspired to be considered in any way cultured, cosmopolitan,
or charming.

Shortly after discovering that Roth was translating the *Kāmasūtra*,
I asked him whether or not, as he was working on Vātsyāyana's text,
he ever got a feeling for the individual, a sense of who the author was
as a man of flesh and blood with his own particular fears and personal
desires.

"No," Roth answered as he turned away from me to open the
Sanskrit-English dictionary that was always on his desk.

LEOPOLD ROTH

I first met Professor Roth in his office in Swinburne Hall in the fall of
1994. I had been accepted into the graduate program in Asian studies
at Western University in California, and he had duly agreed to supervise my work on a doctoral dissertation on the largely ignored genre of
Sanskrit commentarial literature. At the time his eyes were full of
sparkle; he joked continuously, bawdily, and often provocatively. He
did not seem to be in any way an unhappy man. I imagined that it
would be fun to be Leopold Roth.

Roth was born in 1945 in Los Angeles, California. His parents
were movie stars in the forties, fifties, and early sixties. After graduating from Hollywood High School, Roth received his undergraduate
education at the University of California at Berkeley (B.A., 1964); subsequent to a year or so of travel in continental Europe, he was admitted as a graduate student at Oxford University, where he was awarded
a doctoral degree in 1976 by the Faculty of Oriental Studies. Although
Roth's academic credentials were impressive, he published relatively
little during his professional career.

While at Oxford, he met Sophia White (b. 1950 in Reading, England), a fellow graduate student doing research on Restoration litera-

ture, and married her in 1974. A year later, Sophia White-Roth gave birth to twins, Isaac and Leila; the year after that, Roth and his wife received their degrees in the same ceremony in Oxford, and both secured teaching positions at Western University in the Departments of Asian Studies and English, respectively. When their daughter died at the age of twelve, the couple took a year's leave of absence from the university and went to Paris with their son in an attempt to recuperate from their grief. Professor White-Roth accepted a joint appointment in the Department of Women's Studies in 1991 and became dean of Academic Affairs in 1994.

Once every four or five years, beginning in 1974, Roth visited India for several months at a time. Each semester he taught an undergraduate survey course, Asian Studies 150B: Introduction to Indian Civilization (for which I was teaching assistant), and a graduate seminar devoted to the translation and interpretation of a selected Sanskrit text. The last seminar he taught, in the spring of 1997, was on the *Kāmasūtra*. I was the only student enrolled in the course.

As a consequence of the scandal over his professionally inappropriate, adulterous intrigue with Ms. Lalita Gupta, Professor Roth was suspended from teaching during the fall semester of 1997, and his wife of twenty-three years insisted on a separation. Roth's death in winter put an end to the divorce proceedings and his work on the *Kāmasūtra*. An announcement appeared last January in the *Western Crier,* the university's student newspaper:

> Professor Leopold Roth of the Department of Asian Studies was found dead during Christmas vacation in his office in Swinburne Hall. The presence of police investigators on campus, following the death of the faculty member, suggests that there may have been foul play. A secretary in the Office of University Relations, who does not want to be named, had "no comment."
>
> Dr. Roth, it may be recalled, was that Professor who caused so much trouble on campus last semester because of his sexual harassment of a female student from [*sic*] India. The University case against him is still pending. But, because he's dead, they'll probably drop charges.
>
> According to Dr. Paul Planter, Chairman of the Asian Studies Department, Professor Roth, who has published a few reviews as well as some very scholarly articles on India, was working on a translation of the *Kama Sutra,* the famous Indian sex manual that was recently made into a movie. Dr. Planter is preparing an obituary for this newspaper which will be published as soon as he finishes it.

Leopold Roth will be remembered not only as a sexual harasser, but also as a teacher by some undergraduates (who took his Asian Studies 150 class) and by a few graduate students (for his advanced seminars on Sandscript [*sic*]). He may also be remembered as a person by some of the people who knew him.

Roth died of a "subdural hematoma secondary to trauma associated with a basal skull fracture" that resulted from hitting the back of his head on the edge of his office desk in a fall apparently caused by being struck in the face with a large book, Monier Monier-Williams's weighty *Sanskrit-English Dictionary* (1899; reprint, Oxford: Oxford University Press, 1945). The assailant remains at large. Given police indifference to the matter, the question of who killed Leopold A. Roth has, I'm afraid, become an academic one.

Professor Roth had just begun Book Five of the *Kāmasūtra* when he was killed. I do not know to what extent he would have revised his work on the first four books. His translation, as it stands, is very capricious, but so was his life; the translation is, furthermore, often wrong, but no more so than the other published translations of the same text.[1] It has become my responsibility, as the result of my appointment as Roth's literary executor, to edit his translation, to cope with his errors and omissions, his inconsistencies and eccentricities. To this end, I have relied on the seventeenth-century Sanskrit gloss of Pandit Pralayānanga Līlārāja. Roth devoted an entire chapter to that literary figure in his doctoral monograph,[2] and I am writing extensively, in my

1. The text has been translated into English by Sir Richard Burton and F. F. Arbuthnot (1883) and S. C. Upadhyaya (1961), French by E. Lamairesse (1891) and Alain Daniélou (1992), German by Richard Schmidt (1907), Russian by Nikolay Stavrogin (1918), Hindi by Pandit Madhavacharya (1934) and Bipinchandra Bandhu (1943), Panjabi by Kashinath Saighal (1922), Persian by Pralayānanga Līlārāja (1661), Oriya by Vasishtha Mohanti (1939), Zemblan by Romulus Arnor (1956), and Japanese by Henry Kamisato (1996).

2. Roth's dissertation, "*Oflyricheros:* Anagramic Charades and Other Amphibological Verbal Constructions in Sanskrit Literature" (Oxford University, 1976) is a phenomenological study of semantic duplexities. In a "charade" it is not (as in simple anagrams) the order of the letters within words, phrases, sentences, or other semic units that are changed; rather, it is in altering the spaces between those letters that disparate messages emerge. The paronomasial dimension of a series phonemes is not established by the semantic resonances of individual pun-words; new meanings are discovered by dividing a set of phonemes at different points in that set. Thus the nonsense word in the title of Roth's dissertation, *Oflyricheros*, makes sense as "O fly, rich Eros!" and "Of lyric heros." This type of verbal puzzle is much more common in syllabic Sanskrit (in which manuscripts were commonly written without any lexical hiatuses) than in English. Pralayānanga composed a number of them.

own dissertation, about the intentions, conscious and unconscious, underlying Pralayānanga's commentarial discourse. Pralayānanga connects me to Roth.

PRALAYĀNANGA LĪLĀRĀJA

The Taj Mahal was under construction when Pralayānanga left Varanasi to accept a position as scholar in the court of Shah Jahan at Agra. In service of his Moghul patron, the Hindu pandit translated both the *Kāmasūtra* and the *Bhagavadgītā* into Persian, and he wrote original Sanskrit commentaries on those texts, which he then translated into the lingua franca of the court. While my interest has been in his commentaries (and particularly, at present, in his gloss of the *Kāmasūtra*[3]), Roth's scholarly concern had been with Pralayānanga's charadic composition, the *Kāmaśleṣakāvya*. Each of this poem's 181 stanzas, depending upon how the syllables are divided, can be read as the verses of a puritanical religious text or an obscene celebration of sexual love, or both. As the author of the work, Pralayānanga is mentioned in a seventeenth-century account of court life at Agra by the English traveler, diplomat, and linguist Sir Thomas Lovely in his *An Oriental Passage, being the Authentic Account of the Conquest of the East Indies:* "Our Party was well Amus'd by a Venerable Poetaster of the Sunscrit Language under the Patronage of the Drunken Mogul, one Prolayanunga Leeloraj, a Verbalyzer of Rhetorickal Curiosities, who Lectateth in two disp'rate Meaninges at one Tyme. One Stringe of Sounds speaketh simultaneous, hic & hoc, of Strumpette & God-All-Myghtie, & One knoweth not whiche-when."

Roth did an impressive job in his dissertation of translating the abstruse text and delineating the philological, rhetorical, and poetical implications of its verbal charades. He also suggested some of the psychological, epistemological, and metaphysical ramifications of the semantic phenomenon:

---

3. In addition to Pralayānanga's gloss, I have consulted that of Yaśodhara (thirteenth century), the *Jayamangalā* (and occasionally the eighteenth-century commentary of Narsingh Śāstrī). In his notes at the end of each of the seven books of the *Kāmasūtra*, Yaśodhara wistfully confesses that he has composed his scholium in order to find, in that literary endeavor, solace from the pain of separation from his beloved, a cunning and beautiful young girl after whom he has named his commentary (*jayamangalā* literally means "a sign or omen for the conquest [of death]").

Does meaning reside in the utterance, in the sounds themselves, whether or not it is understood or even perceived (as the Indian poet/priest would have it)? Or, as common sense tells us, is utterance, written or spoken, merely the medium for the articulation of a meaning as necessarily consciously conceived by a particular writer or speaker for a reader or listener? Do the ambiguities of language, so vividly demonstrated by charades, wherein two or more incongruous and even contradictory lexemes reside in a single set of phonemes, recapitulate unnameable paradoxes inherent in being itself? Is our understanding of the world simply a question of where we put the blank spaces, of how we, consciously or not, divide ourselves and all that we perceive? The empirical structure of time prevents us, of course, from changing the order of phenomenal events, of having anagrammatic experiences, but nothing hinders our determination of what constitutes the beginning or end of anything. What is the relationship (as either established by or reflected in rhetorical language) between the question ("Am I able to get her?") and the fantasy ("Amiable together")? Once you become aware of charades, you cannot help but take uneasy note of the "manslaughter" inherent in a "woman's laughter."[4]

Lovely gives an intriguing account of the death of Pralayānanga, a story corroborated by Shāhnavāz Khān Khus Emak Awrangābādī in the *Maāthir-ul-Umarā* (2:187–229), elaborated in a nineteenth-century Sanskrit anthology of biographical sketches, the *Vidūṣakamāla* of Bhagavanlal Indraji (4:32), exaggerated in oral folk tales, and summarized in Roth's dissertation as follows:

Māyāvatī was not her real name, but it was what they called her in the royal harem in Agra. She had been the protégée of a famous madam in Varanasi, the proprietress of a prosperous brothel that catered to the appetites of wealthy merchants (or, more often, the sons of those businessmen and their cronies). The pleasures for sale there were not only sexual—one went to that bordello to drink wine (often opiated or spiked with datura), chew betel, smoke tobacco and hashish, eat delicious snacks, listen to music, and watch the dancing of beautiful girls. Māyāvatī, purchased from her father as a child for a considerable sum because of her astonishingly promising beauty, had been well trained by the madam in the arts of giving pleasure as classically delineated in the *Kāmasūtra;* a mastery of the erotic techniques and graceful contortions codified in that text transformed a common whore into a refined hetæra. Māyāvatī was an excellent student. Her talent was so notable, in fact, that her teacher was able to sell her to an agent from the court of the great Moghul.

4. *Oftyricheros,* 418. One might add that, once you become aware of charades, you cannot help but take note of the "old rot" in the middle of "Leopold Roth."

Ibn al-Qifti, the eunuch in charge of the quarters for the female en-
tertainers, a trusted confidante and advisor to Shah Jahan, had special
plans for Māyāvatī. As the Moghul rulers did not observe a policy of pri-
mogeniture, murder was in many situations the most convenient means of
social advancement. The court was a world of intrigue and mistrust; power
was a liability. Anyone in a high position, with any real political influence,
had servants to taste his food and wine for poison, so Ibn al-Qifti developed a secret weapon—Māyāvatī.

A snake charmer who frequently entertained at fairs and festivals in
the fort supplied the eunuch with vials of deadly venom. This Ibn al-Qifti
gradually introduced into Māyāvatī's diet. She ingested only the smallest
drops of it at first, then, after several months, a spoonful, then two, and
within a year she was able to drink a cup of it without manifesting any of
the symptoms of poisoning. After another year had passed, she herself was
as virulent as the deadliest of cobras. Her saliva, sweat, blood, urine, sexual fluids, and tears were lethal.

Awrangābādī estimates that, with the approval of the emperor, Ibn
al-Qifti used Māyāvatī to remove more than a dozen men from the
court.

Although Pralayānanga Līlārāja was essentially a professor, and particularly a Sanskrit scholar, he had, beyond his job as translator and commentator, a variety of functions at court. As a literary critic he was inevitably called upon to judge poetry contests and to evaluate the works of
writers seeking patronage. But he was also expected to be an entertainer,
to dramatically recount Hindu legends of love and death and, even more
often, given his particular talents, to recite riddles, palindromes, and charades, to present the courtiers, for their amusement, with conundrums and
semantic puzzles—anagrams, logograms, and metagrams, acrostics and
amphiboles. Professor Līlārāja was a celebrity; to chuckle in comprehen-
sion and appreciation of his wit was the mark of a clever man.

Pralayānanga had often watched Māyāvatī dance. Although he was
dazzled by her beauty, charmed by her voice in song, and enthralled by
the serpentine movement of her body, he dared not make advances, as intimacies with the female performers were strictly reserved for particular
men of rank as well as for certain diplomats and dignitaries from other
provinces and lands. Such women, it was known, often secretly took lovers
of their own choosing, but they would inevitably be young and typically
dashing; Pralayānanga was a scholar in his fiftieth year.

He was resting in the shade of an ashoka tree after a bath in the Ya-
muna when Māyāvatī first spoke to him. He was startled that not only did
she know his name, but she also could recite one of the puzzle-poems that
he had presented in court.

"I want you to teach me," she said. "I want to learn Sanskrit. A knowledge of that language is the only subject within Vātsyāyana's curriculum
of which I am completely innocent. With a mastery of it, I will be the most
accomplished courtesan in India. After I am too old to work as I do now,

I will be able to have my own pleasure house, and it will be the finest school of all. I will teach my daughters the arts and sciences of love, all of the disciplines in the *Kāmasūtra*. Not only will they speak refined Hindi and Persian with their suitors, they will be able to recite Sanskrit poetry and whisper the most ancient and mysterious words of love."

With the permission of Ibn al-Qifti and the approval of Shah Jahan's office, Pralayānanga became Māyāvatī's tutor. In all accounts of the story, while Pralayānanga had become infatuated with her at first sight, she fell in love with him slowly, gradually, in the same protracted way in which she had acquired her immunity to snake venom.

After months of teaching the girl, Pralayānanga could restrain himself no longer from confessing his overwhelming, all-consuming love. She turned away so that he would not see the tears in her eyes as she told him that, although she loved him as well, adored him with all her heart, they could not be lovers: "You have been different with me than any other man. I find myself waiting anxiously for our lessons. I am always eager for your arrival. I want more than anything to be your lover. But it is impossible." And then she told him why, explaining that to be kissed by her would be the same as to be bitten by a cobra, to be held in her arms would be no different than to be entwined in the coils of a krait. "I am death," she whispered.

The story ends with a strange rape, a curious rapture. As Pralayānanga, protesting that his love has checked all fear of death, forces himself on Māyāvatī, she fights him off. She does so in order to save him, struggling against the desires that are hers as much as his, physically resisting him while crying out that she loves and desires him.

Pralayānanga made love with Māyāvatī only once. In every version of the story, they say that as the professor died, although there were tears in his eyes, he smiled. The nineteenth-century Sanskrit redactor of the narrative adds that "the radiance of the joyous smile was the very splendor of [a knowledge or experience of] eternity."

"Why," Roth asked in a footnote to the story, "I always wonder, are so many people willing, happy, and even eager to die for love in literature, when no one would want to do so in real life?" In some ways Roth's commentary on the *Kāmasūtra* is, I would suggest, an attempt to answer that question.

ANANG SAIGHAL

I first discovered the *Kāmasūtra* in my parents' library. As doctors, they naturally had many medical books in their collection; as a nine-year-old boy, I took a special interest in the obstetrical and gynecological texts. In secret study, I marveled over the extravagantly flocculent mons veneris, the demure prepuce, the pearly clitoris, the shadowy vestibule, the puckered urethra meatus, the yawning labia majora and minora, the ravening vaginal portal, the esoteric fourchette, and the contumelious anus. It was among these texts that I encountered the *Kāmasūtra* of Vātsyāyana for the first time. It was in English, illustrated with racy prints of Indian miniatures and spicy photographs of temple facades, and there was a publisher's note on the first page that made the find all the more thrilling: "The sale of this book is strictly restricted to scholars of Indology and philology, members of the medical and legal professions, and officials of the Government of India." As I clandestinely surveyed the copulatory postures represented by the Indian artists in stone and paint, the book evoked a steamy and hallowed world of luxurious sex, an uncharted land of mountains, deserts, and jungles awaiting exploration and conquest, survey and settlement—my father's world: INDIA. It was to that voluptuous terra incognita that I owed the color of my hair, eyes, and skin, and, I believed, the darkness of my dreams. I imagined that I would someday discover my adulthood and excavate my sexuality in that faraway realm of my paternal ancestors.

I might not ever have gone to India, my father's motherland, if my mother had not died. That she, an oncologist, died of uterine cancer led me to anticipate that my father, a psychiatrist, would someday go insane. In his currently thriving practice in London, he specializes in cross-cultural psychiatry, dealing particularly with the mental health of the Indian immigrant community in the West.

My parents first met as medical students at Washington University in St. Louis and then ran into each other several years later in Indianapolis, where quite coincidentally they had both gone into practice. It was there that they married and that I was born in 1965.

My mother's name was Rebecca. Although neither of my parents were religious in either belief or observance, my mother was a Jew, a racial fact that caused considerable problems not only for her and my Hindu father with their respective respectable families, but also for me, years later, with my doctoral supervisor—Professor Leopold Roth. He considered himself a Jew and me a Hindu, but according to Hebraic law, I am the authentic Jew. My mother was Jewish, his is not—it's that simple. I suspect that Roth resented that fact. Envy would occasionally express itself in unpredictable and unpleasant shows of disdain; belittling my written, academic attempts to articulate insights into

Sanskrit literature, he seemed intent on proving to me that I did not understand India.

I was sympathetic, however, because I envied him as well; I was covetous of his having a mother who is still alive. I believe that if my mother had been there to encourage me, to read to me, to tell me how wonderful I was and how much I was loved, I could exhibit Roth's extroversion and outrageousness, his confidence and willingness to indulge himself so unabashedly and irrepressibly. I would have the forbearance to write books and not merely to annotate them. Furthermore, I would probably have had enough of a sense of self-interest to refuse to edit this text. Yes, instead I would have finished my own dissertation on the forms and functions of Sanskrit commentaries.

After my mother's death, my father, feeling unequipped to care for a young boy, sent me to the Scindia School in Gwalior. They did not teach us very much about India in India; we learned Western things in Western ways. There were no girls at the boarding school, and the British legacy of flogging was the perfunctory punishment for masturbation. Sleepless and restless after "lights out," I'd peruse by furtive flashlight beam the preciously and inspirationally transgressive copy of the *Kāmasūtra* that I had stolen from home and smuggled into that citadel of adolescent castaways. After stripping the book of its jacket, I had disguised the text with the cover from a book that had been a wedding gift to my mother from her father-in-law—Annie Besant's translation of the *Bhagavadgītā*. I was able to earn a bit of pocket money by renting the book out to the other boys for five rupees a night. Its only competition was a pornographic novel, *Dolly, or The Trials and Tribulations of a White Slave Girl* (four rupees per night), in which a young American girl, touring Europe with her parents, is kidnapped in Paris by a Turk and sold to an aging maharaja at a slave market in Istanbul. Taking her, bound and gagged, back to India, the randy potentate, assisted by a staff of lusty male and female servants, forces her to perform, one by one, the myriad sexual acts that are enumerated in Book Two of the *Kāmasūtra*. Actual quotes from Vātsyāyana serve as epigraphs for the lewd episodic descriptions of Indic copulation. The illicit circulation of *Dolly* proved to be good advertising, whetting the appetites of the cloistered adolescents for the copy of the *Kāmasūtra* that I had on the nocturnal market. By the time I packed it up to take with me to St. Stephen's College in Delhi, my book had become ragged and worn by the nervous hands of the pubescent caitiffs in their secret midnight raptures.

In my senior year at St. Stephen's, I wrote a prize-winning paper entitled "Love as Game in Laurence Sterne's *Tristram Shandy*." There were superficial comparisons with the love poetry of Kālidāsa, a selection of whose works I, necessarily and desultorily, read in English. When Vikram Bahadur, my only intellectual rival in English literature at St. Stephen's, reported me to the principal for having a copy of the *Kāmasūtra* in my hostel locker, I evaded expulsion with the inspired explanation that it had been necessary to consult the "normative *śāstra*, not only in order to decode various amorous allusions in Kālidāsa, but also to elucidate the mores of the cultural context and literary milieu in which the essential aesthetic sentiment had been realized by the Indian poet." I claimed, furthermore, that I had reason to believe that Sterne, through his relationship with Mrs. Draper, the woman in India whom he called his "Bramine," was acquainted with the *Kāmasūtra*.

Bahadur's calumnious treachery against me backfired—the principal, a witless (and, at least latently, pederastic) Anglo-Indian pedant, punished poor Bahadur for merely knowing what the *Kāmasūtra* was. It is a dangerous book.

As a consequence of that essay, I was awarded a scholarship at the East-West Center (a name that, at the time, had fatidic significance to the child of a man from the East and a woman from the West) in Honolulu, Hawaii, in the middle of the ocean, a center far away from anywhere, a place from which America and Asia were peripheral and Europe was antipodal. In packing for the new adventure, I tossed my *Kāmasūtra* into a garbage bin together with the only other bits of Sanskrit literature that I had read—my volume of English selections from Kālidāsa, from which I had haphazardly culled quotes for my paper, and my mother's *Bhagavadgītā*. I wanted to leave India in India.

Contrary to my own interest in writing a thesis on Sterne, I found myself compelled to pursue my master's degree in Indian studies simply because, while nothing I said or wrote about English literature had any credibility to my American professors, anything and everything I offered about India or Sanskrit literature was "absolutely fascinating." They were, no doubt, intimidated by the mystic East, if not the entire Third World; they seemed to believe that certain kinds of cultural knowledge are congenital, that the capacity to know is racial, and that the right to know is political. It would have been foolish not to take advantage of their folly. Everyone in America wanted to hear about the

Kāmasūtra and Tantric sex, to know why our women have dots on their foreheads and why we consider cows sacred.

It was relatively easy for me to passably mug up Sanskrit, not only because I knew some Hindi, but more so because I had studied Latin at St. Stephen's. I have always liked languages.

I received my master's degree after writing, with the encouragement and guidance of Professor Lee Siegel, a thesis entitled "Love as Game in the Works of Kālidāsa" (full of quotes from the *Kāmasūtra* that proved the poet's dependence on that text and peppered with epigraphs from *Tristram Shandy*). I resolved to continue on for a doctorate in Indian studies, to matriculate at Western University in California under the tutelage of Professor Leopold Roth, whose dissertation I had read with some interest. Siegel strongly advised against it.[5]

Roth's seminar on the *Kāmasūtra* in the spring of 1997 brought the text back into my life and introduced me to Pralayānanga's commentary. As Roth's only graduate student at the time, I was appointed as his literary executor by his wife at the recommendation of Dr. Paul Planter, chairman of the Department of Asian Studies. "Literary executor" is a rather lofty title for the person given the chore of cleaning out Roth's office, a task which Professors Planter and White-Roth assumed would involve no more than sorting through the deceased faculty member's mail, taking his overdue books back to the library, and throwing away his papers. It was in undertaking that appointment, however, that I discovered, in the office in Swinburne Hall where I had first met Roth, the notebooks that make up the original manuscript for this book.

After struggling through page after handwritten page of often illegible translation and commentary,[6] cutting my way through the autographic and orthographic overgrowth, a discursive jungle of personal

5. Siegel had been a friend of Roth's when they were postgraduate students together in the Faculty of Oriental Studies at Oxford University, but Roth, for some reason, liked to demean Professor Siegel both in print and in conversation. In a scathing review of the publication of Siegel's Oxford dissertation, *Sacred and Profane Love in Indian Traditions* (1979), Roth described the book as "pretentious sciolistic fustian."

6. While Roth certainly knew how to type, and he did use a computer for correspondence, university documents, academic papers, and other projects, he undertook the composition of the present manuscript in longhand, using a Koh-I-Noor fountain pen. "You'll understand, Saighal," he grinned almost demoniacally shortly before his death, "it's one of those charades that we've talked about: 'Penis—pen is.' 'A pen is required to write' equals 'A penis required to write.' Paper is womb, ink indelible sperm, and the charade proves it— 'Ink is semen: Drip erotic all mankind!' equals 'In kiss, emend ripe rot: I call Man "kind."'"

abbreviations and recondite allusions, obscure solecisms and idiosyn-
cratic spellings, frantic cross-outs and crazed catachreses, emotional
digressions and textual lacunae, obscenities and epiphanies, lovesick
rantings and erotical ravings, not to mention sudden and constant fluctuations in form, style, and mood, I felt, for some reason that is still not
really clear to me, that (despite advice to the contrary from Planter,
Siegel, my father, and others) to edit and annotate the manuscript was
the least that I could do in memory a man who died while trying his
very best, with all his heart, to write a book about love. And so, once
again, I opened the *Kāmasūtra*.

Santa Aghora, California
April 1998

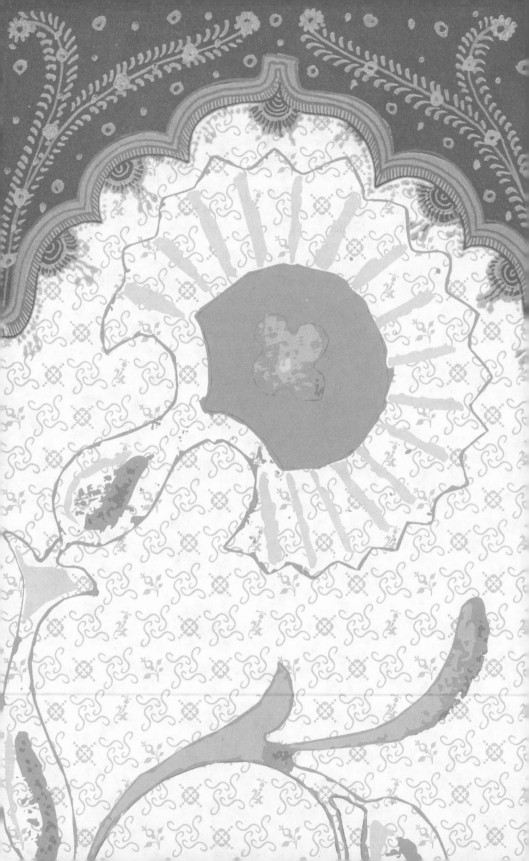

I

PROLEGOMENON

During this painful period in his life, a time in which he felt threatened by what he called his "Oriental distractions," Lee, drinking even more gin than usual, was trying to use writing as a method of dealing with the failure of his erotic impulses, as a way of understanding, if not overcoming, his inability to forge a strong and rational, peaceful and permanent love relationship. Writing was consciously a therapeutic activity meant to keep him out of Bedlam, a means of ordering his emotions and thoughts, his fears and desires. His concern, at least in the particular text that we are considering here, was with the distinctive madness that is provoked by sexual longing, the melancholy that is precipitated by love. Lee wanted to write about love in all its aspects, the most terrible and the most amusing, the most depraved and the most sublime, the most passionate and the most charitable. And while it may be tempting to look for autobiographical reference and indeed outright confession in Lee's work, the text is ultimately not so much either about love or about Lee as it is about the process of writing—writing about love, oneself, and writing.

—Sophia White-Roth, *Love and Madness
in the Life and Plays of Nathaniel Lee:
A Psychoanalytic Approach to Literary Criticism*

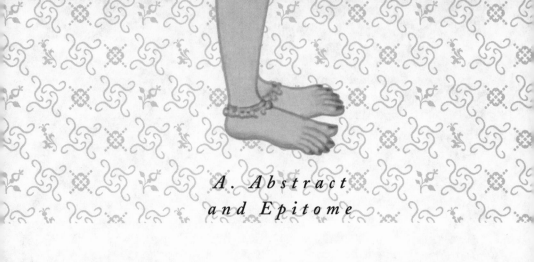

A. Abstract
and Epitome

In the beginning *kama* seized upon an unevolved cosmos and fashioned the imaginable out of the unimaginable. Sages, gazing with wisdom into their hearts, saw the all-permeating power take shape as an omnipotent god—Kama. They made obeisance to the deity, sang hymns of praise, and performed solemn sacrifices. But Kama, rejecting their offerings and songs, laughed. When he so mocked them with uproarious laughter, they were bewildered and asked the reason for it. The god forged his laughter into words: "If a man who is pious seeks merit through sacred acts, I laugh at him. If a man who is intelligent seeks understanding through knowledge, I laugh at him. If a man who is righteous seeks honor through virtuous deeds, I laugh at him. If a man, whether wise or foolish, virtuous or depraved, seeks satisfaction in love, I laugh at him as well. Though he fancies himself my ally, I laugh especially at him." "But why?" the sages asked. And Kama laughed at their question.

—The *Hasyalapa Brahmana* of the *Red Yajur Veda*

1. PREAMBLE

A. TRANSLATION

Blessed be religion, money, and love! [1] And blessed be the professors whose teachings promise that we can understand those things!

In the beginning, the creator of heaven and earth delivered to the creatures he had created a hundred thousand methodological lectures on three primary aspects of existence—religion (morality), econom-

---

1. "Love" is Roth's rendering of *kāma*. The Sanskrit term means desire, pleasure, and sexual love (the desire for it, and/or its objects, and the pleasure derived from it, and/or its objects). *Kāma* was considered both a universal and personal power, an external and internal energy (linking psyche and cosmos). That force, personified as Kāmadeva, was also generally known as Māra (Death).

ics (politics), and love (sex). The gods used the latter revelation to compile a syllabus of sexual love in a thousand installments.

Then the sage Auddalaki [2] digested those erotic teachings into five hundred lessons, which, in turn, were abridged by a board of scholars into one hundred fifty disquisitions organized around seven subjects: general observations, copulation, seduction, marriage, adultery, prostitutes, and erotic arcana.

At the request of the whores of Patna, a certain professor, who was no stranger to the demimonde, transcribed the sixth part of the codex, the homilies on harlotry, into a separate monograph. Likewise another professor redacted the introductory lectures into a discrete prolegomenon. While one scholar handled the handbook of the copulatory sciences (physical and social), another dealt with the (fine and applied) arts of seduction. Yet another editor compiled the dissertation on marriage, while another compiler edited the compendium on adultery. A learned doctor took responsibility for the technical conspectus on sexual esoterica. Thus the encyclopedia, divided up into different parts and written up by so many academics, was fractured; since each of the professors only edited one of the various sections of the magnum opus, that greater, original tome became inaccessible. And that's the reason for the composition of my textbook, the *Kamasutra*.[3]

B. COMMENTARY

Blessed be Lalita Gupta! Blessed is the natural religion promised by imagining Her embrace (O immaculate Lalita of Hindoostan!—intercessoress and sorceress, giggling goddess of grim grace); and blessed are the extravagant economics of Her flesh as it glows in my dreams (O precious Lalita of Golconda!—fleshpot in the flesh, mammary

2. The Brahmin sage Auddālaki was initiated as young man into the sexological school of Vedic liturgy, wherein coitus was practiced as a form of the solemn Aryan sacrifice: "Woman is a sacrificial fire, O Auddālaki: the penis is her fuel and the vulva is her flame with pubic hair as its smoke; when a man enters her that's the stoking; his semen is the offering, and her orgasm is the bright sparks flying" *(Hiraṇyadarpaṇa Upaniṣad)*. The story of the seduction of Auddālaki by a young female student named Vijayā (and how he subsequently began to value sexual union for its own sake, for the intimacy with the girl that it provided him and as a means for pleasure rather than as an impersonal ritual act endowing the community with magical access to the gods) is preserved in Pralayānanga's commentary on the *Kāmasūtra*.

3. Note that Roth abjures the diacritical marks that one expects from an academic Sanskritist (though he did use them in his Oxford dissertation). In these annotations, however, I have maintained the appropriate protocol for transliteration as standardized by the Monier Monier-Williams *Sanskrit-English Dictionary* that killed Roth.

mammon)—the economy of Her breath, the liquidations of Her glance, (what I suppose to be) Her golden touch, and the booty of Her feet—issuing and floating the stocks and bonds of love (the squandered wages of my sins, the loss of interest and all that is invested); and blessed are the politics of this, my newborn lust for the unknown (imperial Lalita, begging begum of the lunatic fringe, maharanical mystress of the house performing acts of congress), the love that She reminds me of (O concupiscent Lalita of Konarka—prurient priestess of the Black Pagoda, devastating *devadasi* and noumenal nautch girl, subaltern subject of my subtext).

Blessed be the Creator for creating Her, if only so that I might recompose Her here, in these notes, my ecstatic excursus, this *Lalita-sutra!* This commentarial re-creation, my diverting recreation, is so that I can see Her naked, stripped by heat and me, and adorned with earrings, nose ring, anklets, bracelets, necklaces, and girdle bells—all silver and shimmering.

Lalita, I want to hear You speak to me someday in tongues, paying lip service; let me taste You (with a kiss that forms a gustatory Mobius strip, organ of taste tastefully tasting the tasty taste of the tasting organ of taste), smell You (alone, I slowly, nervously inhale and tre-tre-tremble with lie-centious anticipations), feel You (right now I rub my fingers lightly over the cover of my ninety-seven-year-old copy of the text and the faded black cotton is the skirt tight around Your hips, and I open up the well-fingered book and You and tenderly rub fingertips across delicate pages that are the color of Your transubstantiated skin, the slightly raised bumps and faint depressions, imprint marks of Devanagari script on both sides of the fragile page, are pores and goose bumps). Will You ever be real to the touch? Will You ever cast a shadow on my wall or be a reflection in my mirror?

In longing to see, hear, taste, smell, and feel Her, I, as a frantic suppliant, chant the thousand names of Lalita.[4] Inspired by Vatsyayana,

4. "I chant the thousand names of Lalita" seems to be a reference to the *Śrī-Lalitā-Sa-hasranāma (The Thousand Names of the Blessed Lalitā* [circa eighth century C.E.]), a devotional text in which the goddess Lalitā is imagined to be the ultimate and absolute reality, transcendent and yet immanent. The universe is contained in her womb, and she is contained in all things. Folded over and inserted in the manuscript of this first notebook of Roth's *Kāmasūtra* were several sheets of lined legal-size yellow paper on which Roth had hand written a thousand cognomina, presumably sobriquets for his beloved Lalita: some phonic (Lolita, Lilata, Lulita, Lewd-Lee-ta, Kalita, Nalita, Jolly-ta, Polly-ta, Bali-ta, Call-ita, Wall-ita, All-eat-a, Tall-ita, Dolly-ta, Moll-ita, Volley-ta, Hall-ita, Pall-ita, Gall-ita,Folly-ta, Fall-ita, Qualita); some anagrammatic (Atilla, Illata, La Tail). The personal as-

I undertake this grammar of love[5] so that it might be more accessible to Lalita. I shall publish it or perish for Her: She must, I believe, learn the history of Her race, remember past lives, and discover the India She magically embodies (Her breasts its mountains, Her hair its forests, Her belly its plains, Her sweat its monsoon rains). It's the least I can do; She is, after all, enrolled in my class—Asian Studies 150B: Introduction to Indian Civilization. My mandate is to teach Her the language of that land, the figures and ornaments, images and metaphors with which She might articulate innate understandings that She does not know She knows and understands. I dream that She might repeat after me, might then sing to me songs that reveal memories of many lives in many ages. I shall offer Her an eternity, one that I might share with Her even for a moment. Lalita Gupta is the reason for this text.

2. CONTENTS

A. TRANSLATION

The *Kamasutra* presents all the topics that were covered in the vast and ancient lost encyclopedia of love in seven concise books.

Book One: introductory reflections on religion, money, and love; a theory of erotic education and knowledge; a survey of the lifestyles of the rich and famous; a classification of friends and paramours

---

sociations around some of the other names (e.g., Sunita, Lakmé, Mayavati, Bramine, Mumtaz, etc.) became clear to me only after a study of the complete manuscript. This note should give at least enough of the idea of the tedious whole to obviate any need to reprint the list in toto.

5. "Grammar of love": Rudolf Roth, a pioneer of Sanskrit studies, wrote an article, *"Eine Grammatik der Liebe und der Sexualität"* (*Zeitschrift der Deutschen Morgenländischen Gesellschaft* [1879], 147–83), in which he argued that Vātsyāyana's *Kāmasūtra* is formally modeled upon the teachings of the grammarian Pāṇini's *Aṣṭādhyāyī* (circa 400 B.C.E.) and that the form of the text is its meaning. The *Kāmasūtra*, he contended, is not a manual (since it covers neither usage, nor style, nor even meaning), but is instead a grammar (elucidating structure, syntax, inflection, and accidence) in which sexual activities are conjugated and sexual objects declined. Leopold Roth claimed (falsely I assume) to be the great-great-grandson of this great, great philologian who, together with Otto Böhtlingk, compiled that incomparable monument to German academic industry, the *Sanskrit-Wörterbuch* (St. Petersburg: Academy of Arts and Sciences, 1875). Had our Roth been using that lexicon instead of the ten-pound Monier-Williams English abridgement of it, he might still be alive—since the *Sanskrit-Wörterbuch* is ten volumes in length (and five pounds per volume), Roth's assailant would certainly not have been able to strike him with it. He would likewise still be among of us if he had been using the dictionary that I used to use, Pandurang Hari's *Sanskrit-English Dictionary for Foreigners*, which weighs a mere twenty-eight ounces and has a soft paper cover.

Book Two: coital conditions in terms of size, time, and circumstance; divers kinds of pleasure; caresses and kisses; scratching and love bites; an ethnographic survey of lovemaking; sexual acrobatics; spanking and moaning; women acting like men; oral sex and aural pleasure; love spats, pro and con; beginning and culminating intercourse

Book Three: choosing the right girl, getting intimate with her, and winning her trust; stratagems for seduction; a hermeneutics of erotic affects; insurance policies for fidelity

Book Four: marriage and the conduct of faithful wives; the deportment of mistresses; the mien of shrews and the demeanor of men in love with multiple women

Book Five: adultery and moral conduct; turning things around; men who are successful at scoring with women; the easy lay; sexual offenses and defenses; sentimental diagnostics and prognostics

Book Six (for harlots): a classification of clients; closing the deal; marketing and public relations; faking it; ways and means of cashing in on sex; symptoms of disaffection; dumping a lover; love and money

Book Seven: cosmetics and patents for potency; reviving lost passion; penis enlargement and vaginal constriction; pharmacological miscellanea

Since a preview of what is to be read is inevitably desired by the educated people of this world, this abstract has explained all that will be covered in the seven books of the *Kamasutra*.

B. COMMENTARY

As Vatsyayana begins by revealing what his text contains, so I, taking him as my model, must do the same. That's one of the rules of my game. I follow him like a shadow.[6]

---

6. And I follow Roth like a shadow of a shadow—where his foot has gone, my footnotes have dutifully ensued. Book One: I was overwhelmed by obscure allusions, unfaithful translations, inflated rhetoric, and embarrassing intimacies. Book Two: I struggled with sorting out chronologies and modulating formal extravagances. Book Three: Not too bad; I felt curiously at home in India. Book Four: Things (people and words) fell apart, turned upside-down and inside out. Books Five and Six: Left me alone, a student without a teacher, an editor without a text, an annotator staring anxiously at a blank page. Book Seven: I still don't know what I'm going to do about it.

Book One: the erotic imagination; who I am, who She is (and why); of India and Lalita, womanifestations geographic and anthropomorphic of one dread power; of phantasies and phrailties. There's psychology and sighcology, and amidst grand theory, I reveal plots and plans.

Book Two: a geology and geography of sex; a poly-sigh and hystery of sex; a grammar, rhetoric, lexicography, and phonology of sex; on the funambulistics, hydraulics, and pneumatics of sex; a gastronomy and anatomy of sex; a malacology, teratology, and volcanology and, indeed, an eschatology and teleology of sex. In my book, as in my life, form is content.

Book Three: An Oriental Passage, being the Authentic Account of the Conquest of the East Indies, with Divers Papers relating to the Antiquities, Amorous Habits, and Statistics of the Land, and Notices on its Wild Races, Venomous Snakes, and Curious Characters, this greatly enlarged by the Author with Poetical Remains on the Subject of the Mysterious Hindoo Woman, A.D. MCMXCVII

Book Four: It was supposed to be about marriage, a place to write about Sophia, how we met, fell in love, married, and had two children; about how her conception of love as the perfection of acceptance and forgiveness allowed me my dreams, transports, and most exquisite miseries. And I was going to write about how Lalita renewed me, amplified my capacities in the give-and-take of love. Lalita and Sophia, two perfections, I was going to say, and describe the perfect resolution of what they are—passion and allegiance, adultery and marriage, fire and water. Both of them were going to love me in a book of jubilations. Instead there was loss and despair. And I am now alone.

[Books Five and Six]:[7]

Book Seven: Sums it all up, explains what love is, and why, and how. The book is definitive, says it all, explains Erotic Apotheosis and Amorous Assumption. It is my Passion Play. I

7. Each of the entries describing the contents of the seven books of commentary on the *Kāmasūtra* was scribbled on a separate page of the notebook for Book One. That the pages for Books Five and Six were blank suggests that, with the completion of each book, Roth would go back to record what he imagined to have been his accomplishments (Indological, literary, and erotic). While Roth's death, at the outset of his work on Book Five, prevented him from describing the contents of Books Five and Six, he did seem to have an idea (grandiose as it was) of what he hoped to accomplish in the final book.

can't reveal the Magnum Mysterium yet; don't look ahead, not until it's time—reading, like love, is a game, and there have to be some rules.

Since a preview of what is to be read is inevitably desired by the educated people of this world, including You, sweet Ms. Gupta, sitting in the second row of the class, third from the end, **this abstract explains what will be covered** in my commentary to my translation—my nightmares and the shadows I have cast.[8]

---

8. "Nightmares and shadows": a somewhat lugubrious play, I assume, on *chāyā*, the Sanskrit word for "nightmare, shadow, shade, or reflection," referring also to a translation or, more precisely, to a textual gloss. If we imagine the *Kāmasūtra* as an opaque disc and the commentaries upon it as light cast by four luminous points (representing Yaśodhara [Y], Pralayānanga [P], Roth [R], and me [S], respectively) arranged as corners of a square (this text), the relationship between the primary text and the sundry commentaries upon it can be diagrammed in such a way that the various meanings, umbral and penumbral, can be distinguished and understood in relationship to each other.

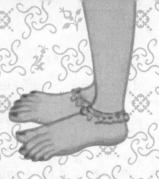

B. Ideals and Fulfillment

Without *kama* there cannot be desire for either wealth or religious redemption, for without *kama* there is no desire nor indeed anyone to desire. Sages who immerse themselves in asceticism do so out of *kama*, out of a desire for the benefits of nondesire. *Kama* is the source of everything, and the end, the well-spring of happiness (if not misery). So, celebrate *kama*—delight with women who have lovely voices, swollen breasts, moist loins, who are elegantly attired, richly adorned, and ever prone to love.

—The *Kamastotra* from the *Blue Yajur Veda*

1. DEFINITIONS

A. TRANSLATION

Human beings find fulfillment in religion, money, and love. For different people, one of these ideals might be more significant than the others; for example, money is the most important to priests and whores. But all three ideals have value, and since life is so very transient, we must cultivate what we can, when we can, and find meaning where we can, if we can.

Because religion is essentially metaphysical, explanations of it are appropriately delineated in scriptures; likewise, the attainment of wealth results from studying books on economics, finance, and business administration. Since sexual pleasure is experienced quite naturally even by beasts, some professors have argued that textbooks on the subject are inconsequential. I maintain, however, that a man and woman who crave sexual union are in dire need of teaching if they hope to find any fulfillment in sexuality as an ideal, as love. And so I,

Vatsyayana, by means of the *Kamasutra*, offer ancient techniques for the realization of love.

Love may be generally defined as a predilection for appreciating other human beings through the senses—the hearing ear, the touching skin, the seeing eye, the tasting tongue, and the smelling nose, as superintended by the thinking mind in conjunction with the conscious self.

B. COMMENTARY

The *Kamasutra*, chrestomathy of love, sexual grammar, and guidebook to pleasure—this text. My commentary, as my reflections on it, is a mirror[1] and I invite Lalita to look at Herself in it, to see Herself as I have imagined Her in ancient India. Since I have assigned the *Kamasutra* to the students in my Asian studies course,[2] Lalita must touch the text (and as I take up the book and gently stroke the page, I feel traces of Her fingertips), must hold what I hold—it's Her homework.

1. As Roth's commentary is a mirror (XO) to the text (KS$_1$), my commentary on that commentary is a mirror (YO) placed at right angle to that of my teacher (XO), unreversing what the first mirror has inverted. A reader (R$_1$) who overlooks or underlooks the commentaries sees but one dimension of the text (KS$_1$) as it exists in the phenomenal, unreflected world, and understands it simply in terms of what is stated on its surface; by means of the commentarial looking glasses, however, a reader (R$_1$) can perceive the text simultaneously in four dimensions (KS$_1$ + KS$_2$ + KS$_A$ + KS$_B$) in relationship to his or her own reflection (R$_2$) and understand it as a conglomeration of multiple surfaces, each defining the other and, in that complex of definitions, providing a sense of the hidden inner space (the unstated or "deeper" meaning) of the text. Place the mirror provided by Yaśodhara at a right angle to my mirror, and that of Pralayānanga at a right to angle to Yaśodhara's, and further dimensions are introduced and multiply each other; new depths are fathomed and one comes closer and closer, in a cool labyrinth of silvery reflections, to a sense of infinite meaning.

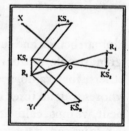

2. The syllabus for the course read as follows:

Asian Studies 150B: Introduction to Indian Civilization

Spring 1997   Instructor: Professor L. A. Roth
MWF 9:30–10:20   A305 Swinburne Hall
Sellon Hall 18   Teaching Assistant: Mr. Anang Saighal

This course is a survey of South Asian cultural traditions, focusing on three Indian normative ideals, the holy trinity of values that epitomizes cardinal Hindu attitudes toward the notion of a meaning or significance to human life—religion, money, and sexual love. In addition to taking a midterm and final examination on the professor's lectures, students must write a paper of approximately ten pages on each of the three required readings: The *Bhagavadgita*, *Power of Gold*, and the *Kamasutra*.

Enrolled in the class, She is constrained to take notes, to write down my words, record my desperate efforts to conjure up Her wondrous land, to bring close something distant in time and space and to substantiate a delicate dream of what might have been, the inconstant subcontinent of my incontinent subconscious.

I have seen Her in two dimensions on the walls of Ajanta and in three on the embellished facades of the Temple of the Sun at Konarak and the erotic monuments of Khajuraho, have smelled Her in white sprays of jasmine and in curling gray wisps of sandalwood incense, and have tasted Her in a golden morsel of sweet halva—light cream and cardamom, dark currants and pistachios.

I've heard the invocations of ancient poets: Her large, dark eyes are the deer eyes of Sanskrit poetry described without fear of hyperbole as reaching in furtive glances all the way to a lotus-adorned ear; Her eyebrows are curved like the bow of Kama; the nectarous moon of Her full face illuminates murky spaces in my anxious heart; the lower lip, blood red and bite swollen, is the quivering lip of an ardent courtesan beckoning Vatsyayana to drink; Her flushed thighs are the firm and shaded trunks of plantain trees, wet with nocturnal rain, or the strong, clutching trunks of frenzied elephants, misted with musk and ichor; and Her breasts, the poets sing, are swollen round and majestic like the sinus lobes on the foreheads of those rutting tuskers. That loses something in translation; but so does *lalita* and Lalita.

Now, finally, the phantasmic avataress of that ecdemic sexuality has descended into my classroom. The history of Indian dance is in the slight tilt of Her head. She's disguised in torn Lee blue jeans (white threads forming an eyelid open around the darkly shining all-seeing knee). On Her raspberry T-shirt is the cipher "I ♥ L.A." There is a hermeneutic to reading T-shirts; I take it as an augury—She will ♥ me, L[eopold] A[braham] Roth].

Crow black hair flies loose ("disheveled," the poet would suggestively note), and the gum She chews is aromatic betel as far as I'm concerned. Traces of datura, I fancy, make Her eyelids languorous. As promised in childhood reveries, She has finally come for me, and the rays of Her smile melt my heart like moonstone.

As if delivered to me by the potency of my own mind, the yogic power (traditionally accrued through ascetic practices) of willing things to happen, She was, less than ten minutes after the first class meeting, suddenly standing at my open door and smiling. Love is all apparition and magic, secret code and Tantric rite, telic correspondences and illusions of control; it generates and energizes symbols that take charge of our souls. Give me a strand of Your hair, a nail paring, or even a glance, and I'll work the beguiling magic of desire.

2. OPINIONS

A. TRANSLATION

Some professors postulate that one shouldn't seek fulfillment or meaning in love, that love is deleterious to the loftier ideals of religion and money. They fancy that love leads to defilement and falsehood, that it forces us into the company of worthless people and drives us mad, that it causes a loss of dignity, judgment, and faith. But love, I maintain, is the very fruit of religion, and it is the most precious thing that money can buy.

According to Auddalaki:

> The man who fulfills himself in terms
> Of religion, money, and love,
> Now and forever attains happiness,
> Both in this world and up above.
> Happiness comes from doing what you please,
> Without worry, without care,
> Without any concern about what might happen
> Now or then, here or there.
> Strive for the rewards of all three ideals,
> All of them have something just for you:
> If not all three, then settle for two, and if not two,
> Then one, if it's love, will do.

I, Vatsyayana, shall expound the ways and means of obtaining all fulfillment through the one, just one—LOVE.

B. COMMENTARY

"Lalita," She said cheerfully. "My name's Lalita—like Lolita but with an *a*." And stunned by the vision, I muttered under my breath, "No, no, my dear Lalita, not an *a*; no, it is rather like Lolita with an *A+*!" And I meditated on the magic syllables, the manumitting mantic mantra, the perfect name, the mellifluous adjective and noun from the verbal root *lal*—"to loll, play, dally, fondle, caress, frolic, to behave loosely or freely"; *lalita*—"artless, lusty, and languid, a lolling lady, charming miss, and graceful girl." O my *lalita* Lalita!

"Lalita Gupta," the apparition said as She walked in and drove philology crazy: *gupta*, "hidden, concealed, secret, private" (the past participle of *gup*, "to guard, defend, protect, preserve"); my *gupta* Ms. Gupta, ravishing descendent of the magnificent Gupta dynasty, the perfection of civilization; Princess Gupta who enchanted the Buddha; a wanton "woman who withdraws from her lover's endearments."[3]

"At registration they said your class was full, but that I could get in if you'd sign this admission form. Fuckin' bureaucracy!" She sighed and sat down. "Will you sign me in?"

My heart lubdubbed itself into a gyroscopic spin. Oh, Her use of the precious present participle, "fucking," from the Indo-European *peik*, cognate with the Latin *pungere*, related to the Germanic *ficken*, purloined from the Middle Dutch *fokken*, associated with the Zemblan *fögun*, universalized in the Esperanto *fuga*. Although She used the lexical indecency unremittingly, there was nothing really vulgar about it—it was rather like the use of *eva* in Sanskrit (the enclitic particle of emphasis meaning "in fact, really, actually, exactly, just, only, quite, the very same," a "meaningless intensifier," according to my Monier-Williams dictionary). Uttered unselfconsciously, it was voiced metrically, just to give lilt and play to a phrase, or phatically, not to express an idea but to establish sociability like the quack of a duck, song of a swan, or purr of a cat. She used it to modify and modulate, to stress and qualify, to punctuate and irradiate. The way She enunciated it brought Her fulgurant teeth to rest on Her lower lip as the upper lip rose slightly in the *f;* and then, for the *u*, Her lips parted as if for a kiss, and they stretched back into smiling as the lexeme culminated so regally in *kin[g]*. It was stunning to witness Her mouth form and release it: "fuh-kin'." Two lips, two syllables, and a smile that merged all twos into one.

"I mean if you can't let me in, it's okay with me. I don't really care, but my parents want me to take courses on Indian culture. Fuckin' India, India, India! They're from India, and that's all they care about; they're pissed off that I don't know anything about it."

"Oh, I can teach You about India," I answered, trying to restrain the regressive quaver in my voice, the adolescent trembling of my limbs; and yes, yes, I told myself, I must teach Her all I know, all that

3. "A woman who withdraws" is a definition for *guptā* given by native lexicographers and cited by Monier-Williams in the dictionary that was the end of Roth. The *Kāmasūtra* was, most likely, written under the patronage of a Gupta sovereign. The name Gupta usually indicates a family of the mercantile or agricultural classes and, in modern times, suggests Bengali origins.

She has forgotten, the knowledge embedded in nucleic acids in the cells of Her flesh. My glance luxuriated in the dark down on Her bare arms, and I imagined the feel of the soft, sweetly sweat-scented, sable *romavali*[4] beneath fingertips and lingering lips.

"The other thing is that my boyfriend, Leroy—Leroy Lovelace, the famous basketball player—is in the class," She continued. "And we like to take the same courses so that we can study together. You know—if I can't make it to class, he can take notes for me, or the other way around."

"I'm very strict about attendance," I interrupted.

"Oh, I don't mind coming; I'll come if it's important to you," She laughed, and my mind played dirty tricks on me, amplifying, against my will, the obscene resonances of Her verb.

"Have you ever been to India, Dr. Roth?" She asked without waiting for the answer. "My parents want me to go. They're on some sort of roots kick. But I don't want to. It's real dirty, isn't it?"

"Yes, I suppose so—that's one of India's charms actually," and my dirty mind made the dirty meaning of "dirty" all that I heard.

"I don't like the food—I mean it tastes okay, but I don't like the way it looks. My mother fixes it all the time, and my father plays the music and rents the fuckin' videos—really terrible movies, unbelievably corny. Yeah, I don't want to go to India—it's hot, and there are all those poor people and lepers begging everywhere." She suddenly laughed. "Well, will you let me in or not?"

I wanted to ask Her the same question. Kama's hook was lodged in my cheek, and I knew that the harder I might try to resist Her, the harder I'd be pulled back, the more the pain would tug me toward Her.

"Of course I'll let You in," I said as I signed the admission slip. "Of course, Ms. Gupta, anything You want. Anything."

"Well, there is something else: one of the textbooks is already sold out—the *Kamasutra*. I guess I can share my boyfriend's copy, but . . ."

"No, no, don't share," I interrupted all too frantically. "I mean it's important to be able to underline, to write in the margins, to record Your reactions to the text, to generate Your own commentary on it. We enter into a relationship with any text we hear or read, like the relationship

4. The *romāvali* (literally, "line of hair") refers to the vertical streak of hair that on many Indian women grows from the pubis up, across the abdomen, over the navel, sometimes all the way to the breasts. In the *Blue Yajur Veda* it is magically equated (for the sake of establishing the efficacy of the erotic sacrifice) with a pillar that connects sky (heart) and earth (womb) without reaching up to heaven (mind). In classical Sanskrit poetry, the line of hair is considered an enchanting mark of beauty, a sign of a girl's transformation into womanhood, the very staff of Kāma. See Martin Merkin's "Body Hair in Sanskrit Literature and Hindu Religious Practice" (*Pilosophy East and West* 18 [May 1959]: 131–41).

with a friend, a lover, or an enemy. A relationship is the ultimate meaning of the text. I have an extra copy. I get desk copies free. You can have this one," I smiled, handing Her my own expensive copy of a Burton translation lavishly illustrated with erotic miniatures and photographs of temple sculptures of copulating couples from Khajuraho and Konarak.

"Isn't this the book about fucking?" She asked, and the sudden use of the word "fucking," with the *g* back in place, to actually refer to fucking made it lewd, arousingly and powerfully distasteful. She had obviously meant to shock me, and it had worked. But I wanted Her to say it again and again—"fuckin'" or "fucking"—to say it sweetly, crudely, lewdly, softly, harshly, loudly, softly, to whisper it in my ear and shout it from the parapets of a fantastic ancient Oriental city.

Struggling not to lose what little remained of my composure, I answered as professorially as Vatsyayana might have done.

"The text is about the transformation of coitus into love, biology into culture, instinct into consciousness. Professor Vatsyayana soberly explains that he composed the book, informed as it is, and ought to be, with dispassion, after strictly observing a vow of celibacy."

She interrupted me with a reading of the cover puff.

"'The complete and unexpurgated text of the famous Hindu study of physical love.' Yeah, it's about fucking all right," She giggled childishly as She flipped the book over and continued: "'This famous Hindu manual of physical love is one of the high points in all erotic literature. It is frank and explicit in its descriptions.'"

"It's a classic of world literature, a key to Indian culture, and I thought the students would enjoy it," I broke in; I was embarrassed, self-conscious, rather pathetically unable to look the young girl in the eyes.

"I'm sure," She laughed in a condescending, supercilious way at, it seemed, two professors—Vatsyayana and me.

We were interrupted by my graduate student and teaching assistant, Anang Saighal, who entered without warning, toting yet another chapter of his dreary dissertation on Sanskrit commentarial literature for me to read.[5] Before I could get rid of him, She had excused Herself and disappeared.

From the moment I handed Her the Burton version (in giving Her the book, I was, I felt, offering Her Her own civilization), I wanted, as an act of devotion and redemption, to transduce the great erotic breviary for Her, to filter the text though my heart (making Vatsyayana's sentiments and sensibilities my own), to make significant all that I had

5. No comment.

learned about India, to whisper the ancient pandit's words to Her and scratch them on Her back, breasts, and thighs. Translation is transmigration: I'd be Vatsyayana reincarnated and She'd be the lover Mallanaga never names, some exquisite hetæra of Varanasi. It is for this reason that I, L. A. Roth, am beginning to translate the *Kamasutra*.

My predecessor, Captain Sir Richard Burton, in a foreword to his translation of the *Kamasutra*, wrote: "All you who read this book shall know how delicious an instrument is the Hindoo woman: when artfully played upon, by an amorously educated man, she proves capable of producing the most exquisite harmonies, of executing the most complicated variations, and of giving the divinest pleasures. She is all but indispensable to the student, and she teaches him not only Hindoostani grammar, but the syntaxes of native life. She has infallible recipes to prevent maternity and augment virility. . . . She is lover in health and nurse in sickness. And as it is not good for a man to live alone, she makes him a fine manner of home." [6]

Dr. Paul Planter, the chairman of my department (who teaches Asian Studies 150A: Introduction to Japanese Civilization) is married to a Japanese woman who does the work for which he takes credit (for example, "his" translation of the erotic *Chin-chin Monogatori* of Sensai Bobo). He justifies and rationalizes this shamelessly: "With love we span the cultures of the East and the West. She comes up with an explanation of the Japanese, and then I lyrically English it; working together in harmony, in love, we come up with a textual transubstantiation, true to the spirit and flesh of the original." With both scorn and envy for this happy man, I feel the inequity and injustice: I am a tenured full professor of Indian studies, a Sanskrit scholar, and yet never, never in my life, have I made love to an Indian woman. Is that just, right, or good? While I have had the oral pleasure of eating Indian food and endured the gastrointestinal torment of Indian dysentery, my psycho-sexo-Indological development has been arrested; I yearn to move on to the phallic and then the genital stages of Indology. Some sort of union, an erotic spanning of East and West, had, before I met Lalita, already become a hope. And now aspiration becomes obsession: I must possess Lalita Gupta for the sake of Sanskrit and South Asian studies

---

6. Roth liked to compare himself to Burton, to mention that they had both studied Oriental languages at Oxford. Roth's identification with Burton seems to have been intensified by the appearance of Lalita; during the last months of his work on this text, he became subject to irrational fears that, as Isabel Burton had burned Sir Richard's commentary on the *Kāmasūtra*, Sophia White-Roth might wish to destroy his.

(not to mention knowledge and truth, let alone pleasure or happiness). My relationship with India has, thus far, been purely voyeuristic—looking at Her, stripped and spread open, from a distance, through a window, with binoculars, only faintly hearing Her sighs and moans. I have smelled Her heady scent, felt Her excruciating heat, but never have I penetrated Her. Lalita is my opportunity to enter India and hold Her in my arms, to be at once outside and inside. India is my text, Lalita will be my data, and love will be my methodology.

Lalita Gupta seems so perfectly and unconsciously an incarnation of a civilization; although She apparently knows nothing about India, one can witness Indianness in Her gait, the long stride taken with arched feet turned out. I have never really been attracted to younger women, and perhaps as a result of that I have never felt old before. Now, for the first time, having just briefly encountered the girl, my age (not the death it brings, but the desexualization that young people attribute to their elders) worries me. Will She consider me too patriarchal to hold Her in my arms? I must show Her how an ancient text, in being reread, becomes young and fresh. I decided to buy some tonic to darken my hair—not dye it, just take away the new traces of gray.

I was standing in the supermarket aisle marked "Health and Beauty" when I saw Her out of the corner of my eye. Yet again it was as if some yogic power or constellationary fate was at work to bring us together once more that day. I hastily put the hair coloring back and rushed to "Liquor" to replace the symbol of anxiety in my basket with one of joy—an overpriced bottle of 1987 Chateau d'Amour rosé champagne. Like a hunter after prey, I snuck down "Automotive Needs and Feminine Hygiene," up "Frozen Foods" and, sighting her by "Bread," I pretended to be surprised.

"Oh, hello! Ms. ah, ah, Das Gupta, isn't it?"

"No, just Gupta," She smiled carelessly, hardly taking Her dark, scanning eyes from the loaves, buns, and rolls.

"Remember me?" I asked. "Professor Roth."

"Oh yeah, sure—you're my astronomy teacher."

"No, no—Asian studies," I answered with a bruised heart. "Indian Civilization."

"Oh yeah, of course—India," She mumbled, looking neither at me nor at my festive wine.

"You're buying bagels," I stupidly observed the obvious; She nodded, mumbled "'Bye," and left me by the bread to wallow in a terrible abyss of silence.

I returned to "Liquor" to wait and watch, and when I saw Her approach a checkout counter, I flew to Her. An old woman, no doubt some protean demoness of Lanka, her overflowing cart a sudden barrier between me and Lalita, beat me to the aisle. I yearned to shove ahead of the crone, to sidle in next to Her, close enough to smell Her hair, perhaps bold enough to ever so gently let some part of my body, seemingly by accident or oversight, touch some part of Her, to look into Her purse when She opened it, to make small talk, to joke about the story in the *Mirror* on the checkout stand ("Sex Secrets of Teenage Girl's 101-Year-Old Lover Boy"), to walk Her out of the store, and ... (oh, I don't know, I really don't know where we might have gone, what we might have said). With only one item (blueberry whole grain bagels) to buy, She vanished in an instant and did not seem to notice me there.

As I waited for the hag's groceries to be checked, I felt a sudden shock, a wave of dread: I sensed the presence of Maya Blackwell in the store; although I could not see her, I knew she was there, spying on me from "Kosher and Oriental Foods."[7]

That afternoon in the supermarket, though absolutely nothing had happened, I felt that, for the first time in over twenty years of marriage, I had been unfaithful to my wife, that the meeting by the bread had been an illicit tryst. I wanted to confess sins that I had not committed, to beg forgiveness for intentions. I was, as Vatsyayana says, by love made to act falsely; love robbed me of dignity and trustworthiness. But, as my teacher proclaims, since life is transient we must do what we must, when we must. I agree with Vatsyayana that neither religion nor economics, neither morality nor money should in any way get in the way of love. I bought the bottle of Chateau d'Amour and took it home.

"What's the occasion?" asked my dear, bright, and beautiful wife.

"I'm in love," I sadly answered, and Sophia smiled.

---

7. Maya Blackwell, who had been a student in one of Roth's classes some years earlier, had apparently fallen in love with her professor. After the murder, I found a large bundle of letters, notes, and cards from her in Roth's desk drawer. Many of them are disturbing:

> When You ignore me, my Beloved, refusing to answer my letters, I know it's just a game to intensify my desires. The exquisite pain of separation from You purifies my love. Perhaps You do not know it, but often You visit me at night in my dreams. Don't worry, I shall not tell Your wife. Secrecy is a necessary ingredient of love. Be not afraid, for I am patient. I derive my strength from the knowledge that if we suffer moments of separation from each other on this mundane plane of existence, it is only that we might realize an even greater love. I know full well that, on the metaphysical plane, we are united forever. There is ugliness here; but only beauty there. And there is where we most truly live.

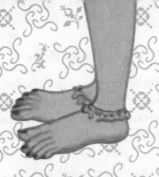

C. Subjects
and Objects

At your insistence, I am now trying to penetrate the Hindu jungle, which had eluded me until now due to a mix in me of a Greek love of limits and a Semitic need for moderation. Professor Richard Schmidt, no doubt in hopes of an endorsement from the scientific community (even if it must come from a Jew!), has sent me a copy of his German translation of a little Indian work entitled *Kamasutra,* with which you are perhaps familiar. He writes that I will "discover that some of your own theories of sexuality were articulated thousands of years ago in India by the learned doctors of the time." I must confess that this is not the case. I can neither make any sense of the book nor appreciate any of the author's supposed contributions to a psychology of love. I'm sending it on to you. If it means as little to you, despite your In-dophilia, as it does to me, you might want to pass it on to your friend Jung. The Swiss Mahatma seems to find some curious enjoyment in such exotic literary frivolities.

—Sigmund Freud, letter to Fritz Jahn (1930)

1. EDUCATION

A. TRANSLATION

To be [considered] truly educated, one should have a thorough knowledge of this textbook, an academic mastery of all of the amatory arts and sexological sciences that are ancillary to the larger and more general topic of love.

At the onset of puberty, girls (no less than boys) should be instructed in erotic theory and practice. While some professors have maintained that it's useless to try to teach such subjects to girls, I, Professor Vatsyayana Mallanaga, would argue that since women are quite obviously capable of fucking,[1] they are also certainly qualified to understand the abstract, theoretical premises upon which the practical, physical applications are based. In an ideal society, all women would be required to study both the philosophy and praxis set forth in the *Kamasutra*.

B. COMMENTARY

"Dr. Ruth, the illustrious professor of Indology?" the voice on the phone blared, continuing over my testy emendation ("Roth!"). "This is Dr. Nilkanth Gupta, M.D., Fellow of the Royal Ayur Vedic Gynecological Society of Bengal, telephoning you, hopefully at a most convenient hour, regarding my own daughter, the highly intelligent and wheatish Miss Lalita Gupta, who is, I thoroughly and correctly believe, currently and felicitously enrolled in your reputed course on the great and glorious civilization of our blessed Bharata. Her devoted mother and I, I humbly assure you, are extremely avid about her highest education and thus heartily wish to converse enthusiastically with you on this and other subject matters germane to all points at hand. You will come to our hallowed home for tea and light comestibles, as is our custom, at your greatest convenience, bringing for your accompaniment and our hospitable inclination, according to the wishes of my very own Mrs. Gupta, your very own Mrs. Ruth, dean I am told, not to mention Dr., Ph.D., and what have you or she."[2]

It struck me as a rather delicious irony that Dr. Gupta, who, in cahoots with the Right Honorable Jaidev Prakash, ringleader of the Indo-American right wing, had previously spearheaded the protest of the Indian community against hiring me for the chair in South Asian studies (calling it, in a letter to the university newspaper, "a neo-

---

1. Since Roth translated this text under the inspiration of, and for the sake of, Ms. Lalita Gupta, whose verbal indecencies were ever flaunted, I suspect that this use of the vulgar English word for the more polite Sanskrit *samprayoga* is a capitulation to the girl's flagrant foul-tonguedness. The brazen use of the four-letter f-word is, however, contrary to the spirit of the conclusions reached by Roth early in his career in his essay, "'Fuck' in Sanskrit?" (published in the now defunct *International Journal of Illicit, Deviant, and Subversive Language* [12 (1976): 47–73]). In this essay, after tracing a history of the verbal root *yabh* through Indo-European, he reflected on the distinctions between learned (archaic, and in that sense "dead" or unevolving) and vernacular languages and then argued that, while there can be licentious expressions in learned languages, there cannot be obscene words: "Obscenity requires regression, rebellion against learnedness, a return to the forbidden, uncodified utterances of childhood."

2. Having had the opportunity to meet Dr. Gupta, I can attest that the man's English (albeit more British than American in accent, vocabulary, and usage) was perfectly re-

Colonial Orientalist plot of the highest and most egregious order") was now inviting me to his home because his daughter was enrolled in my class on Indian civilization.

"Oh, Dr. Ruth, what a felicity!" the gynecologist, a man about my own age, boomed as he greeted me and Sophia one week later with a winking eye, a smiling mouth, and an ear deaf to my correction ("Roth!"). He enthusiastically introduced us to Mrs. Rita Gupta (whose warm brown folds of flabby flesh, dusted with talc like flour on some kneady nan dough, were squeezing out from under the bottom of a pink choli, yeastily rising, then drooping over the top of a purple permapress sari that clashed with Dr. Gupta's plum polyester leisure suit). She sweetly served sweet tea with karanji before performing devotional bhajans for us on the harmonium, songs that were a redemption from the onerous task of making conversation with the couple. While she sang, Dr. Gupta stared at her with glistening eyes. It seemed pro forma for me to look over at my own wife, Dean Sophia White-Roth (who had sighed her consent to accompany me in partial repayment for all the deadly deanly functions that I attend semester after semester for her sake). I'm still and ever dazzled by the crepuscular beauty of her quivering smile, her honeyed voice, and the tentative tilt of her poised head atop the slender, graceful neck, wherein my face has been so many times buried in joy and sorrow. She was wearing my black silk Indian kurta, open at the collar to disclose a silver medallion, Our Lady of the Sacred Heart. She wears it not because she is in any way a Catholic, but because she appreciates the idea of a woman sanctified by the heart, by the most exquisite powers of love. The charm had belonged to our daughter, Leila, and had been a gift, along with an antique heart-shaped mirror, from my mother.

"Now, as the women will naturally want to discuss a variety of fem-

---

spectable and in no way resembled the parodic, exaggerated, stereotypical language that Roth has put into the gynecologist's mouth. The implicit racism of the lampoon is, let me assure you, no less disturbing to me than it must be to any liberal reader. It is, perhaps, some sort of revenge against Gupta for the Hindu's attempt to block Roth's appointment at Western University. Roth never recovered from the indignation of realizing that Indians in California did not want him teaching about India. I was never amused by Roth's bigoted attempts to comically imitate (both orally and in writing) what he considered to be an Indian English parlance and accent. I debated emending Dr. Gupta's language in the manuscript, but decided otherwise on the grounds that, while it tells us nothing about Gupta, the speaker to whom it is attributed, it reveals a good deal about the character of the writer who makes the attribution.

inine topics," Dr. Gupta announced with a cheerful smile as he actually took my hand in his, "we may proceed to my study-cum-library-cum-yoga studio to inspect my priceless collection of ancient Indian medical instruments and texts." With a scampish wink, he lowered his voice into a whisper. "We shall also taste a few drops of whisky."

I could hardly keep my eyes from the framed photograph on his desk, Lalita wearing the mortarboard that marked Her graduation from high school, as Dr. Gupta, after pouring two tumblers of Teacher's scotch, proudly showed me his collection of enema nozzles and pouches (vaginal, rectal, and urethral).

"This is an object of rare and real beauty," he said loftily. "The pouch is made from the bladder of a goat and the nozzle is pure and priceful gold. I can assure you that Sotheby's wants to get their hands on this douche bag." For the sake of what he imagined would be my awe, he displayed an array of antique Indian gynecological instruments including tweezers, forceps, catheters, probes, syringes, and specula as well as an assortment of archaic Indian dildos in a wide range of sizes and made of various materials. "The Hindu of pre-Colonial times was enlightened in all sexual matters. Have another scotch and permit me to expound."

Expound he did, as only collectors over their collectibles can, and throughout his proud pontifications I kept wondering where Lalita was. Would She come home in time for me to see Her? Was She with the boyfriend? She should be reading the *Kamasutra* in preparation for my class tomorrow. Why wasn't She doing Her homework? Where was She?

It was in the midst of this fit of anxiety that it came to me, all of a sudden, an irresistible shining of bright light comparable to the brilliant beam that awakened Gautama as he sat beneath the spreading branches of the Bodhi tree. It came to me! The plan! The perfect plan! I was instantaneously inspired, as if my mind were some sort of magic harp and the wind of the universe had suddenly caused it to vibrate, to sing the divine strategy to me. I was struck by a scheme so brilliant, a plot so simple, an intrigue so elegant—the incontrovertible way and certain means to possess Lalita!

Feigning nonchalance while taking a sip of scotch, I brought it up casually.

"Oh, by the way, Doctor, this summer I'll be taking a select group of advanced students to India for a special summer honors course on South Asian culture. We'll be meeting for discussion with the learned pandits of Varanasi and traveling to Khajuraho in order to take part in an archeological excavation. There will be meditation classes at Sarnath, Odissi dance lessons in Puri, and that sort of thing. Students will be able to earn three credits for the course, for which they'll need to write a research paper. Since standards are rigorous and space is very limited, we are constrained to select only the most talented applicants. So if you happen to know any really bright Indian students, young scholars who are serious about India and their education, you might want to mention it, although, I must warn you, we're already overwhelmed with applicants."

Dr. Gupta took the bait: "My daughter! She is always an excellent candidate!" The hook was set, and all I had to do was give him some line, play with him, and then reel him in.

"Hmmm," I muttered as if trying to imagine the surprising idea of taking Her to India. "Normally two years of Sanskrit is a prerequisite, but, well, I suppose if you are really interested in having your daughter, Lolita . . ."

He corrected me: "No, not Lo-lita, La-lita, Lalita!"

"Oh, yes, of course, sorry. La-lita. If you are really serious about your daughter, Lalita, participating in this extraordinary educational mission, I could probably, given Her background, find out about waiving the language requirement in Her case. I can't promise anything, but I would be willing to discuss the issue with the study abroad steering committee, explaining that, having been raised by you and your so obviously pious wife, Lalita is perhaps qualified by both nature and nurture for admission into the program. On the other hand, your daughter probably wouldn't like to spend the summer studying. She's young. She might rather stay in L.A., going to the beach and having fun. It would probably be difficult for Her to leave that boyfriend of Hers behind for the entire summer. He's a great basketball player. You must be proud that She's involved with him. Still, I suppose you might want to discuss it with Her and with your wife. But remember, I can't promise that She'll be accepted into the program. The competition is fierce this year. But if you are genuinely interested, there can't be any harm in sending you a brochure."[3]

"Our daughter has a natural intelligence, which I am fully confident

3. Roth actually placed an ad in the university student newspaper and had a brochure printed to legitimate his ploy. There were about a dozen inquiries and four or five actual applications (other than the one submitted by Dr. Gupta on behalf of his daughter). Ms. Gupta was, unbeknownst to her or her parents, the only student ac-

would enable her to quickly compensate for any lack of prerequisites,"
he began. "Though she may not have studied Sanskrit in the technical sense, she has since birth heard her mother reciting Sanskrit prayers
during puja, and I myself often lapse into Sanskrit about the house,
dropping this or that pearl of wisdom from *Bhagavadgita*. This course
would be an excellent opportunity for my daughter to behold with her
own eyes the glories and wonders of her native land. Furthermore, she
would have so much to teach the Western students who will be out of
their element. Yes, yes, by all means, send me a brochure."

I was confident that I would be going to India this summer with
Lalita, buying sweets for Her lips and jasmine flowers for Her hair in
Chandni Chowk in Delhi, holding Her hand by the Vishvanath tem-
ple in Khajuraho, putting my arm around Her in the shadow of the
Black Pagoda of Konarak, and making love to Her beneath a mosquito
net in Varanasi where Vatsyayana composed our *Kamasutra*.

As we emerged from the study, I was surprised by what seemed a
sincerity in Sophia's voice as she spoke to Dr. Gupta.

"I'm sorry we didn't really have a chance to chat. My husband mentioned that you're a gynecologist, and I'd like to talk to you about your

---

cepted into the program by the illustrious admissions committee that was composed solely
of Professor Leopold Roth.

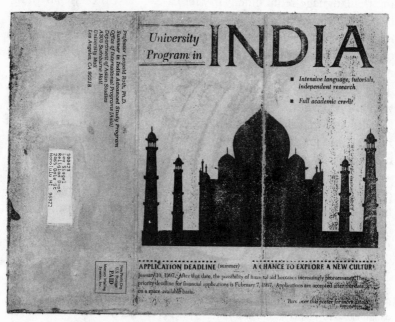

work. A history of the politics of gynecology could be a very intriguing subject to investigate, it seems to me, and the Asian data would be invaluable. I'd like to explore the idea of a manipulation of female sexuality in the name of science as legitimated by the predominately male institution of medicine. I'd be very interested in the Indian material relating to this. Why don't you come for dinner next week? And please feel free to bring your daughter. We'll ask our son Isaac to come as well."

I was utterly dumbfounded by the irony of Sophia's invitation; she would be responsible for Lalita coming to our home. I had nothing to do with it. I am innocent. *Non culpabilis.*

Walking with Sophia, holding her hand in the cool of that evening, I couldn't think of what to say. She too was quiet, and in that silence, thoughts of Lalita yielded to memories of a long stroll with Sophia after Leila's funeral: sighing, I had turned and kissed her, and she had whispered, "My Leopold, oh, my poor dear Leopold. You need so much. So much. I don't know what to do for you, for myself, for Isaac. I hope we can survive this."[4]

Our Lady of the Sacred Heart caught the gleam of the street lights suddenly turned on, and as I squeezed my wife's hand, a shiver of pleasure overwhelmed and dizzied me as one memory faded into another of strolling together, also in the evening, hand-in-hand, legs moving in time, breath in harmony: many years ago, after making love for the first time, walking her back to Lady Margaret Hall through the University park in Oxford, I turned to her and kissed her, and her hand reached under my black cashmere scarf and was warm on my neck. She told me that she would love me forever, and her cheeks were cold white, her mouth, red and temperate.

We went to the Taj Mahal Restaurant and Mogul Lounge for din-

---

4. Leila and Isaac Roth, fraternal twins, were born in 1975. Leila was murdered in 1987. Roth never discussed or referred to it, but I was able to find the following in the *Los Angeles Times* (6 March 1987): "The Leila Roth case ended tragically yesterday with the discovery of the body of the 12-year-old, who was abducted on her way home from school on Valentine's Day. The girl had apparently been badly beaten and traces of semen were found. Leila's family, in seclusion when the news was announced, could not be reached for comment." I say that Roth never spoke of it, but once, while we were reading a Tantric text in our Sanskrit seminar, we came to a rather gruesome passage describing an antinomian rite wherein sexual intercourse takes place at midnight in a cremation ground, amidst burning corpses. "Sex is evil," Roth suddenly said with no expression in his voice or on his face, "truly evil, unless it is tamed, purified, and redeemed by love." And because, moments later, there were tears in his eyes, I reasoned that he was referring to the terrible thing that had happened to his daughter. The crime remains unsolved.

ner. I ordered the Shah Jahan Regal Dinner for myself, and Sophia
played along by ordering the Mumtaz Special. We drank lots of Bombay gin and tonic, laughed about the zany gynecologist, and Sophia
asked about his daughter.

"She seems bright," I answered as lackadaisically as I could.

"What is it, Leo? You're acting funny." The remains of her British
accent intensified as she asked with a smirk, "Do you have a little crush
on the girl?"

"Of course not! She's just a student. She's pretty, if that's what you
want to know, but not my type. Too young. Too, ah, ah . . . Indian."

Sophia laughed and leaned forward to kiss my cheek ("I love you,
Leo. I really do love you"). When we got home, we drank more, got
pleasantly drunk, went to bed, and made love as only people who
have been together for many years, through joy and sorrow, who mutually know each other's bodies as extensions of their own selves, can
do—gently, so gently, with the joy of calmness, in a surrender that
brings the heart peacefully near death with sighed and moaned
promises that something, some serenity or sense of the meaning of it,
will survive, that there is, in some mysterious way, contrary to all the
evidence, an eternity.

2. CURRICULUM

A. TRANSLATION

Now let's enumerate the arts that constitute the curriculum for those
majoring in love: singing, playing musical instruments, juggling, and
dancing; painting, cutting stencils, making floor designs and mosaics;
arranging flowers, tattooing the skin, and dying the teeth; bed making and playing tunes on glasses of water; sorcery, garland making,
and weaving wreaths and chaplets; fashion design, making earrings
out of ivory and mother-of-pearl, preparing perfumes, and doing
magic tricks; preparing ointments and love potions, emetics, laxatives,
and aphrodisiacs; making pessaries and dildos; cooking and bartend-
ing, sewing and needlework; playing cat's cradle and hide-and-seek;
playing the lute, tambourine, and cymbals; telling dirty jokes and
figuring out riddles; reciting tongue twisters and poetry, storytelling,
and acting out the parts of lovers in myths and legends; filling in the
blanks in famous poems and composing verbal charades; rattan bending and woodwork, interior decorating, spinning, carpentry, numis-

matics, malacology, metal polishing, gem cutting, and gardening; staging ram, cock, and partridge fights; teaching parrots and mynas to speak; hair dressing, shampooing, and massage; Sanskrit, sign language, and secret codes; speaking foreign languages (vernaculars, dialects, and slang); fortune telling and chariot repair; mnemonic games, wordplay, and a thorough knowledge of dictionaries; prosody, rhetoric, etymology, and metrics; mimicry, impersonations, literary forgeries, and putting on disguises; skill with dice and gambling, backgammon, chess, pachisi, and other board games; making children's toys and animal sounds; a mastery of etiquette, yoga, plumbing, military science, and gymnastics.

Any beautiful and virtuous woman who masters the arts and sciences of love will have an honored place in society; such a woman is respected, praised, and desired by one and all. She can, by her amatory expertise, captivate any man. Likewise a man who is a master of these liberal arts can seduce any girl.

B. COMMENTARY

If I were making this up or fantasizing it, I could not imagine a plot more perfect. My plan was working better than I ever could have dreamed. The day after our visit to the Gupta home, an anxious doctor, appearing in my office with his daughter's high school transcripts and diploma, a ribbon that She had won in an eighth-grade gymnastics contest, and a certificate of music study from Bhatkhande Community Night College in Artesia, beseeched me to do everything in my power to help Ms. Gupta get accepted into the summer study in India program.

"You will, my esteemed professor," the doctor proceeded, "shortly be receiving highly relevant letters of reference, including the eulogistic epistolary proclamations of the Right Honorable Jaidev Prakash, venerable trustee of the Los Angeles Indo-American Republican Party."

Dr. Gupta brought me a bottle of Teacher's scotch, as a bribe I assume, and despite university regulations, I insisted that we open it right then and there in my office in order to offer a toast in hopes of his daughter's success with Her application to the program. The booze made him all the more exuberant.

"We are, of course, yearning for our dearest daughter to know the traditional Indian arts—cooking (curries and kabobs, savories and sweetmeats, rotis and pickles galore), spiritual disciplines (*Gita* and yoga), domestic arts and sciences (bed making and shopping, washing and ironing, sweeping and the like, all done with a feminine smile), fashion (sari wrapping) and traditional cosmetics (lac, kohl, and mahendi, decorative bindis and sectarian tilaks), and language training (mellifluous Hindi and divine Sanskrit). If there is anything a mother or father can do to expedite and enhance the higher educational processes to which our excellent daughter is being subjected in your university, let it be your duty to so inform us of the same. That she go to India for the consummation of that education is most desirable. The instruction of women is an ancient and holy tradition in India. That the woman of the Indian household was ever and always, at all levels of society, in charge of keeping the domestic accounts, preparing the budget, and supervising the purse certifies that all women in India, before the Muslims and the British, were lettered, learned, and literate. Naturally we want our highly astute daughter to be no less sapient. Education is of the utmost importance for an Indian woman; it is through being highly learned that she is capable of being the most excellent wife and superlative mother. Let us refresh ourselves and make ourselves even more convivial with two more drops of Teacher's, my humble offering to your good self."

He explained how important it was to him that his daughter go to India and witness first hand a society in which the benefits of arranged marriages are so apparent.

"Based on the ancient Hindu science of eugenics, we are dutifully arranging a marriage for Lalita so that she can enjoy that highest spirito-physical experience as described by our ancient rishis. Naturally she is, under the sway and swirl of Western influences, resistant to the ideal at this time. But just as the frolicsome filly must be broken, so our daughter (more dutiful than she knows because of influences and outfluences of genetics, family upbringings and uptakings, and past lives) will also be broken, and once tamed and ridable, like the noble animal in question and analogous, she will be happy to participate in the divine domesticity that is our Indian way and means. Yes, we are arranging her marriage, and this summer study in India will surely make her an all-the-more-marriageable candidate for the most suitably qualified boy. She will yearn for the highest love. And what, you are inevitably asking, is the basis of that true love according to the Hindu understanding? Obedience to our parents' wishes, whims, and wisdoms. From this love comes the immanent bliss of transcendental understanding and the transcendental bliss of immanent experience, or vice versa. Once you are on that plane, it is all one and the same through and through. That is what *Gita* says. Let's have just a few more drops of drink."

He picked up my Monier-Williams *Sanskrit-English Dictionary.*

"In this heavy tome, there are more words for 'pure love' than there are words for 'white snow' in the Eskimo dictionary. That is because the ancient Hindu knew every form and facet of that emotion. Our daughter must imbibe that wisdom in preparation for marriage. It is yet another imperative reason that she must go to India with you this summer during the marriage season, when she will note what great bliss will be in store for herself when she accepts the matrimonial arrangements made on her behalf."

Without asking, he poured each of us another tumbler of Teacher's.

"My dear professor, I speak to you man to man, doctor to doctor, father to father. I am worried about Western influences. My daughter has made friends with one Mr. Lovelace, luminous star of your own university's illustrious team and basketball champion of the highest rank and file. That is all well and good for I am highly open-minded about racial issues. It is not his color per se that is such a damn botheration to me, but I do not want Mr. Lovelace convincing my innocent daughter that American culture is greater than Indian culture on the grounds that, for example, India has never produced a basketball star of any greatness. Indian ideals of purity, chastity, and morality must be safeguarded abroad. This is not, you must be assured, some rank puritanism of the British sort on my part. It is that, in my hallowed tradition, virginity lends beauty to a girl. With profound hopes that it is not already too late, I pray to God that our daughter's hymen remains intact until marriage for the sake of Indian culture. Let me be frank with you: I am anxious for her to accompany you to India so that her relationship with the basketball player does not develop any further. If she goes to India with you, she will forget about him in no time. In India she will be exposed to a more excellent category of morality."

The doctor had finished the last of the Teacher's and it had made him weepy; tears formed as he made his final, dire supplication:

"You will, Professor, do everything in your power to help my daughter. Her mother and I wish her to be the perfection of Indian womanhood. We have tried, to no avail, to send her to my family village near Patna. You are our hope for our daughter to discover the glories of being from India. She must go to India with you this summer. You must take her!"

He said it. I am innocent. I proclaim it again: *Non culpabilis.*

Moved by the display of paternal devotion, I smiled reassuringly, took his hand in mine, and opened my heart to him:

"I promise you that I will do all that I can do for Lalita."

D. Lifestyles of the Rich and Famous

I had quite a thrill the other day when I visited the set of *Taj Mahal* and saw all the oriental knickknacks, the pretty garden, and a replica of the world-famous monument to love that I have heard so much about for so many years. Big bucks have been spent on rebuilding it right here in movieland Mecca for what moguls at the studio are calling "The Greatest Love Story of All Time." Didn't they make that one last year? Or was it the year before that? Anyway, the big surprise came when urbane man-about-town Eddie Edwardes invited me for lunch in the "harem room" of the palace. Even though I've known Eddie for years, I hardly recognized him in that colorful oriental costume and make-up. He looked great! We were joined for lunch by Eddie's beautiful wife, Tina Valentina, and their little boy, Leo. Just in case those of you who miss seeing Miss Valentina on the silver screen these days wonder what the heck she's doing, Tina's been busy lately playing the part of Mom! I asked the boy if he wants to be actor like Dad when he grows up. "Nope," he said. "When I grow up, I want to be the King of India like Dad." Isn't that cute? I just had to ask Eddie what the movie's all about. "Love," he said. As if we hadn't suspected!

—Hedda Hartman, "Hartman's Hollywood"
Los Angeles Herald-Examiner (July 1955)

1. ROUTINES

A. TRANSLATION

After a fellow has graduated from college, done some traveling, and figured out a way to earn a living, he ought to set up a household in the big city in a manner befitting a sophisticated man-about-town.[1]

1. "Man-about-town" is Roth's translation of *nāgaraka*, the person about and for whom the *Kāmasūtra* was written—a city slicker and ladies' man, a leisured playboy, the urbane, mannered gallant, a connoisseur and bon vivant with savoir faire, a dandy whose

He should acquire a comfortable home with a separate study and a large master bedroom that is decorated with seasonal flowers and graciously furnished with a king-size bed; there should be a bedside table with drawers that are well stocked with rubbing oils, pomades, cosmetics, and perfumes as well as citron peel and betel nut. There should be a spittoon, cages with parrots in them, musical instruments, art supplies, and writing materials. The garden should have plenty of water, a canopied swing hanging from one of many shade trees, and a bench surrounded by arrangements of potted flowers.

Upon awakening, our cosmopolite brushes his teeth, puts on cologne, and in front of a polished mirror, applies lip gloss and mascara. After breakfast, he teaches his parrots racy bons mots. There may be a little gambling, poetry composition, or reading, and then it's time for lunch, followed by an afternoon siesta.

In the evening he oils his hair and sharpens his nails before going out to drink and dine, listen to music, and watch beautiful women dance. After inviting at least one of the ladies to his home, he returns there ahead of her, changes his attire, lights incense, rearranges the flowers, and places out snacks and wine for his guest. Once the girl arrives, he amuses her with charming banter, playful civilities, spicy jokes, and the naughty noises he has trained his parrots to intone.

If there's been a storm and the girl's clothes are wet, he himself redresses and readorns her. Thus the man-about-town whole-heartedly devotes himself to attending to the needs of loving women.

B. COMMENTARY

After graduating from college, figuring out a way to make a living, and traveling in India, I set up a household in the big seraphic city of my birth. A comfortable house with a separate study. A garden with a brightly canopied Indian swing. I bought the swing in Delhi for Leila when she was four years old. I still hear the child's squeals of thrill, expressing a delight tinged and intensified by traces of terror as I pushed the swing, back and forth, higher and higher, and she stretched out her legs then curled them under; the little girl would throw her head back, extend her delicate arms while holding onto the ropes for dear life, and giggle, "Don't stop! I want to go higher, higher, higher!"

When I'd tuck Leila into bed at night, she'd ask me to read to her

---

life is consecrated to the pursuit of elegance and pleasure. For the *nāgaraka*, love, the sentiment formulated in and by poetry, is the only justification for human existence, which is, in all other respects, ultimately banal.

from *The Girl Who Charmed Serpents:* "Because her father was Inspector of Railroads, it was required that he travel all across India. Her
mother, who loved to visit with other English ladies, always went with
him. And so the little white girl [I'd substitute the name "Leila" for
"Mary"] was left in the care of an ayah, a brown angel who loved Leila
as much as any parent could. Children are gods in India. In the warm
spring afternoons, as Ayah pushed the little Memsahib in her swing
in the garden, Leila would giggle, 'I want to go higher, higher, all the
way up to Heaven!'"

While Sophia was reading stories of the Wild West to Isaac in the
next room, Leila would inevitably make me promise to take her with
me to India next time.

"Is it beautiful?" she'd ask. "Is it like the book?"

"Yes," I'd say, that she might share the burden of my infantile Indian reveries. It started in childhood for me as well, in childhood where
all of our capacities for love are established; infancy leaves indelible
marks of vulnerability, solitude, and melancholy. All of our lives, it
seems, we ache the ache of the cradle; that ache is for what we, for lack
of a better word, call *love.*

It's difficult to discern the line between memory and imagination
as, with eyes closed in a game of blindman's buff, I stumble with arms
outstretched through obscure paradises of childhood and history.

My fantasy of India, with its myriad sentimental audacities, began
in bed. Once upon a time, just as I was later to take Leila to the lush,
mysterious India of a book, my mother took me, tucked under warm
covers, to the India of *The Jungle Book,* acting out the parts (growling
Shere Khan's lines and hissing the utterances of Kaa): "It was seven
o'clock of a very warm evening in the Seeonee hills when Father Wolf
woke up from his day's rest."

My mother was an actress not only naturally, but also by profession.
The studio had changed her name from Clementine Bell to Tina
Valentina. Though she considered herself some sort of Christian, she
had flirted with theosophical musings that she associated with India,
and for a month or so, she had been a follower of Swami Paramahansa
Yogananda because, she confessed, "as a movie actress, I like the idea
that everything is an illusion. And I loved going for walks with your father at the Self-Realization Center on Sunset, near the beach. It was
so calm there, so wonderfully calm. They said it didn't matter what
your religion was, that all religions were different paths up the same
mountain. India must be a tranquil place. Hindu philosophy has given

me a sense of peace, Christianity has given me a love of music, and Judaism gave me your father, the great Eddie Edwardes." She also consulted by mail a psychic reader in Orlando, Florida, named Maharani Kalidevi, who in 1953 advised her to give up acting in order to take better care of her eight-year-old child.

Although my father never talked about Judaism, once a year he burned a yahrzeit candle for his father, who he claimed had been a rabbi. No one ever called my father by his real name, Joseph. Eddie Edwardes began his movie career as a matador, then he was a Mexican bandit in *Love in Laredo,* then a bedouin in *Saharan Serenade,* and then he played the maniacal chief of the Thugs in *The Curse of Kali.* Scantily clad nautch girls danced for him, bowed down, and beseeched him to choose them to be sacrificed.

Although my parents did, in the early fifties, briefly cohost a television show called *Celebrity Charades, The Curse of Kali* was the only movie in which they ever appeared together. As a kidnapped Memsahib, my mother begged my father, the terrible Thug, not to harm her as he stared deeper and deeper into her eyes, softly whispering hypnotic mantras *("Om kali om chinga linga dinga om")* that would have made her submit to his every perverted sexual whim had she not been saved in the nick of time by the dauntless Jock Newhouse as Colonel Sleeman.

Perhaps it was because he was so convincing as the evil Hindu priest in *The Curse of Kali* that Eddie Edwardes was cast in 1955 to play the Great Moghul, Emperor Shah Jahan, in Hollywood's epic love story, *Taj Mahal.*[2]

2. I recently found a poster for the never-released film in a shop selling Hollywood memorabilia. As this collector's item was far too expensive for me to purchase, I wish to thank Mr. Kaminsky, proprietor of Kaminsky's Hollywood Memories, for permission to reproduce it here. Kaminsky laughed over it: "Edwardes collectors are real connoisseurs. This is esoteric stuff. I mean the guy was one of the worst actors of his generation; he was so bad that you almost have to love him for having had the guts to get in front of the camera. He's kind of a cult figure in the world of movie kitsch."

It was because of that movie that I encountered an Indian woman for the first time—Sunita Sen, an actress brought from Calcutta to play the part of Mumtaz Mahal, the Light of the World. The film was to open with my father imprisoned in the Agra Fort, wistfully looking out over the river (to strains of sitar music that faded into the grander symphonic sounds of the Hollywood Philharmonic Orchestra) at the exquisite monument to love, the tomb he had built for his beloved so that the world would always remember their love for each other. The emperor, clad in simple white muslins, would narrate the story of the monumental love affair as Hollywood had reconstituted it: prince and begum would fall in love, marry, become powerful, and after battle scenes and murders, court galas and love scenes, she would die in his arms. All of this would be intercut with scenes of the building of the Taj Mahal. One of the greatest pleasures of my childhood was going with my father to the lot and watching the workers reconstruct the Taj Mahal in Culver City. I loved the cavernous sound stages swarming with serpentine cords and cables, vaulted with drops, lights, pulleys, and lifts. So many places to hide and, like all children, I loved to hide. I ate lunch with my father, sometimes in the harem room of the palace, but most often in what was supposed to be his cell in the fort, where I ran my fingers over cardboard made to look like red sandstone latticework covering the window that faced a backdrop painted with a misty image of the Taj Mahal. I recognized the great monument from the illustration in the copy of *The Jungle Book* that my mother kept in the top drawer of my bedside table. When I went with Sophia to the Taj Mahal for the first time, I was not as enchanted by the real mausoleum as I had been by its plaster, paint, and paper replica in the studio; the original posed a dreadfully seductive promise in cool marble of a strangely painful loveliness, a lover's lie that death itself might in some mysterious way, because of love, be lovely.

My father called me down to the living room in my pajamas and robe to meet the guests: the studio doctor and his wife, Noreen Nash; Jock Newhouse and the recent winner of the Miss Indiana beauty pageant; Fritz Jahn, the urbane German director of *Taj Mahal;* and the ravishing Sunita Sen—all of them gathered convivially in the Edwardes salon for cocktails before going to the Club Malabar to drink, smoke, sup, joke, laugh, dance. My father made a gin and tonic for Miss Sen.

Sunita Sen set down her cigarette in the crystal ashtray to shake my hand. The black eyes, shaded by the long lashes that deer have, matched the night. The curious dot on her forehead matched in color the purple silk sari embroidered with gold. The anklets and bangles, nose and toe rings, and the matchless natural perfume of her enthralled my childish heart. Whenever I drink a gin and tonic, I think of the Bengali actress and can see the large and darkly mascaraed eyes, the hair parted in the middle (the part tinged with vermillion), and the long shiny braid—a serpent whose venom is love.

"Would you like to visit India someday?" she asked with a demure smile.

"Yes, I'd like to ride an elephant like Mowgli in *The Jungle Book*."

"He's a sweet boy," she laughed, and then sipped her cocktail. "It's so strong. I'll be quite scandalously tipsy in no time."

After being kissed by my mother and father in ritual preparation for bed, I shook Sunita Sen's hand again and did not want to let it go. I went upstairs and tried to read *The Jungle Book* but could not concentrate because I was falling in love with Mumtaz Mahal, Jewel of the Seraglio and Light of the World.

The next morning, alone in the kitchen, I saw the crystal ashtray full of cigarette butts, and some of them, all the imported Rothmans, were marked with lipstick that matched that on the rim of the highball glass from which the Light of the World had been drinking gin and tonic. My heart was pounding in anxious terror that I would be caught indulging in a transgressive pleasure. I rubbed the lipstick off the glass onto my finger, smelled and tasted it; I stole the butts of the cigarettes that she had smoked and, as if sharing in some forbidden delight with her, smoked what remained of each one of them, the dizziness that it caused but another dimension of the complex of emotions that I was realizing constituted love.

I went to the set one day to watch the shooting of a scene in which my father sat upon the Peacock Throne with Sunita at his feet resting languorously on red silk pillows and cooled by feather fans waved obsequiously by dusky servants. The wife of Jahanghir, Nur Jahan (played by an elderly Ariana Arundel), stood attentively behind him. My father recited his lines grandiosely: "Today I dispatched orders to Zafar Khan, my governor in Kashmir, to assemble his troops and invade Tibet. Some of the ministers have asked me why. It is, I explain to them, for Mumtaz Mahal—you, my beloved. Men give gems to their women as tokens of love. Since I love you more than any man has ever loved a woman, I want to bestow upon you the Himalayas as a string of jewels, Tibet its center, an ornament almost grand enough for you. All that I do is done for love." They had to reshoot the last line in close-up: "All that I do is done for love." Again: "All that I do is done for love." Again, again, again: "Sound. Take number 28. Action." *Clack!* "All that I do is done for love."

My father had to age over fifty years in the two-hour film, to begin as a young man of twenty and end as an old man of seventy-four. As a youthful prince he attended a New Year's festival in the Moghul garden. There was a fair with extras dancing, juggling, and playing odd games, ornately caparisoned elephants, and a tiger on a jeweled leash; in the garden there were stalls where women were being auctioned. Shah Jahan walked toward Mumtaz Mahal's booth, and Eddie Edwardes took Sunita Sen's gloved hand in his, looked into her eyes, and as the microphone boom lowered and an elephant shrieked, he spoke: "Oh, that I were this glove upon thy hand."

"The Greatest Love Story of All Time" ended in disaster. The director was stabbed to death with an Indian *bichhua* dagger, a prop purloined from the set by Sunita Sen. The headlines in the *Los Angeles Herald-Examiner* were more titillating than any movie or fiction could have been: INDIAN VIXEN MURDERS LUSTY LOVER AT HOLLYWOOD ORGY. The scandal ruined my father's career. He had been at the sordid party that was described by Hedda Hartman in *Confidential Magazine:* "Character actor Eddie Edwardes, who will always be remembered for the chills he made run up and down our spines in *The Curse of Kali*, was literally caught with his pants down at a seamy soiree, proving he would have done a great job playing the part of an oversexed Mohammadan Mogul in the now nixed production of *Taj Mahal*. Wife Tina Valentina was at home taking care of the Tinseltown twosome's little boy, while Eddie burned the midnight oil boning up on his *Kama Sutra.*"

My mother told me not to believe any of it.

"What's the *Kama Sutra*?" I asked her.

"Just some Indian book about love," she answered.

I asked my father, "Why did she do it?"

"She loved him," my father said so sadly. "All that she did, she did for love."

He took me back to the studio, held my hand, and we walked through the streets of Laredo to the lot where the workers were deconstructing the Taj Mahal, the great monument in which love and death were linked by beauty. We strolled across the black and white checkerboard linoleum that would have passed for rare marble. The fronts too seemed perfectly marble, though their backs were wood, chicken wire, and plaster. The bits of paint, from a distance, were truly inlay of jasper, agate, lapis lazuli, carnelian, and bloodstone. The silver doors that had been stolen by raiders from the real Taj two hundred years ago had been seemingly retrieved from history for the movie only to be cracked apart with axes, revealing tin gilt over pasteboard. Pick-up trucks hauled away chunks and splinters of dadoes, arches, filigreed panels, bas-relief irises, grillwork, fantastic balustrades, and dirty white plaster detritus that could no longer be identified.

It had been Eddie Edwardes's ultimate aspiration "to be the star of the greatest love story ever made, a romance that will live forever." He had been confident that he would win an Oscar and, more importantly, that his foot- and handprints would be immortalized in cement in front of the theater on the corner of Beverly Drive and Burton Way that was being rebuilt with a great breast-shaped roof that replicated the dome of the Taj Mahal. Because of the scandal and cancellation of the film, the theater remained just the Beverly-Burton, not the Taj as proposed; today the building, its Oriental dome still visible, houses the Discount Bank of Israel. Like the matching Taj Mahal in black marble that Shah Jahan had wished to build across the river from his beloved's white sepulcher as a memorial to himself and to love, the cement commemoration of my father's contribution to the cinema and to love was never realized. Though there are miles of celluloid images of my father and a mine of memories, nothing solid abides. That's why I too light a yahrzeit candle each year, on the eighth day of June.

Shah Jahan's hair turned as white as the Taj after the death of Mumtaz Mahal; my father's hair did the same with the cancellation of the picture. He would wear the costume around the house: the lavish yellow brocade shirt; the tight red silk pantaloons embroidered with violet flowers visible through a diaphanous skirt; an emerald green sash with purple and crimson paisley leaves; a turban plumed with black and white feathers (on one side an emerald green piece of glass as big as a walnut, on the other a diamond clear piece of glass the same size, and in the center a larger ruby red, heart-shaped ornament); violet buskins, embroidered with pearls of paste, the toes pointed and curling; armlets, bracelets, and rings on every finger. Sometimes, in play with me, he'd draw the gold-painted wooden sword from the red velvet scabbard. It was a melancholy game, painful as all games become when they go on too long—over ten years. Beardless and without the Eddy Leonard makeup, my father looked a pale emperor dressed in that outfit each evening while he and my mother drank gin and tonic and played backgammon, a game he said came from India. He'd recite the lines that had been meant to quench the thirst for romance of massive lovelorn audiences, the last utterance in the script: "Forgive all those who are lost in sadness and allow them, O Lord, to enter the Garden where True Love abideth."

He died of a heart attack three hundred years after the death of Shah Jahan, dressed in that ridiculous costume. My mother insisted that her husband be buried in the emperor's clothes under a memorial stone that she had designed for him; while I thought it lacked dignity, Tina Valentina maintained that it made sense of my father's life.[3]

I had to capitulate to his wife then, but twenty-one years later, I refused to comply with her preposterously bathetic designs for the wording on Leila's gravestone; with a teary smile, my mother more than recited the sentimental lines—she performed them:

> She would have loved, had she the chance;
>   Instead she teaches angels how to dance.
> She would have wed and worn a ring;
>   Instead she teaches angels how to sing.

Leila, who wanted to be an actress like her grandmother, is buried near my father. Against all reason, logic, and common sense, there's solace in that for my mother. At the funeral, instead of flowers, she placed upon the grave the medallion of Our Lady of the Sacred Heart that Sophie now wears and a little heart-shaped hand mirror that I keep in a bedside table drawer. Occasionally I look into it with vague hopes that I will see Leila there. I long to gaze at the smile and to hear the voice: "Is India beautiful? Is it like the book?"

When I go to see my mother each Sunday at the Stars of David Home for Retired Members of the Film Industry, she inevitably wants to talk about the great Eddie Edwardes, to reminisce about the parties, the galas, the Club Malabar, and the ephemeral salon that was their home.

Very often, before I can get to her room, I'll be stopped by the al-

3. I have taken a snapshot of the grave site at the Hollywood Hills Haven of Hope; the stone is modeled after the stars of recognition on Hollywood Boulevard, where Edwardes goes unremembered.

EDDIE EDWARDES

1900   1966

THERE'S A NEW STAR IN HEAVEN

ways impeccably dressed Jock Newhouse: "Psst, Roth, Roth, come in here, kid." Jock Newhouse ("It means Jacques Casanova in English," he'll say with a racy wink), for his cinematic debut, had rakishly played the part of Casanova, the quintessential man-about-town, and often recites his lines from the movie: "The chief business of my life has always been to indulge my senses; I never knew anything of greater importance. I felt myself born for the fair sex—I have ever loved it dearly and have been loved by it as often and as much as I could." I have known Newhouse (born Lev Vogel) since childhood; he had, according to my father, the reputation for having the biggest penis in Hollywood: "Ten blackbirds can perch on it." Newhouse always feigned modesty in response: "Your dear father exaggerated—the tenth bird has to stand on one leg."

Recently, Jock had announced with youthful exuberance, "I'm writing my own memoirs, a happy confession with no holes barred. I don't want it to be like all of those self-aggrandizing, bullshit, ghost-written Hollywood chronicles. I want to tell the real story of my life and loves. The problem is that I don't know how to type or use a computer, so I've got to find somebody who can take dictation. Somebody with big tits. Maybe you've got some coed around the university who wants to earn a few extra bucks."

Last visit, he signaled to me as usual.

"Psst, Roth . . . Roth, come in here. Come on, have a glass of champagne with me to celebrate. It's the good stuff—Chateau d'Amour, your father's favorite. I got the good news today—I'm celebrating. I've finally won my case." It had been in the court for over a year: when he had arranged for the surgical implant of a penile prosthesis,[4] the directors of the Stars of David Home had informed him that, as he was already causing enough trouble by sexually harassing all the women in the institution, he would be evicted if he went ahead with the operation that would provide him with an eternal erection. "The new amendment to the OBRA Act of 1993 requires that the home respect all my rights, grant me my dignity even if, as in my case, dignity means having the right and opportunity to be undignified. I don't really need the implant—I still get a hard-on most mornings, but occasionally I can't get it up at night anymore, and that's when I need it around here, at night when the place goes quiet and all the ladies are lying around

4. On penile prostheses and dildos, see *Kāmasūtra* VII.2: "The penis should be perforated and then fitted with a choice of artificial aids, rough or smooth, some with thorns, some with bells."

in their beds dreaming about the good old Hollywood soirees. You wouldn't think an old folks' home would be a good place for pussy, but I can tell you, it's better than a sorority house."

Newhouse had been at the infamous party, the scene of the love crime that ended my father's career. The sex scandal had the opposite effect for Jock Newhouse; it enhanced his persona and made him a bigger star than ever.

The real reason Newhouse usually invited me into his room was to solicit my services as his go-between: "Listen kid, think of your father. Don't you think he'd want me to schtup your mother in his memory? Your mother seems shy about it, or she's playing hard-to-get. Put in a good word for me. Help me make her happy. It's for your father, the great Eddie Edwardes."

I always promised him that I would see what I could do, but whenever I brought him up, my mother just chuckled, "Oh, he's much too old for me."

Tina is always dressed for visitors, her strawberry blonde wig perfectly coiffed, her face powdered, cheeks rouged, eyes mascaraed, lashes curled, lips glossed—all of her elaborate makeup meant to compensate for what the many little injections of collagen and pinches of cosmetic surgery were failing to maintain. She always smiles, although sometimes there are slight, delicate tears in her loving eyes.

"Isaac and Leila came to see me the other day," she said.

While I, no less than Tina Valentina, need to modulate reality according to my own fears and desires, regrets and hopes, I was unable to restrain myself from correcting her:

"No, that was Isaac with his girlfriend, Aphra. Leila is dead." One of Aphra's books, a romance novel entitled *Fires of Love,* was on the bedside table.

Ignoring what I was saying to her, my mother told me that last week a fan had written to ask for a pair of her underwear.

"I mailed him a pair of black lace panties," she giggled. "I know it was naughty of me, but I couldn't help it. It was so flattering. He's probably homosexual anyway—most of my fans are. I wonder why that is."

It's always the same scene. I take her in my arms and tell her how very much I love her and she reciprocates: "I love you too, Leo. But sometimes I worry about you. You just seem to need so much. You always have. You've never been able to be alone, not even when you were a little boy. I think you were born that way. I shouldn't have gone on location to Mexico for *Curse of Kali.* That's what Maharani Kalidevi said. You'd cry and cry if I left you alone in the crib, but the second I appeared and took you in my arms, you'd smile and drool."

Then I inevitably ask her to leave the home where I see her fantasies indulged to such a degree that I fear her illusions are turning into delusions. "Where would I stay?" she always asks, to which I answer, "In Leila's room." And ever able and eager to ignore realities that do not conform to the sweet movie of a life that she writes, directs, and stars in, she smiles, "Oh, no, I wouldn't want to inconvenience her."

This time, seeing how sad I suddenly became when she spoke of Leila, she repeated her expressions of love, stroked my cheek, and then, as if I were still eight years old, she offered to read some of *The Jungle Book*. She still had the same book that had been in my bedside table when I was a child, a leather-bound edition illustrated with engravings of the Taj Mahal and the Black Pagoda at Konarak, nautch girls and a child bride, fanatical yogis and fearsome fakirs, an elephant and mahout, a snake charmer with his cobras, and a tiger hunt. The engraving of Shah Jahan had been cut out.

"That's okay, Mother, I have to go now anyway. I really do," I said with my hand resting on her arm. "I love you, but I can't stay any longer. We're having a party at the house tonight, and I've got to go to the restaurant to pick up the food."

"A party," she laughed youthfully. "Oh, how I love parties. What is more wonderful than a party? People being happy together, a whole room full of pleasure. Eddie and I use to give such wonderful parties. Good parties are the sign of a great civilization."

2. PARTIES

A. TRANSLATION

The man-about-town frequents fairs, salons, cocktail parties, picnics, and other revels.

Fairs

On a regular basis, town officials should rally in the Temple of Sophia[5] to plan fairs that include such festivities as erotic farces performed by

---

5. Roth has, I suppose in homage to his wife, translated Sarasvatī as "Sophia," the gnostic personification of wisdom. While there is some degree of coincidental similarity, Sarasvatī is invoked by Vātsyāyana as the tutelary deity of music, poetry, speech, and learning, or as Pralayānanga maintains, as a sort of a patron saint of the urbane who practice the fine arts ancillary to the arts of love. She came into existence when Brahmā, the creator, alone

itinerant actors, magic shows and puppet plays, exhibitions of snake
charming and juggling. There should be gambling and lots of games
(such as charades, hide-and-seek, and catch-as-catch-can).

Salons

Whether it's chez some demimondaine or at the home of a boulevardier, there should be parties at which people can discuss the arts
and sciences of love; the most brilliant, interesting, and stimulating
of the party-goers should be so honored. When attending a salon, if
you want to be popular, it's best not to speak in pure Sanskrit. Remember that nobody likes a bore.

Picnics

Accompanied by fun-loving, shapely women, the man-about-town
should occasionally go horseback riding in the country. When his
party arrives at a picnic area, they might enjoy watching a cockfight,
playing a game of dice, or doing a little dancing. When they return
home for the evening, they ought to take with them a bouquet of
flowers, a wreath, or some other such souvenir of the day, a *memento
amatoriae* of the pleasures they have enjoyed. In summertime such
garden parties should include frolicking in a swimming pool.

Listen to Auddalaki:

> Let there be feasts to celebrate the moon,
>   both when it's full and when it's new;
> Let there be celebrations of Kamadeva,
>   for what you give to Love, Love gives to you.
> Let the laughter of lovely ladies and urbane gentlemen
>   set the festive, gala tone;
> But he who is most wise will not forget how to laugh
>   when it's dark and he's alone.

B. COMMENTARY

"I can't believe I invited the Guptas to dinner," Sophia sighed, finger-
ing the silver medallion of Our Lady of the Sacred Heart, a gesture that

---

in the universe, used all of his power to make his body half male and half female. Falling
in love with his female half, Sarasvatī, Brahmā mated with her, and she gave birth to human
beings. Sarasvatī's love for her consort is chaste, an expression of wisdom rather than passion. Similarly in Gnostic mythology, Sophia emerges from the separation and reunion of
an androgynous creator God, and in her association with Mary, becomes, like the Hindu
goddess, a representative of wisdom as the full and pure realization of love.

always means she is bothered or anxious. Anxiety also intensifies her English accent. "You must forgive me, Leo. How could I have done it to us? An enthusiasm of the moment always seems to be my downfall. I've invited the most absolutely boring people imaginable. Perhaps I can cancel it, explain that we have to attend the Deepak Chopra lecture at the university that night."

Afraid of losing the opportunity to have Her in my home, I tried to play it cool and detached, not to seem too eager to meet with the admittedly boring parents who would be bringing the lusciously lovely Lalita to me.

"Don't give it another thought, darling. It's okay. Look on the bright side of things—we know lots of boring people. In fact, now that I think about it, all of our friends are boring."

"I don't mean to sound cruel, but none of our friends are quite as boring as the Guptas," she said as she started toward the phone.

Once again panic yielded inspiration—I proposed a game, a little contest, a wager worthy of the wit of Vatsyayana's man-about-town.

"Wait a minute. I have an idea. We'll have the dinner party as planned, but I'll invite three other people that we know, and I'll bet you anything, anything you want, that I can come up with three guests more tedious than the Guptas. It's a redemptive idea, don't you see? The more monotonous the party is, the more exciting it will be for us!"

Sophia's mildly bemused smile gave me hope that my scheme was working.

"Okay, you're on," she laughed, "but you'll have to make that four. I told Isaac that he could bring Aphra. We can't count Isaac. We can't ask ourselves if our son is boring. That's too harsh. But I want Aphra on my team. I don't want to cook, though. Let's pick up take-out food from the Taj Mahal or the Ganges Grill. The loser does the dishes and cleans up. So, who's on your team?"

"You'll have to wait and see," I answered, playfully pulling Sophia toward me for a kiss and already beginning to put a squad together. Lalita, I reckoned, would be the weak player on Sophie's team, the one who most threatened to be interesting; but still, I had to have a strong game plan to come up with a crew as boring as Dr. Gupta, his blessed wife Rita, and Aphra Digby.

We often had to endure Aphra, a rather masculine woman in her forties, since she was supporting our son, something that, quite amazingly, she was able to do with her earnings as a writer. We were, nevertheless, not so happy that she had convinced Isaac that being a poet was a good career choice.[6] In Vatsyayana's time the profession promised fame, fortune, the love of women, and the respect of men, not to mention a higher birth in the next life. But no longer; we live, as everyone has surely noticed, in tawdry times in a banal world.

Not even Isaac knows Aphra's real name; in her actual life she adopts whatever nom de plume she's using for the particular literary project that she's working on at the time: she was Victoria Seaman as an occasional scriptwriter on the television show *The Love Boat;* Leigh Larus was the name of the author of her Harlequin Romance, *Fires of Love;* Candy Clitterson wrote her porno novel, *Confessions of a Cock-eyed Coed;* Norma Zeale made a small fortune with the self-help book, *The Power of Passionate Thinking;* and as Alana Agrona she produced

6. Aphra, as she explained to me that evening at the party, had encouraged the young man to write a book, a long (fifty-five pages) autobiographical poem, which through her efforts, was published by Occidental Press last year. It is an odd book to say the least. The preface (which appears in the back of the book) and the afterword (in the front) were written by Ms. Digby under the name of Naomi Mihrof (which I realize is "For him I moan" spelled backward). She also takes responsibility for the title: *Mirror Retro (Or Terror Rim* backward). The text represents Digby's efforts to help the boy to transform a disorder into art. The sole symptom of his particular illness manifested for the first time in 1987, when Leila was murdered. At that time, while living with his parents in Paris, Isaac began to suffer from bouts of a transient right-sided hemiplegia, manifesting as a derangement of the visual component of speech, during which he, though normally right-handed, would write with his left hand mirror-wise, like an impression on blotting paper, reversed and made legible only by holding up a mirror to it. The states in which he, quite unwillfully, lapsed into mirror writing came and went without warning. I wrote to my father with questions about the neurological aspects of this syndrome only to learn that patients, during these states, "typically become subject to the independent activity of stored up memories localized in the right hemisphere of the brain. Retrography, while not uncommon in patients who have suffered particular kinds of stroke or who are victims of violent trauma to the brain, is relatively rare in patients suffering from emotional trauma." The text of Isaac's poem was printed in reverse, as written, and came packaged with a mirror to enable readers to decipher the strange script. I quote one of the 111 stanzas of the poem (#18) as an example of an odd poetic accomplishment, a risky publication gesture, and as an illustration of a neurological anomaly. You will, I'm afraid, have to provide your own mirror.

> laughter I am told is the meaning of my name
> after the son of one who'd bow to such a
> savage god and kill for him in spite of the love
> ravaged body of the woman who laughed in the
> face of god and wept for a girl whose name meant
> night, who inverted darkness in a heart-shaped mirror to
> light, the day on which she died for me and turned me
> around as a reflection of herself, still and buried in a
> ground that's barren despite the god, a realm of children
> slain, sacrificed to ideas of love, dreams without the
> pain or pleasure, without the naked flesh that shows in mirrors

a "gardening book for lovers" entitled *Roses Are Red, Violets Are Blue.*
Sophia was counting on the certainty that at the party we would be
hearing in tedious detail all about Aphra Digby's current literary endeavor.[7]

I had a simple but effective strategy for victory: I would invite only
academics; my colleagues, I was confident, would be magnificently,
stupendously, and exquisitely boring. I had the dream team. First were
Dr. Paul Planter, chairman of my department, and his boring wife
Pimiko—he'd be sure to recount every lurid detail of the most recent
chairmen's meeting, and since Pimiko doesn't speak English and always just sits there smiling admiringly at her illustrious husband, I
reckoned that, even without a Ph.D., she'd be pretty dull. Second was
my esteemed colleague, Dr. Christopher Cross, gastropodologist ex-
traordinaire, who would, undoubtedly, have lots to tell us about the
anatomy, psychology, and social life of snails, about his fellowships and
grants to do research on the habits, if not the wit and wisdom, of *Helix
hermaphrodites.* And finally, I had just heard from Saighal that his former teacher, Professor Lee Siegel, was visiting from Hawaii to give
some sort of lecture on "Jews of India" for the Hollywood Hadassah
chapter.

Unfortunately Siegel explained that he couldn't make it, giving the
lame excuse that he had to attend the Deepak Chopra lecture at the
university that night. So I invited his protégé, my teaching assistant,
Anang Saighal, a good pinch hitter, I figured, in that he'd probably talk
about his dissertation, his comps, his committee—all those excruciat-
ingly wearisome things that graduate students think fit for conversation. And even if I didn't win, even if, against all odds, Saighal, Cross,
or the Planters let me down by being mildly interesting, I was happy
because that night I'd have Her in my home.

One of my team members was first to ring the doorbell.

7. Sitting next to Aphra Digby on the couch at one point during this party, I was among
those who were informed of the details of her current project, *The Latin Lover,* a novel about
a classicist, an elderly professor of Latin who is translating Ovid's *Ars amatoria.* "He has led
a solitary life, has never married, and has never, except once in his youth, been sexually involved with a woman. His failing health constrains him to hire a nurse, Carmena Penista,
a young and beautiful Mexican (i.e., Latin) maid with training in geriatric care. The aged
scholar and the barely literate, very promiscuous young girl fall in love. Though they never
actually have sexual intercourse, I use poetic language to evoke the intensity of the erotic
power that informs their alliance. The theme is the relationship between past and present,
between literature and life, and between the mind and the heart as the respective seats of
the intellect and the emotions."

"Sophia," I called out with pleasure, "Anang is here. And guess what! He's brought a chapter of his dissertation on medieval Sanskrit commentators. Fascinating, don't you think so, Soph? I'm anxious for our guests to hear all about it."[8]

The Guptas were next. She stood behind Her mother, who stood, bearing an offering of karanji for us, behind Her father, who stood in front of me, his hands joined in the traditional Indian greeting as he beamed and boomed, "Dr. Ruth, illustrious professor of Indology! What a pleasure to have this sight of you!"

When I corrected him ("Roth, not Ruth!"), he smiled.

"May I call you Dr. Lee?"

"Leo, not Lee. My name is Leopold Roth. Leo like the Holy Roman Emperor, like Delibes, Buscaglia, and the astrological sign. Leopold like the king of Belgium, like Loeb and Leopold . . ." I was stopped short by the realization that he wasn't listening to me. He was wearing a black dress suit and a Loma Linda Medical School tie. His women were clad in saris; Lalita's was purple silk embroidered with gold.[9]

As they entered, I looked straight into Lalita's lovely eyes, as I did not dare to do in class, and offered to take Her shawl that I might lightly, tenderly touch Her shoulders. She insisted on keeping it.

"But you may take my wooly," Mrs. Gupta announced with a wobble of the head.

Dr. Gupta, who wanted to know if I had received his daughter's application for the study tour of India, kept winking at me as if we had made some sort of deal.

"Are You eager to go to India, Lalita?" I asked with a cordiality that was well tempered by professorial civility.

"No, not really, but my parents want me to," She answered frostily. "Do you have a phone I could use?"

After directing Lalita to the telephone in the bedroom, Sophia opened the door for the Planters, who had given Cross a ride. Mrs.

---

8. I only brought a chapter of my dissertation with me because Professor Roth had asked me to do so.

9. Lalita was not wearing a sari, but rather khakis and a red cardigan over a white blouse. The rich blackness of her luxuriant hair as it curled down over the crimson of the sweater made her look very beautiful indeed. Since at the university she always wore jeans, I supposed that her parents had obliged her to dress up to impress her professor and director of the summer study in India program. I wonder if Roth really thought she had worn a sari, perhaps because he refused to acknowledge her distance from her cultural traditions, or if he is simply lying.

Planter bowed obsequiously as her husband slapped me on the back, fulsomely expressing his pleasure to see me—rather odd, I felt, since he sees me every day at the department and usually doesn't even say hello.

Cross entered the house like a champion racehorse lunging out of the gate.

"Snails, Leo. I just heard today—I got the NSF grant for the research. Let's celebrate! I can't wait to tell you." Those were his first words, uttered before he had even taken off his coat. Luckily for me, he was clearly raring to talk *Gastropodae* tonight.

"Great, Chris," I said. "You'll have to tell all of us. Everybody likes to hear about snails."

Lalita returned from the bedroom as I was beginning to offer drinks to go with the spicy Indian snacks set out in Indian brass bowls for the guests. I was disappointed that She wanted a 7^{UP}. I'm not sure I can really love someone who doesn't drink; I imagined Her imbibing cool reflections of a full moon from a cup of heady wine, getting drunk with me, letting drink dissolve all boundaries and erode all sense of time and place.

Aphra, last to arrive, announced that Isaac couldn't make it and joined Saighal on the couch. This woman, old enough to be Isaac's mother, in her dark glasses, torn jeans, and a sweatshirt with a portrait of Dostoevsky on it, was as underdressed as Gupta was overdressed.

Lalita, now on Her second 7^{UP}, once again wanted to use the phone. I liked it that She was in our bedroom and hoped that She'd sit on the bed while talking on the phone so that after Her return to the living room, I could approach my bed as a shrine, like those in India that have the footprints of Vishnu on them, and rub my hands over the indentation She had made unknowingly for my sake. "*Om śriye lalitāyai nitambinyai namaḥ.*"[10]

After She emerged, duly accepted yet another 7^{UP} from Sophia, and sat down with the same weary expression on Her face that She frequently had in class, I went into the bedroom to worship Her impression on my side of the bed next to the table and phone. The bed, however, was desolately flat, unimpressed by her buttocks, and I felt cheated by that, as if a secret assignation had been missed. I sniffed the smooth, clean bedspread for some possible lingering scent of Her. Nothing. She must have stood impatiently during the call. Upset,

---

10. Literally, "[Devotional] salutations to the blessed goddess Lalitā, with the beautiful buttocks." I supplied the diacritical marks in the text.

ruffled, and driven by pangs of infatuation, I picked up the phone, pressed the redial button, and after one ring heard a man's hello.

"Lovelace?" I made a good guess.

"Yeah, who's this?"

"Phil Jackson, coach of the Bulls."

"No shit?"

"Listen son, I don't want to hear that kind of language from you. Pay close attention. I've seen some of the tapes of your games, and I like what I've seen. I want you to fly out here to Chicago as soon as you can, on the very next plane. I believe you've got what it takes. Grab a cab at O'Hare and come over to my place, 5801 South Ellis Avenue. I'll pay you back for the plane and the cab, of course, but be sure to bring the receipts. And, of course, I expect you to fly first class. I gotta go now, kid. Get here right away. See you soon. And remember kid—'Go Bulls!'"

The moment I hung up I was terrified that he might have recognized my voice; he was, after all, taking my class. I was consoled by the thought that he was frequently absent and that, when he did come, he often slept. But what if he actually did go to Chicago and then figured out that it had been me on the phone? And what if he doesn't have a sense of humor (he never laughs at my jokes in class)? He might beat me up, come into my office and roll my bones and flesh into an unrecognizable ball of gore. But terror, because of love, gave way to thrill: oh, oh, oh, to suffer for the beloved, the glorious martyrdom of love, the ultimate fulfillment of exquisite passion; and Lalita would then find his youth, strength, and agility crudely brutish and would be moved with sympathy for me, the older, gentler, and wittier man-about-town who suffered for Her sake. His virility is in his limbs, mine in my heart and soul. I wanted him to try to kill me. And if I were badly injured, Sophia wouldn't have the heart to be angry with me.

I returned to the living room to find the boring party in full swing—the monotony had reached an electrifying pitch, the humdrumness of the banter was sensational. Chris Cross, having announced that he was sorry to be missing the Deepak Chopra lecture at the university that night, was telling the Guptas about the chemical makeup of the slime that constitutes the snail's tracks. Aphra was on the couch next to Saighal telling him about her latest book. Planter was ponderously translating all the boring things that the others were saying into Japanese for his expressionless wife. The game was rousing. Alone in the bleachers with Sophia, I was silently cheering for my team of champions: "Come on Saighal, tell them about the commentary you found listed in the *Catalogus Catalogorum*—you know, the Hindi commentary on a Prakrit commentary on a Sanskrit commentary on a nonexistent text. Come on Cross, that's it, way to go! Interrupt Saighal to tell him what you wrote your dissertation on when you were a graduate student! Come on Planter, speak some more in Japanese! Way to go team! Push 'em back, push 'em back, waaay back!"

At half time, the players left the field to line up for their choice of take-out Indian food. Mrs. Gupta announced that she was a vegetarian, "for the sake of kindness to other dumb animals." I was grateful that I had a vegetarian and teetotaler, Mr. Anang Saighal, on my team as well—they're always boring.

When Lalita emerged from the bedroom smiling for the first time that evening, displaying a genuine happiness about something, Sophia's team was going strong. Dr. Gupta was claiming an Indian origin of scotch.

"It should not be called 'Scotch whisky,' but 'Indian whisky,' because it was, in fact, invented and enjoyed five thousand years ago in India and relished in that finer time and clime by royalty in luxurious palaces as well as by the lowly in humble hovels. But this is typical of the British Imperialism which has credited my great civilization with only India ink, Indian wrestling, and Indian giving. Similarly tea from Darjeeling is called 'English Breakfast Tea.'"

Aphra was blabbering about her literary accomplishments to Pimiko Planter who, despite the fact that she probably didn't understand a word of it, kept nodding and smiling politely.

"I've dedicated my life to writing about love. I have defined love in many ways: pornographically, as an experience of intense sexual arousal and release in *Confessions of a Cockeyed Coed*; romantically, in *The Fires of Love*, as an experience that gives meaning to life, an access to higher and deeper levels of being; psychologically, in *The Power of Passionate Thinking*, as a source of energy that can be applied for the sake of success to all aspects of life, an energy that begins with a certain positive attitude toward oneself; and philosophically, in my new book, *The Latin Lover*, as the principle which binds opposites together into new, unique and dynamic, whole beings.[11] It's all of these and none of them;

---

11. I've recently gone through Aphra's books to try to find her definitions in context.
Romantic *(Fires of Love):* "Sebastian's caressing hands were suddenly still. 'I didn't mean for this to happen, Heloise, believe me. Please believe me!' he said with tears in his handsomely limpid eyes. She realized that what had just happened was as un-

these are merely perspectives valid for certain people at certain times in certain predicaments. No definition is adequate, and thus a novel is the only way to get at it. Anything you say with a straight face, sincerely, about love is a cliché and that's unforgivable, but for a character in a novel to utter a cliché is appropriate. My books are nonclichéd juxtapositionings of clichés. *Confessions of a Cockeyed Coed*'s the only one that's been translated into Japanese. Have you read it?"

Pimiko smiled and bowed several times.

My team was putting up a good fight: while Planter explained to Mrs. Gupta why Japan was so much cleaner than India, Saighal was trying to interrupt Cross, who was explaining the sex life of snails to Sophia (who smiled over at me), to whom Dr. Gupta was boasting about the extraordinary accomplishments of himself, his daughter, and India.

"Of all sentient beings," Professor Cross lectured, "snails have the richest and most fulfilling love life. First of all, their genitals are in their heads, which is a much cleaner, safer, and more reasonable place for them than between the legs, all mixed up there with the dirty parts.

---

planned for him as it was for her, and in her heart she struggled with all her might to rise above the most earth-shattering and soul-stirring experience of her entire life. Never before had she wanted a man to come that close to her. 'This must be love,' she thought, but trying to seem unconcerned, she said, 'Perhaps you'd better leave now.' Sebastian, the fires of love burning in his heart no less feverishly than they were burning in hers, rose, put on his overcoat to protect him from the storm, and walked to the door."

Psychological *(Power of Passionate Thinking):* "Love is the key that opens the door to success. 'Everybody loves a lover,' the old song goes, and it's true! But we don't become lovers by accident; we have to make it happen! It begins with self-affirmation and self-acceptance, a celebration of our own individual uniqueness. That is the foundation of an ability to respect the other's individuality and to genuinely appreciate his or her growth. When two people do that spontaneously, sharing all that is positive about each other, that is the beginning of real love. Real love grants freedom as well as wholeness and wellness, meaning and success!"

Pornographic *(Confessions of a Cockeyed Coed):* "The dormitory was pretty quiet since most of the girls had dates on Saturday night. 'I shouldn't have fallen in love with Professor Spiegel,' I said sadly as hot tears trickled down my cheeks. 'He told me he loved me, but he was just using me. I was just a toy for his ego and his cock. I'm not sure which one was bigger. It hurts being in love.' 'It doesn't have to,' the dorm mother sweetly smiled as she sat down next to me. 'College is a place to learn things, not only about anthro and psych, but about love too.' As she spoke she opened my bathrobe and began flicking my nipples with her fingertip, making them big and hard. 'There are many kinds of love. But if it doesn't feel good, it's not really love. If he hurt you, he didn't love you; and if you were hurt, you didn't really love him.' As she spoke,

Each snail has both male and female organs, and their sexual union is simultaneous: the male part of one mating with the female part of the other and vice versa. Snails experience true, whole, and equal love. In the laboratory I've watched them in the throes of passion, dancing for each other, kissing, smacking, bumping, drawing themselves erect, tentacles quivering wildly, and then when the genitals make contact, each exudes a dagger that enters the flesh of the other, wounding the other, making him/her twitch, convulse with rapture, and then each produces a long whip-like penis that is wiggled into the seminal vesicle of the other. The male aspect of each snail is satisfied only when its female side is satisfied which can happen only when the male side of the partner (also dependent on its own female side) is satisfied. When the snails separate, having experienced the very essence of love, they slowly wander away from each other and resume a solitary life in their garden. They don't need to talk. If we could be as the snails, informing love with mutuality, simultaneity, a perfect and exquisite inability to distinguish our pain and our pleasure from that of the beloved, moments of love, such as the snail knows, would suffice,

---

she stuck her finger in my cunt and began wiggling it around. Before I knew it, I was on the floor, and her tongue was where her finger had been. When she began to finger herself at the same time, I got really turned on and understood what she had said. 'It feels good,' I moaned. 'So good. I love you,' I cried out. Her muffled voice responded, 'I love you too.' Her words, tongue, and finger all worked together to make me erupt like a volcano, and when I came, it made her come too. I was beginning to know the meaning of love."

Philosophic *(The Latin Lover):* "Professor Larus, seated comfortably at his desk, looked up from the text at Carmena, who was folding his clothes. Taking a sip of the tea she had made for him, he felt the warmth of the cup in his fingers as her warmth, the recalescence of the hand that had carried it to him, and the fervency of her smile too, and of her sympathetic and humored glance; it was also the fever of the body that had embraced so many boyish lovers. He felt no jealousy (although he no longer permitted her to tell him about her sweethearts), no need to possess her (although he had made her promise to come to his funeral and to shed one tear ['Just one, and then I want you to smile for me']), and no desire to limit her in any way ('For your sake, I hope you'll find better work soon'). He read the Latin aloud to her: *Saepe tamen vere coepit simulator amare, saepe, quod incipiens finxerat esse, fuit* (she listened as intently as one who understood Latin might have done), and then he translated it for her: 'Often the pretender begins to truly love her whom he has pretended to love, and he comes to really be what he has merely pretended be.' She smiled her approval, appended the text ('that's as true for her as it is for him'), and threatened to learn Latin in order to read the book if he died before finishing the translation. 'When you first came to work for me, and I realized how very beautiful you are in every way,' the old man said as she

fulfill, and bestow happiness upon us. The evolutionary process that has deprived the male of a vagina and the ability to bear young as it has deprived the female of a penis and an ability to inseminate has been, in human beings, compensated for with language. We have developed language in order to replace our missing sexual organs and capacities, to attempt to overcome the biological inequalities that exist between us. Men talk and write because they don't have vaginas, because they cannot give birth; women talk and write because they don't have penises, because they cannot fructify." And so on, and so on, and so on.

Suddenly Dr. Gupta, no doubt to further ingratiate himself to me on behalf of his daughter, offered to make his wife to do the dishes.

"Oh, just leave the dishes," Sophia laughed. "Leo will do them after you're gone."

"No," Planter jumped in. "Please, let my wife do the dishes. It's part of her religion. It's her meditation. It's a Japanese thing. We got rid of our dishwasher at home because the technology had removed Pimiko from the joys inherent in a timeless and universal activity. It's a Zen Buddhist practice. She closes her eyes and listens to the sound of the tap water as it speaks of the evanescence of things; she opens her eyes and sees the steam, breathes it in and smells the life-affirming fragrance of lemon-scented Joy; she reaches through the soap suds, pondering for a moment the way in which our lives are like bubbles; and she experiences what the Japanese call *mono no aware*. It's an untranslatable phrase suggesting beauty, transience, the bliss inherent in sorrow, the and-yet-ness of being, and that sort of thing. Then suddenly her hands are warmed by the water and a feeling of well-being comes over her, an understanding of why we are here, a why that cannot be answered in words. The sink becomes an external metaphor for an in-

---

put his shirts in the open drawer. 'It made me sad that I am over sixty years older than you. But that's not so anymore. When I look at you I see the girl, but I also see the woman there who has yet to present herself to the rest of the world. There are so many things I would not be able to see if I were a young man.' He fell silent because he saw the old woman in her too, infirm like himself, and he also saw the skull and bones and dust. The vision did not make him sad, but he was afraid that it might frighten her, that she would not understand that it was not a bad thing to die. He himself had just learned it; the understanding had come from contemplating her as she moved around him, from loving her in ways that they did not discuss, and from knowing that having loved her, he could die without fear that his life had been unbeautiful or without meaning."

ternal world, which she orders and purifies as she rubs each dish clean, so perfectly clean, carefully drying it with infinite care before returning it to its proper place in the universe. It's a ritual, a lustration, a form of prayer and meditation, at once a path to enlightenment and an expression of it. It is an art. Please allow her."

All the while Pimiko was smiling and bowing, and I was confident that the speech made Planter a front runner until Dr. Gupta began to explain that the "art of dish washing" had originated in India and had been taken to Japan with Buddhism.

Confident of victory, Sophie refused to let either Mrs. Gupta or Mrs. Planter do the dishes. I offered coffee and postprandial drinks to our thrillingly boring guests. Without mentioning it, I served decaffeinated coffee to Sophia's players and caffeinated to mine. Then I worried about it: should it have been the other way around? Would stimulants make the players more or less boring? Mrs. Gupta, who had put seven spoonfuls of sugar in her coffee, hardly needed caffeine; she was playing well for Sophie. She drank so many soft drinks that she had to use the toilet as often as her daughter had to use the phone.

When Aphra abruptly announced that she had to go to pick up Isaac, it gave the other bores, all of them fairly bored I think, an excuse to leave.

"We really must be making our adieu," Dr. Gupta exclaimed grandly and apologetically, as if anyone would protest his departure. "Dr. Ruth—or may I, now that we have fraternized, call you Dr. Lee?—you were an excellent host. Erudite and beneficent, a bit humorous and highly respectable in each and every way. I am most sorry to be exiting, but we must convey our diligent daughter home for the sake of her study. Typically unafraid to burn the midnight oil, she is assiduously convening with another student for the purpose of scholarship."

Fearing that that other student might be Lovelace, I did not want to let Her go. But for the sake of propriety and discretion, I had no other choice but to say good-bye.

"I'll see You soon."

"You will?" She asked.

"Yes, in class," I muttered, hardly able to conceal my wistfulness.

"Oh, yeah, right, class . . . "

"I need to do some work as well," Saighal said, and I wondered if maybe he was going to be meeting Lalita later. He had been looking at her strangely. There was betrayal in his eyes.

When everyone had left, Sophia and I sat down to determine the results of the game. I would have been willing to call it a draw, to admit that it was pretty close all around, but Sophie thought otherwise.

"The envelope please," she laughed. "And the winner, the most boring guest of the night is . . . Ms. Lolita Gupta."

"Laaalita, not Lolita," I snapped, and then, catching myself, lowered my voice to a whisper. "She wasn't that boring."

"Don't be a bad sport, dear," my wife smiled. "I was proud to have her on my team. She was a champion, gold medal all the way. If she would have just continued to frown as she did the first half of the evening, that would have been almost interesting. The glower gave an impression that she actually had something on her mind, that she had sufficient depth to be troubled about something. But then for the second half of the party, she just grinned that inane smirk, creating the impression of a limited emotional, psychological, and intellectual range. She kept rolling her eyes in adolescent disgust whenever her parents spoke. But best of all, she never said anything all evening except, 'Can I use the telephone?' That was excellent. The real *coup d'ennui*, however, was that she bored others more than anyone else because she herself seemed so much more bored by everyone else than anyone else."

She laughed and said, "Good night, Leo. I'm going to bed."

I would have argued with her, explained how fascinating and wonderful Lalita had been to someone who really kept an eye on Her, but I realized that that might reveal my illicit sentiments; and so I went into the kitchen, and as I stood over the sink, the hot water running, thinking of Vatsyayana's man-about-town (who surely wouldn't ever wash dishes), I was suddenly aware that I had begun to dislike my life—it had become boring.

After turning off all the lights in the house, I reclined on the couch to smoke the last Viceroy of the night and drink one more Bombay and tonic. I imagined one of the parties about which Vatsyayana had written: when we returned home for the evening, we brought a bouquet of flowers with us, a memento of the pleasure we had enjoyed. "Tomorrow," I whispered. "Come with me. Yes, come through a secret passage I have found that leads to an ancient world of love. Come, come to timeless fairs and festivals where we shall worship Kama. Let there be galas in the moonlight and get-togethers in the afternoon. Come with me to drinking parties, picnics, and other revels. Please, come with me."

E. Paramours
and Comrades

MALA BABA [Eddie Edwardes]
[Chief of the Thugs and High Priest
of the Cult of Kali]
You dare to accuse me of lust, O ignorant foreigner to this mystic land! You dare, O Englishman, to accuse me of seducing these beautiful women! Ha! They are not bewitched! They long
for eternity. They yearn to be sacrificed! They
are the chosen nourishers of Kali Ma. Hail Kali
Ma! I am but the humble servant of Kali Ma! Hail
Kali Ma!

COLONEL SLEEMAN [JOCK NEWHOUSE]
[Superintendent of Operations for the
Suppression of Thugs]
That's a bunch of baloney and you know it! You're
nothing but a cheap barbarian trying to pass or-
gies and murder off as religion. You and your
comrades are just a bunch of goons, and we're
here to put an end to your shenanigans once and
for all. Hail Victoria!
—*The Curse of Kali* (RKO Pictures, 1949)

1. LOVERS

A. TRANSLATION

Love, when its object is the generation of bull-like sons who have an
honorable place in society, must, according to the scriptures, be gov-
erned by caste restrictions. It is not, however, unauthorized to enjoy
intimacy with fun-loving ladies, regardless of their caste or social sta-

tus, when the object of love is pleasure. The professors who contributed volumes to the original encyclopedia of love enumerated the kinds of women who are unsuitable as paramours: lepers, lunatics, hags, albinos, hunchbacks, foreigners, nuns, and the wife or mistress of your teacher. The seduction of any other woman is neither a malfeasance nor a crime. I, Professor Vatsyayana, maintain furthermore that, if accomplished with intelligence and sensitivity, seduction is a fine art and lovemaking an exact science.

B. COMMENTARY

It is, I believe, appropriate to this commentary for me to inventory certain "fun-loving ladies" whom I found "suitable as paramours"—not necessarily the girls or women who have meant the most to me, but the ones whose love has had Indological resonances and ramifications, whose being has connected love and India and me.

Clover Weiner

When Miss Bonellia, the second-grade teacher at Burton Way Elementary School, announced that we were going to do notebook projects on the countries of the world, I was assigned India because she had seen *The Curse of Kali*. Clover Weiner (who had been given Israel) invited me to her house with the explanation that her parents, who were on a tour of the Orient, had sent her lots of postcards from India. I could have them to paste into my notebook with the other images that I had already collected: a beautiful woman in a sari, wearing lots of bold jewelry and with a diaphanous shawl over her head, from an old *National Geographic*; a haggard woman in rags holding out a begging bowl, from a newspaper; a child suffering from malnutrition; and photographs of a Bengal tiger, Gandhi, Paramahansa Yogananda, and Queen Victoria, the Empress of India. As I looked through her postcards (I remember the Taj Mahal, a snake charmer, and a dancing girl), Clover announced that she had to "go number one." Divulging that no one was home and that she was afraid to sit on the toilet alone (because she sometimes had a dream that there was a snake living in her toilet and that when she sat down it would come up and bite her "tushy" or push its head into her "peepee hole"), she implored me to accompany her into the bathroom. After she pissed for me, I pissed for her. "I've never done this with any other boy before," she whispered with a bashful tenderness and beseeched me never to tell. I solemnly promised (and have kept that avowal until this very moment); I was no cad and, overwhelmed by the thrill of the sweet transgression and intimacy, I was in love. Whenever we could get away by ourselves, we'd drink pitcher after pitcher of cherry Kool-Aid together in order to subsequently and joyfully urinate for each other.

I imagined that I'd probably marry Clover someday. I loved her until Sunita Sen, the darkly beautiful actress from mysterious India, expelled, without knowing it, the little pink, white, and golden Clover from the tenebrous mansions of a child's erotic imagination. Even the most impassioned love can be indiscriminate when it comes to its object.

Leona Sealman

Each morning as I watched the freshman girl ride her bicycle into the Hollywood High School parking lot and up to the bike rack, I contemplated each push of her foot against the pedal, the reverberation of sexual power up through her calf, flexing through her thigh, crossing her groin to descend the other thigh and down the other calf to the other foot and pedal, only to bounce back again, and again, and again, up and down, a vigorous crotch clutching the leather seat, a lithe torso rocking back and forth, lowering and rising rhythmically with burgeoning breasts apparent, neck arched, head erect, glistening beads of sweat on her forehead, teeth biting her lower lip; it took my breath away. Watching her wipe her face, untie her blonde hair, and lock the bike, I plotted our encounter: I'd wait at the bike path and, pretending not to see her as she approached, I'd step out in front of her. Then, having run me over, she'd feel guilty and repentant, ask if I was hurt, dress my wounds if I was lucky enough to sustain any, hold me in her arms, care for me, and nurse me back to life; she'd become my friend, then girlfriend, then lover, whore, and perhaps someday my wife. I'd teach our child how to ride a bike.

Too often the sweet schemes of love go sour: swerving to avoid me, she lost control of the bicycle, fell, and broke her arm; the bone came through the skin, blood gushed, and she went into shock. A crowd converged. There was screaming and panic, then the siren shriek of the ambulance, and I had to go to Latin class to recite *amo, amas, amat* before finding out if Leona Sealman would live.

Not only wouldn't the Sealmans allow me to visit Leona in the hospital, they also sued my parents and (because of the large "NO PEDESTRIANS" signs in the school's driveway) won the case—eighteen thousand dollars in damages. It wasn't until almost a year later that she approached me in the cafetorium, apologized for the lawsuit, and explained that she wanted to thank me because, with the money that she had been awarded by the court, her parents were going to buy her a bright red MG sportster for her sixteenth birthday. "I'm going to take you out for a ride in it; we can go wherever you want," she giggled naughtily. Suggesting that we didn't have to wait for the year and a half to pass before having our first date, I invited her to a Valentine's party that my parents were having the following week, promising her that we'd be able to secretly scavenge drinks, including French champagne.

In bed embracing my soft pillow, in the shower with my lips against the wet tile, in the back yard with my arms around a eucalyptus tree clad in peeling bark, I rehearsed the first kiss.

She appeared at our door on Valentine's Day afternoon only to remorsefully explain that when her mother had discovered that the party was at my house, she had refused to give Leona permission to attend. Deeply disappointed, of course, I politely offered to at least show her around our Hollywood home. I escorted her to the pool house, which after the production of the ill-fated *Taj Mahal*, had been redecorated, transformed from a Hawaiian luau hut (so decorated after my father's appearance in *The Sailor and the South Seas Siren*) into a Moghul harem room: there were silk pillows on a low divan, fake lattice windows, burnished brass lamps, a hookah, and other props scavenged from the broken-down set. On one wall hung a framed print of the Taj Mahal. I decided that I would tell her about the unfinished film, recounting the love story of Shah Jahan and Mumtaz Mahal, and then try to kiss her. If she kissed me in return, I'd reach around and feel the side of her breast; if she let me do that, I'd touch her breasts from the front; if she let me do that, I was prepared to unbutton her shirt and reach over or under her brassiere, or even to unhook that mysterious undergarment. If she'd let me do that, I'd be as happy as the Great Moghul himself.

I was, in fact, more shocked than happy: the moment we reached the pool house, Leona sat down on the divan, reclined, and bent her knees in such a way as to purposefully reveal an inviting absence of panties. I dropped my jeans down around my ankles, pushed back her skirt, and awkwardly entered her. Closing my eyes I, for some strange reason, pictured Sunita Sen. I could see her more vividly than ever before, could smell her skin, feel her hair on my face, taste her cheek, and hear her voice: "He's a sweet boy." We were making love in the Taj Mahal. Afterward we smoked the Viceroy cigarettes that I had stolen from my father, and I blew smoke rings to impress her.

Leona and I, illicit lovers in the sense that her parents refused to let her see me, continued to meet in the Indian harem room most days after school. One afternoon, after making love, she asked me if I "believed in foreplay."

"Yes," I said, taking the hint to heart. The next day—during foreplay, in fact—she asked me if I "believed in God."

"No," I said—not that I had thought much about it, but I sensed that, like my "yes" to foreplay, it was the right, more sophisticated and manly answer.

"Good," she answered. "Neither do I. Because if there's really a God, then you and I are going to go to Hell, where we'll suffer for all eternity."

"Why?" I asked and really wondered.

"For smoking and having premarital sex. God really hates that."

Leona broke up with me before she got the red MG; by that time she no longer dated high school boys. A desire to become an actress inspired her to change her name to Loni Leigh and to give herself only to older men who had some clout in Hollywood. Years later Jock Newhouse confessed to me that he had made love to her. "I wouldn't have done it if I had known she was only sixteen." I wondered what happened to her. "She went the porno route, called herself Lana Lamange," Jock told me. "She was actually pretty good in *Box Lunch.* The last time I saw her was in *Southern Comforts.* She was looking a bit over-the-hill for the genre."

Eve Christ

By the time I was a senior in high school, I considered myself rather a man-about-town, a boulevardier so sexually sophisticated (thanks to Leona Sealman's hint about foreplay) that only an older woman who smoked and drank, who wore black and liked art, was suitable to become my paramour. It was affectation, I confess, that sent me to the avant-garde concert at the Heidegger Coffee House and Bookstore. On that amazing evening, Eve Christ, completely naked, sang the "Bell Song" from Delibes's *Lakmé,* that romantic operatic celebration of love and death in India. When, after thoroughly enjoying the Edenic nudity of Eve Christ, not to mention her impressive coloratura, I went back stage to get her autograph, I found a very distraught artiste complaining that the police, not having raided the show as expected, had thereby deprived her of the opportunity to be dramatically arrested and then to prove in court that her performance was art, not obscen-

ity. "The line is so fine," she explained to me with an awesome intensity, then invited me to her apartment to smoke *ganja*. I asked her what
that was. "It's Sanskrit," she replied, "for pot."

Upon awakening in the morning, it pleased her to learn my name.
"That was Delibes's first name, the French guy who wrote the song I
was singing. Not only that, I'm a Leo—it's my astrological sign. It
must be fate that brought you to me. I can't believe your name is Leo!"

I couldn't believe her name was Eve Christ, but it was—I swear—
her real name. If this were a novel, it would be literarily ungainly to give
a fictional character such an unlikely appellation; or if the author,
confident in his readership's willingness or ability to suspend disbelief,
were to use such a name, Eve Christ would no doubt have greater
affinities with the primal woman than any other woman has, and she
would more significantly incarnate some aspect of the Son of Man than
any human being does; but no, there was nothing about her that was
significantly like either of those figures or even anything that was no-
tably or ironically unlike them. A character named Eve Christ would
undoubtedly tempt the hero—me—with all kinds of fruits of all kinds
of knowledge; the fictional persona, to live up to her Christian name,
would lead me into defiance and sin, and then, to make momentous
her surname, she would redeem me, die for me in order that I might
live on, transformed through the power and glory of the bread of her
flesh and wine of her blood.

If this were a novel, Sophia would mean "wisdom"; my wife would
not be merely a woman who breathes, perspires, menstruates, urinates,
defecates, and someday dies. If this were a romance, I would be in control, able to determine who lives, who perishes, who finds happiness
in love, and who experiences desolation. If this were a saga, L.A. would
have to do with angels, and Oxford would not be merely a city where
I happen to have studied—it would be a symbol of Orientalism,[1] and
India too would be a symbol of so very many things.

I admit that sometimes I pretend that my existence is a fiction,
some entertaining drama (its tragedies cathartic, its confusions and

---

1. "Orientalism" is, in this usage, a term coined by Edward Said (in a book of that
name) to refer to Western academic research on, and writing about, the Orient. "Orientalism," Said argues, is "a Western style for dominating, restructuring, and having authority over the Orient." It is perhaps germane to an understanding of Roth's scholarly endeavors to further quote Said on the Orientalist construction of Eastern sexuality: "The
Orient was a place where one could look for sexual experience unobtainable in Europe, a
different type of sexuality, perhaps more libertine and less guilt-ridden."

mishaps comedic), in order to allow myself the diversion of seeking meaning in it, of discovering some significance in insignificant events, of seeing the people I know as pivotal characters in a great play engaging in activities as dictated by the structure of a profound unfolding plot. The problem with life, however, at least in my experience of it, is that it is not literary all, that it has no real beginning or end, no really bad or good characters, no plot, no structure, and certainly no moral or meaning.

Eve earned her place in this list of women who connected me to India not only by teaching me my first Sanskrit word *(ganja)* and singing Lakmé's song, but also because of an Indian calendar (printed in Germany): the 1962 Kama Sutra calendar. When I saw it for sale in the Heidegger Coffee House and Bookstore, it struck me as something that she'd appreciate, admittedly not so much because of India as because of sex. For each month there was a reproduction of some erotic Indian miniature, each one depicting a different sexual position, each one accompanied by a poem. I gave it to her for Christmas.

Halfway through the calendar, because my parents thought I ought to go to college, I said good-bye to Eve and left for Berkeley. If this were a novel or a romance I would have gone to Harvard, and I would not choose to inflict on her, here in ink, what real life, which makes no choices, forced on her in blood. Before she could get through all twelve postures for sexual union, she discovered, after a fall in which she broke her hip, that she had bone cancer. She died in early November. I should have taken leave from college to spend October with her, holding her in my arms, naked as she loved to be, beneath the autumnal painting of the beautiful Indian girl sitting astride a supine man-about-town. I remember the poem:

> Purple clouds gather, and thunder shrieks,
>> Winds blow ferociously, elephants stampede.
> As days darken I take my place over you
>> Just to keep you here. To keep you.
> Pray, leave me not this month, no, no,
>> For separation is datura poison and
> I want . . . to live. Yes, oh yes, to live,
>> My love.

I should have stayed with her but didn't. Does it matter? She's dead. The fallen leaves of autumn have scattered, are gone forever, and dry earth, threatening us again with barrenness, awaits no lover but the frost. The deathly beauty of turning leaves, the vividness of the reds and yellows, fades. No one cares to endure the pain of remembering. Nothing means anything except in books.

The day I heard from my mother that Eve Christ had died, I decided not to go to class. Trying to write a poem about love and death (in which suddenly her name, against my will, took on meaning), I realized that literary gestures have a way of devaluing life, of making it trivial by trying to make it profound. Meaning is demeaning.

Over and over I played the record, listening again and again to the great diva, Anna Maria Leonardi, sing the "Bell Song." A girl who lived in my apartment building knocked on the door to ask me the name of that beautiful music, but I won't write about her here, about our love affair, because she had nothing to do with India. Thoughts of that civilization came back into my life one day while I was sitting on a bench in Sproul Plaza thinking about Eve Christ.

There were tables lined up around the square where students could sign petitions and get information about a variety of organizations, groups, societies, and movements. As my eyes focused on the Peace Corps table, I felt that Eve's death would be in some way worthwhile if I learned something from it, allowed it to redirect my life in some consequential way. Suddenly, impulsively, I wanted to devote all my energy to helping other human beings, as an atonement, I suppose, for not having dropped out of school to be with Eve in the chilly fall. I impetuously decided to join the Peace Corps. The young woman at the table, after perfunctorily giving me booklets, pamphlets, fliers, and an application, asked me what area of the world interested me.

"India."

"Why India?" she probed. As the answer would have necessitated an account of at least my second grade notebook project, postcards to Clover Weiner from her parents, *The Jungle Book*, Sunita Sen, *The Curse of Kali*, my parents' pool house, the "Bell Song," *ganja*, and the calendar on the wall above Eve's bed, it seemed more conveniently succinct simply to answer that I wanted to meet Indian women.

The Peace Corps representative recoiled in disgust.

"We don't become sexually or romantically involved with the people in the countries of our service. We're there for them, not for ourselves."

I was rather startled.

"Do you mean to say that if I go out to India, and I am stationed in some remote village helping the natives all day in that heat and with their sewage system, I can't go out at night with any of the girls, can't ask even one to come and sit with me beneath a banyan tree so that I can wrap my arm around her and give her a little kiss?"

"Of course. You can't date village women," she scowled. "What do you think the Peace Corps is for?"

"You mean I might go for two years in India without love, or sex, or even a little light petting? Does Kennedy know about this? Why does anybody join?"

She explained that she didn't think I was Peace Corps material, that I had a very bad sense of international service, that my motives were repugnant, and that, furthermore, I obviously had a fatuously stereotypical notion of Indian culture, no doubt based on "watching some bad Hollywood movie [true!], seeing, and completely misinterpreting, reproductions of ancient erotic sculptures on Indian temples [true!], or hearing about a few ancient Indian books like the *Kamasutra* [true!] which aren't really about sex anyway, at least not in the gross, carnal sense of the word." She was adamant: "India's not like that." Pointing to a table nearby (right next to a table for the Young People's Socialist League [YPSL]) where information was being distributed by the League for Sexual Freedom (LSF), she sneered, "I think they've got more to offer along the lines of your interests."

Relieved that I didn't have to go to India after all, I returned the materials she had given me and followed her advice. Sexual freedom—Eve would have approved, I reckoned. So would have the Great Moghul.

Isabelle Eberhardt

That wasn't her name, but try as I might, I can't remember what it was. I call her Isabelle after the rebelliously mystical sensualist who left Europe to live in the Sahara, taking one Arab lover after another, smoking hashish, drinking absinthe, and indulging in every religious and erotic excess that she could imagine and actualize; she was a celebrant of a rapturous Oriental disorientation and an intrepid champion of sexual freedom. Like that Isabelle, my Isabelle dressed like a man and had masculinely cropped dark hair—but wide green eyes proclaimed gynic wonders within. Isabelle, the woman manning the information table for the League for Sexual Freedom, gave me a few fliers and asked me to sign up ("only ten dollars for men and women are free") for a "Pagan Christmas Orgy," an event that proved to be disappointing to say the least: a naked young man with acne, dark glasses, and a pointed party hat, holding a helium balloon with the words "Get Wild" on it, opened the door to an apartment that had Indian bedspreads for curtains and a dirty floor strewn with beanbag chairs and lots of big pillows.

"Slip out of your clothes and join the fun," he mumbled without even bothering to smile, take my admission slip, introduce himself, or ask me what I was majoring in. There were about ten rather pathetic guys, who looked like they were studying engineering; there were only two girls, one very white, one very pink, both very obese, and a haggard older woman with frizzy gray hair and sagging, wrinkled breasts who was rubbing oil on the body of the only boy in the room with either an erection or a smile.

"Want a grape?" the pink fat girl asked, and the league member who had let me in again commanded me to take off my clothes.

"I'm not actually attending the party. I'm just here to see one of your members. I've got to find her. I don't remember her name. She was sitting at your table in Sproul Plaza signing people up. I've got to talk to her. It's very important. It's an emergency. Her family's trying to locate her."

"She's not a member," he explained, "she just works for us. How is it that her family has you looking for her and you don't even know her name? Take off your clothes and get wild."

I left and spent Christmas Eve clothed, alone, and not very wild, wondering how I could find Isabelle. Because it was Christmas vacation, there were no tables in Sproul Plaza, but as soon as classes resumed, I returned to the great square to find the woman who would help me let go of Eve. I was still jealous of death, yearning to someday possess a woman as completely as death possessed Eve; I had not understood until she died that I loved her .

Discovering on the first day of spring semester that the League for Sexual Freedom table was being manned by the very white fat girl from the orgy, I ended up talking to the more attractive woman at the table next to it, the representative of the Young People's Socialist League, who urged me to attend a meeting of YPSL in order to learn about "real liberation" and "to get involved in the common struggle of students, factory workers, migrant laborers, and Negroes." There were photographs of oppressed masses from all over the non-Communist world. The ones of women laborers in India doing road work were especially heart-wrenching.

Several weeks later I ran into Isabelle at Gaylord's Café and stood over her angrily as if I had the right, because she had not been at the orgy, to act like a jilted lover. I was hurt that she didn't seem to remember me. My story, how I had gone to the "Pagan Christmas" to see her, amused rather than moved her. "What a group of losers," she laughed.

What does Isabelle have to do with India (other than the fact that Gaylord's serves Indian food)? She told me about a splinter group that had broken off from the LSF, the Kama Shastra Society (KSS), "a very exclusive association formed for the sake of studying the existential aesthetics of sexuality and radical cultural alternatives to Western models of interpersonal interaction. It's run by a religion professor; he actually interviews all applicants. Members have to be healthy, attractive, have at least a 3.5 average, and have to have gotten above a 1300 on their SATs." Finally inviting me to sit down, she revealed that she herself was a member in good standing of the KSS. That I wasn't doing well enough in school to apply provided an inspiration for me to study more assiduously in the future. College began to mean something to me.

Since Isabelle was an anthropology major, I signed up for anthropology classes in order to have an opportunity to run into her and seat myself next to her. A subtle reference to my bottle of Dexedrine got me invited to her apartment to study on the eve of the first midterm in Cultural Anthropology. We stayed up all night quizzing each other on the terms: consanguinity, caste, matrilineal, ethnocentrism, commensality, hypogamy and serial polygamy, liminality, naive realism, taboo, uterine descent, uxorlocal residence, stimulus configuration. After the exam we went back to her room, and when, while lying in my arms, she told me that she was having an affair with a certain married Asian studies professor, I could not imagine how she could find a man so much older than us sexually attractive.

The second time I made love to her, as we were lusciously locked in each other's arms, I was happily anticipating the melting away of boundaries between ego and id, subject and object, when she suddenly growled:

"Say it, say what I want to hear, say it, baby, say it."

"I love you," I moaned, unabashedly wanting above all else to please my beautiful Isabelle, delectable doyenne of the Kama Shastra Society.

"No, not that, not that, baby. Say it!"

"What, my darling?"

"Say 'Fuck, fuck, fuck.' Talk to me, baby. Talk about fucking me, fucking my cunt with your cock, fucking, fucking. Say 'Fuck, fuck!' Say it!"

The way she grunted it was monumentally and painfully obscene.

Not wanting to be a party pooper, however, I cleared my throat and I tried to utter it, but just couldn't get the intonation, pitch, or any of the other suprasegmental, psycho-acoustic properties of the word right enough to create the desired psycholinguistic effect. I just didn't know the language. I think it was at that moment that I decided to stop seeing Isabelle, to give up my efforts to get admitted into the Kama Shastra Society, and to start majoring in linguistics.

The discipline required that I take a course in Sanskrit. Thus, I suppose, if I had been able to say "fuck" better thirty years ago, I wouldn't be translating Sanskrit now. The *Kamasutra* would not play a part in my life. I liked the idea of studying a dead language. I fantasized that in a dead language I would be able to speak to Eve again.[2] I liked it, furthermore, because California gubernatorial candidate Richard Nixon, in a speech promising to cut the university's budget if elected, said, "Students who don't know how to wash the dishes, change a lightbulb, fill out an income tax return, or respect the American flag are at the university at our expense studying things like Sanskrit." Since I hoped never to wash any dishes, change any lightbulbs, fill out any income tax forms, or honor the flag, I decided that I would study Sanskrit in graduate school.

Theresa Berkeley

I recall her name even though I never knew her very well; I remember asking her if she decided to attend Berkeley because that was her name ("No," she said, and remarked that her brother, Cal Berkeley, had gone to George Washington University). I met Theresa, who called herself "Tess" after the titular character in the Hardy novel, at a meeting of the Young People's Socialist League, a function I attended not because I wanted to join the proletarian class in their struggle for the just appropriation, ownership, and control of the socialized means of production, but because I was lonely and wanted to have a love affair—I was sure that Commie chicks, in defiance of bourgeois morality, would put out. Standing next to the table supporting a jug of Italian Swiss Colony wine, paper cups, a box of saltines, and a package of Velveeta was the gray-haired woman from the orgy. When I remarked that I recognized her from that meeting, she inquired as to whether or not we had had sexual intercourse. She accepted the news that we hadn't

---

2. Sanskrit is, of course, not actually a "dead language." The news is broadcast in it each morning in India, pandits still to speak it, and literary texts continue to be produced in it.

in good spirits ("Well, some other time maybe") and proceeded to reveal her hopes to merge the two groups "in order to psychotechnically evaginate society by means of a revolutionary resexualization of all existing political systems." She was delineating the details of her plan for "the perfectly classless and fully orgasmic society" when we were approached by one of the other ten or so party-goers (most of whom, I figured, were undercover FBI or CIA agents), the only attractive one (thus definitely not an agent), a straight-haired blonde in a blue work shirt whose sensually swollen lips insinuated a softness and longing behind a severe facial expression.

"Tess, this is . . . What did you say your name is?"

Upon hearing the answer, the stunning socialist looked me in the eyes and exclaimed, "Like Trotsky! But are you a Trotskyist? Or are you a Leninist?"

Since I didn't know the right answer, the most sexy one, I quickly responded that I was a Maoist. I couldn't have done better even if I had known anything about Communism. My testimony, together with my name (she was, in fact, a Trotskyist), resulted in her taking me back to her room in the house in Oakland that she shared with two black men with Muslim names, whom she said she wanted me to meet so that I could discuss Mao's visionary plans for Africa with them. Needless to say, I was relieved that they weren't home. The only thing I remember about making love to her is that, right after we finished, she suddenly, quite adamantly and sincerely but completely inexplicably, said, "Feuerbach really pisses me off."

"Me too," I sighed.

Because I spent money (that could well have been used to buy gin, cigarettes, or drugs) on posters of Mao, books on revolution, and even a flag from the People's Republic of China to suitably redecorate my apartment so that I could invite her over to my place, I was disappointed when, after only three dates, she insisted that "our sexual interaction threatens to inspire the kind of possessiveness, gender inequality, and counter-revolutionary sense of beloved as object and property that typifies the bourgeois institution of love."

The Theresa-India connection is rather poignant. Years later in Oxford, the year I married Sophia, I was reading an article in the *Sunday Observer Magazine* about foreign women in Third World prisons. One woman, newly arrested, insisting upon her innocence, explained that she had not known that the Indian with whom she had become involved in Thailand, and with whom she had subsequently traveled to Calcutta, was a Naxalite.[3] She had been arrested for treason, and the United States government was unresponsive to her family's requests for intervention. "My god! It's her! It's Tess!" I cried out to Sophie. "It's Theresa Berkeley. She was a friend of mine. I went to college with her!" Last year, there was a woeful photograph of her in *People* magazine in an article called "American Women behind Foreign Bars" in which she, still in prison but now in Gwalior, spoke of being repeatedly raped and beaten during her more than twenty years of incarceration. "I want to go home," she said in the interview. "My crime was that I fell in love with the wrong person. I've paid for that now. I want to go home."

Miss Something-Das or -Ji

Once I had seen the beautiful Indian girl in the sari with the red bindi on her forehead in my Comparative Phonology class, I threw out the Mao poster, folded up the Chinese flag, and bought a poster of the Taj Mahal and a print of Krishna playing his flute for love-enraptured, dancing milkmaids; I also purchased some sandalwood incense, a few Ravi Shankar records, and exchanged my Communist propaganda literature for some used books: the *Bhagavadgita* and *Kamasutra,* the autobiographies of Gandhi and Paramahansa Yogananda, a picture book on Khajuraho, Sir Thomas Lovely's travels, and something about *devadasi*s by Edward Sellon.[4] I placed bookmarks well into all of them

3. Naxalites were an outlawed Marxist-Leninist revolutionary group whose violent rebellions in the late 1960s were intended to represent the interests of India's agricultural laborers.

4. Edward Sellon (1818–66), an Englishman who had entered the army at sixteen, was dispatched to serve in India, and in his over ten years of service there, rose to the rank of captain. In addition to pornographic works set in India, Sellon wrote a quasi-academic book on Indian temples and phallic cults. His tormented autobiography, *The Ups and Downs of Life* (1862), deals extensively with his years in India and particularly with his sexual relations with Indian women, whom he preferred to their European sisters. In *The Oriental Epicurean, or The Delights of Hindoo Sex, Facetiously and Philosophically Considered, in Graphic Letters Addressed to Young Ladies of Quality* (1865), he devoted considerable attention (in terms that must have fulfilled Roth's most delirious Orientalist fantasies) to *devadāsī*s, literally "female servants of the deity," but more precisely dancers married to the idol enshrined in a Hindu temple. This is presumably the book to which Roth is referring. Sellon described the *devadāsī*s as "loose sluts who are consecrated in the worship of the perverted prickly gods of Hindoostan."

The service they perform consists of dancing, singing, baring their bodies, and, most sacerdotally, sexually honoring wealthy patrons of the temple. Their dancing is executed in lascivious attitudes and lustful motions. Their chanting is of obscene songs. Their displays of nakedness inspire offerings to the deity, and copulation is performed under the pretext that the god, carved as he is of wood and garishly

and left them scattered conspicuously around the apartment. All this was to impress the attractive Indian student if and when she'd accept an invitation to dinner at my place; take-out from Gaylord's, I figured, would win her heart.

"Thank you very much for the hospitality of your invitation," she said, "but it is neither my habit nor my custom to visit the home of a gentleman without being chaperoned by either my elder brother or my parents. And as they are in India, it is quite out of the question."

Professor Karen K. Karamazov

The anthropology course that Isabelle and I had taken together was taught by a woman who, as a result of having done fieldwork in India, had exotic jewelry. For the required term paper, I chose the topic "Love in Ancient India" so that I could get some use out of the books I had bought to impress the Indian girl. Professor Karamazov was interested in the theme; following her doctoral dissertation on sexual relationships among some tribal group in Orissa, she had construed and inferred theories for a paper, which she assigned to us, entitled "Love in the Pleio-Pleistocene Era." This study of protohuman romance defined *love* (I got it right on the midterm exam) as "a ritualistic byproduct of aggression, a calculated metamorphosis of individually instinctual antagonisms into a cooperatively constructed strategy for survival. Love, then, marking as it does a stage in the development of human consciousness, involves the unique idea (practiced but not conceptualized by other animals) that survival is not an individual need but a communal achievement."

Despite her initial interest, however, the professor didn't seem to care for my paper, deeming it "romantic drivel trying to pass itself off as anthropological analysis" and giving it a *C*. As my feelings were naturally hurt by that evaluation of my very sincere, although admittedly underresearched, ideas about love as "average," I went to her office to discuss the grade, and since this was long before anyone had ever heard

---

painted, takes some pleasure from it. As soon as these so-called religious duties are over, they convert the temple itself into a whorehouse. Extravagant are the allurements and charms which these enchanting sirens display to draw customers and increase the temple revenue. From infancy they are instructed in the various modes of kindling the fire of voluptuousness, as taught by their scripture known as "Kam Sootra": myriad postures and attitudes for fucking, means for keeping their cunnies tight, sweet and fragrant, formulae for enlarging the penises of their lovers and making those instruments as firm as that of the wooden god.

of sexual harassment, I didn't think it particularly inappropriate that she invited me to her apartment for dinner (a meal that consisted of SpaghettiOs, Hershey's Kisses, and LSD). Ignoring all of my attempts to bring our discussion around to the topic of my grade, she tirelessly recounted autobiographical anecdotes about sexual relations with tribals, "men so primitive, so cut off from the world, that they've never heard of India. They make love with an urgency and ferocity that no civilized man can even imagine."

As a result of her ethnographic research, she had concluded that "the Pleio-Pleistocene man always mounted the woman from behind in order to keep his eyes open and on the lookout for an attacking enemy. In this vulnerable situation, the male endeavored to climax as quickly as possible; the female compensated by developing the ability to have an orgasm in a matter of seconds. Their intercourse was informed with a perfectly balanced mixture of desire, pleasure, fear, and wrath." This idea, she hoped, would earn her tenure and promotion.

"Well?" she asked, and since the LSD made me hesitant to come to any conclusions about what anything meant, I responded, "Well, what?"

"Well, do you want to try it?"

"You mean Pleio-Pleistocene style?"

"Yeah. Do you?"

I think I said yes, but actually, I really don't remember much about my undergraduate education.

Sophia White

I met her on my first day in Oxford at the Sea Gull and Child pub, where she was sitting with an iceless gill of gin and an ashtray full of Capstan butts, reading Lee's *The Rival Queens*. There has always been something sexy to me about watching a woman read: she is there and yet elsewhere, absorbed, still, and concentrated (it promises an occasion late at night in bed). She was wearing chocolate brown wool gloves that had the fingers cut off (she'd lick a fingertip to turn a page) and that was sexy too, and so were the matching wool scarf and the well-worn rough-out leather boots.

"Excuse me, I'm new in Oxford and I was wondering . . . "

I've forgotten what I said to her, but it must have been the charming, witty, or urbane utterance of a man-about-town because I remember a warmly hospitable smile and an invitation to sit down. When the pub closed we left together, and I walked her to the forbidding doors of Lady Margaret Hall, in front of which I could not muster the courage to kiss her good night. She must have sensed it because, as she squeezed my hand reassuringly, her fingers seemed to whisper "next time" into my palm.

Without the pluck to telephone her college, I returned daily to the Sea Gull and Child in hopes of running into her again. Several weeks passed before she materialized. I was pleased that she remembered me.

When I told her that I was in England to learn about India, she said that her father had been in India before Independence in some capacity that had always been unclear, and being unclear it must be clear that there was espionage involved; her grandfather, Brigade-Major Francis White ("a blackguard despite the name") had, furthermore, served in the Bengal Lancers and had privately published a limited edition of his memoirs that she would show me someday. "It's shameless in every way—erotically, morally, politically, religiously . . . even rhetorically. My grandmother accepted the fact that her husband was sexually involved with what he called his 'little native nigger girl' because, I suppose, she did not quite consider that dark child a human being in competition with her as a white woman."[5]

Sophia, beyond these personal connections, had some academic interest in India in that she had discovered, among Lee's unpublished papers, a correspondence between her mad poet and the English traveler Sir Thomas Lovely that described the "Tage Mehale" to Lee in lyrical terms, going so far as to say that there was nothing in Europe "so bold or majestick." Apparently inspired by this, Lee had, at the time he was committed to Bedlam, begun making notes for a play that was, because of his madness, never completed—*Mogol Chah Jehan of Hindoustan, or The Triumph of Love, a Tragedy.*

When we were turned out of the closing Sea Gull and Child, I nervously invited her to come to the bar at my college where we drank gin and Indian tonic until we were so drunk that she couldn't bicycle home and had to stay in my room. We lay down next to each other under the duvet, fully dressed (my shoes were cuddled up to her leather boots by my desk), and only when I was certain that she was asleep did I

---

5. Brigade-Major Francis White (1845–1919), as a boy of thirteen, volunteered to serve his Queen in India. He returned to England only once, and very briefly, to marry Beatrice West (in 1877); he fought in the Second Afghan War (1878–81) and the Third Burmese War (1885), after which he retired to spend the rest of his life in Orissa despite the protests of his family in England. His autobiography was privately published in 1900.

˙softly, so softly, kiss her cheek. It was a full year before she confessed
to me that she had been awake.

When Sophia announced that she wanted to introduce me to her
"other American friend, who is also studying Sanskrit," Lee Siegel, I
was, for no reasonable reason, jealous—had she slept with him too? I
didn't want anyone else to ever have made love with her. I had never
in my life felt particularly possessive or jealous before. In fact, normally
in my relations with women, I preferred it if they were, or had been,
promiscuous; my other lovers' other lovers relieved me of the burden
of a feeling that I owed them something in return for their affection
and their sex.

Sophia, indulging my Indological aspirations, bought me a gift the
first Christmas after we met: the Monier Monier-Williams *Sanskrit-
English Dictionary*—not the reprint nor the pirated Indian edition, but
the hefty Oxford original—and she inscribed it "What, my darling, are
the words for 'love' in this language? Whisper them to me. Your
Sophia. Xmas, 1974."

She argued that I didn't need to go to India since I was writing
about ancient India, a vanished civilization, and about Indian texts,
more of which existed in the Bodleian Library than in Indian collec-
tions. But I was adamantly intent upon excavating the present for remains of the past. Against her natural impulses, but encouraged by her
supervisor to go there in order to follow up on "Lee's India connections," she finally agreed to come with me in the summer of '75.

Everything there amazed and dazzled me. Because India is everything I am not, I experienced myself in new way. Sophia was saddened
by the poverty (which made me feel rich), revulsed by the filth (which
made me feel clean), repelled by the lepers (who made me feel healthy).
"My grandmother and mother were victims of men who loved India,
or rather victims of that love," she murmured. "Is that going to be my
story too?"

In hopes that she might be infected by the romance of it, I took her
to the Taj Mahal. She was annoyed by the swarming hawkers and
flocking tourists and unmoved by my stories of the love affair of Shah
Jahan and Mumtaz Mahal. "I'm sorry Leo, it just makes me too sad.
It's just too painful. And having diarrhea is hardly sexy or romantic."

Perhaps I married her after our return to Oxford as an apology, as a
way of thanking her for coming with me. Perhaps I married her so that
I wouldn't have to think about love anymore, so that I could take
courtship and sex, happiness and comfort, companionship and fulfill-

ment all for granted. I married her because, of all the women I had ever met in my life, she seemed the most suitable of mates. And I was always faithful to her, faithful in the sense that I never made love to another woman. But there was India. I went there again and again without her. India was my transgression, my mistress and whore, the female with whom I was having a torrid affair. But Sophia seemed to give me permission for that; she herself often used the phrase "Leopold's love affair with India." I once heard her say to Isaac on the phone, "Yes, that's right, he's going to India again this summer. He's persisting in the love affair, even though he knows the love is unrequited."

2. FRIENDS

A. TRANSLATION

A friend is someone influential during childhood, someone who comes to your defense, someone with whom promises are exchanged, someone with whom secrets are shared, someone with whom a mutually beneficial pact is made, and someone in whom you can confide (the man-about-town often needs a man who can be trusted to assist him with the many little details that must be taken care of in romantic plots, erotic schemes, and strategies for the seduction of girls).

Auddalaki says:

A man who's self-possessed and has a lot of friends
(One who's truthful, one who lies, another who defends),
This man, if knowing when and where to make his passes,
Will surely captivate even the most obdurate of lasses.

B. COMMENTARY
Someone Influential during Childhood
JOCK NEWHOUSE

Jock is a perennial juvenile delinquent, ebullient and adventurous, recklessly charming and urbanely immature in his dotage, resiliently fighting time-tainted nature to the bitter end and making a game of the battle. He knows how to play ontological charades. Whenever he came to our house, it was with a woman for himself, a bottle of champagne for my parents, and a gift for me—once he brought me the sinister black bull whip that had been his weapon in *The Return of the Son of Casanova*.

The sharp-eyed, smiling actor generously initiated me into the danger-tinged pleasures of tobacco. Although I had already tried to smoke Sunita Sen's lipstick-marked Rothman butts, I didn't really know what I was doing until Jock became my professor. "You're thirteen," he grinned, "and you still haven't experienced the best things in life: smoking, drinking, and schtupping women." He snapped open his silver cigarette case and I reached for my first real smoke. Jock smoked Luckies and still does, lots of them, every day. He taught me how to blow smoke rings like a man-about-town, the art that a few years later, as a postcoital divertissement, amply impressed Leona Sealman. By the time I met Sophia in the Sea Gull and Child, I could puff one silken white ring through another, and there was something stirringly erotic about the hazy vision of penetration and merger, the smoky fusion of two into one from the inside out, the dissipation of boundaries, ethereal and transient. What, I always wonder, do people who don't smoke do after making love?

Jock taught me drinking too—gin and tonic, the libation of the Raj, with that bit of quinine to ward off Indian malaria, that tad of vitamin C in the lime to prevent scurvy, and that dose of juniper, an aphrodisiac according to the *Kamasutra*.

"There can be no true friendship," Jock rhapsodized, "without drinking. Without drinking there can be no good party, no true feast, no real celebration, secular or religious. Drinking is camaraderie and communion." He laughed and downed his grog. "But do you know what's better than drinking, better than smoking, better than anything in the world?"

"Doing it with girls?" I answered confidently, not sure that it was true, but secure that it was the answer he wanted, if not needed.

"*A+*, kid, *A+*! That's the greatest thing, Leo, to schtup women. You have a lot to look forward to. Do it as often as you can, do it with all your heart, your soul, your might, happily and heartily, religiously, with joy and the knowledge that you're affirming life, doing just what God created you to do. When both the man and the woman have pleasure, God Himself shivers with delight and takes pride in what He has made." I love happy Jock, Saint Jock, the priapic priest of the cult of glad love, because he really believes that stuff and wants me to believe it too. It was that genuinely innate, adolescent joie de vivre that came across so vividly in his movies. It made him a star.

Not so long ago, Jock telephoned from the hospital, where he was recovering from the implant operation, waiting anxiously to try out his new penis and a bit testy because the nurses wouldn't let him smoke. Hoping that they might ignore a few cocktails or even join him, he asked me to bring a bottle of Bombay gin, some tonic, and limes. But that was, I think, just an excuse to get me there so that he could show off the two new things that were the compatible sources of a fresh, and clearly expansive, delight—his revamped penis and his latest girlfriend.

He started with the penis: "I didn't want the one you have to pump up. This beauty is always erect, always hard enough for penetration, but flexible enough so that it can be comfortably held down by tight underwear while not in use."

It was, I must admit, a magnificent sight even with the stitches in it: large, firm, and seemingly proud to be a vehicle and symbol of pleasure and virility, seemingly happy to have had a long life and looking forward to new adventures, defiant of death and hell, pointing straight and eternally toward heaven. It would be erect even in the grave. In Hindu terms it would be considered a manifestation of god, an epiphanic source of blessings, sanctifying the life of anyone who beheld or touched it or made offerings to it.[6] In Jock's terms it was a monument erected to the seminal virtue of fun. Jock always has, as long as I've known him, wanted to have fun, struggling heroically in every situation, always with all his heart, to make others laugh and to laugh himself. Love and sex for Jock Newhouse are, above all, sovereign wellsprings of mirth, emancipated from the procreant urge, freed from everything but themselves as experiences of pure pleasure, of perfect and holy fun. He was my father's best friend, his only real friend at the end.

Next, his other new pride and fresh joy, his "girlfriend":

"Let me show you something," he winked as he reached for the copy of a pornographic magazine called *Cocktail*. Opening it to a

6. The reference is to the Śiva-linga, the phallus of the deity that is venerated in India as the primary phenomenal manifestation of the god. Pralayānanga, in the context of his commentary on the discussion of penile prostheses in *Kāmasūtra* VII.B, explains, "All pious people are eager to worship the linga in the shrine [thus it follows]: A man [should], upon waking up in the morning and before going to bed at night, make reverential salutations, offering benedictions and hymns of praise or supplication to the linga on his own body, placed there as the god, by the god, for the god; a woman [should] consider any assignation with a man as a visit to a shrine and [should] bow to his linga (as a manifestation of god) and make offerings of ghee and curds, flowers and incense to that holy form."

spread of a spread-open young girl with one high heel pointing to the ceiling, one hand squeezing her breast, the other hand separating the swollen labia of her glistening vulva, and her tongue lewdly extended, he smiled. "Isn't she beautiful? I'm in love with her, really in love. Her name's Bonnie Ray Oswald, but she uses the stage name Venus Doudounes—I helped her come up with that one. She wants to be an actress, not the porno stuff, but real movies—art, cinema! She's wonderful. And she knows how to type a little—she's helping me with my memoirs."

On the next page Venus was joined by another woman for a performance of mutual cunnilingus; I asked Jock if that bothered him.

"No, that's Thelma," he said. "Cute girl, real bright and lots of fun. She's in law school. Do you want me to introduce you to her?"

"Jock, my life is a mess already," I suddenly said, and surprising myself I told him about Lalita, confessed my plan to take Her to India. "I've never been unfaithful to Sophia. I don't know why I'm so suddenly obsessed with the girl. I don't even know Her. She's just in my class. It probably doesn't really have anything to do with Her. This may sound ridiculous, but it has something to do with India. I've dedicated my life to studying Sanskrit, to learning about India, yet I've never made love to an Indian woman."

"Yeah, you've got to do something about that," he said with utter sincerity, as if what I was saying actually deserved to be taken seriously. "Life is too long to forgo doing what you know deep down you need to do. Don't worry about being ridiculous. You've got to schtup her. That's all there is to it. I'd like to go to India someday. Maybe we should go together. Do you remember me in *The Curse of Kali*? Damn, I was good. Eddie was good. Tina was good. We were all good, and we were all having fun down there on location in Mexico. Too bad about the *Taj Mahal* picture. Do you remember Sunita Sen? That's the only Indian I ever schtupped, as far as I can remember. I mean Indian from India; there was Loretta Eagleheels, of course—she was an Indian from America. I met her on the set of *Darkness over Dakota*—God, I loved her."

I brought him back to Sunita Sen.

"She was hungry," he sighed with sympathy, "really hungry—she wanted to be loved so desperately, more than any man could ever love a woman. Her problem was that she didn't care about having fun, only about being loved."

When I asked him if my father had an affair with her, he laughed. "Everybody had an affair with her."

I wished I could have been older; I would have loved her, and she wouldn't have needed to be so desperate. I would have cared for her, adored her, worshiped and protected her. I felt I understood her and knew she would have responded to that.

When Venus suddenly arrived in the hospital room, Jock's pecker was still on display.

"It's wonderful," she smiled genuinely, and the beam of her expression, it was plain to see, made Jock smile in turn with unequivocal joy, and it seemed that his smile broadened her smile. With peroxided hair, long eyelashes and Lee Press-On Nails, monumental breast implants, and wearing a tight black spandex miniskirt and a T-shirt (emblazoned with the phrase "HAVE FUN!"), she looked rather like a parody of female sexuality. As I shook her hand, I felt disapproval naturally arise out of a reasonable suspicion that she was only bothering with old Jock because she imagined he could do something for her movie career, or perhaps she thought that she might soon inherit some of his money.

She had brought red roses for him and a get-well card which, when opened, played a little tune ("All You Need is Love"). Jock passed it to me and I read, under the printed words to the song, Venus's inscription: "I can't write 'get better' because you're already the best! With all my heart, all my flesh, and all my soul, Forever, Your Goddess of Love."

"It's amazing isn't it?" Jock smiled in awe. "I mean the electronics and technology that go into a little gizmo like this! A card that plays a tune! It's miraculous. It's giving me an idea, a wonderful idea. I've got to talk to my doctor. I want one of whatever is in this card implanted my in my scrotum so that my schlong can croon! Yeah, I want it to stand up and serenade my Venus with some fantastic aria as all the other parts of my body form a chorus and hum along. Wouldn't that be spectacular?"

I had to agree that it would be rather sensational.

"I showed Leo your layout in *Cocktail,* honey. Why don't you autograph one for him?"

Jock wouldn't listen to my insistence that I didn't want to take his magazine.

"I've got plenty," he said proudly. "Sign one for him, darling. He's a great kid." She did as she was told, and there were tears of joy in Jock's wide eyes, really and truly the look of love, as he gazed at her. You could tell that he felt he was a lucky man.[7]

Someone Who Comes to Your Defense

DR. PAUL PLANTER

I have to admit it: Professor P. Planter, chairman of the Department of Asian Studies, did come to my defense against the Indian community of Southern California and the protests of Dr. Nilkanth Gupta. By Vatsyayana's criteria, I must consider him a friend (even though I don't actually like him) because, with tireless conviction, he wrote countless memos and letters on my behalf, supporting me as the best available candidate in the world (civilized and uncivilized) for the professorship in Indian studies, asserting that, far more than any of the other candidates ("Asian or Western, female or male, disabled or not"), I was able to "analytically integrate a penetrating linguistic and metacultural knowledge of Indian civilizations into a global reconceptualization of universal issues and phenomena, and to do so with unique methodological prowess and hermeneutic acumen. The issue is not a geographic area, but an academic discipline. India in this case, like all countries and cultures, at whatever period, is but a context, as defined by arbitrary cartographic imperatives, for data out of which the scholar has an intellectual mandate to exegetically establish metaphors and semaphores that serve intracultural, discur-

---

7. I found the copy of *Cocktail* in Roth's desk when, as literary executor, I was going through his papers. "Any friend of Jock's is a friend of mine," Ms. Doudounes had written, and signed it, "Love, Venus." I rarely look at this sort of publication, and so, while I certainly do not consider myself a prude or in any way a sexual spoilsport, I must admit that I was somewhat shocked by the magazine with its utter lack of text (other than obviously fictional confessional letters passed off as nonfiction and an illustrated story about a Mexican houseboy entitled "Training Manuel") and its endless pages of lurid photo-illustrated ads for phone sex, videos, and such products as penis enlargers, vibrating dildos, aphrodisiacs, and life-size inflatable dolls. It is pornographic rather than erotic in my estimation, the latter being literature or images that are about sexuality, about arousal, as opposed to the former, which is literature that tries to be sex, to substitute for sex, to arouse rather than illuminate. It's a question of intent, of both *intentio auctoris* and *intentio lectoris*. And what does my definition make of the *Kāmasūtra*, not only the original Sanskrit text but the innumerable illustrated editions, from Indian palm leaf manuscripts commissioned by impotent maharajas to modern Western versions for the coffee tables of the fallen and faded equivalent of Vātsyāyana's ancient man-about-town? And what does my definition make of Roth's attempts to arouse Lalita with language? That was, I am convinced, ultimately his intent, the *intentio amatoris*. Aphra Digby has explained another way of distinguishing between pornography and art: "If you want to turn a dirty book into literature, just introduce death into the discourse. Death makes sex profound. It turns pornography into pornosophy" (personal communication).

sive representations of ontological processes in ways and terms that challenge established assumptions, while functioning socially to reaffirm the academy as the locus for the continuousness of a redis-cernment of a meaningfully linked series of the processive phenom-ena that come to be accepted as 'reality.'"

In return for thus defending me with semantic misdirection, how-ever, he expected me, for the many years that followed my appoint-ment, to cover for him whenever he needed an alibi for his frequent marital infidelities. I warned him that Sophia was, as dean of Acade-mic Affairs and chair of the Committee on Sexual Harassment, quite serious about putting an end to intimate interactions between faculty and students.[8] Unperturbed by the caveat, Planter cheerfully contended that as a dedicated scholar, wholly devoted to the life of the university, the only women he had an opportunity to meet and seduce were stu-dents. "But don't think that I don't love my wife. The girls are impor-tant. They keep me in touch with student life, with what the kids are thinking about these days. It's always consensual and, I swear to you, I never let it affect my grading," he said without the slightest trace of con-trition. "It's important when you're married to a foreign speaker, par-ticularly an Asian, to make love in English once in a while." He assured me that Pimiko approved. "Japanese women expect their husbands to go out drinking with their colleagues several times a week and to use that as an excuse for adventures with other women occasionally, if not regularly. Don't you see? I need you to lie to her, even though she knows it's a lie, so that she can pretend it's the truth. If I didn't do it, she'd lose face; she'd think I was professionally irresponsible and sexu-ally underdeveloped. She couldn't be proud of me. I'm unfaithful to her for her sake, out of respect for the erotic conventions of her culture."

One night when I was playing the beard for him, after he had told Pimiko that we were comparing Sanskrit and Japanese versions of a Buddhist text on "discipline for nuns," Sophia telephoned to say that she had a late deans' meeting with the president, and my stomach

8. The University Policy on Sexual Harassment, which was indeed written by a com-mittee chaired by Professor Sophia White-Roth in her capacity as dean of Academic Af-fairs, states: "The respect and trust accorded a faculty member by a student as well as the power exercised by the faculty member in giving grades and recommendations greatly di-minish the student's freedom of choice should the faculty member's requests for sexual fa-vors be included along with his or her legitimate expectations. A faculty member who en-ters into a sexual relationship with a student where a professional power differential exists must be aware of the possible consequences of even an apparently consenting sexual rela-tionship."

churned with unfounded suspicions and irrational fears that she might possibly be with Planter. I don't really believe that it was so, but in relations between men and women, I have discovered, anything—absolutely anything—is possible.

Someone with Whom Promises Are Exchanged

DR. NILKANTH GUPTA

Leaving his office for my office immediately after receiving official and formal notification that Ms. L. Gupta had been "accepted into the Advanced Program for Summer Study in India," Dr. Gupta arrived late in the afternoon.

"You are a friend, my great Professor, and I am obliged and thoroughly indebted even so much that I must humbly ask pardon that, in a previous time, unknowing of your beneficence and prestige, I was somewhat equivocal about your appointment to the esteemed Indological Chair upon which you now sit as a befitting throne to your erudition. You are, my great one, more than a friend—you are a brother, and I am confident to the utmost that, as a brother, you will look after my daughter as your own kin."

Despite his exuberance, I could tell there was something bothering him.

"I am proud to know you," Dr. Gupta said sincerely, but rather sadly, and then hesitating, the gynecologist lowered his voice. "You are my friend and I am, likewise, your friend. Isn't it so? The ancient Indian sages opined that friends must assist each other in every way at all times. Thus you must help me with one small problem which threatens to become large. Now that my fine daughter has, because of your concern and understanding of how important it is for a person to be educated in the ways and means of their own culture, been appropriately accepted for the India program, she refuses to go. Women! It is, I am certain, because of the basketball player, the famous Mr. Lovelace. She insists with a melodramatic *Mississippi Masala* sort of histrionics that she doesn't want to be parted from the fellow. Imagine giving up Indian civilization for a Negro in short pants who spends his time throwing a rubber ball into a basket placed high up, for no good reason, on some wall! The young are prone to confuse infatuation with love. You must, as the esteemed director of the prestigious program, convince the child that she will have a rollicking good time in India. While I, of course, expect you, dedicated scholar that you are, to demand diligent study once there, I want you, as my friend please, to give her, at this time, the impression that it will be so much fun there—fun, fun, and more fun in the sun. Tell her how romantic India is. Yes, feed the love fantasies of a young and inexperienced girl."

I promised.

"But then, my friend, once you are in India," he gazed at me plaintively, "please promise me that you will keep a protectively well-peeled eye on her. She is so naive, and thus some scoundrel could attempt to take advantage of her. Promise me that you will be strict with her night and day. Promise me that you will take care of her in every way."

I promised.

"I knew," he said, "that I could count on you, my friend."

Someone with Whom Secrets Are Shared

MS. LALITA GUPTA

The very next day, right after class, Lalita (the assigned *Kamasutra* and the notebook for my course, cradled in her arm, were adornments to Her natural beauty) came to my office.

"Professor Roth, you've got to help me. I need your help. Can I close the door?"

When I explained that the university's sexual harassment policy precluded shutting the door and that the regulation was strictly enforced by the department secretary, Ms. Naper, She lowered her voice to a whisper.

"Listen. My father is, as you may have noticed, obsessed. India, India, fuckin' India—that's all he thinks about. This summer study scheme of his is just a ploy to separate me from Leroy. He wants to arrange a marriage for me in India, to some Indian guy who I don't even know. The whole thing's ridiculous, and I don't want to go. My father's a racist. I'm not going. That's all there is to it. If he insists, I'll run away with Leroy. He's going to Chicago after graduation. Please, help me. Please!"

"Well I think it is important to be respectful of Your parents' wishes," I admonished, disappointed as to the reason for Her visit. I had hoped that She might have come in response to my comments on the paper that She had written on the *Kamasutra* for my class.

"I figured that's what you'd say, that you'd be on their side and not mine. So what's the point of talking to you about it? I had hoped you'd put in a word for me and maybe tell him that, on a previous trip, a girl got pregnant or something, that you disclaim any responsibilities as a chaperon, that you can't supervise the fuckin' sex lives of the students in the program. If he thinks that I'll be screwing around, there'll be no way he'll let me go. Please help me. I love Leroy. I mean I really love him. Do you know what it's like to be in love? If I go to India, it'll be over. Leroy will find someone else. I want to marry him and spend the rest of my life taking care of him. I love him. Please help me."

As she spoke, an extraordinary thing happened, a change in me, a realization that this was not merely some midlife sexual surge, some minor infatuation, but rather a breakthrough for me in terms of my understanding of love: all selfish motives were eclipsed by a kind of transcendent love, a love that yearns to give to the beloved, to free, rather than possess, Her. I listened to myself vowing to help Her.

"I'll tell your father that the trip has been canceled due to lack of enrollment or some such thing. Let me work it out. I want to help You. I do care about You. I really do."

"Oh thank you, Professor, thank you! I can hardly believe it! Thank you!" She cried with an exuberance that reminded me of Her father, and then She actually leaned forward in the chair and put Her hands on my hands, which were on my knees. I could feel Her warmth radiate up my thighs, into my groin, through my stomach, up my back, and into my shoulders, and I missed a breath.

"Yes, I'll help You, Ms. Gupta," I said slowly and purposefully. "I want You to have what You want."

She smiled, stood, and when I rose to see Her to the open door, She suddenly, without warning, surged forward and kissed me on the cheek.

"Thank you Professor Roth," She said from the doorway with an open and radiant smile. "You're a friend, really a friend. And that means a lot to me."

Is friendship a kind of love, I wondered, a sentimental subcategory of it, or a larger class of emotion that subsumes love? Or is friendship a response utterly distinct from, or even anathema to, love? There is none of the violation, ferocity, urgency, or thrill of love in friendship; there's none of the trust, ease, or taking-it-for-granted-ness of friendship in love. In my experience, any time a woman has said to me that she "wanted to be friends," it has meant "I do not want to be physically intimate with you," if not "I find you completely disgusting." But suddenly, I said to myself, "No. Love *is* an aspect of friendship. Friend-

ship is, indeed, the highest expression of love, freed as it is from need."
For the first time in my life I believed that the Pauline *agape*, the theologian's *caritas*, was not a construct reflecting a repression, or even a sublimation, of a more primary *eros*, the libertine's *amor;* I understood that all the saints, the holy ones of both India and the West, were right, that true love is gratuitous and kind, unblemished by possessiveness, envy, lust, jealously, anger, disappointment, or fear. It is a friendship. The truth was so obvious. One does not desire to have the beloved; one desires for the beloved to have. Because I truly loved Her, I wanted Lalita to find fulfillment in love with the man She loved—Leroy Lovelace.

I might have actually continued to desire that for Her, to give Her up for myself for Her sake, in the name of true love, even to believe all that stuff about a higher love, about charity, selflessness, and friendship, if Mr. Leroy Lovelace himself had not, only fifteen minutes after Lalita had left, arrived in my office. It would have been such a beautiful story, all amatory sacrifice, self-discovery, and high ideals. It would have been good. But it would not have been true.

Someone with Whom a Mutually Beneficial Pact Is Made

LEROY LOVELACE

I assumed that Lovelace had come to discuss the failing grade he had just received on the paper on the *Kamasutra* that he had submitted in my class.[9] But he didn't seem to care about that.

"You've got to help me," he said quite sadly. "I need your help, man. Can I close the door?" As I explained the university's open-door pol-

---

9. The failing grade was hardly contestable. Parts of the opening of the paper rang a bell since I, undoubtedly like Mr. Lovelace, had perused the entertainment section of the *Los Angeles Times* that week. Compare the first page of his paper with the ad for *Kama Sutra* that appeared in the *Times:*

> The Kama Sutra, a very well-written and in all respects excellent, informative and educational book by a great author from India named Vatsyana [*sic*] Mallanaga, is drop dead beautiful. It is truly a rhythmic, sensual book, amazingly sexy. It is luminous, exotic, and alluring. It is also sensual, triumphantly sensual and sumptuous. I would even go as far as to say, sumptuous beyond description. Furthermore it is a lush storybook dream and a tale of love. It was highly readable. I especially liked the beginning when the two naked girls were swimming around under water, and I thought the heroine of the book looked real good. I'm glad you assigned the book to us to read because I think everybody ought to read it at least once in a lifetime. I know I'm glad I did [etc.].

icy to him, I noticed that he was carrying the *Kamasutra* and his note-book for my class.

"Listen, Professor, I want to talk to you man-to-man, like a friend, okay? I know I'm not that good a student or anything, that you and I have nothing to talk about when it comes to India or intellectual shit, but a man is a man, if you know what I mean, and so I know you can understand what's on my mind. When it comes to pussy, it doesn't matter if you got a Ph.D. or if you're illiterate; it doesn't matter if you're the NBA Player of the Year or some spastic who couldn't even get on the Special Olympics team; it doesn't matter if you're on *Lifestyles of the Rich and Famous* or on some CNN special on the homeless; it doesn't matter whether you're white or black or yellow or even green for that matter. As men, when it comes to women, we're all in the same love boat. And as men we got to help each other out. Right?"

Expecting him to make the pitch that Lalita had already made, to enlist me as a go-between responsible for propitiating the Guptas, I was more than surprised by what he had to say.

"Look, I've been getting it on with this Indian chick in the class, Lalita—I'm sure you've noticed her and how she can't keep her

When I encouraged Roth to see this film, he sneered disdainfully, claiming that he didn't go movies because he couldn't smoke in them. But I suspect that his resistance was because he felt a kind of possessive-ness, that in translating the *Kāmasūtra* and writing a commentary upon it, he had an intimate relationship with it; it was to him, I think, as if, in allowing it-self to be made into a movie, the text had be-trayed him, had been un-faithful to him as its lover. The book had become what it is about.

hands off me even in class. Hey, she's a sweet girl, don't get me wrong. She's a good girl, good in bed, pretty smart, and nice, real nice. But the problem is, she's gotten possessive and that just don't work for me. I mean I gotta move on—you know? I'm graduating. I'm going to play in the NBA, man. The NBA! Yeah, I'm going to have a Lamborghini and lots of pussy. It's unbelievable how it happened. Some mutherfucker pulled a prank on me—called me up, said he was Phil Jackson and that he wanted me to come to Chicago. So I went. How was I to know it wasn't really Jackson? I had the wrong address, but finally, after calling the stadium and getting one number, then another, and another, I'll be damned if I wasn't talking to the coach of the Chicago Bulls, the real man himself—Phil Jackson. He said he never called me! Shit, I was embarrassed, man—confused, mad, and I didn't know what to say next. The amazing thing is that he believed me. The man figured out that it must have been a joke. Phil's real smart. Not only that, he's nice, real nice. He laughed about the whole thing and then said he'd watch me play, you know, since I had come all that way an' all and spent all that money. The rest is history, man, fuckin' his-to-reee! I'm going to play for the Chicago Bulls—me, little old me! We got all the technical hassles with the draft and my contract worked out. The asshole who tried to fuck me up actually got me into the NBA! So who's laughing now? You understand? You see what I'm saying? I can't let this chick get in the way of the Bulls' future, can I? Now I like the girl, don't get me wrong. Maybe I even love her. Yeah, I do love her. But I'm just not ready to settle down with one lady, you know? There's a world out there. I mean I'm a young man. You know? You understand; you remember when you were young. You didn't want just one pussy, right? No man does."

Simultaneously I detested him for being so unappreciative of Lalita and loved him for being so willing to let Her go. I was proud to have helped him in his career and genuinely looking forward to taking full credit for it when he went on to lead the Chicago Bulls to another NBA championship.

"What exactly do you want from me, Mr. Lovelace?" I asked sympathetically.

He leaned forward and put his hands on my hands, which were on my knees.

"I want you to call me Leroy for starters. Like a friend, man. Listen. I've got a plan. I want you to tell Lalita that you've arranged for me to go on the summer trip to India. We'll tell her that we're keeping it a secret so that her father and my coach here don't find out. We'll tell her that Phil Jackson is the only other person who knows about it, and that he said it was alright for me to go. She'll believe it, and then she'll agree to go on the trip. And once she's out of town, well, that'll be it. I got it all figured out. I'll give you a note to give her once you're on the plane, or over there in India—whenever you think the time's right—explaining that it's best for both of us to say good-bye to each other and get on with our lives. It's the right thing for everybody. I mean I'm not doing it just for me but for her too, and her parents. And for the Bulls of course. I've thought a lot about it. It's the best thing for everybody. Don't you think so?"

"Oh, absolutely," I assured him, so thrilled with what I was hearing that I wanted to kiss Mr. Lovelace just as Lalita had kissed me, a kiss of friendship and gratitude. Rather than kiss him, however, I shook his hand and assured him that, as a man, I understood his feelings, that as men there was an incorruptible bond between us—a camaraderie. I vowed to help him, explaining that, in my opinion, following the edicts of Vatsyayana, to help another man with a woman is to help oneself as a man. In return he gave me tickets for the next home basketball game, and in a show of good faith, I raised the grade on his paper from an *F* to an *A*.

He reiterated the plan: "Now remember, we've got to convince her I'm going to India with you. She's got to believe it, or she won't get on that plane. I'm going to tell her that I talked to you, and because you're such a big basketball fan and a fan of mine in particular, you arranged to get me into this weird-ass India study thing just to help her and me out, to give us a chance to be together, really together, without her parents bothering us and without me having basketball practice all the time. We want her to dream about India, picturing herself there with the man she loves, being with him night and day. I'm going to tell her what a great guy you are, and that you've got a real soft spot for people in love."

"Yes," I said as I shook his enormous hand, "tell Her that all I do, I do for love."

Now both Lalita and Leroy smiled at me continually during class. And I smiled back at them. Everyone was happy. My dear friend Dr. Gupta telephoned to thank me.

"You are wonderful! You are great! I don't know how you did it. Now, much to my astonishment, but in keeping with my prayers, my blessed daughter wants to go to our India with you! You must have quite a way with women! You certainly seem to have a way with my daughter, and she, I must admit, can be quite obdurate. You are quite a man, my friend!"

"Oh, please," I responded with humility. "It's really my pleasure."

Someone in Whom You Can Confide

ANANG SAIGHAL

My graduate student and teaching assistant, Mr. Anang Saighal, asked me today if he might be permitted to use my office this summer while I am in India. After agreeing to it, and feeling confident that he (reliant upon me, as he is, in his hopes of successfully completing his dissertation and being awarded a doctoral degree) would not dare to betray me, I have decided that I shall, just prior to my departure, confide in him. I need someone, a man, as Professor Vatsyayana teaches, **who can be trusted to assist with the many little details involved in romantic plots, erotic schemes, and strategies for the seduction of girls.** I need someone to cover for me in case there are inquires about the program.

On the surface our relationship is professional and respectful, formal but friendly; one level down, right beneath the cordial facade, however, we annoy each other (he disapproves of my drinking, if not my scholarship, and I'm impatient with his moral stodginess, if not his academic fastidiousness); yet another level down and we are more interested in each other (me in the young man who is some of the things that I would like to have been, and he in the old man who has some of the things that he hopes to have); one more layer of the onion, down another floor, and we detest each other for some reason I do not quite understand; one more plane, another layer, deeper down, there in the basements of our selves, there in the darkness, we do, I think, understand each other and are the closest of friends for some reason that I do not comprehend (although I know it is the same reason that makes us dislike each other up above).

Yes, I'll confide in Saighal. There is no pleasure in deception, I've discovered, unless someone knows the truth; without that person, there's no one to appreciate the skill of the deceiver, to recognize the artfulness of the lies and hoaxes; it's as if there is no priest in the confessional, no reader of the book.

Here Ends Book One of the *Kamasutra*.

II

FUCKING

I want to write about fucking. Fucking happily, gloriously, freely, and, above all else, lovingly, getting pleasure by giving pleasure by getting pleasure by giving pleasure in a fantastic dizzying spiral of infinite delight. For eighty-four of my ninety-seven years on this wonderful earth—made so enchanting and lush by floral, faunal, and human fucking—I've fucked as often as I could, joyfully giving myself over unceasingly to my instincts and discovering that when we so surrender, we realize that our urges are marvelous and good and do no harm provided they are given unbridled dominion over the soul. I want to write about fucking, my razzing answer to death, my most spiritual experience of love, my holiest communion with God, my ecstatic celebration of the miracle of life, the obvious reason for my existence—both its cause and mandate. Yes, I believe in God, just like I believe in fucking. Someday maybe I'll write about God, but now I want to write about fucking, and I want all the women who read what I've written to be pleased, to feel that they have made love with me, or at least that they'd like to. And I want the men who read this to feel that they've made love to the women that I've made love to, or at least that they'd like to. I want to write about fucking, but I'll be damned if what is so beautiful when you're doing it, dreaming or thinking about it, or talking about it with the one you've done it with doesn't become something else on paper. Descriptions of fucking fall flat. And that's why, as you read these pages, I'd like you to reach down and touch your genitals, as kindly, sweetly, and tenderly as you can, just so you'll know what I'm talking about. It's okay, you can do it. Because I'm playing with myself as I write this, I hope you're doing the same as you read it. Otherwise there's not much point. Go ahead. Don't be shy or modest, prudish or self-conscious. That's it. It feels nice, doesn't it?

—Jock Newhouse (with Venus Doudounes), *The Silent Years,*
vol. 1 of *Memoirs of the Vagabond of Love*

A. Mix and Match

"Opposites attract," the professors say, and it's damn true. The old white worm can't say no to a fresh brown burrow, whether it be in Nubia, Abu Sinnel, or the Malabar Hills, where I was stationed when it occurred to me that Man has not Free Will, not a piss of it, despite the musings of this metaphysician or that, epicure or epicene. It was as that pucka native mopsy sat wiggling rampant in my lap, giggling as I fucked her, that I realized it's all just and only chance. We're haughtish tempted to reckon we choose our mate or poke, or that she's destiny's cumshaw, if not God-given or Satan-sent. But no, beyond the laws of magnetism, governing the universe as they do, it's chance. Of course, you've got to be skilled at the game so you don't lose what chance presents you.

—Edward Sellon, *The Ups and Downs of Life: A Discursus on Man and Woman, Lingam and Yoni, Old and Young, White and Black, West and East, for Better or for Worse, &c. and &c.* (1865)

1. BIG AND SMALL

A. TRANSLATION

Men may be categorized according to penile dimensions as *rabbits, bulls,* or *stallions;* women may be catalogued according to cuntal capacities as *does, mares,* or *she-elephants.* There are sexual *fits* (doe-rabbit, mare-bull, elephant-stallion) and *misfits.* The *misfitian* (or *mixed*) sexual union is subcategorized into *high* (when the penis is bigger than the vagina [and this is, in turn, sub-subcategorized according to how much bigger]) and *low* (when the pudenda is bigger than the mentula [and this too is sub-subcategorized by degree]). *Matched sexual union* is best, but *high copulation* is better than the *low fuck.*

B. COMMENTARY[1]

1. Here Roth's commentary takes the form of a Kāmasūtra game. Essentially an adaption of Book Two, the game incorporates each chapter into some aspect of play, thus

Kamasutra

The Game of Love

A GAME FOR TWO PLAYERS

PLAYERS:
 a man (*nagaraka* or "man-about-town")
 a woman (*ganika* or "courtesan")

CONTENTS:
 1 *Kamasutra* (illustrated text and English translation of Book Two)
 1 game board
 6 pawns (representing Vatsyayana's classification of lovers according to genital dimensions [*K.S.* II.A]):
   3 male: rabbit, bull, stallion
   3 female: doe, mare, elephant
 64 *Kamakala* cards (representing each of Vatsyayana's 64 Arts of Sexual Love)
 1 pair of dice

OBJECT:
 To be the first player to move all three of his or her pawns into the *Kamaloka*,
 the World of Eternal Pleasure.

THE BOARD:
 A. Men's Court *(Sabha)*
 B. Women's Quarters *(Antahpura)*
 C. Dicing Hall *(Akshabhumi)*
 D. Vatsyayana's School *(Goshtishala)*
 E. Eightfold Path *(Ashtamarga)*
 F. Circles of Transformation (*Chakra*s)
 G. World of Eternal Pleasure *(Kamaloka)*

SETUP:
 The female player sits in the Women's Quarters (the corner of that chamber
 pointing toward her, the Dicing Hall on her right). The male player sits across
 from his opponent (at the corner of his court, with Vatsyayana's School on his
 right).

 The woman's pawns are in her quarters; the man's are in his court. The pawns
 are placed in the circles designated for the particular animal classification of
 men and women that each represents.

 The sixty-four *kamakala* cards are shuffled and placed face-down in the designated circle in Vatsyayana's School.

 The dice are placed in the Dicing Hall. Each player makes one roll of the dice;
 the higher roller starts, then the players alternate turns.

A. MEN'S COURT *(SABHA)*

Vatsyayana's debonair men-about-town, the *nagaraka*s [*K.S.* I.D], would gather
in halls or other meeting places to exhibit their wit and intellectual prowess, their
social graces and mastery of the arts. They would discuss language and literary
composition and would speak of women, adventures, and love. In dedication to
maintaining and refining those conventions that had the potential to invest their
lives with elegance, they would pass the afternoons in cultural endeavors, joking
perhaps, composing erotic poems, or reciting tales of love. And then, in the

evenings, it was time to enjoy the pleasures upon which they had reflected during the day. It was time to play the game.

To move out of the Men's Court, the man-about-town must, before rolling the dice, choose a pawn and place it in one of the two entry squares (x) adjacent to the court. Only one pawn may be put into play at a time, and once in play, a pawn may not return to the court. Each pawn's designated space within the court will become the area in which the *kamakala* cards drawn by that pawn during play are kept (face up). Selected cards always belong specifically to the pawn who draws them (rather than to the player who is in command of that pawn).

B. WOMEN'S QUARTERS *(ANTAHPURA)*

In salons, harems, and chic bordellos, urbane ladies, *ganika*s [*K.S.* VI], (young girls as well as more experienced women of the world) would convene to teach and learn the arts of love, to become more erotically cosmopolitan and sexually sophisticated, to master the graces and skills of sensual expression that would refine them and make the world all the more beautiful for their presence in it [*K.S.* I.C]. They were intent upon the most sublime and delicate of delights, the sweetest interchanges, the give and take of pleasure with the most suave and accomplished of paramours. And like the men, they waited for the evening. Drawing, painting, dancing, singing, exchanging secrets, laughing, perhaps dozing and dreaming, they were eager to play all of the games of love.

To move a pawn out of the Women's Quarters, the courtesan must, before rolling the dice, place her pawn (as chosen before the roll) in one of the two entry squares (y) adjacent to those quarters. As with the male players, only one pawn may be put into play at a time, and once in play, a pawn cannot return to her quarters. Each pawn's designated space within the quarters will become the area in which that pawn's *kamakala* cards are kept (face up) as they are collected during play.

C. DICING HALL *(AKSHABHUMI)*

Vatsyayana includes skill in dicing and a proficiency in various board games in which dice are used in his list of talents to be acquired by those men and women who hope to experience fulfillment in amorous pursuits. There is the luck of the throw, the chance of the roll, the fate of the game: the skill is in knowing what to do with the numbers on the dice—what pawn to move and what square to enter, when, where, and with whom, to give oneself over to love.

With the throw of the dice into the Dicing Hall, a pawn may be moved in any direction (but in only one direction for that roll) along the Eightfold Path according to the roll of the dice. Once all three of a player's pawns are on the board, any pawn may be moved. A player may move either one or two pawns on his or her turn (for example, if a player rolls 4 and 3, a single pawn can be moved 7 spaces or two pawns can be moved—one 4 spaces and the other 3 spaces).

Note that the four double spaces in the centers of the four edges of the board give flexibility to the movement designated by the throw of the dice: they can be used to change the destination of the moving pawn by plus or minus one space, depending by which of the spaces adjacent to these double spaces the pawn chooses to enter and exit.

C

E

F

Cremation Ground

Linga Puja

Shrine of Kama

Marriage Hall

E

F

F

X

X

B

♀

5

D. VATSYAYANA'S SCHOOL *(GOSHTISHALA)*

The *Kamasutra* is an academic textbook and Professor Vatsyayana undoubtedly had students who went to him to study the ancient amatory arts and traditional sexual sciences. His scholastic enumeration of the sixty-four classical Arts of Sexual Love is preserved on the *kamakala* cards (which players attempt to collect for each pawn as a record of their sexual education, of the knowledge acquired in the school and put into practice by playing the game of love).

The *kamakala* cards, round in the traditional Indian style, each depict of one of the sixty-four erotic activities constituting the Arts of Sexual Love as delineated and described by Vatsyayana in Book Two of the *Kamasutra*. There are eight suits, distinguished by background color and corresponding to Vatsyayana's classification of the eight modes of erotic enjoyment [*K.S.* II.B–I]. There are eight cards in each suit, representing Vatsyayana's descriptive lists of, and technical terms for, the ways of indulging in those eight categories of sexual dalliance:

> 1. *Embraces (red)* [*K.S.* II.B]: *frottage, grab bag, bump-and-grind, crush, creeper, climber, sesame-and-rice, milk-and-water*
>
> 2. *Kisses (orange)* [*K.S.* II.C]: *hard-pressed, reverential, gentle, passionizer, gambit, alarm clock, phantom, trompe l'oeil*
>
> 3. *Scratching (yellow)* [*K.S.* II.D]: *crescent moon, half moon, tiger claw, peacock foot, leaping hare, lotus petal, beeline, zigzag*
>
> 4. *Biting (green)* [*K.S.* II.E]: *hider, hickey, sweller, dot-dash, coral reef, dotted line, broken cloud, boar tusk*
>
> 5. *Coital Postures (blue)* [*K.S.* II.F]: *Uprising, upsy-daisy, full nelson, yawner, crab, lotus, nail pounder, bamboo splitter*
>
> 6. *Spanking (purple)* [*K.S.* II.G]: *paddle, slapper, jab, punch, wedge, scissors, tweezers, tongs*
>
> 7. *Woman-on-Top Techniques (black)* [*K.S.* II.H]: *Butter churn, thruster, hula, dreidel, vice, swing, sparrow hop, rub-a-dub-dub.*
>
> 8. *Oral Sex (white)* [*K.S.* II.I]: *Lip service, sidewinder, tip-topper, inside-outer, mango munch, slip-slurper, sucker, him-hummer*

When a pawn lands in a square occupied by a pawn of the opposite sex, both pawns pick one or more *kamakala* cards from the top of the deck in Vatsyayana's School. Each card depicts one of the sixty-four codified acts of lovemaking, which the pawns will enjoy together in the square. The pawn entering the square draws first. The number of cards drawn depends on whether sexual union is *matched* (3 cards), *high mixed* (2 cards), or *low mixed* (1 card), following Vatsyayana's categorization of men and women (based on genital size) and his evaluation of the varieties of union between those lovers [*K.S.* II.A]:

♀ \ ♂	rabbit	bull	stallion
doe	matched—3 cards	high mixed—2 cards	high mixed—2 cards
elephant	low mixed—1 card	matched—3 cards	high mixed—2 cards
mare	low mixed—1 card	low mixed—1 card	matched—3 cards

If more than one pawn of the opposite sex occupies a square, all the pawns practice the arts of love together, each picking the appropriate number of cards for lovemaking with each of the other pawns of the opposite sex in that square.

When a pawn enters a square occupied by one (or both) of the other pawns of the same gender, trading between them can, optionally (at the discretion of the player in charge of those pawns), take place (representing vicarious enjoyment and the exchange of sexological information).

The goal is for each of a player's pawns to have experienced all eight acts of lovemaking, for each pawn to have collected one *kamakala* card from each of the eight suits. Once those eight cards are in a pawn's possession (kept in his or her home circle), he or she may proceed out of the Eightfold Path and up through any one of the four central columns containing the Circles of Transformation (*chakra*s), the five steps leading into the World of Eternal Pleasure *(Kamaloka)*.

E. EIGHTFOLD PATH *(ASHTAMARGA)*

The Eightfold Path consists of eight blocks of streets in an ancient Indian city. Along the pathways are homes and shops, places to rest, eat, or drink, parks or gardens in which to have a chat or enjoy a secret rendezvous. Moving in any (but only one) direction, men and women roam the streets seeking sexual experience and knowledge, amassing the *kamakala* cards that will qualify them to transcend the world of transient pleasures. Along these roads are certain sacred or profane squares, each of which has a particular significance in terms of lovemaking (as tallied by the collected *kamakala* cards):

1–2. The Shrine of the God of Love (Kama) and the Forest Pavilion: As these places are particularly erotically auspicious, pawns landing together in these refuges draw twice the number of cards due them for the assignation—in these spots, they make love twice as much for twice as long (for example, a mare and a bull together here would draw four rather than two cards).

3–4. The Drinking Hall and the Temple of Sarasvati [*K.S.* I.D]: Men and women meet in these places not for sexual union, but for communal fun, for flirtation and mirth. Here no cards are drawn. By landing here, however, male and female pawns, at the discretion of the players in charge of them, are entitled to make bargains for the exchange of cards in their possession.

5. The Marriage Hall: Women may be tempted to land here—when a female pawn enters the Marriage Hall, she draws three *kamakala* cards, provided there is no male pawn in the square. If, however, a male pawn lands in this square while it is occupied by a female pawn (if she has not been able to leave the square in time), the female must give six *kamakala* cards to the male as a dowry.

6. The Brothel: Men are tempted to land here—when the male pawn enters the Brothel, he draws three *kamakala* cards, provided there is no female in the square. If, however, a female pawn lands in this square while it is occupied by the male (if he has not been able to leave the brothel in time), the male must give six *kamakala* cards to the female as the price of a lavish night in the demimonde.

7. The Ashram: Both men and women will be motivated to land here if they possess a large number of cards in general, but are lacking a card of one or more particular suits; by stopping in the Ashram, a pawn may exchange up to three cards from his or her collection (placing them at the bottom of the deck in the Vatsyayana's School) for the same number of cards from the top of the deck. Sexual intercourse is not permitted in the Ashram. Thus, if a pawn of the opposite sex enters the Ashram while the pawn who has exchanged cards is still there (if

he or she has not been able to leave the square in time), the resident pawn must hand over the newly acquired cards to the pawn who has just entered the Ashram.

8. The Cremation Ground: In this square couples practice a Tantric sexual ritual wherein the normal rules of the game are reversed: the pawn entering the square draws second; *low mixed* union entitles the pawn to three cards (rather than one), *high mixed* to two, and *matched* union draws only one (rather than three). If a third pawn of either gender enters the Cremation Ground, thus catching the lovers (who have just drawn their cards), that pawn takes all of the cards collected in the ritual by both Tantric pawns.

9–10. Untouchables—Foreigners and Tribals: Even though by landing in a square with Untouchables a pawn loses one card (to be placed at the bottom of the deck), pawns with more than one card of a suit will not be unwilling to make such a forfeiture. A pawn with no cards is considered an Untouchable and thus receives one card for landing in this space. No sexual union may take place here. Thus, if two pawns of the opposite sex land in this space, both pawns must put all of the cards in their possession at the bottom of the deck (note the advantage of this for a pawn with few cards if and when he or she lands in one of these squares while it is occupied by an opposite-sex pawn possessing many cards.

11–12. Linga Puja and Vedic Sacrifice: In as much as both the worship of the phallus of Shiva and the performance of the Vedic sacrifice are noncopulatory erotic acts and sources of fertility, any pawn who lands in one of these two squares receives one *kamakala* card, provided no other pawn of the opposite sex is in the square. No sexual union may take place in these spaces. If a pawn lands in this space while it is occupied by another pawn (male or female) the resident pawn must return the card that he or she has just picked and must, furthermore, leave the square on the next roll. If the other pawn, the one remaining behind in the square, chooses not to leave on his or her next roll, that pawn draws one *kamakala* card (and is subject to the same regulations that applied to the previous pawn).

F–G. CIRCLES OF TRANSFORMATION (*CHAKRA*S) AND THE WORLD OF ETERNAL PLEASURE (*KAMALOKA*)

Once a pawn is in possession of at least one card from each of the eight suits (i.e., once he or she has mastered the art of at least one practice of each of the eight modes of erotic activity), that pawn may enter the internal, yogic path leading up through the Circles of Transformation (*chakras*) and into the *Kamaloka*. The *Kamaloka* may only be entered by an exact roll of the dice and no pawn may be moved into a *chakra* occupied by another pawn of either gender. Once the *Kamaloka* has been entered, once the transient pleasures of this world have been realized and transcended, the pawn achieving that state shuffles his or her cards and places them at the bottom of the deck in Vatsyayana's School.

> The first player to move all three of his or her pawns up the *chakras* and into the *Kamaloka* wins the perpetual pleasure of eternal erotic Love. He or She is the Winner of the Game.

2. YOUNG AND OLD

A. TRANSLATION

For the purpose of fulfillment in marriage, the man should be three times older than the girl; for the purpose of pleasure in love, however, age is secondary to other considerations. Men are classified as *youthful, mature,* or *elderly;* women are classified as either *young* or *old.*[2]

People may be further classified, according to their sexual propensities, as *phlegmatic* (while fucking, they're apathetic [like an *elderly* man]), *balanced* (they're erotically equilibrated [like a *mature* man]), and *choleric* (they're hot-to-trot [like a *youthful* man]).[3] Age does not apply to women here; young or old, they may fall into to any of the categories above, depending upon their feelings for the man.

B. COMMENTARY

I, Professor Leopold Roth, also have a theory of equal and unequal unions based on age. I argue that teenagers should be with teenagers: they should experiment together in the back seats of cars to the brutal beat and cool cacophony of liminally lubricous music, indulging in perfunctory petting and puerile panting, saying no and yes and no, no, no, and yes, yes, okay, yes, oh yes, let's do it, in heated heartbreaking, bowel-churning gasps, giggles, and gurgles of ambivalence and ambiguity as trembling, sweaty hands explore unfamiliar and

---

providing a way of playing rather than reading the book (concomitant with Roth's notion of hermeneutics as a ludic activity). Before leaving for India, where he commissioned craftsmen to make the cards and pawns, Roth had sent this mock-up to Romulus and Rowley Puzzles and Games, Inc.

2. Pralayānanga elaborates: "The ideal marriage is between a man aged twenty-four to thirty-six and a girl between the ages of eight and twelve. It must be remembered, however, that it is forbidden by all accepted [Brahminical] codes and law books that the marriage be consummated before the girl's first menstruation. This age ratio, however, applies to marriage only [i.e., where love is not a relevant issue]. In matters of love, as the story of Auddālaki illustrates, an elderly man will inevitably be made to appear foolish by a young girl; the greater his pleasure with her, the greater, ultimately, will be his despair. Love makes men blind to their own age; because of that blindness, they will trip over many an unseen obstacle and fall; because of such falls, they will become [socially] crippled. On the other hand, the man should be sufficiently older than the girl if he hopes to have any authority or control over her."

3. Roth has ignored Vātsyāyana's mathematical observation that there are, in terms of duration, nine possible classes of sexual union; figure into this the nine types of sexual union based on the dimensions of the genitals and you get 729 kinds of copulatory matchings; add the classifications based on age and there are 26,244 kinds of union—Narsingh Śāstrī gives the technical nomenclature for each and every one of them.

hitherto inviolable anatomical precincts. To the beat of spurting of estrogen and androgen and sudden pituitarial surges, amidst sprouts of hair and drops of blood and semen, let them feel and imagine that they understand. May they steal sweet liqueurs from parents' locked cupboards, drink too much, and vomit together in swells and torrents of teenage love. Let them get hurt; let them be sentimental; let them not even think about the inconsequentiality of their inflated passions.

At the age of twenty (± a few years), however, it's time to turn to an older, more experienced person for initiation into the adult realm of sexual love. Young men should be with older women, young women with older men. I envision a civilization wherein fulfillment in love would be eminently possible. A boy of twenty needs a woman of forty (± a few years) to transform him into a man: she can teach him to please a woman, how to be tender in word and action; she can transform his sexual urges and aches into sensibilities and sensitivities, instructing him in the subtleties of erotic etiquette, the tender manners of love and sweet politics of passion. She, in turn, is in control and guiding, ripe and sophisticated (thanks to her former lover/teacher); she reaps the benefits of a fresh and pure virility, a curious and innocent heart. And when that boy has become a man of forty, he's ready and mature enough, well enough versed in the arts of sexual love, sympathetic enough to a woman's fears and desires (thanks to the pedagogical acumen of his former lover), to tenderly initiate a girl of twenty into womanhood, to teach her how to please a man, and to appreciate her womanhood and all that she learns from him.

It's fair (isn't it?): women in their forties having boys in their twenties, and men in their forties having girls in their twenties. It's equitable, judicious, and even beautiful, isn't it?

The girls in my perfect world will bear children with their older lovers. Once these children are approaching their twenties, my women, now mature and ripe for fresh sexual exploit and amatory accomplishment, will be ready to take on and tutor callow lovers, boys in need of their love.

Like Vatsyayana, I anticipate objections. What happens to us when we're old? When the forty-year-old men and women become sixty, they will, in my erotically perfect society, release their younger lovers, relinquish them to the still younger lovers for whom they have been prepared. And then, ready only then, in full maturity, lovers in their sixties will turn to each other, and at the very period when people in our unruly and unkind society are feeling the despair of aging, my lovers will be perfectly matched, contented and calmed in each other's experienced embraces. Fully fulfilled sexa-, septua-, and octogenarians will, like teenagers, have their equals in intimacy, companionship, and mutual understanding. Looking at each other they'll see youthfully radiant smiles on aged wrinkled faces. They'll laugh at youth and age, time and death, and at others and themselves. The elderly in our society are deprived of the erotic epiphanies and amorous annunciations that my moral policy and code has to offer.

Literature influences life too harshly, in revenge, no doubt, for life's excessive regulation of literature: inevitably, in novels and romances, the old man is either a cuckold or a sadist when sexually involved with a young girl, who is, correspondingly, either a whore or a victim. Stories of old men cuckolded by young women are always comedic; what is so sad in life is laughable in art. Stories of dirty old men who possess young women are always pornographic; what is so revitalizing in life is always wicked in art. If this were a novel, Jock Newhouse could be only a fool or a villain, pathetic or dirty. But Jock (as in -strap and -ularity) is a sage and a hero, admirable and clean.

Speaking of Jock, I received this in the mail:

Jock Newhouse and Venus Doudounes
request the pleasure of your company
at a
Champagne Drinking Party
to celebrate their marriage
on Friday, the thirteenth of June,
nineteen hundred and ninety-seven,
at sundown.
The Polo Lounge
The Beverly Hills Hotel

While it's Jock's first marriage ("I've waited for the right girl to come along," he told me), it's the third marriage for the bride, who is seventy years younger than the groom ("I know that this one is going to last," Venus smiled).

I visited the Stars of David Home not long after getting the invitation. The ambulance pulling away silently as I drove in frightened me with a premonition that Jock or my mother might be in it. But no, Tina Valentina was chipper as usual, and Jock, forbidden to smoke inside the home, was outside in the garden.

"They say it isn't good for me," the ninety-seven-year-old pornerast, carefree and exuberant as ever, complained as he blew a perfect smoke ring, motioned for me to sit down next to him on the bench, and offered up a Lucky Strike from his silver cigarette case. "I'll miss my friends here, but I'm glad to be leaving. There are too many rules and too many people dying. Venus and I have found a cozy little apartment overlooking the La Brea Tar Pits."

He explained that the ambulance had been there to take Ariana Arundel's body away.

"She was going to play your father's mother in *Taj Mahal.* Too bad about that movie. They found her dead this morning—one hundred and sixteen years old. It's too bad. I loved her. I've always loved older women, and there aren't that many of them around anymore. Did you know her? Ariana, Ziegfeld girl and then sex siren of the silents, big-eyed, big-boobed, big-hearted star of *The Drums of Desire*? She was the first movie star I ever schtupped. It was in 1921, when I first got to Hollywood. We were talking about it just the other day. She remembered everything about the evening. Everything, every detail of what happened the first night we went out in her Pierce-Arrow to the newly opened Coconut Grove, where we ran into Adolph Zukor. She remembered what we ate (terrapin à la Bengal, pommes de ville, sloe sorbet, and I can't remember what else) and what we drank. 'Jock, honey, do remember that 1915 Chateau d'Amour Rosé Imperial? That the grapes had been picked by prisoners of war gave it its special charm. Remember the palish gold, fine and prickly mousse of small and steady bubbles, hmmmm, sound as a bell, and that lusciously nutty Pinot bouquet? I can still taste it. Oh, what I'd give for a glass of that now. Do think there's a bottle left anywhere in the world? One that hasn't gone bad, that still has its sweetness, its sparkle and bubble?' She remembered the tunes we danced to ('Jungle Love,' 'Native Night Song,' and 'Ain't Got No Pajamas'), what we talked about as we drove along Sunset back to her bungalow, and then undressing me (the sound of my gold shirt-studs bouncing on the Italian marble floor, the sight of my bow tie curled into a question mark on the blue Persian carpet), asking me to remove her fur (making that little mink open its clip of a mouth to let go of its tail, unsnapping the lacy garter, slowly rolling her silk stocking down her perfect leg), and then more champagne (a sweeter, more amber in the candlelight Veuve Clicquot 1914), and then making love and the tapers burning out and the light of dawn breaking through the window with me still in her arms, a light that was still in the clear azure eyes that were set into the now mottled and wrinkled circles of aged skin. She asked me about it. 'It's been a long time Jock. Do you remember too?' she whispered. Just the other day she was talking to me about it. 'Tell me, honey, can you still smell my scent, the scent of that part of me that's down there, smell what it smelled like then? Can you still taste my neck, my arms, my legs, my toes? Can you still taste all the parts of me that you kissed that night?' God, I'm, going to miss her," he said with tears rolling down his cheeks. "Venus wanted her to be the bridesmaid at our wedding." He wiped his eyes with a fine monogrammed handkerchief and laughed.

As I apologized to Jock that I wouldn't be able to attend the celebration, that I would be in India, I reminded myself to send the couple a sumptuously illustrated copy of the *Kamasutra* as a wedding gift.

He hardly paid attention to my expression of regrets, as he was quite obviously distracted by the loss of Ariana Arundel. He continued to eulogize her, to recollect all sorts of intimacies. He lit up another Lucky.

"About two weeks ago, her great-great-granddaughter came to see her, bringing her little one-month-old great-great-great-granddaughter, who was named Ariana after the old movie star herself. I was visiting her room, telling her about the wedding plans. Old Ariana was holding the newborn Ariana in her arms, and as I looked at them, it struck me as so wonderful that out of the womb of the old Ariana, out of her spreading legs, came a little girl who grew older, old enough to open her legs and give birth to another little girl who gave birth to another little girl, like a series of flowers opening and pushing forth new flowers, or like those little painted Russian dolls. And I could see the whole series, the generations of women, the persistence of sex and love and life. I looked at that old woman holding that infant girl and I saw it all. It was a mystical kind of thing, sort of a religious vision. I had seen the womanhood that is in each and every woman. When we see that, when we can feel and sense that, when we completely lose ourselves in that, that is the greatest thing a man can know. That's salvation on earth. That's perfection. That's truth."

He laughed and put his hand affectionately on my knee.

"So you can't come to the wedding. Well, too bad. Off to India again. I remember. You're taking that Indian girl there so that you can schtup her."

"Well it's not just that," I began to defend myself and then hesitated. I wanted Jock's advice. "Maybe I shouldn't go. Maybe I should just force myself to forget about this girl. I love Sophia. I really do."

"Loving more than one woman is a symptom of generosity," Jock said confidently, moving in closer to me and putting his arm around my shoulders. "Acting on it is the mark of bravery. Being able to pull it off is a sign of creativity. Not hurting anyone is the index of compassion. Generosity plus bravery plus creativity plus compassion add up to gallantry. To be gallant is to rise above other men and to be a hero for those other men to follow." He was, I think, reciting his lines from *The Vagabond of Love*.

I left him to go to my mother's room. She told me how happy my father was going to be to see Ariana Arundel again.

3. FAST AND SLOW

A. TRANSLATION

Men may be sexologically categorized, in terms of how long it takes for them to have an orgasm, as *speedy*, *average*, or *prolonged*. There's a controversy when it comes to the categorization of women in terms of the rapidity of their sexual detumescence, and there is disagreement among the specialists as to the qualitative and quantitative relationship between the male and female orgasm. Professor Auddalaki argues, "A woman does not ejaculate like a man does, with a sudden burst of pleasure, but rather enjoys the steady delight that results from having her sexual itch appeased by a man. The bliss that she derives from sexual union is a different kind of satisfaction than the orgasmic joy experienced by the man. Since a woman can't know what the man experiences, how can she feel his pleasure? And how can a man ever ascertain what a woman feels?" I, Vatsyayana, on the other hand, maintain that men and women experience the same pleasure. There are, obviously, differences both in the roles played by the man and woman in the sexual act and in their respective attitudes toward coition, but such distinctions do not necessarily determine a difference in sensation or experience. Men and women making love, like wrestlers in a match or rams butting heads in battle, feel the same feeling in the end.

B. COMMENTARY

I probably wouldn't have accepted Professor Cross's invitation to have lunch at the House of Lee if the ancient Sanskrit text hadn't actually made me wonder. Not that it mattered Indologically or erotically, or that there was anything at stake scientifically or literarily, but for some reason I was curious to know if contemporary biological science had any light to shed on the Vatsyayana-Auddalaki debate. It could, I felt, make an interesting footnote.[4]

I posed the question, "Is the male's experience of orgasm different from the female's experience of it? I'm asking you as a scientist, a biologist. What do you think? Do we feel the same thing similarly, the same thing differently, a different thing similarly, or a different thing differently?"

4. And since Roth didn't write the footnote, I suppose I must. For a detailed study of the question, see "Written Descriptions of Orgasm: A Study of Sex Differences," by E. B. Vance and N. N. Wagner (*Archives of Sexual Behavior* 5 [1976]: 87–98), two psychologists at Washington University. I became aware of this article through my father, who had been one of the seventy consultants serving as judges in an experiment that attempted to determine whether or not there is any qualitative difference between male and female experiences of orgasm. The judges were presented with forty-eight descriptions of orgasm (twenty-four written by men and twenty-four written by women, students in an introductory psychology course). That the judges could not correctly identify the gender of the person describing the orgasm suggested to the researchers that the experience of orgasm is essentially the same for males and females. The descriptions were judged by "professionals," according to the article: gynecologists and urologists, psychologists and psychiatrists. Perhaps if they would have chosen literary critics, poets, translators, or even theologians adept at hermeneutics, the conclusion would have been different. The researchers included, as an appendix to their article, the descriptions that were written (without indication of the gender of the students), many of which described orgasm as "indescribable." The recurrent words were "tension, relief, spasm, tingling, fluttering, pulsating, explosion, flash, vibration, surge, rush."

My interest in this is rather more rhetorical than sexological. I've begun to look for descriptions of orgasm in literary texts by men and women. I found the following in *Confessions of a Cockeyed Coed*, by Candy Clitterson (aka Aphra Digby): "As I began to come my cunt muscles flexed and constricted around Professor Spiegel's pulsating prick so powerfully that he began to grunt as if being choked. Suddenly I was cunt from head to toe, polymorphously pussy, every part of me just extensions and appendages of the swollen, sucking, and bubbling orifice. The legs that stretched away from it trembled as I screamed, 'I'm coming, I'm com-co-co, oooo ohhh, oh god, oh aoo ooomnnnnnnnnn ahhhhhh, yes, yes.'" I have counted twenty-two descriptions of orgasm in that particular book. I have also found what I believe to be a description of male orgasm in Isaac Roth's poem, "Mirror Retro":

> i'm on the edge and ledge of a mirror, poised for love's blind jump
> time to breathe darkly the thrill shrill gasp and feel the deadly thump

The young poet's association of orgasm and death, epitomized by the French phrase for it, *le petit mort*, seems universal. That the French also call it *l'extase* gives it religious, rather mystical, connotations that are also universal. What is more interesting to me than the comparison of orgasm (an experienced experience) to other (actually unexperienced) experiences (whether it's volcanoes erupting, canons firing, clouds bursting, whirlpools whirling) is the

"Well, snails certainly experience the same thing," he began, and lapsed into an ecstatic, if not envious, encomium to the hermaphroditic amatory customs of *Helix pomatia,* a lurid account of enormous erectile penises wiggling and waving at each other as ravenously twitching vaginas gape and gasp to gobble, each like the other, as the other, male and female, bathed in each other's slime, simultaneously giving and receptive. "Oh god," he sighed. "Don't you sometimes wish you were a snail?" He asked if I could bring some snails back from India for him; as I was using Indian texts for my research on love, he would use Indian snails for his research on sex.

I reiterated my question: "Does the female part of the snail experience the same thing as the male part of that same snail? I want to believe that men and women feel the same thing, of course, to feel that I know what Sophia feels and that she knows what I feel. That would be very, very nice. But if men and women don't feel the same thing, then heterosexual lovemaking doesn't really make us more intimate; it is rather something that further marks our difference and accentuates the very distance between men and women that sexual love tries to span. That's very sad. You're a scientist. I want a scientific answer, not a political one, not a poetic one, not a sentimental one. I want to know the truth, not just some facts about snails, but some truth, just a little truth, about people."

He told me a story, swearing that it was true, and I, in turn, swear that in telling the story that he told me, true or not (confession or fantasy, record or romance), I am telling the truth:

"Even as a child I loved snails. I've always been crazy about them. So

---

comparison of other experiences or situations to orgasm: Aphra Digby, in *The Latin Lover,* compares the death of Professor Larus in the arms of the young and beautiful Carmena Penista to orgasm (reversing the cliché); Siegel, in *Laughing Matters,* compares laughter to orgasm as a way of explaining the pleasure of comedy; Sophia White-Roth, in *Love and Madness,* compares Lee's uncontrollable "poetic outbursts" to orgasm; Francis White, in his *Indian Adventures,* used orgasm to describe the thrill of sticking a pig; and Leroy Lovelace, in a recent *Cocktail* magazine, compared sexual climax to basketball's alley-oop: "The perfect timing, the leap, the slam, the trembling of the net, the quiver of the backboard, the bounce, bounce, bounce and—hey baby—it's two points. And it feels good, real good."

In writing about sex generally, but about orgasm specifically, we encounter the limits of what words can do, the impotence of the lover who dares to write, the ultimate failure of language and the emptiness of the literary endeavor. Writing about love and sex is not so much writing about love or sex as it is, and cannot escape being, writing about writing. This is, I suppose, why I find comfort in being a commentator rather than a writer. I do not try to write about experience, but only about writing; I am safe in forewords and footnotes as I use words to explain only words.

it was natural for me, when it was time to go to college, to study inver-
tebrates in the zoology department at Washington University in St.
Louis. That was in the sixties. One day I saw an ad in the university
paper asking for volunteers for some experiments. It paid minimum
wage. No one had heard of Masters and Johnson then. I volunteered
and got chosen. I can tell you, it was harder getting accepted into the
experiment than it was getting into graduate school. I mean I didn't
have to show my penis to the graduate chairman of the zoology department! But Masters and Johnson wanted to make sure there were no
physical abnormalities. And, of course, they had to be certain that volunteers weren't motivated by the opportunity for exhibitionism or getting laid, that you weren't some sort of Reichian orgasm junkie or a
Communist.

"I'll never forget my first orgasm in the clinic. It was one of the most
beautiful, almost spiritual, experiences of my life. It took place in a
plain and luminously white room, windowless and spotless, with a high
white bed covered by a crisp white cotton sheet, and there was all that
fantastic monitoring and recording equipment. A woman entered the
room in a white lab coat, white like a wedding gown, and asked me to
lie down. She wrapped the sphygmomanometer around my arm to
monitor my blood pressure, pumped the bulb, listened to my heart
with her stethoscope, then dabbed my chest and legs and arms with
cool conductive petroleum jelly and strapped on the sensors for the
electrocardiogram, and pricked my scalp to wire me for the electro-
encephalograph, running one of the leads to my lower rib cage to get
a read on my respiration. It was foreplay as far as I was concerned. She
asked me, 'Mr. Cross, my records show that you are able to mastur-
bate without the aid of a marital surrogate, photographs, or other visual or mechanical stimulators. Is that correct?' 'Yes,' I answered
proudly—I had been quite a champ as a high school student when it
came to beating off.

"'We will be filming the ejaculation,' she informed me, 'noting color
variations in the glans, scrotal shifting, position changes in the testes,
and other reactions. We'll also be monitoring external sphincter contraction and reactions of testes, prostate, seminal vesicles, Cowper's
glands, and rectum. You may begin whenever you like.'

"That was such a sweet thing for a woman to say. It so touched me
that I found myself staring at her face and thinking that she was really
very beautiful—ten or fifteen years older than me, but very attractive.
And as I masturbated I kept looking at her, at the probing but wholly

nonjudgmental eyes, the kind and accepting smile, the calm posture and demeanor, the clean dark hair. I loved the grace with which she held her clipboard and how her pencil moved as I masturbated in the cause of science. And then an extraordinary thing happened. At the moment of ejaculation, I cried out uncontrollably, 'I love you!'

"Later, while debriefing me, she asked if I had said 'I love you' as a way of heightening stimulation or bringing on the release, if I usually used those words while masturbating. 'No,' I confessed. 'I meant it. Absolutely. I do love you, really love you, and I want to marry you.'

"She didn't believe me, of course, just as you probably don't believe me. She thought I was joking. But I swear that I'm telling you the truth. I was in love with her. I telephoned her, the very next day, at the clinic. Since she didn't recognize my name or voice on the phone, I had to remind her: 'Cross, the really good masturbator.'

"When I invited her out for coffee, she explained that technicians at the institute weren't allowed to become socially involved with subjects of the experiments. So when we finally did get together, it was quite illicit, and that, I think, made it all the more powerful. It wasn't until about six months later. I was on all fours in the bushes in one of the gardens in St. Louis Municipal Park collecting snails when I heard two women on a bench arguing about something. They didn't know anyone could hear, so they were speaking quite freely and angrily too, having a lovers' quarrel—jealousy, resentment, feelings of rejection, all the usual stuff. Then one stormed off and the other started crying. The sound of her weeping was so moving that I couldn't help myself—I crawled out of the bushes and asked if she was okay. It was her! The love of my life! And the amazing thing was that she remembered me! I guess I had impressed her. She dried her tears and invited me to sit down with her, and I showed her my snails. She wanted to know why I was interested in snails, and I told her all about the hermaphroditic thing. She liked that. She understood it. We went for coffee, and for the first time in my life, somebody actually seemed interested in what I was doing. Somebody finally understood my love of snails and why I would want to dedicate my life to them. I took her to dinner and she was sweet. She even asked if it would bother me if she ordered the escargot. That's what I call considerate! I told her about how much the experience with her in the Institute had meant to me, that I thought of her every time I masturbated, that I always ended it by whispering 'I love you,' and that the 'you' was truly her.

"Two weeks later we were married. Masters was the best man and

Johnson was the bridesmaid. And the first six months of our marriage was the happiest time of my life. I talked to her about my work with snails and she talked to me about her work with orgasms. We shared everything. I understood what it meant to be truly and perfectly in love. I believed that the end of the story would be that 'they lived happily ever after.'"

Cross paused and I realized that I had never, in all my years of knowing him, seen him look truly sad before.

"Now I suppose you're wondering what this has to do with your question. Do men and women experience the same thing during sexual union? Is there a qualitative difference in male and female orgasm? Masters and Johnson had concluded that there was indeed an orgasmically based equality of the sexes. My wife objected, and believe me, she knew her orgasms. She felt that the sexologists were skewing the research results for political reasons, that they were interpreting the findings in a way that distorted them in support of liberal democratic values that asserted an equality of the sexes. As a result of standing up for the truth, for what she believed in, she lost her job. She, a mere graduate student, had published her argument against the now famous authorities on human sexuality."

Cross subsequently sent me her article (published in *Archives of Sexual Behavior* [1966]) by campus mail:

> Researchers who argue that men and women are the same in regard to orgasmic experience ignore the physiological fact that accounts for temporal differences: men ejaculate and women do not. In order not to distort their findings, these scientists have refused to acknowledge the clear distinction between orgasm (the neuromuscular discharge of accumulated sexual tension that they would like to say is equivalently experienced by men and women of all ages) and ejaculation (experienced only by postpubertal males). The categories and classifications obfuscate as much as they clarify. It is precisely because of ejaculation that men have a different feeling, a sensation of urethral contraction, penile choking, a feeling of being milked, and then the uncontrollable sudden burst of semen under pressure (described by one experimental subject as being "like a shaken champagne bottle uncorked. Ka-booooom!"). None of the women whom I interviewed during my work at the Institute ever articulated their experiences in terms of either champagne or any other sparkling beverage. An exemplary female description was of "warm chocolate dripping off a spoon, sloshing into meringue, spasmodically bubbling, oozing and seeping into thick whipped cream with hot pralines sinking into it." Female subjects reported clitoral pleasures distinct from (but not unrelated to) other sensations permeating the pelvis, warming, swelling, and opening

it up like (to use the words of another female informant) "an enormous ripe squash spilling its insides, seeds and pulp and sticky stuff, as its rind softens and breaks down from the rising heat of the oven." Universally reported by women, and entirely unreported by any of the men in our experiments, there was a rhythmic stirring, a warm-to-hot syncopated trickling, a build up, and then some release and a subtle throbbing, more release, release in various or many directions and dimensions. Male orgasm is always unidirectional and unidimensional.

My data clearly indicate that all male primates detumesce in the same way and feel the same thing, while there's a wide spectrum of female sexual response, a vulvic variability and vaginal virtuosity in a complex repertoire that includes shifting plateaus, radiating refractions, explosions and implosions, dips and dives, stimulation and simulation, trickling and tickling, penetration, opening, and spreading, with clitoral, labial, uterine, fallopian, rectal, and transinguinal contraction and constriction, convulsive or non-convulsive, ecstatic and/or peaceful, like birth and death and everything in between all at once, on and on, in endlessly intricate combinations and configurations, certain ones of which they note as orgasm. The female orgasm is subjective, the man's, objective. No woman subject ever stated anything like what was commonly heard from the male participants: "I shot my wad." There are psychological ramifications of these findings: women are happy after orgasm if they feel loved. If not, there's the dark melancholy of the post-coital abyss, made all the darker by the uniquely female orgasm. Orgasm is *in* the woman and *out* of the man. The pleasure men feel in orgasm is a self-aggrandizing one, the ego's delight in being even transiently reaffirmed; loving or being loved is irrelevant, made all the more irrelevant by the fact that "the wad has been shot" and is gone. The male and female orgasm are analogously related by context but in no way homologous in terms of cause, effect, or function.

Naturally I had to ask him what had happened to his wife; I had been unaware that Cross had ever been married, or ever been even interested in women, or in men for that matter, or in anything other than snails. She had left him to go back to her previous lover, the woman with whom she had been arguing in the park. He was telling me all about how heart-broken he had been over their divorce when, all of a sudden, it happened again. My stomach turned, my chest felt tight. I became completely flustered. Casually looking around, I saw her, staring at us through the window of the restaurant, her image disrupted by the reversed Chinese characters—Maya Blackwell.

"Chris, look over at the window," I said, interrupting his amorous lament. "Do see that girl staring at us?"

"What girl?"

The stalker had vanished, but I was still trembling.

That night Sophia took my hand and asked, "Is anything wrong?" She was beginning to ask that rather too often, and it was making me uncomfortable. "You can tell me." she said. "You can tell me anything. We've been together a long time. Over twenty years. We know each other completely. We are a part of each other. I feel that something is wrong. You can tell me. You don't have to. But please, my darling, tell me when you're ready. I love you. Here, let me hold you in my arms."

The next day I telephoned the police about Ms. Blackwell. A Detective Chan said that there was nothing that the police could do unless there were actual attempts on my life or at least some explicit death threats; anything less was not sufficiently substantial to warrant a restraining order. He did not consider this letter grounds for police action:

> My Love,
>   We are one above, and in Death shall merge and know the ecstasy that is rightfully ours. It is, I understand, because You are afraid of Death that You deny that we are meant for each other for all eternity. And Your fear forces You to resist our fated union, to deny reality and Love; it forces You to struggle against accepting me in an evanescent world which You so wrongly mistake for reality. But You will give in, like all of us, to destiny. You will return to me, enter me, and be absorbed by me. I am waiting for You. Do not be afraid. There is one woman who can give You the unqualified Love that You crave, need, and deserve. I worship You.
>   Forever,
>   Maya

The detective laughed over the letter: "Love! Twenty years on the force has taught me a thing or two about love. It's behind murder, kidnapping, abuse, fraud, forgery, breaking and entering, disturbing the peace, speeding, and even double parking."

B. Squeeze and Squirm

In proceeding with our *Sanskrit-Wörterbuch* we must somehow find the confidence to imagine that what we experience and feel here and now is what they experienced and felt there and then. Do we dare to even ask ourselves the question: What is the difference between love *(kāma)* and love *(Liebe)*?
— Rudolf Roth, letter to Otto Böhtlingk (1869)

A. TRANSLATION

The ancient erotologists established a technical nomenclature for caresses. There are embraces employed by couples who have just met: *frottage*, when a man and woman allow limb to touch limb under some false pretext; *grab bag*, when nobody's around and a man teasingly pinches a woman's tits or grabs her butt. There are embraces for lovers who know each other a little better: *bump-and-grind*, when, in the dark or in a crowd, a man and a woman take turns bumping up against each other; the *crush*, when a man presses a woman up against a wall or a post. Getting down to actual foreplay, there are four more embraces, two of which stimulate passion, and two of which are expressions of that passion: the *creeper*, when, like a vine around a tree, a woman entwines a man and, softly sighing, she cranes her face toward his for a kiss; the *climber*, when a woman, as if scaling a tree, places one of her feet on the man's foot, wraps her leg around his thigh, reaches around him with one arm, and puts one hand on his shoulder in order to lift herself, grunting and groaning, up for a kiss; *sesame-and-rice*, when, with arms and legs entangled, a man and woman recline impassioned; *milk-and-water*, when a man and woman, blinded by erotic ardor, embrace one another as if to enter each into the other and become one.

B. COMMENTARY

"*Kamasutra*," Aphra enunciated with delectation, balancing each syllable on her tongue like a morsel of savored food, "*Ka-ma-su-tra*." She sucked and swallowed, adjusted her dark glasses, stretched her legs up and put her Converse high-tops up on my desk, lit up one of my Viceroys, and inhaled more smoke through a transient frown than she exhaled through her tough smile. "What translation should I read?" There was a disconcerting food stain on the severe mouth of the portrait of Thomas Chatterton on her sweatshirt.

"Burton," I answered.

"Isaac told me that you're translating it."

I was, that evening, working on this very section, which I passed to her with a perfunctory apology about it being a first draft.

She read out loud: "**The ancient erotologists established a technical nomenclature for caresses. . . .**"

Her unexpected entry into my office at night had startled me. How did she know that I was there? How did she get into the building? Had the janitor left it unlocked again? Because of Maya Blackwell, I had asked him to secure the building after six o'clock.

"Let me explain my interest, Professor Roth," she began, "and why I'm here. I've got a new idea for a new book and a new name for the new woman who is going to write it. I'm ready to get started on the research and I want your assistance. Isaac said that you'd be enthusiastic, that the whole thing is right up your alley. My agent loves the idea, really loves it. We may not be talking Pulitzer here, but we're talking mega-money. Look, Roth, I know that you don't approve of my relationship with your son, but I want to work with you. This could be really big financially for both of us. This is going to be the *Dead Sea Scrolls* of sex. Listen. Under the name of Tajma Hall, I'm going to translate an ancient Sanskrit text, a text that has just been discovered by a woman archeologist named Montana Smith."

"Do you know any Sanskrit?" I innocently asked.

"No, of course not. Why do you think I need you? But don't get ahead of me. During an excavation in the Himalayas, Dr. Smith has unearthed an ancient manuscript that she identifies as some sort of *Kamasutra*, a text that, at first glance, seems to be a variant or recension of the already known *Kamasutra*. But then it turns out that the unknown text predates the famous *Kamasutra*. And this newly discovered version was written by a woman! The realization is that Vatsyayana actually plagiarized the female version of the text. We'll prove that. Dr. Smith takes the manuscript to her old friend, Tajma Hall, for a translation. The two women realize that the text is unknown because phallocratic Brahmins, later supported by sexist Western scholars, suppressed it from the very beginning; men couldn't handle the idea of a woman writing a sex book. But now it's been discovered. And it's going to be a best-seller. Now let me tell you about Tajma Hall. I've written her bio for the dust jacket: 'Tajma Hall is the nom de plume of a famous Indian movie star who must keep her real identity a secret. After a life of extravagant sensual indulgence and great financial success, Tajma took a vow of silence and chastity to devote the remaining years of her life on this plane of existence to the study of Sanskrit, the pristine language of the Goddess, and to the translation of ancient scriptures written in that language by the great women of India, the mystic land where the Goddess reigns supreme.'"

I asked her what, other than another one of my Viceroys, she wanted of me.

"For the introductory essay, in which I prove that the sexist who wrote the renowned androcentric *Kamasutra* actually plagiarized from the liberated and sexually enlightened woman who composed my text, I'll need you to come up with some Sanskrit. I want plenty of Sanskrit terms to sprinkle into my book, some verbal spices to give it that Indian flavor. Sanskrit words in parentheses will make the whole thing believable. That's the kind of thing that makes writing academic. The difference between scholarship and fiction is that scholarly books have foreign words, footnotes, a bibliography, and an index. Say, professor, what's the Sanskrit for *labia majora*. I want that in my index. Do you know the Sanskrit for that?"

"*Yonyoshthau*," I answered in the nominative dual.

"And what about *clitoris*?" she challenged.

"*Kamachatra*," I responded, "'love's umbrella,' or *kamankusha*, 'the elephant goad of love.'"

"Beautiful. Very exotic," she said with a happy smile. "We're going to make a brilliant team. Together we'll be able to pull the deception off. I don't really mean 'deception,' not in the sense of fraud, or even hoax—it's really more of a game. Do you like games? Do you want to play?"

While I didn't really approve of Tajma's deviousness, nor condone the proposed literary subterfuge, I was seduced by the idea that, if I were to help her, she might try to smooth things out between Isaac and me. I did it for my son. I gave Tajma Hall both the title of the text to be forged and the name of the woman who wrote it: the *Ratisutra* of Jayamangala. I further helped her by suggesting that we could give real credibility to the whole thing by forging a letter that we claimed had recently surfaced at an auction in Bombay, "a letter from Sir Richard Burton to Bapoojee Hurree Patel, a clerk from Booldana district, Hyderbad," a letter in which Captain Burton thanks the Indian gentleman for providing him with a manuscript of the *Ratisutra*: "The text is, contrary to my initial suspicions, much more than a literary curiosity. It is remarkable indeed that a woman in ancient times, within the Sotadic zone no less, could have penned with such sublimity, softness, and sensuousness, so learned and unabashed a treatise on this subject. There is not a trace of prudery to be found in these verses. European ladies have much to learn of love from their Oriental sisters." I also supplied the information, to be included in her introduction, that would account for the disappearance of Burton's copy of the manuscript: "Upon Burton's demise, his wife Isabel burned large portions of his collection, including a revision of his *Kamasutra* and this *Ratisutra,* as well as all correspondence and papers that had anything at all to do with erotic phenomena or pornographic literature." And I came up with the idea to claim that, in a letter from the seventeenth-century English traveler Sir Thomas Lovely to the poet Nat. Lee, there is mention of a "lewde Chapbooke in the Sunscrit Language by a genteel Lady of Olde Hindoostan relatinge to the Habites of the Hareem & sparing naught in regards to Delicatries I fain would mention here." Aphra was delighted by my contribution: "This is just the sort of lie that makes it seem true."

Noticing the words on the spine of the *Sanskrit-English Dictionary* on my desk, she picked it up and opened it at random.

"All the little words we'll need to give credibility to our project are right here in this book." She shut the lexicon, commented on how heavy it is, put it back on my desk, helped herself to another one of my Viceroys, thought for a moment, and then, suddenly, out of the blue, asked me point blank: "So, are you messing around with that little Indian girl who came with her parents to your dinner party that night?"

Utterly shocked by the question, I denied the crude accusation. She laughed.

"Isaac thinks you are, or that, at least, you want to. I told him that she was at the party. 'My father,' he said with some amusement, 'is really into this Indian thing. He doesn't really want to seduce the girl as a person, but as India. He wants to fuck India.'"

"Why is Isaac so distant from me lately, so scornful of me?" I asked his lover.

"You take so little interest in him. You haven't even read the book that he published, his poem. There's a lot about you in it, you and your wife, and his sister. He can't understand why you don't want to read it."

"Of course I want to read it," I insisted. "I'll get to it, but I've been very busy with my own work, with my translation. And, well, it's hard to read," I defended myself. "I mean, it's printed backwards!"

"You look in the mirror, don't you? And that's backwards," she laughed. "Come on, you can tell me. I've confided in you, told you all about my game, the new book—my little deceit. So why not tell me what it is that you're hiding. Why not? Are you having a little affair with the Indian girl? Come on, tell the truth."

I stressed my dedication to Isaac's mother.

"What interests me is conjugality, passion in the service of companionship. I wouldn't allow random desires, even if I had them, to destroy the life I've built with Sophia. I'd be crazy to do that."

I was so startled by her impertinence that, in all honesty, I actually don't remember the rest of the conversation, and I do not want to risk recording here anything that is not true. Whatever lies I might have told in my life, I am, in this commentary at least, wholly dedicated to the truth, to discovering it, telling it, and writing about it. Truth is truth whether anyone believes it or not.

C. Kiss and Tell

India's far far'way and vast
So raise now up thy Jigger Mast.
Come conquer me and taste my Spice!
Oh kisse my lips, yes, kisse me twice,
On the Lips of both my Mouth and Cunt.
Pray let me speake this Matter blunt:
Explore the torrid wet, exotique Land
With a Tongue led on by scouting Hand!
 O timid Lover, I give Breath to this:
 My barbarian India awaits thy Kiss.
—Thomas Chatterton, "Her Oriental Letter Paraphras'd"[1]

A. TRANSLATION

It's appropriate to kiss the forehead, cheeks, neck, eyelids, breasts, and lips of your beloved as well as to put your tongue in her mouth. Oriyas like to kiss the twat, but, obviously, even though there are some people who, in the throes of passion, are prone to lick such parts of the body (in accordance with their own particular cultural traditions), such osculatory practices are not for everybody.

Kisses may be classified in terms of the parts of the body that are kissed (as well as according to the zest with which they are executed): *ordinary* (appropriate for the face, crotch, and armpits); *hard-pressed*

---

1. Note that Thomas Chatterton (1752–70), well known for his literary forgeries and for the despair that drove him to poison himself at the age of seventeen, uses "India" as metonymic for the female genitalia (and "barbarian" paronomastically coalesces the "wildness" of the land and with the "beardedness" of the anatomical part). This euphemistic usage of "India," more literary than colloquial, can be found in the works of Nat. Lee, Thomas Lovely, Laurence Sterne, Edward Sellon, Leopold Roth, and John Donne (who was, I suspect, the originator of the trope) in "Love's Progress": "And Sailing toward her *India*, in that way / Shall at her fair Atlantick Navell stay."

(right for the chest, cheeks, and vulva); *reverential* (good for the forehead, chin, and sides); and *gentle* (meant for the eyelids and brows). Kisses may be further categorized in terms of the occasion on which they are given: the *passionizer*, when the girl, gazing at the face of a lover who has fallen asleep, suddenly kisses his mouth; the *gambit*, when a girl gets a man's attention by kissing him when he's busy reading or writing, or when he's arguing with her or wanting to go to sleep; the *alarm clock*, when the man comes home late at night and kisses a mistress who is fast asleep (it's a good erotic stratagem for a girl to wait up for her lover, but to feign sleep in order to get these sweet kisses); the *phantom*, when a man expresses his affection by kissing his beloved's shadow on a wall or her reflection in a mirror (if it's a portrait of a girl that the man kisses, it's called the *trompe l'oeil*).

It is not immodest to kiss a woman's hand in public, at a family gathering, or some soiree. There are also occasions when it's appropriate to kiss the feet of the beloved.

"Kiss as you are kissed," Auddalaki says, for love should be reciprocal:

Kiss
tongue to tongue and lip to lip;
kiss
tit for tat and sip by sip.
For love asks
an eye for an eye, a tooth for a tooth;
while love gives
a truth for lie, a lie for a truth.

B. COMMENTARY

"kiss the twat"

Eve Christ imparted to me the knowledge of the tempting fruit; she said, "This is my body; take, eat. Do this in remembrance of me." She taught me the linguistics of desire and gave the taste test of sex. Love, for Eve, was music. "The clitoris is the reed," she explained, "in the mouth of the instrument of pleasure. Play me, play me, play the delirious fugue for two organs and two hormonicas." And, with the Christwoman's legs wrapped around me like curved tubes of fleshy brass, an allomorphic and polysonic instrument (part cuntralto bassoon, part tender tuba), I played dream songs, improvised duets and sextets, learned the rapturous registers, mastered the modulations of pitch that are achieved by changing lip pressure, the force of breath, and manual manipulation of the valves and holes. And it was my breath that vibrated through her, emerged as her melodic moans, rhapsodic murmurs, and climactic cries. "*Bois*," the naked Lakmé, carnal coloratura, sang before her death, "*et tu m'appartiendras. Bois!*" She smiled. "The clitoris is a reed."

Jock Newhouse has another metaphor: "The clitoris is to the vagina what the mezuzah is to the threshold of the Jewish home. It must be kissed before entering. It's a mitzvah. That kiss blesses all that goes on inside" *(Memoirs of the Vagabond of Love)*.

"particular cultural traditions"

Sir Monier Monier-Williams, without whose monumental *Sanskrit-English Dictionary* I'd be dead as a scholar, was received by the Viceroy of India, Lord Ripon, in Calcutta in the hot summer months of 1883. With the Viceroy's encouragement, he made an ethnographic tour of the Indian subcontinent (accompanied by one of his students), which resulted in the publication of his erudite "Report on the Osculatory Customs of the Natives of the Sundry Lands under Jurisdiction and Protection of the Empire" for the *Journal of the Anthropological Society of London* (January 1885):

> While kissing enjoyed great popularity in Britain in the seventeenth century as attested by the infantile doggerel of Nat. Lee and the no less famous epistle of Erasmus, it has, as we have become more civilized (and thus more conscious of hygiene), become a thankfully less fashionable pursuit (at least in Oxford). While the Brahmins of India share our oral propriety, the less educated and more humbly bred indulge in a fantastic variety of osculatory activities. The Romans classified the kiss into three types in terms of both place of application and sentiment expressed (*oscula* [cheek/friendship]; *basia* [mouth/affection]; and *suavia* [lips/passion]); the more extravagant Hindus, in contrast, have no fewer than sixty-four classifications for the act as codified in their *Kāmasūtra*.
>
> I have observed a wide range of osculatory indulgences in India, some suggesting the backwardness of our charges, others intimating manners in which we, in our pursuit of evolutionary success, would be wise to emulate. The Muria of Madhya Pradesh (who describe coitus as "the *membrum virile* and *pudendum muliebre* joking together") believe intercourse will not result in impregnation if the partners do not kiss; the kiss, they quaintly imagine, breathes life into the fœtus. The Lepcha of Sikkim, who do not associate sexual intercourse with conjugal affection, regard the kiss as cannibalistic; that their mountain cousins, the bearded Palchas of Sgaw Vale, refer to the kiss as "pressing vulva to vulva" (*akunāpidipanūka*) suggests that they deem it a tribadic activity. Among the Somavansi Kshatriyas, who abjure the idea of an exchange of saliva, kissing involves the mutual rubbing of chins, cheeks, noses, foreheads and even ears (in the case of the highly impassioned). The Andamanese have a predilection for sodomy; and rear entry obviously obviates the European mouth kiss. Among the Bhandaree of Orissa, males refuse to kiss the breasts of their females, maintaining that such action, associating one's mate with one's mother, is in gross violation of their incest taboo. The most bizarre prac-

tice is of certain mountain Kadars who, in imitation of their hunting dogs, kiss the recta of their wives. His Highness, The Maharajah of Chhokrapur, well-versed in the kissing conventions of Europeans, has confided in me that, while he enjoys a multitude of the pleasures of the bed with his wives, he saves passionate mouth kisses for his "little lover-boys."

"when the man kisses a lover who is fast asleep"

There was to be a kissing scene in *Taj Mahal* between Shah Jahan and Mumtaz Mahal, the Light of the World, between my father and Sunita Sen.

```
INT. WOMEN'S QUARTERS—NIGHT

EXTREME CLOSE SHOT. ILLUSTRATED KAMA SUTRA MANU-
SCRIPT ON A BEDSIDE TABLE. A LOTUS BLOSSOM AND
STALK FALL ACROSS THE EROTIC ILLUSTRATION TO CON-
CEAL THE EXPLICIT PARTS. The CAMERA slowly pulls
back to reveal MUMTAZ MAHAL asleep on the luxuri-
ous bed, canopied by diaphanous curtains that
tremble in a midnight breeze. WIDE SHOT of the
candle-lit room reveals LADIES-IN-WAITING cir-
cling the bed of the BEGUM. They prostrate them-
selves solemnly to greet SHAH JAHAN. He silently
gestures for them to leave and they obey. CLOSE
on SHAH JAHAN revealing the longing he feels for
his Queen. MEDIUM SHOT of MUMTAZ MAHAL sleeping.
The CAMERA explores her body through the curtains
from the P.O.V. of SHAH JAHAN.

                SHAH JAHAN (V.O.)
Oh would that your silken pillow were my lap
to cradle you and guard your sleep no less than
my armies guard the Empire. But I dare not
awaken you, for you are perhaps dreaming of
me now, and in our dreams, yours as well as
mine, there is an eternity that the waking
life does not allow us. But if I forgive the
world, it is only because it has permitted me
this glimpse of you, this taste of love in
which there is no division. Your joys are my
own as are your sorrows; in that oneness, I
find rest, and in that rest, I do not age.


The curtains part. CAMERA CLOSES on the BEGUM.


            There are no concealments.
```

The fingers of SHAH JAHAN gently caress the face
of MUMTAZ MAHAL and a slight smile indicates a
sweet dream.

                                          DISSOLVE

SFX—MUMTAZ MAHAL'S DREAM
We are floating in a lush, soft valley of muted
pinks with no hard lines or edges. CAMERA pulls
back slowly and we emerge from deep within the
center of a lotus blossom. The flower fills the
screen, and as we continue to pull back, we see
that SHAH JAHAN is holding that flower. He extends it. REVERSE ANGLE. MUMTAZ MAHAL accepts it,
smiles, smells it, blows gently into it, and then
flinches.

                 MUMTAZ MAHAL
       (with playful panic)
       Oh! There's pollen in my eye. I can't see!

                 SHAH JAHAN
       (bemused)
       Let me help. Here, come here, my beloved.

MEDIUM SHOT. SHAH JAHAN blows pollen from MUMTAZ
MAHAL'S eyes. She closes her eyes, and he gently
kisses one eyelid and then the other. EXTREME
CLOSE UP. SHAH JAHAN'S lips on MUMTAZ MAHAL'S
eyelid. The CAMERA pulls back to reveal that we
are once again in the women's quarters with SHAH
JAHAN seated on the bed next to MUMTAZ MAHAL. Her
eyes slowly open and the lovers gaze at one
another longingly.

                                          CUT

MUSIC. EXT. WIDE AERIAL of TAJ MAHAL—DAWN

"kissing his beloved's shadow on a wall"

I'm haunted by an image of Lee in Bedlam as described by my wife in
her *Love and Madness in the Life and Plays of Nathaniel Lee:*

> Lee was often chained up at night and confined to darkness by day.
> Dr. Edward Draper, physician at Bethlehem Hospital from 1684–1707,
> put the dramatist on a milk diet (which surely must have aggravated the
> pained alcoholic). Hospital nurses stopped whipping Lee only when Dr.

Draper realized how much delight that gave him. Pleasure was not, at that time in England, deemed salubrious for the insane. As documented and described in the anonymous *Complaints and Romances: Recollections of the Reign of Charles II,* Lee was exhibited as a freak to fashionable ladies and urbane gentlemen. A poem dedicated to Lee by Sir Thomas Lovely indicates the madman's state at one such divertissement in Bedlam:

> Like a regal fool in a royal court,
> Thy want of wit provides good sport;
> When thou fucked thy shadow on a wall,
> I didst laugh whilst thou didst bawl.
> Though her cunt was but a rustie grate,
> Thou didst seem to love thy penumbral mate!

Lee had apparently fallen in love with his shadow and would, as described in a letter from Aphra Behn to Lovely, "dance with her." According to Behn, Lee, whose head had been shaved upon admission to the asylum, carried a miniature portrait of his younger self (painted by Sir William Monier-Digby) with lush long hair. He would display the image with explanations that it was "his beloved Leah. Look at her hair, her beautiful hair!" And then he would kiss the portrait "with unnatural rapture." A secondary narcissism seems to have been the major symptom of his nervous breakdown. Narcissistic themes and images (mirrors, pools, shadows) abound in the practically illegible fragments of *Crown of the Seraglio,* the Oriental extravaganza that he was writing during his incarceration (MS in the Bethlehem Royal Hospital Archives, Collection of Poetical and Dramatick Miscellany).

Lee, also at this period, kept hidden in his cell a small hand mirror, which he would show to visitors and then whisper, "Look. Look there. 'Tis a portrait of one who wishes to murder me. Look carefully. And when the murder's done, bring that soul to justice."

"to kiss a woman's hand in public"

Jock Newhouse is my authority on this, and there is something appropriately kamasutric about the urbanity of his disquisition. It's from the manuscript of his memoirs-in-progress that he has asked me to read before going off to India.

When I first came to Hollywood, it was still the custom to kiss the hand of a woman to whom you were introduced. It is, indeed, a grave loss for civilization that the genteel gesture has become an extinct species of erotic felicity.

You know nothing other than her name, uttered just before the moment of truth, but if you are astute, if you've trained your senses, you can, in kissing a woman's hand, learn everything that there is to know about her.

Where does her glance fall as she extends her hand to you: upon your hand, her hand, or your face? How anxiously and quickly, tentatively and slowly, or comfortably and naturally does she extend it?

As you receive her hand, your index finger should provide a comforting balance as it touches the spot where her index finger is fixed to her palm. As you turn your gaze to the hand that you have just received in your own, let your fingers spread just enough so that, while your index finger remains in the crucial spot, the tips of your other fingers each find a place in the corresponding curves of hers. Your pinky should very gently touch the tip of hers. Does she withdraw her pinky slightly? Apply pressure to yours? The signals will most likely be unconscious on her part; she will be telling you things that she does not even know, or if she knows them, would not dare to utter.

As your face lowers toward the hand, note well its position: does it veer out from the wrist, away from her body, in, or straight ahead? Does she place her thumb above your index finger, below it, or to the side? This is the most basic aspect of the exegesis: what rings or bracelets are on display and what do they blazon? The nails are easy to read: what care has she taken to groom them? Do they intimate vanity, pride, fastidiousness, hygiene, lust? And there are more subtle questions: are the fingers held close together in modesty, spread apart in wantonness, or do they find their own natural comfort? Is there a tremble or a steadiness?

Still scrutinizing the hand, before the kiss, while feeling and taking account of its warmth or coolness, note well the muscle between the thumb and the index finger: is it concave, convex, or flat? Since the skin that gloves the hand is, unlike the facial skin, certain to be devoid of makeup, you can, by inspecting it, become acquainted with the skin of her entire body, its texture and its color, its suppleness and its resilience. I look for a slight lump on the inside of the middle finger to discover, provided that she is right-handed, whether or not she writes; a woman who writes is always romantic. Writing of any kind is inevitably an erotic activity, full of longing and fantasy.

Now slowly lower your head, slightly pucker your lips, and elevate her hand with playful solemnity: does she make an effort to raise it, to lighten it, or does she surrender it to you, allowing you full control of that exposed and extended part of her body?

Breathe in deeply to smell it: smell the glove that has been removed for you, smell the soap that has washed that naked hand and the parts of her body that remain, for the time being, clothed. There is, no doubt, a hint of perfume and powder as well. Lilac, lavender, and sandal are good signs. The palm of a woman who has potential as a lover is slightly moist, and that perspiration contains the fragrance of the whole person.

Listen! What does she say during the public hand-kiss, and when and how and why does she say it? Silence suggests that she's savoring the touch and is impassioned. Imagine kissing that hand again, in the future, after intimacy, and savor the intimation of what it will be like to run your tongue between those fingers, into the four little crotches of her hand, across the clitoral knuckles, and then into the palm to taste passion's stigmata.

And when the act is complete, do not simply drop her hand. Make a gesture as if giving it back to her, as if it has been something with which she has entrusted you, and you have taken care of it. Give her back her hand as if for safekeeping, and independent of her will, that hand will want to return to your lips like a bird returning to a safe and comfortable perch. And then, as you let go of it, look deeply into her eyes and smile slightly, only slightly, but in a way that suggests that you want to beam with joy and are restraining yourself only because others (her lover, her husband, or her friends) are present. Absolutely nothing has happened and yet two people, unbeknownst to anyone, have, in a fleeting moment, had the love affair of a lifetime.

"to kiss the feet of the beloved"

My chairman, Professor Paul Planter, using his wife to explain the Japanese, produced a coffee-table porno book, the *Chin-chin Mono-gatori* (reminiscent, with its *shunga* paintings and woodcuts, portraits of lovers in a variety of sexual postures, of the illustrated *Kamasutra*s of Moghul India). In one chapter of the book, a courtesan, formerly a Buddhist nun, tutoring the hero, a dissolutely priapic Chinese monk and scholar, in the arts of love as she has learned them, turns to the topic of the pleasures of foot kissing:

> The floating trade is one that a girl learns by being apprenticed at a house of pleasure. One must study the new fashions in intimacy so that the customer will be able to have experiences unknown to the ordinary townsfolk. He pays for refinement. Just as each cook at a fine inn, though knowing how to prepare many kinds of noodles, will have his special dish, and just as each monk, trained in all the words of Buddha, will know how to recite one particular sutra, so each courtesan must have her special erotic talent. Mine is foot kissing *(ashi-seppun)*. When I take my customer to the bed chamber, when he has taken a seat, I do not undo my sash, nor do I seem anxious for him to disrobe. With great care I remove his tabi and begin to massage his tired feet, singing as I rub:
>
>> Dew formed on your feet as you waited
>>   all night, outside, for me, for me.
>> Such is the melancholy state of lovers
>>   on the bridge to the floating World.
>> Love may be bitter because nothing persists,
>>   but the taste of the dew will be sweet.
>
> And then, after washing his feet in warm sake, I begin to kiss the toes of my client. This causes great pleasure to the man. I respond by licking the toes, one at a time, starting with one foot, with the small toe, working my way toward the big toe, and then to the other foot, starting with the big toe and working my way down to the little toe, licking, sucking, and blowing on them lovingly. This is what Lord Buddha has chosen for me as my way to spread happiness about in a world of sorrows.

The charm of this stuff is mitigated, for me at least, when, later in the chapter, the courtesan explains how she goes on to encourage the

man to insert his big toe into her vagina: "With that part of myself I
suck on his toe while my mouth chants the holy Buddhist formula, *Om
Mani Padme Hum* ('The Jewel is in the Lotus'), that delivers my client,
together with all humanity, from misfortune."

"kiss as you are kissed; love should be reciprocal"

"I had a dream last night," my mother confided in me when I went to
visit her at the home this afternoon, "a wonderful dream in which you
asked me to come to India with you. I didn't want to, but you per-
suaded me by saying that you needed me because you were writing a
book about love in India. I've never been able to deny you anything.
You said that you were convinced that men learn about love only with
the help of their mothers. How sweet of you to have such a thought.
You needed me to untangle love for you."

Once we got to India I apparently disappeared from the dream, and
she was inside the Taj Mahal by herself:

"It was dark in there. At first the fragrance was very faint. But it got
stronger and stronger until I realized what it was: I could smell him, that
perfume he used to mix up like a secret potion so that he wouldn't smell
like anyone else. And then I heard his voice, the beautiful acting voice
of Eddie Edwardes, resonant even in whispers. 'Tina,' he said, 'Tina,
come here. I've missed you. What took you so long?' I turned around and
there he was, in his Indian costume, that beautiful outfit that the
wardrobe department let him keep. He looked so handsome, just like the
Emperor of India, and alive, so very much alive, and I reached for him
and he kissed me and I kissed him just as he kissed me. And he kissed
me as I kissed him. And it was so wonderful and real. And then, just as
he was beginning to undress me, just like he used to do, kissing me on
the neck as he did, making some naughty little joke, I suddenly remembered that he was dead, and I became very frightened—not afraid of him,
but panicky, confused, bewildered. 'I can't kiss you,' I cried, 'because
you're dead, Eddie. Damn you, you're dead!' And then he just laughed,
just like he used to laugh whenever I got upset at him about anything.
'Tina, your kiss has brought me back to life. A kiss to make it well. I'm
not dead anymore. I'm alive. It's true. Here, feel the heat of my hands.'
And he caressed me and I felt his warmth. He was alive. And as I kissed
him, I breathed into his mouth and he breathed into mine, kiss for kiss,
breath for breath. My clothes seemed to dissolve. My hair was long and
loose, and Eddie kissed my breasts and then held me very close to him
so that I could feel that he was breathing. And then we were making love.

When he was alive and we made love, I always felt that I was dreaming. Now I was dreaming and, as we made love, I felt I was awake, more wide awake than I have ever been in my life! What a wonderful dream!"

She laughed with tears in her eyes. "This is hardly the kind of thing a mother should be telling her son. But it made me so happy. It doesn't matter that it was a dream. That didn't make it any less real. Oh, Eddie Edwardes! He understood love, how to love and how to be loved. And because he loved me so much, he came to me in my dream. He must have realized how much I've missed him. It had been so long since I had kissed him. He promised me that he'd come back again. Maybe soon. Maybe. I hope so."

Because of the dream, I suppose, my mother asked me to take her to the cemetery, not something that I particularly enjoy. I hadn't been there in a long time. As we drove in, she asked that I not go with her to the grave site, explaining that she wanted to be alone with him: "The last time I ever kissed him was here. Right over there in the memorial hall, just before they closed the coffin."[2]

2. This presses me to recall, with some sadness I must confess, kissing my mother in her coffin. As Joseph kissed his dead father to revive him, to prevent his soul from escaping through his mouth, so I wanted, under the pretext of kissing her good-bye, to imagine that I might do something about death, to believe that love gives us some defense against its bite. Although she looked like my mother, her forehead beneath my lips did not feel like hers. The kiss was bitter. It was a moment of realization that she was gone forever. Not only was it true, it was the Truth. Several times, when I've kissed a woman, the recollection of that dark childhood kiss comes back to me: I've trembled and become upset; I have had to struggle to put it out of my head. The memory mocks me as it tries to convince me of the utter impotence of love and the inviolate futility of each and every kiss.

The last time I kissed my mother before she died was in the hospital. She had made me sit next to her on the bed while she assembled a jigsaw puzzle, a reproduction of Botticelli's *Birth of Venus*, trying to convince me that I was somehow, in some way, actually helping her. She spent the last months of her life putting puzzles together. "Here, take this one, Nangi," she said. "Do you see where it fits? Up a little higher. That's it. What bright boy you are!" Then there was only one piece left, making it obvious, of course, where that piece fit. As I started to put it into its place, she stopped me, folded my hand around it, and whispered, "Keep the piece. Keep it as a little memory." And then she kissed me on the cheek and turned her cheek to be kissed

in turn by her child. I didn't want to: she had lost most of her hair, her skin was white and dry, her flesh smelled like rancid milk, and I was afraid of her sickness and thus, in a way, of her. I had to force myself to kiss her, to do it out of obedience rather than feeling, and although she surely sensed my repugnance, she must have understood or at least forgiven because she told me, in words I don't quite recall, that she loved me. I have kept the piece to the puzzle.

D–E. Tooth
and Nail

—"*It was love*"—for during the three weeks she was almost constantly with me, biting ✴ ✴ ✴ ✴ with her teeth and scratching ✴ ✴ ✴ ✴ with the sharp nail of her delicate hand, night and day—I can honestly say, an' please your honour—that ✴ once.

—Laurence Sterne,
The Life and Opinions of Tristram Shandy, Gent.

A. TRANSLATION [AND/OR]
B. COMMENTARY

Editor's Note

A photocopy of a two-page mockup for a proposed Classics Illustrated edition of the Kāmasūtra *was stuck in the translation notebook for Book Two at this point. Thus, I suppose, the comic begs to be read as some sort of translation of, and commentary on, K.S. II.D–E on "erotic biting and sexual scratching."*

VATSYAYANA INSTRUCTED THE URBANE CITIZENS OF PATNA IN THE ARTS AND SCIENCES OF SCRATCHING AND BITING....

AS PASSION INTENSIFIES ONE SHOULD ASSAULT ONE'S LOVER WITH TOOTH AND NAIL.

OOOH

AAAAAAAAAH

AS BITING AND SCRATCHING ARE SURE TO AROUSE A LOVER, PERSIST WITH TOOTH AND NAIL, DESPITE RESISTANCE, UNTIL SURRENDER, UNTIL RAPTURE.

THE PLACE: SCRATCH THE CHEST, NECK, BACK, WAIST, BUTTOCKS, AND THIGHS. BITE ALL THE PLACES THAT YOU WOULD KISS...

THE TIME: BEFORE LEAVING ON A JOURNEY; RETURNING FROM A JOURNEY; WHEN THE LOVER IS ANGRY, AROUSED, SLEEPY, OR DRUNK; IN JOY AND IN SORROW.

AAAAAAAAAH

WHEN A STRANGER SEES BITES AND SCRATCHES ON A WOMAN, LOVE'S SOUVENIRS, HE BECOMES ENCHANTED.

F. Poses and Postures

Every writer should have a position. What you write is your way of explaining that position, why you favor it, and why you think others should adopt a similar position.

—Nancy Bartz, *How to Write Term Papers*

Editor's Note

Roth neither translated nor commented upon this famous section of the Kāmasūtra *on sexual positions. At this point in the notebook for the commentary on Book Two, he merely tucked in a copy of the first five pages of a twenty-page paper that Ms. Gupta had written for his class on the chapter in question. The comments in the margins are mine, duly placed there in partial fulfillment of my responsibilities at Western University as Roth's teaching assistant for the course on Indian civilization during the spring semester of 1997. The grade and remarks on the title page are Roth's: he relegated the niggling task of correcting spelling and making specific comments to me; higher judgment was a prerogative reserved for the professor himself. I would have given the paper a C grade at best; in pedagogy, as in love, I believe, it is often kinder to be harsh, more generous to be honest than to write or say what the student (or beloved) wants, or hopes, to hear.*

THE MOUNTAIN OF ECSTACY, THE OCEAN OF BLISS:
Positions for Sex in the <u>Kama Sutra</u>
Compared to Indian Dance and Yoga
as well as to Chinese Tai Chi Chuan
and International Gymnastics

by

Lalita Gupta

A+

an excellent paper — see me for further discussion. You might want to go on to do graduate study, to turn this into a dissertation or a book!

Forgive the TA's sarcastic comments — I don't think he understood your paper.

This is brilliant work — original & energetic & sensitive — a pleasure to read. I wish I had more students like you!

Term Paper
Asian Studies 150B
Introduction to Indian Civilization
WESTERN UNIVERSITY
Professor L.A. Roth
Spring Semester 1997

> There is nothing mysterious or magical
> about coital positions. They have the
> potential to add a dimension of adventure
> to sexual intercourse. And adventure, as
> the ancient philosophers observed, is a
> necessity of love.[1]

Introduction

In this paper I will show that the different
positions for sex that Vatsyayana enumerates in his
famous <u>Kama Sutra</u> are related to and connected with
the yogic postures and dance poses of old India.

The position that I would like to take in this
paper is that the relationship between them implies
that, in ancient India, sex, yoga, and dance were
simply three paths (one erotic, one spiritual, and one
aesthetic) up the same mountain. Or, to put it another
way, these were three sacred rivers into the same
ocean. In order to show that this ocean has a shore
on many lands, I plan to compare the Indian stuff with
the art of Tai Chi Chuan as developed in China[2] as

---

[1] R.R. Rosemont, <u>The Ins and Outs of Human
Sexuality</u>, p. 169. This was the textbook for an
excellent course I took at this university from
Professor C.Cross (General Science 350: Biological,
Psychological, and Social Aspects of Human Sexuality).
Dr. Cross explained that a variety of sexual positions
was one way that human beings have compensated for their
lack of the feathers, fur, bristles, claws, fangs,
antennae, horns, tails, trunks, bills, etc. that make
sex so exciting for animals.

[2] I learned about Tai Chi Chuan in the other half
of this course (Asian Studies I51B, Introduction to East
Asian Civilizations) taught last semester by Professor
Planter. Dr. Planter gave the course an experiential

ARE YOU SUGGESTING INFLUENCE OR MERELY COINCIDENCE?

2

well as with gymnastics which is international as
Nancy Bonellia explains in her book:

> Ancient records have been discovered in
> China, India [italics mine], Persia,
> Egypt, Greece, and the Americas that
> describe and/or illustrate that gymnastics
> is a universal [italics hers] pursuit of
> mankind. Man has always felt the need to
> tumble.[3]

Sex Positions in the Kama Sutra[4]

Chapter six of part two of the Kama Sutra deals
with "the different ways of lying down, and the
various kinds of congress." Vatsyayana begins by
distinguishing the best positions for "high congress"
in which the little yoni[5] needs to be expanded for the

---

component that made the class really enjoyable. We
practiced Tai Chi Chuan and Zen meditation.

[3] Nancy Bonellia, Beginners' Guide to Gymnastics,
Calisthenics, and Tumbling, p. 13. We are using this
book in my Floor Exercise Gymnastics class this semester
(Physical Education and Recreation 185).

[4] The translation quoted through out this paper is
by Richard Burton, the one assigned in this class. I
look forward to Professor Roth's translation that he
said in class he was doing. Burton's is too hard to
read; try to do yours in plainer, more modern English so
this great book can have more relevance for young people
today. Burton's is so old-fashioned; but what can you
expect from someone who was married to Elizabeth Taylor!

A DIFFERENT RICHARD BURTON!

[5] Yoni is defined by Webster as "a stylized
representation of the female genitalia symbolizing the
feminine principle in Hindu cosmology" (New Collegiate
Dictionary, p. 1351). This implies that, because of the
way "language constructs thought" (as we have been
informed in this class), women in ancient India realized
that between their legs they had something cosmological.

3

big (<u>maha</u>) <u>lingam</u>[6] (these are the "widely-open,"
"yawning," and "wife-of-Indra" positions) vs. those
which are best suited for "low congress" in which a
big vagina needs to be contracted for a little
penis(these are the "clasping," "pressing," "twining,"
and "mare" positions). For very low congress the
author recommends dildoes, vibrators, and things like
that. Scholar that he was, Vatsyayana cites Babhravya
as the source for the above and notes that another
sexologist adds other positions to the list: "rising,"
"pressed," "half-pressed," "bamboo-splitting,"
"fixing-a-nail," "crab," "packed," "lotus," and
"turning" positions. Since some of these require
great balance and coordination, Babhravya recommends
practicing them in water. Vatsyayana doesn't agree
and neither do I: even though it sounds like it's
going to be nice, making love in the water is too
squeaky. Vatsyayana's rational has to do with it
being contrary to some religious law.

Next the <u>Kama Sutra</u> gives two standing-up
positions ("supported" and "suspended") and various
rear-entry positions, each named after an animal: cow,
dog,[7] goat, deer, ass, cat, tiger, elephant, boar,
horse. What's really amazing is that the book says
that when you take that position you should act like

---

[6] <u>Lingam</u> is defined by Webster as "as a sytlized
phallic symbol of the masculine cosmic principle and of
the Hindu god Siva" (Ibid. p. 663). This implies that
in ancient India men realized that thier penises were
gods and cosmic symbols.

[7] I wonder if it is because of an Indian
influence that we too call it "doggie style."

(handwritten annotations: "WHERE'S THE ANALYSIS?", "THIS IS MERELY DESCRIPTIVE", "IDENTIFY!", "THIS IS EMBARRASSING TO READ!", "WHICH LAW?", "WHY AMAZING?", "THIS IS ?", "NO!")

4

the animal: mooing, barking, bleating, braying,
meowing, growling, roaring, snorting, neighing. This
suggests that we have the potential during sex to
realize and get in touch with the ways in which we are
animals (something that we too often forget) and to
take pleasure in that. The author later adds that "an
ingenious person should multiply the kinds of congress
after the fashion of different kind of beasts and
birds."

The classifications continue: one woman with
many men; one man with two or more women; and, last
but not least, "congress in the anus" (Yuck!) There
are whole chapters dedicated to blow jobs (2.9) and
the woman getting on top of the guy (2.8)
respectively.

The chapter ends with the sweet but pretty
sexist assertion that by mastering these positions men
can "generate love, friendship, and respect in the
hearts of women." There's a great footnote by Burton
on this:

> The reader will bear in mind that the
> exceeding pliability of the Hindu's limbs
> enables him to assume attitudes absolutely
> impossible to the European, and his chief
> object in congress is to avoid tension of
> the muscles, which would shorten the
> period of enjoyment.

The <u>Kama Sutra</u> had a big influence Indian art as is
obvious from the famous temple freezes at Konarak and
Khajuraho. Although on those temples the sexuality is
symbolic, metaphysical and spiritual. People acting
out the divine ground of the universe in wierd
positions are common in Indian art.

5

Many Westerners reading about all the positions
in the <u>Kama Sutra</u> might get the idea that people in
ancient India were "lascivious, salacious,
concupiscent, lickerish, and lubricous."[8] But actually
they were highly sophisticated and ahead of their
time. Only recently, thanks to pioneers like Freud,
Masters and Johnson, have we in the West come to
understand that wierd positions are good: "Modern
sexologists agree that for most people a certain
agility and willingness to experiment increases coital
gratification."[9]

IMPLICATIONS?

Animals have sex in only one position. They
don't do it symbolically and are never aware that they
are the divine ground of the universe. Coming up with
new positions is part of being human. Creativity can
turn reproductive biology into art (related to dance);
contemplation can turn it into spiritual practice
(i.e., yoga and Tai Chi Chuan); and playfullness can
turn it into fun (related to gymnastics). Thus, in
the next parts of this paper I will explain all of
that.

Dance and Sex

Every body knows that dance and sex are related:
both involve partners (usually male and female),
rythmic gestures, tandem body movements, and shifting
positions. Both are enjoyable and make you sweat.

NOT NORMALLY CITED AS A SOURCE.

---

[8] Roget's <u>Thesaurus</u>, p. 629.

[9] R.R. Rosemont, op.cit., p. 170. The author,
incidentally, catalogues only a measely sixteen basic
positions, only half the number the ancient Indians knew
about.

G. Spanking
and Moaning

I have the right to wear men's clothes: the man in me thrilled over the exquisite brutality and bloodlust of the Bône riot; the man in me thrilled with that same dark ecstasy over the opportunity to whip Rakhil the Jewess (who, at first, thought I was a boy). But I am much more of a woman than you imagine: the woman in me took pleasure in letting the sun blister the skin on my cheeks and breasts as I lolled naked on the rooftop of the house in Akaba; the woman in me took the same dark delight in the voluptuous tortures dispensed upon me by Mahmoud Saadi (when he discovered that I was a girl). I have realized in myself a capacity to enjoy pain (whether inflicting it as a man or receiving it as a woman) provided that the pain is allied with love. In this way only am I a Christian.

—Isabelle Eberhardt, *Ivre au pays des sables*

1. SADISM

A. TRANSLATION

Love is mortal combat. It's manly to be rough, tough, and sadistic; women are by nature vulnerable, weak, and masochistic. Sometimes, however, either out of passion, proclivity or perversity, or just for fun or experimentation, the gender roles will be reversed. But it never lasts long—the innate sexual tendencies of men and women will inevitably reassert themselves.[1]

1. Roth has left out Vātsyāyana's taxonomy of the blows, categorized in terms of the place on the body that is struck: the *spike* on the chest, the *dagger* on the head, and the *drill* on the cheeks. Our good commentator, Yaśodhara, describes the position of the fingers for each blow in a way that is redolent of the *mudrā*s of religious practice and the conventionalized hand gesticulations as enumerated in the *śāstra*s of dance and drama. Pralayānanga warns sadomasochistically inclined lovers to be careful: "King Chitrasena became so blinded by sexual passion that he murdered a courtesan with a violent blow known as the *spike;* the king of the Kuntalas slaughtered his queen with a whack called the *dagger;* and the

The authorities explain that the erotic deportment of one who has not studied the sexological textbooks will be dictated by impulses rather than by rules. Indulgences that are driven by passion alone are bound to be as chaotic as our wildest dreams. Just as a galloping horse, blinded by speed, is oblivious to posts, potholes, and ditches in the road, so ardent lovers, in the heat of sexual combat and the scotoma of rapture, are not in control of what they do. But those who have properly studied such scholarly texts as the *Kamasutra* will be mindful to remain aware of their own strength and to always appraise the delicacy and mettle of their lovers.

B. COMMENTARY

The following account of that mortal combat that is euphemistically characterized as "making love" is from the brazen memoirs of my dear wife's scurrilous grandfather: *The Indian Adventures of Brigade-Major Francis White of the Bengal Lancers in the Service of His Empire & Himself* by Himself ("Cosmopoli: MDCCCC: for the Corinthian Club of Calcutta, the Crimea, Paris, Oxford, & the Sandwich Isles, & for Private Circulation Only"):

[7 July 1896, Juggernauth Pooree]: I'm a lucky-get-happy jasper with my store of Murreee beer & Burma cheroots, enough pink gin & ruby port to slake a regiment, & sufficient imsauk & majoon to keep the old pig-staff stiff; I lackadaze in my planter's long-sleever on the veranda with my suitably sycophantic John fanning me.

In order to reserve full officer's pay I was obliged to pass the Higher Standard in Oreeya parlance. As I had, with congenital facility, passed similar examinations as set in Hindoostanee, Bengalee, Pushtu, & Lephcha, it was not of great concern to me. But I dispatched my John to fetch me an Oreeya lass in the bagh-bazaar, that she might, for bangles & baksheesh, tutor myself in her curly-cued patter & idiom.

He engaged a regular strapping black-nippled nugger-naree, my little Rum-Jenny, & though she was full of Dom blood, she played the royal courtezane, some Your-Highness-of-a-Whore, Princess Pudenda, Our Lady of the Pompoir, right from the palm-leaf paginations of the *Kameh-Sootreh-Bible*. My nokar-boy John quipped of her, *"Chuchoondur-key sirpur chumbeylee-k'teyl,"* which is bustee-Hindustani talkee-talk for "There's jasmine perfume on the head of a muskrat."

Commander-in-Chief of the Gupta Armed Forces put out the eye of a beautiful dancer with a jab termed the *drill*." The commentator continues: "A man who enters the bed of a woman as if entering a field of battle will enjoy success as a lover; so too a man who enters the field of battle as if entering the bed of a woman (receiving wounds of arrows and spears as if they were the bites and scratches of a lover), will enjoy success as a warrior."

Moorullee, she appellated herself: "Little Bird Girl." In time my bawdy bayadere, my Maharuttee Devee & Jaungha-Mutaunee, seemed at starters a toyish niggeree with just budding breasts, a tiger-pussy teener. The nippy demoiselles of humid Hindoostan, however, as if ripened by the weather, maturate much faster than our English maidens.

The gup-gup at the club was that my cocket had gone all junglie, that there wasn't a white quim I'd touch, & that wasn't far unfair, for our sallow Mem-Sahibehs cannot keep up with woggy wenches when it comes to fucking. The luscious spread of crimsonated clam, haloed with a fleecy nimbus of pickaninny down, all set in subtle shades of brown from coir to resorcin, is a spectacle more puissant than that provided by the puny pink & creamy cunts of Albion. These nut-brown native strumpets, experts in the use of pessaries & pikes, know & train their russet cunts. She fancied what she called *chootree*, Oreeya-jabbery for "buttockry" of a scrupulous kind wherein the compliant gent grips, squeezes & fiercely beats the nates of her behind whilst she squeals & screams, hisses & moans, ululates & vellicates, thereby allowing me to master the nasal, guttural, sibilant, & palatal tones which I myself needed to learn if I was to speak her Oreeya.

One hot day it occurred to me that my little bird girl was, in some profound sense, India incarnate & that India is, in another not less profound manner, herself a rutting woman with whom John Company is having a long, dangerous & delicious fuck. It's a big Imperial puck-puckeroo if there ever was one, & if we don't swive her good, there'll be mutiny, adultery, & she'll cut our balls off in the night. But if we can keep it up & fuck her right, pleasing & punishing her with judicious simultaneity, she'll be on her knees begging for the service of John Company's Imperial Pego. But beware John Company! Apply boudoir lessons to Colonial rule. The pego arrogantly reckons he's Sovereign of the Seas; but he's easy prey for the ultimately victorious Yonee. *Vicisti, O vafera Vulva! Et væ virilis victus!*

Don't inaccurate my words: I'm no bloody sluggish pervert, not one of those poggy swipes for whom the rod's the endall. No, for me it is the means. I whip my steed to speed & take the jump. It's preparationary. My Moorullee confessed that after I had treated her swashy posteriors to my strict Assamese pizzle, she felt all the more warmth during my hot gallop in her paddy-field. Fucking was then reward & solace, balm & salve for body & soul. *Coitio ergo sum.*

As long as I live I shall never forget or in any way disregard the sublime vista of my Jaungha-Mutaunee's tantalizing twitchings during the beatings that I so lovingly rendered. O sweet chastisements! It's spiritual endeavor: the more the sullen body's punished, the more awake & holy she becomes. Ask Our Lord, if you have doubts or misgivings.

I took to opiated claret in the afternoons & languored on the veranda with her, perusing the palm leaves of a little *Kameh-Sootreh-Bible* which my John had unearthed for me in the bazaar. Each leaf had a fuck-posture incised with primitive innocence & Sunscrit lingo in Oreeya script.

Supinating in the chopper cot, white veiled by mosquito net, fine dolly-donned in the choicest saree with which I had gifted her, Moorullee was whimpering. With a perturbation that does not become me, I upped the netting & sat down, hoisted the saree like a sail to expose chocolatey buttocks, removed my riding glove & trailed my fingers up her leg toward the ravening ravine. Strumpet thighs closed clam tight in clenchy pudendal resistance as she moaned through tears with a voice immensely melancholic: "How can I trust that thou still lovest me, Master? Thou hast not beaten me even once in the past four weeks. Hast thou tired of thy slave?"

It was whispered so plaintively that it drew tears to my eyes though I am not a sentimental man so easily provoked to weeping. I entreated her pardon with solemn peccavis & promises to make it right at once &, drying up effeminate tears, I went resolute to fetch my pizzle-crop from where I had left it hanging on a brass hook by my Leela's stall.

I pushed her down across my legs, hiked up the silken saree & commenced the whipping, first slow & soft, then swift & hard as she womaneuvered under the bills & blows, rocked & gasped & shook. Like my Leela on the trail of a pig, responding to the crop, she picked up speed, cantered to full gallop, faster & faster, harder & harder, white frothing at the trou, legs bending, bowing, opening wider & wider, faster & faster, & then, as when I'm astride my Leela & we've touched top speed, I took up my sticking pole. Lifting her up & hunching her over, I leaned across her back as over my Leela's fierce driving, thrusting neck, & with pointed pole poised, I entered & rode, faster & faster, tugging her hair as I yank my Leela's glossy mane, still flogging her to greater speed, & then, all at once, as when I stick a pig, there was one last thrust all the way to the bone & my valourous pego was drippy wet like my stick with pig's blood & just as my Leela, at that moment when I extricate the lance, will turn, rear, snort, & whinny loud, so my Moorullee rolled, groaned, rose, fell back, & I collapsed into her arms to gently stroke her hair, all tenderly & lovey.

And all the while I was fucking her, my John was outside pulling the punkah cord, & he heard the final moans of our excruciating ecstasy, he cried out, "Huzza Huzza! Hip hip hurrah! Rule, Britannia! Long live the King! Long live the Queen! Long live India! Long live everybody! Ram-Ram!"

"Oh, shut up, John!" I had to yell out &, hearing his savage guffaw, I vowed to give him a sound flailing. No, no, no, I don't trust my nigger John-boy as I suspect a fancy for my beloved Jenny-girl &, armed with Lee Enfield, he'd purloin her just like some baboo-extremist Partitionist who'd expropriate Bengal. These fellows feign they're chaste bramucareyas, but it's all persiflage & raillery. They worship linghums &, with the incitements of their lecherous gods, they lust in measures beyond civilized comprehensions. The *Kameh-Sootreh* is their Holy Gospel, Vatsyayuneh their Saint Paul. Fucking, which is a mere, though thoroughly engrossing, diversion for the Christian soul, is, alas, their religion.

2. MASOCHISM

AN OPERATIC TRANSLATION IN ONE SCENE
Cast of Characters:

LALITA, a courtesan ....*soprano*
VATSYAYANA, a professor ....*bass*
LILA-RATHA, a *nagaraka* ....*tenor*

A full moon and oil lamps illuminate a garden shaded with ashoka, bilva, and mango trees, and ornamented with creepers, bamboo, and flowers; a shrine to Kama stands at the back beside a stream just showing through the trees. The sage Vatsyayana sits cross-legged beneath the largest tree on a raised mound of dirt to the side of a pavilion at center stage. There, upon a bed of lotus petals, are two lovers: Lalita and Lila-Ratha.

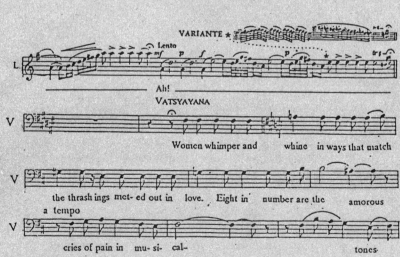

Lila-Ratha begins thrashing Lalita, at first gently, playfully, but with mounting ferocity; the force and sites of his blows change and with each change there is a different moan, cry, or sigh.

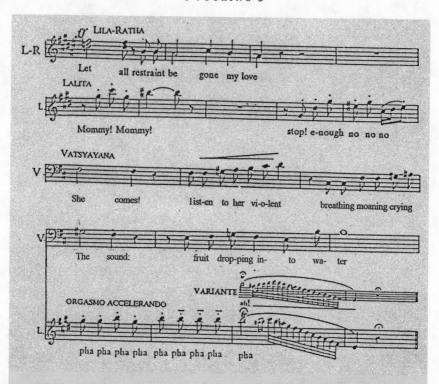

A cloud passes over the moon, and though Vatsyayana is no longer visible, the lovers, languidly resting in embrace, are softly illuminated by the flickering lamplight. Dawn is approaching and with it come the songs of the various birds that the *Kamasutra* has designated as those whose cries are to be imitated by women during the act of love: first the nightingale and then doves, cuckoos, sparrows, parrots, partridges, ducks, and geese.

THE END

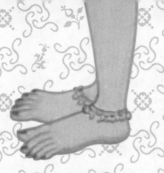

H. Topsy-turvy and Vice Versa

Literary forgeries, like the feigned heights of venereal excitement in coition for which harlots are renown, are reprehensible or admirable depending on the quality of the forgery and the motive of the forger. Art, like love, is alas all masquerade. You chastise me for my forgery, Sir, and yet is not the forger, with his furnace and molten metals, his anvil and hammer, the one to whom we owe some of the most esteemed and indispensable instruments and implements of civilization? And is not God the forger of all creation? Your Bible deems it so—or is that a forgery as well?

   —Thomas Chatterton, letter to Laurence Sterne (1768)

The wide, melancholy eyes of Thomas Chatterton stared at me, and looking back at the adolescent face on her sweatshirt, slightly distorted by her breasts, of that restless and duplicitous boy who in 1770 committed suicide at the age of seventeen, I said, "Hello, Aphra." She corrected me: "Tajma, Tajma Hall." At her request, I had let her read a portion of my translation of the chapter in Book Two of the *Kamasutra* that deals with women getting on top of their lovers during lovemaking; she had forged her translation of the equivalent passage from her fabricated *Ratisutra* that she would claim Vatsyayana had stolen from Jayamangala. It was time to compare the texts:

A. TRANSLATION

The *Kamasutra* of Vatsyayana (II.H)	The *Ratisutra* of Jayamangala (II.H)
How to Open a Woman	**How to Master a Man**
Having approached the girl, and then sitting down next to her, the man should distract her with conver-	Having gone to his office, or some such place where he feels in control of the situation, the woman should

sation as he unknots the clasps of her garment; if she protests, he should, while flustering her with kisses—first on the cheeks, then on the mouth—continue to fondle her until his penis becomes erect.

If it's the first time they've made love, the man will probably need to pry open thighs that will inevitably be bashfully clamped together. The same holds true if she's a young girl. In any case, he should squeeze her breasts, tickle her armpits, and caress her neck. If she's a sexpot of whatever age, however, the man can proceed by doing what comes naturally, what follows from grabbing her chin, kissing her, pressing against her bosom, and ferociously pulling her hair. The young girl may close her eyes in embarrassment or modesty, genuine or feigned.

The secret ways to please a girl, according to Auddalaki, are revealed by observing where her eyes fall as one makes love to her—that's where one should strike. The affective indicators of female sexual pleasure during intercourse are: relaxation of the limbs, blinking of the eyes, excessive expressions of shyness or shame, trembling, moans of "oh, no," sweating, sighing, and an unnatural shaking of the head.

ask him to speak of his work or some such topic upon which he feels expert. Not listening to a word of what the fellow is saying, the woman should move slowly toward him, constantly staring him in the eyes, and then she should reach down to slowly, but purposefully, loosen his belt. If he protests, the woman should stop the flow of his words with her tongue in his mouth while continuing to undress him, feeling, as she does, for the stiffening of the lingam.

If the woman has never made love to him before, or if he's a young and inexperienced boy, he'll probably try to make physical advances as evidence that he knows something about what he's supposed to be doing. In this case, pushing his hands away or holding them tightly to indicate that she does not want him to make the advances, the woman should lean forward to kiss his neck, chest, nipples, stomach, and so on, and so on, until he surrenders to her control.

The secret of being pleased as a woman, according to Mahayogini Kalima, is in the realization that each woman herself contains her pleasure and that boys and men are merely instruments for the activation of that enjoyment. The indicators of a man's submission are: grunts, groans, grimaces, sweating, muscle flexing, and verbal expressions of love, obscene utterances, cries of "oh, yes," grinning, and making snorting sounds.

If, after the man has ejaculated, the girl hasn't been satisfied, she'll swear, bite, kick, and refuse to let the man stand up. In order to prevent such a scene, before actual intercourse, the girl's vulva should be hand-stirred, as if by an elephant—ah, yes, that will make it soft.

When the woman takes the man's position, on top of her lover, there are three conventional acts: the *vice*, in which the penis, caught in the grip of the vaginal lips, is forced in and pushed out, over and over again; the *dreidel* (which takes practice to master), which involves revolving around the man, like a wheel around an axle, an action requiring the lady to elevate her pelvis; and the *swing*, in which the woman gyrates and rocks her pelvis in every direction. In case she tires, she should rest her forehead upon her lover's forehead.

Once a man has surrendered to the woman, he should be coaxed to stimulate the vulva, using his hand as the elephant uses its trunk, or his tongue as the cow licks her calf. When the woman realizes the activation of pleasure, it's time to direct his lingam into the yoni.

Taking her usual position on top of the boy or man, the woman should proceed to perform the conventional acts: the *vice*, in which the lingam, caught in the grip of the yonic lips, is forced in and pushed out, over and over again; the *top* (which takes practice to master), which involves revolving around the lingam like a wheel around an axle, an action requiring the woman to elevate her pelvis; and the *swing*, in which the woman gyrates and rocks her pelvis in every direction. In case the man tires or seems ready to ejaculate, the woman should slow her movements down, or even stop without removing the lingam from the yoni, and warn her lover that if he comes too soon or is too fatigued to continue, she will spread word about that he is impotent, and she will seek out a more adept athlete of love.

According to the sexological sages:

Although a sexy woman may try to hide her real emotions by masking their affects, once she gets on top of a man her true nature will, by the power of passion, be revealed.

A woman's behavior during that form of lovemaking, while she's wholly absorbed in sexual pleasure, should be ob-

According to the priestesses of Rati:

Although men try to be in control, imagining that they have some power over women, once they are mounted, their real nature, which is vulnerable and weak, becomes apparent.

A woman should constantly watch the man from her place above him, taking note of how and what he does

served in order to know her true disposition.

One should not cause a woman to make love in the manly position if she's very fat, if she's menstruating or has a small vagina, if she's pregnant or has recently given birth.

down there, so that she can judiciously determine whether or not it's worth keeping him in her erotic service.

One should not ride astride a man if he's underweight or if his lingam is piddling, if he's prone to either premature ejaculation or impotence.

B. COMMENTARY

"Well, it's absolutely and perfectly faithful to the original," I was able to say with an encouraging smile. Since is there is no ancient Sanskrit text, of course, her translation *is* the original.

"I compared your translation to Burton's," she responded. "His is so charming in that kinky Victorian way. Yours is, I assume, more correct. The question is, not only as a translator, but as a man, would you rather be charming or correct? And which do you think Vatsyayana would advise you to be?"[1]

---

1. In all fairness, or unfairness, to Roth, he does not always stack up favorably in terms of correctness to Burton, nor unfavorably to him in terms of charm. Compare Burton's version of a passage from this very section, II.H, with the same passage as transformed by Roth (for Ms. Gupta no doubt) from a detached description into a sort of impassioned poem merely by a shifting of the distant third-person singular feminine pronoun into the more intimate second person:

BURTON:

With flowers in her hair hanging loose and her smiles broken by hard breathings, she should press upon her lover's bosom with her own breasts; and lowering her head frequently, she should do in return the same actions which he did before, returning his blows and chaffing him. She should say, "I was laid down by you and fatigued with hard congress; I shall now therefore lay you down in return." She should then again manifest her own bashfulness, her fatigue, and her desire of stopping the congress.

ROTH:

And there are blossoms in
    Your tousled locks and laughter
in Your gasps and sighs
    as our faces touch right after
You jostle me with Your breasts
    when You bow Your head
to me as You do and are
    what I have done and said;
"Now I lay you down to keep"
    You tease and torture me
and then, all at once, You seem
    shy, beg to rest and be
The woman that You are
    and not the man You see.
      "Stop"

I changed the subject.

"How's Isaac? He doesn't call me, or come by to see me. What's going on with him?"

"He's fine, just fine," she answered lackadaisically as she lit up one of my Viceroys. "He doesn't call you because he's waiting for you to telephone him, to tell him that you've read the mirror book. But that's not my concern."

She pulled the Monier Monier-Williams *Sanskrit-English Dictionary* toward her, opened it, and after seeing that the order of the alphabet was not that of English lexicons, she asked me to help her find *rati*.

"I want to know what the word in my title really means." She read aloud: "'Repose, pleasure, enjoyment, delight in, fondness for, the pleasure of love, sexual passion or union, amorous enjoyment, personified as one of the two wives of Kama; the pudenda; a magical incantation said over weapons; the name of a meter; a game; a plant *(Datura stramonium);* the name of a queen; a kind of bird *(Larus indicus).*' And on and on and on. All the definitions are so long. All of these words mean so many things. This dictionary's so big. It's heavy. Be careful not to drop it on your foot. You could break something." She hesitated. "Okay, be honest with me. Do you think I can pull this *Ratisutra* thing off?" She looked me straight in the eyes. "Tell me the truth."

That command again and again. The dreadful imperative tense. It's the injunction given to all translators and lovers. It's a reader's command, a woman's demand. Sophia asks it of me; everyone I've ever loved has asked me to tell them the truth. It comes with the deal; it's a line in the book, a play in the game.

I told her what she wanted to hear.

"If I do pull it off," she said quite seriously, "you won't ruin it, will you? You won't expose me? Can I trust you?"

That question again and again and again. The discomforting interrogative. It's a question asked of all translators and lovers, a reader's query, a woman's question. Everyone I have ever loved has asked it. "Can I trust you?" The answer is always the same: *Yes.*

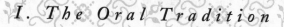

I. The Oral Tradition

Never ask a man-about-town, "Fancy a blow-job?" Never! Only little street sluts express themselves like that. Instead, as a demonstration of your sophistication, whisper demurely and softly in his ear, "Would you, Sir, care to make some use my mouth?"

—Edouard Lamairesse, *Le Kama Sutra: Un manuel Indien de civilité pour les petites filles à l'usage des maisons d'éducation adapté pour les femmes occidentales*

A. TRANSLATION

Duplex est tertia species, aut forma muliebri aut forma virili. Hic species forma muliebri prædita feminæ vestitum, vocem, naturam, consuetudinem, teneritatem, timiditatem, simplicitatem, preferendi imbecillitatem, pudorem imitetur.[1] Since this fuck is in the mouth rather than in the cunt, it's called the *blow job.*

B. COMMENTARY

Non culpabilis.

1. Roth's perverse endeavor to translate the section on fellatial procedures in a way that reverses the conventional nineteenth-century practice of rendering the transgressive texts of a foreign-language discourse into Latin, to put the clean parts in Latin and the dirty parts in English, did not go very far. This is all of the translation of the chapter that I have been able to find except for the following marginal note in English: "What we call 69, they call the *crow*"; and this into Latin: *"Quæ res cum secretum aliquod atque mens varia sit, quis igitur est, qui disceptare possit, quis aut quando aut quo modo quidgue conficiat?"* In his early article, "'Fuck' in Sanskrit?" Roth had compared Latin and Sanskrit obscenities, arguing that, while those languages had, of course, many terms and countless idioms for sexual intercourse, they lacked any word equivalent to "the deliciously illicit morpheme that is so profoundly *dirty* not because of what it means (which is hardly dirty), but because of how it sounds and, much more crucially, because of its forbidden history. It has taken many mouths, the buccal cavities of many transgressors shouting it out in many contexts, to invest the word with its very unique lectional power."

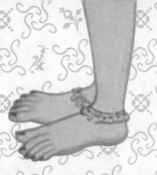

J. Alpha and Omega

No fixed centers, for starters—and no edges either, no ends or boundaries. The line vanishes into a geographical landscape of an exitless maze, with beginnings, middles, ends being no longer part of the immediate display. Instead: branching optional menus, linked markers and mapped networks. There are no hierarchies in these topless and bottomless networks of evenly empowered and equally ephemeral window-sized blocks of text and graphics.
—Robert Coover, "The End of Books"

1. FOREPLAY

A. TRANSLATION [AND/OR] B. COMMENTARY

Editor's Note

I have had to compile this entire section from scattered documents, fitting them into a congruent whole as one would some sort of puzzle: pages were stuck into the two notebooks for Book Two of the project (the one for "translation" and the one for "commentary"); there was a manila file folder in the second drawer of Roth's file cabinet (where he was keeping his clothes at the time of his death) containing crumpled pages of the Devanagari text with various traditional commentaries in Sanskrit, Hindi, and Oriya; in his desk drawers I found a set of illustrations, random graphics and sketches, copious notes (many illegible or senseless, or both), correspondence, and other materials. "Afterpiece" is, incidentally, the only section in which Roth, translating more as an accomplished scholar than as a hopeful lover, uses the diacritical marks as conventionalized by the dictionary that killed him.

Seedy-R0M-Antics ● Multimedia Development
719 North Sterne Street • Shandy Hills, CA 90318 • (310) 278-6666

Buddha's Birthday
April 8, 1997

Dear Professor Roth:

Your name was given to me by Professor Lee Siegel of the University of Hawaii in response to a letter I wrote to him regarding our interest in developing software for a CD-ROM version of the famous Indian erotic text, the *Kama Sutra*. I am an Indian National working as a director in the Multimedia Development division of Seedy-ROM-Antics, an innovative new company, dedicated to exploring the frontiers of an exciting new industry. Books, we believe are an outmoded and profoundly limited means of conveying information.

Siegel informed me that you are working on a new translation of the *Kama Sutra*. You are to be congratulated on that project (I have long wondered why the translation of the Orientalist, "Dirty Dick" Burton, keeps being reprinted and reissued). I would like to propose that you work on that project in consultation with us.

We are particularly interested in producing a line of materials dealing with human love and sexuality. Among the projects currently under development here are "The Physiology of Sex," "The Art of Making Love," "The Psychology of Sex," and "The World History of Love." We have also produced such adult interactive games as "Porno Producer," "Beverly Hills Dick," "Tit-Tris," "Domination Dominoes," "Ice Hickey," and "Strip Stud Poker." The *Kama Sutra* will fit in nicely and even give a perhaps needed cultural dignity to our endeavors.

As an Indian (though not currently a practicing Hindu), I have always been proud of the great accomplishments of my forefathers including such architectural wonders as the Taj Mahal and the erotic temples of Khajuraho, as well as such literary masterpieces as the *Bhagavad Gita* and the *Kama Sutra*, two of the greatest texts of all times (one for the body and one for the soul—understood in unison they offer wisdom to the whole being). Thus I have come up with the idea of producing a CD-ROM *Kama Sutra*, a project no doubt more commercially viable than a CD-ROM *Bhagavad Gita*, although that will certainly be accomplished (funded by the proceeds from our *Kama Sutra*—the flesh will serve, not hinder, the spirit) in the future; all texts, I am certain, will ultimately be delivered from books, like souls from temporal bodies, to be resurrected and reincarnated in more enduring multimedial forms. As we at Seedy-ROM-Antics say, "Books are a thing of the past." We salute the ravenous bookworms with a big '*bon appetit.*'

-2-

As in so many domains (mathematics, erotics, and aeronautics, to name but a few), my forefathers were characteristically ahead of their time: It seems to me that our ancient Indian palm leaves (like those upon which the *Kama Sutra* were scratched) were essentially lexia, discursive units that could be manipulated non-linearly, non-hierarchically, more rhizomatically and axially. They foreshadow the floating networked windoids, the units (comprised of scriptons and textons) that comprise an ergologically dynamic hypertext.

Literacy (a problem in my country) will soon be recognized as but a historical step toward a technological hyperliteracy (which promises to redeem my country from its present economic limitations), an ability to comprehend ('read' will be a word to describe what people used to do with those cumbersome and static [not to mention dystopic] things called books) lexially protean hypertexts in which distinctions between writer and reader (like the differentiations between lover and beloved in sexual union) disappear as participants experience technologically generated meanings. The individual or collective participant in the *Kama Sutra*, in control of the peripeteia of the text, will deliver it from the the tar pits of antiquity to the boundless cyberspaces of a luminous present. What was sound (Vatsyayana speaking), became (through the endeavor of scribes) a set of palm-leaf lexia which, in turn (through the endeavor of Western Orientalists), became ink-cellulose which, in turn (through the efforts of myself and hopefully you, Professor Roth), electron-phosphor. Shakti, the goddess who is power—electronic and nuclear (not to mention metaphysical)—will live in the hypertext just as she lived in mythological consciousness of India's Golden Age!

If you are interested in this exciting, and I believe lucrative, enterprise, please contact me by telephone, mail, or E-mail on the Internet (cdromporn@multisex.net) at your earliest convenience.

Cybernetically yours,

N.V. Sundaralingam
Executive Manager of Production

Seedy-R0M-Antics ● Multimedia Development
719 North Sterne Street • Shandy Hills, CA 90318 • (310) 278-6666

Passover
April 21, 1997

Dear Professor Roth:

Thank you for telephoning me so promptly. I very much appreciate your interest and enthusiasm, not to mention your insights and ideas. Let me suggest some of the ways in which you might begin thinking non-linearly about this (ad)venture, some of the ways in which the new technology will let all of us understand a discourse more metaholistically by providing us with a new, multidimensional access to it, by transforming what was confined as text into a liberated hypertext.

I was particularly impressed by your statement that this project in no way compromises the text, that the *Kama Sutra* has had many forms and incarnations, that it has been an oral text at times, an illustrated text, an enacted text, and that its publication in book form, mere black print on a white page, limits the text. Yes, you reiterated my sentiments exactly! Working together, we shall bring the *Kama Sutra* back to life and, having breathed a photonic *prana* into it, set it free! Everyone who sits on my large staff is excited!

In order to give you an example of the kinds of things I envision, let me take a portion of the text that particularly (despite Dirty Dick's Orientalist overlay) interests me. I have a nostalgia, I confess, for the way of life that we in India used to enjoy. It's the first paragraph of the tenth chapter of the second book:

> In the pleasure-room, decorated with flowers, and fragrant with perfumes, attended by his friends and servants, the citizen should receive the woman, who will come bathed and dressed, and will invite her to take refreshment and to drink freely. He should then seat her on his left side, and holding her hair, and touching also the end and knot of her garment, he should gently embrace her with his right arm. They should then carry on an amusing conversation on various subjects, and may also talk suggestively of things which would be considered coarse, or not to be mentioned generally in society. They may sing, either with or without gesticulations, and play on musical instruments, talk about the arts, and persuade each other to drink. At last when the woman is overcome with love and desire, the citizen should dismiss the people that may be with him, giving them flowers, ointments, and betel leaves, and then when the two are left alone, they should proceed as has been already described in previous chapters.

-2-

How charming! What a lifestyle! Who can read such a passage without yearning to live in ancient India? That's what we want our customers to experience through the unique interactive technology under development. Let's think virtual reality (not to mention holography)! There are no limits as to what is possible through digitalization!

But okay, for the time being, let me give you some sense as to how we might deal with such a passage and then, when you've thought it over and come up with your own ideas, get back to me. Remember to think metasensually, to envision hypervisually, to hear sounds, music, voices. We want the experience of the *Kama Sutra* to be a technosexual one for our consumers. Imagine a man and woman spending the evening together (naked perhaps) at their computer, exploring a web of infinite amorous links, a Boolean network of erotic data bases, an electronic orgy participated in by lovers from all over the world, past (thanks to us) and present (thanks to users of Internet); imagine them transported by the technology back to that flower-decorated pleasure room! I can hear the music, smell the perfumes, taste the drinks, and see the beautiful woman on my left!

How can we—you, the brilliant, Western Sanskrit scholar and me, the no-less-brilliant-at-what-I-do, Indian multimedia-guru—go wrong? We're talking a state-of-the-art, cutting-edge, high-tech, post-post-post-modern interfacial marriage of ancient Indian erotic wisdom (thanks to you) and modern technological achievements (thanks to me). It sends chills up and down my spine!

But let me be specific. The most obvious of various ways of accessing this passage would be choosing "Two: Sexual Union" from a contents menu, then "Ten: Beginning and End" from the sub-contents menu, and then "One: Beginning Congress" from a sub-sub-contents menu that includes "Two: Ending Congress," "Three: Kinds of Congress," and "Four: Love Quarrels."

Now let's think audio tracks: imagine the text read in Sanskrit by a pandit or in English by an actor (we could get Ben Kinsley or Roshan Seth); there could be a choice of night *ragas* to accompany the passage and evoke the mood, or even some modern ambient music. Highlighting "They may then sing," could result in a sound clip that lets the consumer hear a classical Indian song or something masala-hot and sexy from a Hindi film (do you know "*Meri chhatri ke niche a jao*" ["Come join me under my umbrella"]?).

Now let's think visual displays: from an "Illustrations" menu one might pick either verbal illustrations (from Sanskrit literature, depictions in this case of women arriving at trysts with their lovers), or graphic illustrations, either still (reproductions from Indian art) or video clips (from Hindi films, or XXX films shot especially for this project [these will be especially useful for the chapters on sexual positions, oral sex, etc.]).

-3-

Using the Topics tool you can see what's available on subjects like dildoes, menage á trois, positions for loving, infidelity, orgasm, aphrodisiacs, etc., and using the Search tool you'll be able access engrossing discussions of such specific things as clitoris, erection, hickey, nipple, etc. We want our customers to enjoy using their Tools.

Think interactive, if not hyperinteractive (not to mention interhyperactive): Each consumer will be able to enter their own commentary on the *Kama Sutra*, to a part of the text, bringing their sexuality, their own dreams and fantasies, their own unique understanding of the mysteries of love to the text. Isn't that what the literary experience (not to mention the sexual or amorous experience) should be? Each reader of the same text, like each lover of the same woman (or the other way around), modulates that text, transforms that lover, finds in it/her/him something that has never been discovered before. Don't you agree?

Remember, we are capable of morphing anything, of 3-D and realistic fractal texturing. I know that Vatsyayana would be thrilled to know what we are doing with his text.

Get back to me with your comments and reactions.

Intratextonically yours,

N.V. Sundaralingam
Executive Manager of Production

P.S. Yes, I do think it's a good idea for us to meet (since you don't have e-mail) and, yes, I do know the Taj Mahal Indian Restaurant and Lounge and, yes, Thursday for lunch would be just fine. Shall we say at noon? Yes?

WESTERN UNIVERSITY
Department of Asian Studies
Swinburne Hall
2530 Eastland Avenue
Los Angeles, CA 90220

N.V. Sundaralingam
Executive Manager of Production
Seedy-Rom-Antics
Multimedia Development
719 North Sterne Street
Shandy Hills, CA 90318

April 25, 1997

Dear Mr. Sundaralingam,

It was a pleasure to meet with you at the Taj Mahal for lunch. I am indeed intrigued by the project (although I'm afraid that many of my concerns might be a bit too academic for you). I am, you must understand, above all else, concerned with language, with translation, with semantic transformations, particularly in respect to erotic discourse. Is language necessarily an impediment to the full expression of emotion and sentiment, or does it have the potential to be a faithful articulation of sexual desire and the ache and joy of love possible? Is it that we do and can love only because we have language, and that eloquence is actually a state of the heart? Do words stand between us and our beloved, or are they the only bridge? These are the kinds of questions that inspired me to begin a translation of the Kamasutra.

I think it is imperative (and legitimating) that we provide the Sanskrit text in Devanagari script and in transliteration into a variety of other scripts including, of course, Roman (and both Braille for the blind and sign language for the hearing impaired); and then there should be a choice of translations, English of course, but also French, German, Spanish, Arabic, Japanese, Chinese, Hebrew, Hindi, and indeed as many as possible (including Yiddish, Lepcha, Zemblan, and Esperanto).

At any time, the user should be able to press a
"commentary" button to find out what Yashodhara or the other
traditional commentators have had to say about the passage in
question. I envision the text in Sanskrit: one can block any
portion of that text, from one word, to a whole chapter, to
the whole text, and then push a "translation" button. It
would be an inspired use of the medium, I feel, if at any
time, one could click on a "MS." button in order to see
actual palm leaf manuscripts. It would be valuable to
scholars, furthermore, if one could use the technology to see
variant readings and thereby to create a critical edition of
any portion of the text. So, for example, from the passage
that you've cited, if I am aware of the vario lectiones I
realize that, depending on whether one reads
kṛtasnānaprasādhanaḥ or *kṛtasnānaprasādhanām*, it is ambiguous
whether it is the man who is "bathed and dressed" (as I would
propose), or whether it is (as Burton suggests) the woman.

It would be valuable if one could highlight any word in
the text and use that word to access contextual information.
So, for example, highlighting "citizen" (Burton's English for
nagaraka, the urbane and sophisticated man about town, one
could be taken directly to the chapter within the *Kamasutra*
(i.e., I.D.) that describes the figure and through that
section, one might access descriptions of him from other
literary texts as well as images of the *nagaraka* from Indian
art; there could be a history of the well-dressed man about
town in India from the earliest times up to the era of the
Nehru jacket. Highlighting "perfumes," "refreshment,"
"musical instruments," or "betel" in the same extract would
access illustrated discussions of those things in ancient
India.

I completely agree with your observation, by the way,
that since the Kamasutra did not exist in Vatsyayana's mind
as a linear text, but rather as a ganglionic mass of
interconnected images, sounds, memories, perceptions, and
ideas, we are, through the power of a new technology,
redeeming the text from a dead language, bringing it back to
life, electrifying it.

The point of hypertext is, I assume we agree, to free a
text from an identification with its writing or its manifold
readings and to stress the ways in which reader (receiver)
and writer (sender) become indistinguishable like a lover and
beloved in sexual union. We should try, I think, to create

a text that is like a woman, to provide an experience of that
text that is more like making love than reading. Each man
who makes love to her (a woman or our hypertext) experiences
her differently and in doing so changes her for her next
lover. To make love to a woman is to annotate her. Every
woman, I would imagine, has many readings.

 I have lots of ideas and am anxious to talk to you
about them. Shall we have lunch again? I like the House of
Lee in Artesia for Dim Sum. We must talk soon as I am
leaving for India in a few weeks and will be gone for the
summer (I'm conducting a study abroad program there).

 In the meantime, I am enclosing a sample of something
specific. I take up the text where you've left off to show
you what I would do with what you have called "Two: Ending
Congress," what I've titled "II.J.2 Afterpiece." Let me know
what you think. I look forward to continuing our discussion
of love and sexuality in India.

 Wishing you well,

 L.A. Roth

 L.A. Roth
 Professor of Indian Civilization
 Department of Asian Studies
 Western University

2. AFTERPIECE

A–B. TRANSLATION[1] AND COMMENTARY

In order to ascertain what people in ancient India did after lovemaking, one might, for example, highlight on the screen the touching vignette from Vatsyayana's prescriptive description of postcoital behavior and manners (screen 1),[2] and then (if you can resist the "Video" button) click on "Transliteration" and select "Roman" and any graphic font from the font dialogue box (screen 2).

Depending on one's mood or philological frame of mind, one might chose to click on "Translation (German)" and an appropriate font (screen 3).[3] With that velar fricative of theirs, Germans can say things that we can't, can make unique invitations to sexual intercourse by passionately forcing sauerbraten-fragranced breath through the moist narrowing formed as the back of the tongue touches the quivering soft palate. The sound belies both the delight and disgust that are complicitous in all sexual desire. Germanic *Liebe* can be growled, howled, hailed, and *Sieg-Heil*ed. As I whisper *"Ich liebe Dich"* into Your ear, You must realize that the only difference between *You* and *me, ich* and *Dich*, is one little *D*. There is an ecstasy possible in a German that is well suited to erotic verbal ejaculations, a grandeur unimpeded by prosodic self-consciousness and intensified by capital letters *(love* for them is *Love): "O Stern und Blume,"* the great Meister of the German Liebes-Lied sings, *"Penis und Vulva, Liebe, Leib, Leid und Zeit und Ewigkeit!"* It can't be translated.

Das Deutsche, with its inflections and syntactical precision, is utterly authoritarian, all grammatical rules and semantic regulations. Speech is

1. Since Roth did not provide an English translation of the passage under consideration, I have attempted to do so: "Retiring to the roof terrace of the mansion in order to revere the moon, the lover attends to his beloved there with agreeable stories. While she is seated on his knee and gazing at the moon, he should point out the constellations to her, enabling her to identify Arundhatī, Dhruva, and the Seven Rishis." I'm not quite satisfied with "agreeable story" for *anukūla;* the English phrase cannot convey what is expressed by the Sanskrit poetical term for a romance, particularly a love story that ends happily after a series of woes, calamities, and mishaps.

2. The nonhighlighted portion of the text explains that after lovemaking the man and woman should go to separate toilets to relieve themselves and wash. They should then join each other once more to chew betel and massage each other's bodies with sandal unguents. The man, Vātsyāyana notes, should caress the girl, mutter sweet nothings, and invite her to drink with him. Then they should chat and enjoy a pleasant meal—perhaps a light consomme, some spicy meat kabobs, mixed fruits and fresh vegetables, a bite of karanji, a bit of candied lemon, and a tamarind sorbet.

3. The translation, published in Berlin in 1907, is by Richard Schmidt (1866–1939).

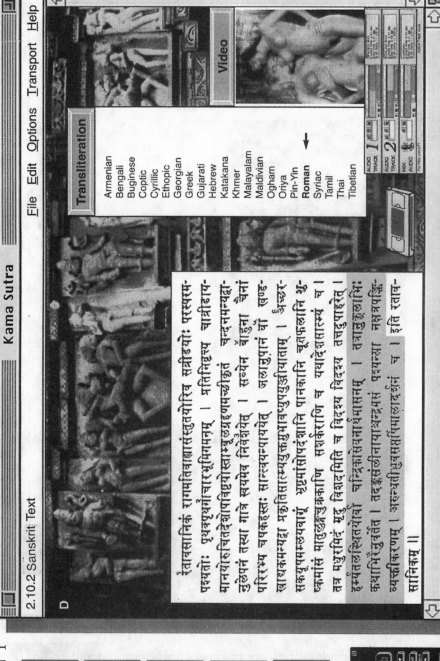

SCREEN 1

2.10.2 Sanskrit Text

Transliteration

Armenian
Bengali
Buginese
Coptic
Cyrillic
Ethopic
Georgian
Greek
Gujarati
Hebrew
Katakana
Khmer
Malayalam
Maldivian
Ogham
Oriya
Pin-Yin
Roman
Syriac
Tamil
Thai
Tibetian

Video

AUDIO TRACK *1*
AUDIO TRACK *2*
MIX AUDIO

SCREEN 2

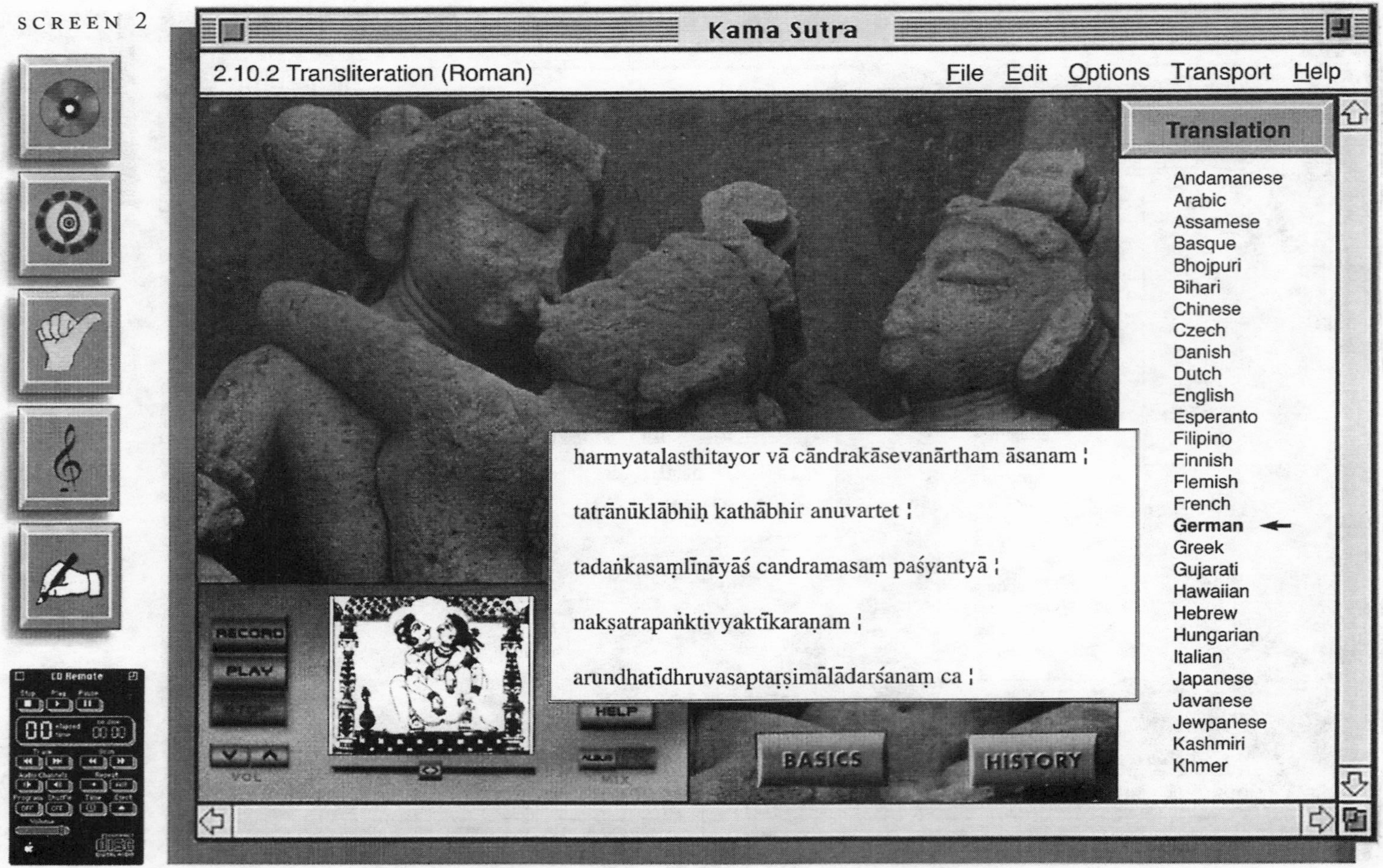

Kama Sutra

File Edit Options Transport Help

2.10.2 Transliteration (Roman)

Translation

Andamanese
Arabic
Assamese
Basque
Bhojpuri
Bihari
Chinese
Czech
Danish
Dutch
English
Esperanto
Filipino
Finnish
Flemish
French
German
Greek
Gujarati
Hawaiian
Hebrew
Hungarian
Italian
Japanese
Javanese
Jewpanese
Kashmiri
Khmer

harmyatalasthitayor vā cāndrakāsevanārtham āsanam ;

tatrānūklābhiḥ kathābhir anuvartet ;

tadaṅkasaṃlīnāyāś candramasaṃ paśyantyā ;

nakṣatrapaṅktivyaktīkaraṇaṃ ;

arundhatīdhruvasaptarṣimālādarśanaṃ ca ;

BASICS   HISTORY

RECORD   PLAY   VOL   HELP

CD Remote

SCREEN 3

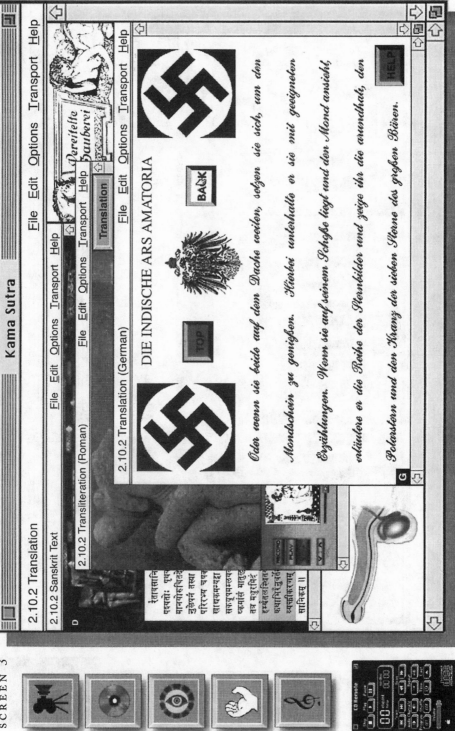

Kama Sutra

2.10.2 Translation

2.10.2 Sanskrit Text

2.10.2 Transliteration (Roman)

2.10.2 Translation (German)

File Edit Options Transport Help

File Edit Options Transport Help

File Edit Options Transport Help

File Edit Options Transport Help

Bereitefte Zauberei

Translation

DIE INDISCHE ARS AMATORIA

BACK

TOP

HELP

Oder wenn sie beide auf dem Dache weilen, setzen sie sich, um den

Mondschein zu genießen. Hierbei unterhalte er sie mit geeigneten

Erzählungen. Wenn sie auf seinem Schoße liegt und der Mond ansieht,

erläutere er die Reihe der Sternbilder und zeige ihr die anmuthat, den

Polarstern und den Kranz der sieben Sterne des großen Bären.

G

D

CD Remote

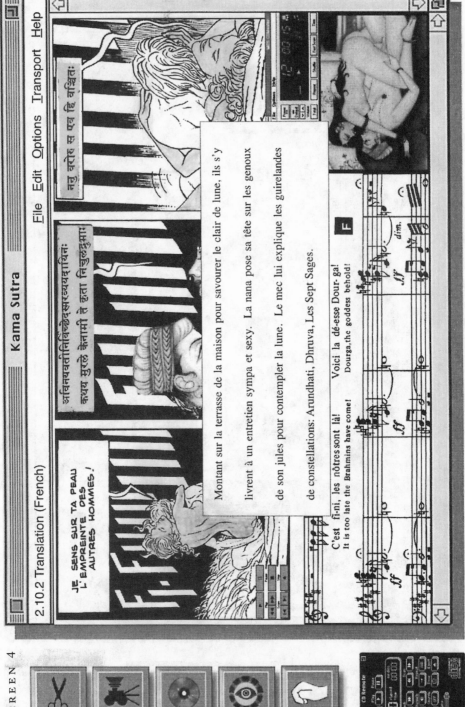

SCREEN 5

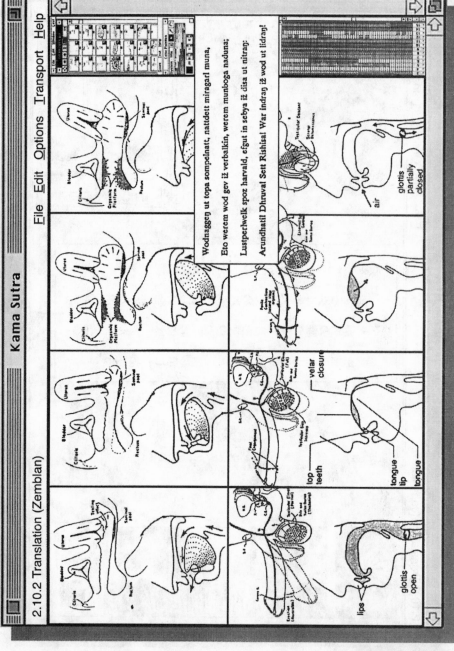

Wodnaggen ut topa sompelnatt, nattdett miragarl muna,

Eto werem wod gev iž verbalkin, werem munboga naduna;

Lusterlwelk spoz harvald, efgut in sebya iž disa ut nitrag:

Arundhatil Dhruval Sett Rishisal War Indrap iž wod ut tidrap!

glottis
partially
closed

air

velar
closure

top
teeth

tongue
lip
tongue

lips

glottis
open

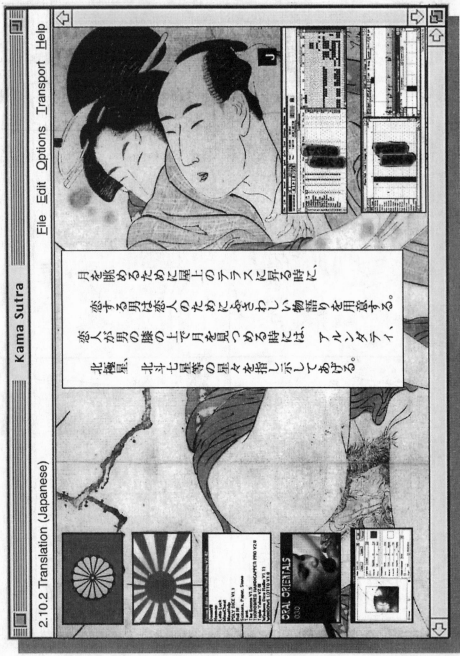

月を眺めるために屋上のテラスに昇る時に

恋する男は恋人のためにふさわしい物語を用意する。

恋人が男の膝の上で月を見つめる時には、アルデバイン

北極星、北斗七星等の星々を指し示してあげる。

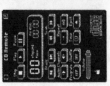

SCREEN 8

If it is warm inside the house and the moon is shining, the lovers will want to climb up to a terrace on the roof where they can enjoy the moonlight, the coolness of night, and a pleasing tête-à-tête. They'll take betel to chew whether it's hot or not, and once they're up on the roof, the man, having seated the girl on his lap, tells her love stories; and since women don't know much about astronomy, he explains the constellations to her: "There's Arundhati, the tiny godess of conjugal delight; if you can't see her, beware—you'll die within six months!" "There's Dhruva, the fixed and constant pivot of the planets; if you see him before nightfall all sins will be absolved." And there are the Seven Sages, all in their right places!"

SCREEN 9

Ursa Major, The Great Bear (Big Dipper)

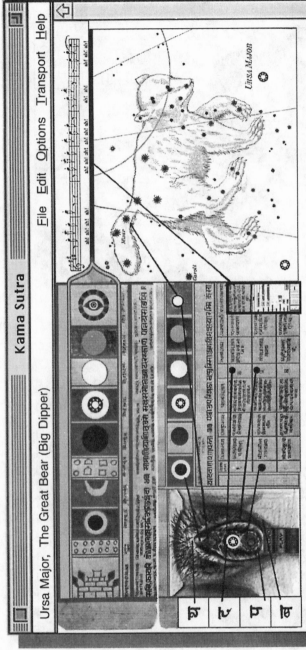

Ursa Major

The Seven Rishis or Sages are the seven stars that comprise the Big Dipper in Ursae Majoris. When Agni, the god who is fire, fell in love with their wives, the Krittikas (our Pleiades), his own wife Svaha (the personification of the sacrificial oblation) magically took on the form of each of them in turn and made love to Agni while he imagined that he made love to the wives of the Sages. When wandering celestials, who happened to witness this sidereal lovemaking, spread the gossip that the Krittikas were unfaithful, all of them were banished except Arundhati (the small, faint star Alcor [g Ursae Majoris]), who remains near her husband, the sage Vasishta (ζ, Mizar, the middle star in the handle of the Big Dipper), because he trusted her and affirmed her fidelity. She is invoked as the model of conjugal fidelity at the Hindu wedding ceremony.

SCREEN 10

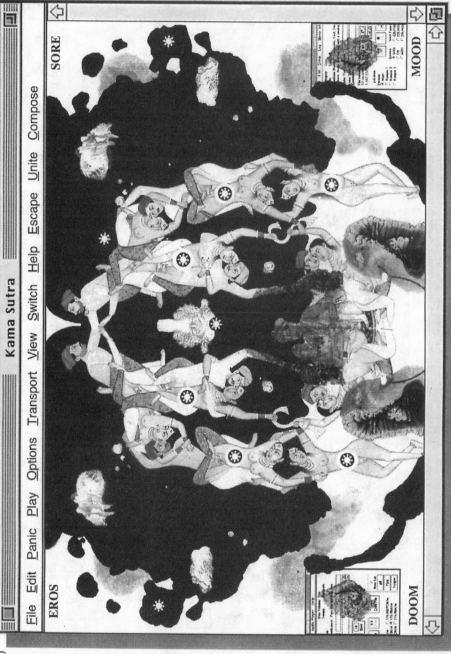

Kama Sutra

File Edit Panic Play Options Transport View Switch Help Escape Unite Compose

EROS

SORE

MOOD

DOOM

serious business. It is a precisian's system that orders the chaos of thought. *"Was ist denn Liebe?"* their *Denker* ask in a seriousness Teutonic. It was only in German that Wagner (having, incidentally, heard of the *Kamasutra* through Schopenhauer, who was given a copy by his good friend, the gymnast Friedrich Jahn) could imagine creating a new religion of love. The Germans do not speak of love so casually, do not use their *lieben* as freely as the French, who utter their *aimer* even more liberally than we intone our *love*. Sexual love, articulated in German, is at once and inevitably fascistic, grandiose (it's those *O*'s and those caps), and vulgar (those gutturals and fricatives do the trick). And so Schmidt, the old *Lustmolch*, in his translation of the *Kamasutra*, has to lapse into Latin when the Sanskrit becomes too literal to fit comfortably into his mouth: *"Libidinis tempore dorcas in alta coniunctione vulvam quasi amplificans inter coitum procumbat."* While his excuse was to make chaste the sentiments by putting them into a dead language, the learned parlance of taxonomies and tongue of doctors, philosophers, and theologians, the effect, he surely knew, was quite the reverse—it's the language of Ovid and Catullus, Nero and Caligula, not to mention Abelard, the father of academic sexual harassment. The dirtier it is, the better it sounds: *"Profert Sophia scorteum fascinum, quod ut oleo atque urticæ trito circumdedit semine, paulatim cœpit inserere ano meo."* You just can't say something like that in English or German without sacrificing the waggery or wit that made the Circus so much fun. So click on "Translation (Latin)," or if you've had enough Classicism and are ready for some Romanticism, "Translation (French)" (screen 4).[4]

"Le clair de lune" is so much more sonorously lovely than *"den Mondschein"*—*n'est-ce pas?* When Sophia and I spent our year in Paris, after Leila's death, I heard my father speak French (a language of which he knew hardly a word) in *Le fléau de la Déesse,* the dubbed version of *The Curse of Kali,* which appeared on French television one night. It was then that I realized for the first time French's potential in matters of sexual love. Before sacrificing a white colonial virgin (my dear mother, Tina Valentina, cast for the part because she looked so innocent), he tried to hypnotize her so that he might make love to her, and in that act, consecrate her as an offering to the Goddess Kali: *"Dans le noir nous—toi, la vierge sacrée, et moi, le Fakir mystique—verrons le clair. Dans les labyrinthes nous, nous ensemble, trouverons le désir parfait, et dans*

4. I am unable to determine the translator of the text; it is from neither of the published French versions (Lamairesse [1891] or Daniélou [1992]). The use of argot, however, suggests that the translation is probably by Roth himself.

l'abîme nous, purifiés par notre vigueur, révélerons l'amour." The ridiculous English line, despite my father's ludicrously demonic histrionics,
had attained a certain power, an erotic wickedness, in French. Bathos
verged on pathos. The American audience had snickered where the
French fans sighed. That their word for *sex* is *amour* is really quite
charming. The French have a tradition on their side, a history of
philosophers who have taken love seriously. Delibes understood that
"to sing a love song of love is to make love."[5] *"L'amour est . . . "* (fill in
the blank with any French bon mot, any noun or adjective, and it)
sounds profound; translate it into English and sex becomes different
than love, and philosophy degenerates into psychology.

German and French translations already exist. The CD-ROM
provides the opportunity to fulfill more exotic linguistic impulses. So
one might choose "Translation (Zemblan)" (screen 5),[6] Japanese
(screen 6), or Chinese (screen 7).[7]

The Indologist might be interested in "Commentary (Yaśodhara)"
followed by a click on "Translation (English)" (screen 8). Or one
might, using the same procedure, call up an English translation of either the commentary of poor Pralayānanga, the rather puritanical eighteenth-century Sanskrit commentary of Nrisimha Shastri, or the more

---

5. Léo Delibes, letter to Rudolf Roth and Otto Böhtlingk of 25 April 1897, in Léon
Chagale, ed., *Delibes, l'homme, sa vie, ses amours, ses maladies, et son oeuvre operatique*, 18.

6. The *Kāmasūtra* was translated into Zemblan verse in 1945 by the poet Romulus
Arnor (1914–58), who had retired to an ashram in Rishikesh during World War II. He also
translated the *Bhagavadgītā* from Sanskrit (1943), as well as Ovid's *Ars amatoria* from Latin
(1925). The graphic images on screen five represent one of the semantic curiosities and
wonders of Zemblan. When a woman says "I love you" in that language, the mouth replicates the actions of the vagina in orgasm from the excitement phase (I/*jo*) through the
plateau phase (love/*leva*) to the resolution phase (you/*zūa*); so too, when a man says "I love
you" in Zemblan, his tongue imitates the movement of the penis from the flaccid (I/*ya*) to
the erect stage (love/*lev*) and back down again (you/*vi*). The breath is different too. This is
in part a result of the fact that, in Zemblan, all personal pronouns (not simply the third-
person singular ones as in English, nor only the third-person singular and plural ones as in
French and Sanskrit) are gendered. The word for "I" or "me" is different for a man than for
a woman; so too the gender of "you" is always indicated, whether male, female, or both.
Zemblan is an intensely carnal language, giving verbal expression to anatomical, physiological, and glandular activity. It is ejaculatory parlance. To say "I love you" is to make love.
To hold those words back, restraining premature articulation, intensifies the final release.
In Zembla, being unable to speak of love is considered a kind of linguistic impotence or
frigidity. "I *(jo/ya)*" brings a drop of mucous to the lips; "you *(zūa/vi)*" causes contractions
of the larynx; and "love *(leva/lev)*" requires a high level of cortical activity. Zemblan, like
many Sanskritic languages, is well suited to charades, hence Roth's interest. The great Con-
mal termed Zemblan "the forked tongue of tongues."

7. Professor Paul Planter provided the Chinese and Japanese translations.

touching nineteenth-century Hindi commentary of Pandit Bhagavan-lal Indraji (from MS Bodleian Cod. Sansc. 1608).[8]

Going in a completely different direction, as made possible by the technology, one might highlight "Arundhatī," "Dhruva" (the Pole Star), or the "Seven Rishis" in the text, the transliteration, or any of the translations (i.e., *saptarṣi, les Sept Sages, den Kranz der sieben Sterne des großen Bären, Sett Rishisa,* the Seven Rishis), select "definition," and thus retrieve an illustration of our Ursa Major (screen 9). But is there really either a bear or a dipper in the sky, or are there seven sages or anything else but random, coincidental chaos in the heavens above us? Is the cosmos anything other than a Rorschach test? If there is anything out there, why not men and women making love (screen 10)?

If reading this sequentially, one would turn next to a taxonomy of passion, a classification of erotic feelings. The beauty of the CD-ROM networked hypertext is that, at this point, perhaps a bit bored with Sanskrit, with French, German, Chinese, Japanese, and Zemblan translations, having had just enough of commentary and digressions on astronomical legends, and uninspired by the thought of reading a set of definitions, one can click on "Video" and go right into a 3-D environment (a moonlit, pillow-strewn terrace on the roof of an ancient Indian mansion perhaps) to an interactive segment of the *Kamasutra,* the digital porno movie that is included as part of the package.[9]

8. Bhagavanlal Indraji was commissioned by Foster Fitzgerald Arbuthnot to do a Hindustani gloss of the *Kāmasūtra* with a rough English translation, which was then reworked by Edward Rehatsek, the Austro-Hungarian Sanskrit scholar who had gone to India in 1847 to teach German, French, Zemblan, and Latin (as well as comparative philology and systematic phonology). Retiring in 1871, Rehatsek began to wear Indian clothes and to cohabit with a "native girl in a house of reeds." In July of 1876 Rehatsek, Arbuthnot, Francis White, and Richard Burton met (as reported by Isabel Burton in a letter to Nikolay Stavrogin) with Indraji in Bombay to discuss the English translation of the *Kāmasūtra.* As no printed version of the text had as yet appeared in India or anywhere else, Indraji was dispatched to make a collation of manuscripts cached in libraries in Varanasi, Agra, Puri, and Calcutta. Rehatsek's version of Indraji's version and commentary was amended by Arbuthnot, whose version was revised and polished by Burton. There is a great leap from Pandit Bhagavanlal Indraji's rough rendering to Sir Richard Burton's witty re-re-re-rendition. In a manuscript in the Burton collection at the Huntington Library, Roth had discovered remains of the first stab, among them the good pandit's translation of the passage in question: "Veranda going for moon orb watching, Sahib and Memsahib are talking, talking most talkatively. Sab is saying this star and that star are this and that."

9. Vātsyāyana goes on to explain that it is important to remain affectionate after lovemaking and to express that affection with loving glances and tender words. The man is encouraged to tell his beloved love stories and to reminisce as to when he first met her and how he fell in love at the first sight of her; he should, furthermore, describe the sorrow he has felt in times of separation from her. Is it not odd that Roth would leave that out?

3. MIDDLEMAN

A. TRANSLATION

A woman who loves a man becomes agitated if he wants to end their relationship or if he travels abroad with another woman. Such a love-piqued, sexually rankled woman will sit by the doorway cursing, will scream with anger and weep with sorrow; she'll strike her lover or pull his hair, fall to the ground, and rip off the ornaments that he has given her. When this happens (and if it is truly love, it surely will), the man-about-town should coolly, calmly, and collectedly soothe her with sweet words as he takes her in his arms and carries her to a bed. By persisting with adamant professions of love and subtle apologies, the man should make it possible for the woman to forgo weeping and taunting, to allow herself to give her lover permission to embrace her. If this fails, the lover must resort to a middleman to make peace with the beloved. One must, however, be warned that the passions of such go-betweens, in many cases, have overruled a commitment to duty.

Auddalaki says:

Woman's anger excites a man, but it should not become a bore
For lovers love their misery, but its placations even more;
Jealousy without propriety transforms lover into fool:
While women should be hot-headed in their love,
    men should play it cool.

B. COMMENTARY

I am the middleman for both Mr. Leroy Lovelace and Dr. Nilkanth Gupta, dutifully acting in their behalf with respect to Ms. Lalita Gupta, for the good of Whom both are, like myself, so deeply concerned. Both of them thanked me sincerely for my assistance, for taking Ms. Gupta to India.

"Thank you, thank you," Dr. Gupta said, visiting my office on the Friday before the imminent passage to India and shaking my hand warmly. In addition to his check for Her tuition, fees, and travel expenses, he gave me ten thousand rupees so that I could "treat the blessed and brilliant daughter of Mrs. Gupta and my good self to a special treat if she becomes disconsolate or downtrodden due to the circumstances of being in a distant clime, far away from a devoted mother and dutiful father." He beseeched me to take good care of Her, and I promised that I would do everything in my power to make Her happy in India.

"Thank you, thank you," Mr. Lovelace said, visiting my office no less than fifteen minutes after Dr. Gupta and shaking my hand warmly. He gave me the letter that he wanted me to give to Lalita once I was on the plane with Her. He asked me to take good care of Her and to convince Her that it was all for the best, and with all my heart, I promised him that I would.

Once he was gone I couldn't resist opening the letter.

Dear Lalita,

I love you. I swear I do. That's the honest to God truth. I love you. I really do. But I got some bad news for you. I'm not coming to India. I'd like to, but I just can't. I got summer training. I can't be traveling around. Sweet girl, I'm going to be playing for the Chicago Bulls. I'm going to be famous! I know that you love me, just like I love you. So I know that you will understand if I have to call time out on this thing we've got going. Understanding is what love's all about. I know that if you really love me, you will understand that I can't be tied down at this stage in my career by a woman, no matter how beautiful she is. And you are beautiful. Because I love you, I understand that, even if you don't want to go to India without me, it's important for you to go there and find your roots. I know Doc Roth will do his very best to help you. He's not such a bad guy. Because I love you, I want you to have a good time in India. If you meet a guy, I want you to feel free to be with him in any way you want. That's what love is. And because you love me, I know you will want me to be with a woman if I meet one who is nice. Because I love you, I want you to be happy. And if you really love me, you will want me to be happy. Because we love each other and want each other to be happy, we have to break up. That's what love's all about.

Have a good trip. I love you, I really do. Please be sure to drop me a post card to tell me how you are doing. I'll miss you. I really will, because I love you so much.

Love,
Leroy

Oddly, as I licked the new envelope into which I had put the letter, I was aware of how much I'm going to miss Sophia this summer ("I really will, because I love you so much"). I will always love Sophia. Always. As I read the letter I could not help but remember a conversation that Sophia and I had long, long ago in the Sea Gull and Child in Oxford: a young man and woman, students full of amatory hopes, talking about love as it is constructed by convention and intellect, imagination and inspiration in literary texts. They agreed that love was a function of language, the hypostatized foundation of an aesthetic sentiment, and that that accounted for it being so seemingly different at different times and different places, despite the intractable universality and uniformity of the sexuality that it abstracts and disembodies. Slowly, gradually, after drinking lots of gin, they drifted from books to life. And he dared to ask her what she thought it really was.

"Love?" Young Sophia laughed, paused, smiled, and then spoke with disarming sincerity. "That's the difficult one. No matter what we say, it sounds wrong, either too trivial or too grand. It's acceptance I suppose. And understanding. Yes. And that acceptance requires real and unqualified forgiveness, yes. An appreciation that lasts as long as one lives? I think so. And it would last longer if there were anything after we die; still, even though there isn't anything after death, love asserts itself as if there were. (Again, and inexplicably, she laughed.) That's partially what's so pleasing, so moving, about it. It's also what's so melancholy about it, I suppose. Love challenges and defies oblivion, even while realizing that it must lose. That's its nobility, I think, its insistence on making sense of itself even though it makes no sense. (She paused.) I'm sorry, I'm not making any sense myself. I'm not really sure I mean any of this. My efforts feel and sound, I'm afraid, more literary than natural, more academic than personal, not that I want them to be, but I can't help that. Why is it so hard and sad to speak of love? Why does speaking of it make me so self-conscious, so aware of my limitations? It makes me feel false, pretentious, pompous. I'm sorry, I'm being indulgent. I'm being boring. And I think I'm drunk. You tell me what you think, Leo," she laughed. "You wouldn't have asked me if you didn't already have your own answer ready."

I don't remember what I said to her, how I defined love at the time, but it must have been good, because I do remember that she took me to her room that night. And last night, over twenty-three years later, I made love to her again, and it was as moving as the first time, as full of pleasure, beauty, and sadness. I will always love Sophia.

But now it's time to go to India, land of the *Kamasutra*.

Here Ends Book Two of the *Kamasutra*.

III

SEDUCTION

The exotic is only different from the erotic with respect to one letter. The pleasure of the exotic is an erotic one through and through, although the reverse, unfortunately, is not always so. The appeal of Oriental antiquity, where the murkiest longings are enjoyed and the most barbaric fantasies are realized, is in the promise of an unknown experience of love, a greater, darker, and more mysterious love than that which is conceivable here and now. Since that detestable British critic, Monsieur Sellon, noted in the papers that I have not been to the Indies, everyone inquires whether or not I have such plans. I refuse to go! "It is," I insist with my deepest artistic convictions, "in operatically portraying the East Indies as an imaginary country and personal revery that I have the potential to come closest to a perfect depiction of a reality." My friend, Herr Rudolf R., who has just returned from a voyage in the East, laughs: "No, no, my dear Leo. An exacting and realistic depiction of the actual country—strange Agra, Banaras, Jagernathpuree, and other places—would amount to the composition of an *opéra fantastique* beyond anything that anyone might imagine or dream." Herr Rudolf brought a gift for me from Banaras, a curious little Hindoo catechism of love entitled *Kama Sutra* and translated into English. The book is not without interest.

—Léo Delibes, *Journal Intima* (1884)

A. The Pick

Life is trying in Delhi. It is hardly an arena for a LADY of Sentiment or a GENTLEMAN of Manners. Love is a scarce luxury in the Orient. There's little music in the air and it is Satanically hot in more than one manner. Sindhia is the True Sovereign here despite what is officially decreed, and I do not believe he fancies OUR KIND. Mr Draper tells me the Mahrattas suspect we might someday attempt to overthrow them! He freely speaks of Governmental suspicions but not of those in his own heart. "The Oriental does not surrender easily," he announces, preferring to talk of India, the Company, of Sindhia, the Viceroy, or even Doojee, the shoemaker, than to acknowledge ME. Whilst I have repeatedly reminded him that I consider our marriage a mortifying difficulty, he refuses, despite the rumours he has heard about US, my dearly Beloved White Bramin, to give up hope of living with me on peaceable or creditable terms. I yearn to be in Shandy Hall, set Free from Draper's Colonial Peace, LIVING Redeemed with Thee. I remain an Indian Lady Unfortunate in LOVE & Your Bramine For Ever.

—Mrs. Draper, letter to Laurence Sterne (1765)

1. GOOD CHOICE (TO THE EAST)

A. TRANSLATION

A man should choose a girl who comes from a prosperous family; her mother and father should still be alive, should not be older than the man, and should support the liaison. To be truly loved, the girl must be beautiful, healthy, amorous, and have a good figure and proportionate limbs as well as sharp teeth and nails manicured to points. It is the solemn duty of friends to warn the man of any problems that they foresee as possibly arising from the union. That a girl might initially resist the man should not discourage him from choosing her; often the most obdurate of girls, if patiently pursued and artfully seduced, become the most passionate of lovers.

B. COMMENTARY

Premsagar Guest House
Kamnagar, New Delhi
Eighth Night of the Dark Half of Vaishakh [May 29]
Moharram

"Yes, yes," I optimystically reassured the frightened face in the men's room mirror at the airport. "If patiently pursued and artfully seduced, the most obdurate of girls will become passionate lovers. We must face the fact that initially She might not be pleased by Her predicament, but once She accepts the reality of the situation, She'll be seduced by India, utterly fascinated and dazzled by the exotic land of Her ancestors. She'll come to love India and you, distinguished and urbane professor of Indology, intellectual curator of India's amatory glories."

Lingering in the lavatory in order to avoid the Guptas (fearing that the Hindu gynecologist would want to meet the other students in order to determine whether or not they were up to cutting his blessed daughter's mustard), I applied nicotine patches to various parts of my body so that I would be able to endure the long no-smoking flight. Not until it was the last call for boarding did I rush toward the gate, allowing myself only a moment to console Mrs. Gupta, who was pathetically weeping in the arms of Dr. Gupta, who after urgently supplicating me to take care of his daughter, did, as predicted, ask me where the other students were.

"I'm sure some of them are already on board," I told him, "but most of the students from Western were not accomplished enough to be accepted into the program. The majority of them, the ones flying in from Harvard and Yale, Oxford and Cambridge, the Sorbonne and Sophia, Berkeley and Hawaii, will be meeting us when we change planes in London. I've got to board now. Don't worry about your young scholar. She'll love India. How could She not?" It was deeply gratifying to be able to comfort the proud progenitor in that painful moment of separation from his beloved offspring.

"She is in seat 18A," Mrs. Gupta moaned. "Kindly double-check her comforts."

Lalita greeted me anxiously as I settled, politely smiling with feigned disinterest, into the seat that I had reserved next to Her.

"Where's Leroy?" She asked nervously. "Where is he? They're about to close the fuckin' doors. God, I hope he's not late."

I consoled her with words that I had rehearsed for the purpose of preventing Her from fleeing the plane before takeoff:

"Don't worry about a thing, Ms. Gupta. Mr. Lovelace told me to tell You that he was taking a different flight for fear that he might run into Your parents at the airport, afraid that if they saw him, they wouldn't let You go."

"Leroy is so smart. That's brilliant!" She said with a smile of relief. "He thinks of fuckin' everything."

"Yes, he probably does," I remarked as I fastened my seat belt. Then, as the 747 lost touch with the earth, I took the envelope containing Lovelace's letter from my pocket. "Oh, I'm sorry, I almost forgot. He told me to give You this letter. It'll probably tell You which flight he's on."

It was only a matter of seconds after opening the envelope that Her smile vanished, and much to the disgruntlement of the passengers in front of and beside us, She started shouting, "Fuck! Fuck it! Oh, fuck him! Fuck! Fuck! Fu-uh-uh-uh . . ." Tears choked Her; She coughed, gasped, whimpered, sniffled, and then, to my great joy, She grabbed my arm, turned Her face into my shoulder, and sobbed. I lightly stroked Her luscious black hair in a fatherly manner, and I was warmed by the touch and fragrance of the weeping girl.

"Is something wrong?" I asked innocently. For the moment She was too upset to speak, but by the time the captain had turned off the seat belt sign, she had started again.

"Fuck! Fuck! Fuck!"

"What a woman!" I thought to myself. "What heart! What feeling! What passion! What a capacity to love."

She suddenly straightened herself up in the seat.

"I've got to go back."

"Should I ask the stewardess for a parachute?"

"That's not funny. I've got to get the first plane back to L.A."

When I ordered Her a double Bombay gin and tonic (to calm her down) and the same for myself (to celebrate the fact that I was, really and truly, on my way to India with Lalita Gupta), the stewardess asked to see Her passport as proof that She was old enough to have a drink. "Are you traveling together?" she asked, and Lalita answered (angrily) before I could (politely), "What are you getting at? He's just my professor and that's it. We're together, but not *together*, as if that's any of your fuckin' business anyway." What spunk! I love that in a woman!

Soon She was sobbing again, couldn't eat any of the meal nor watch the movie (Eddie Murphy in *The Nutty Professor*); I missed the second half of it myself after swallowing two Halcyon, drinking three more double Bombay and tonics, and reading an article in the inflight magazine:

> Since the dawn of time travelers have gone to India in search of majesty and mystery, for spices and romance, for adventure and spiritual enlightenment. They've come in groups like the Greeks and the Persians, the Portuguese and the Zemblans, the Dutch and the French and of course, the British, whose legacy will astound you. Or they have come questing as individuals like Alexander the Great, Marco Polo, Thomas Lovely, Rudyard Kipling, Richard Burton and the Beatles. Columbus was trying to go to India when he stumbled on America. Today you can follow in the footsteps of these travelers, marveling at the same sights they saw and experiencing the same romance!
>
> You'll discover that a trip to India is much more than a vacation. It's an education! Ever fascinating Delhi is an excellent point from which to start. There, age-old traditions and contemporary fun seem to go hand-in-hand. Mystic monuments are a stone's throw from trendy discos. In the morning you may hear the chant of the Imam calling the pure in heart to pray in the Jama Masjid, and in the evening, you'll hear the rap of the DJ calling the young at heart to dance the night away at such chic hot-spots as the Club Om-Shanty or Chez Krishna. Perhaps you'll shop for exotic curios in the chic Kamnagar Bazaar of bustling New Delhi. Perhaps you'll eat kabobs in exotic Old Delhi. No matter what you do, you are certain to thrill over the experience of a lifetime! From fabulous Delhi you can go to enchanting Agra, that Mecca for lovers from all around the globe, to behold that incomparable monument to eternal love, the world-famous Taj Mahal.

It wasn't really a dream (I hate dreams in books as much as I hate books in dreams), but more of a revery to the lull of the hum and tremble of jet motors, through the haze of Bombay and Halcyon: the construction of a beautiful monument to eternal love out of illicit wishes and deviant hopes somewhere between sleep and wakefulness, between heaven and earth, East and West. The plane of consciousness was on automatic pilot. All was dark. Intrusive thoughts of this intractably real world were forbidden. Private. No Trespassing. Beware of Cobras. Waiting for Her, with eyes closed, I listened to the faint music of the sweetly sandal-scented breezes of Malabar stroking the strings of a lute hanging on an ivory peg. There was a silver bowl of dark wine-red apples on the table, and next to it, a dagger with a curved blade. In the distance, echoing from the jungled hills of Seeonee, I could hear the exultant cries of wild animals. I realize that I'm embellishing the dream as I write it down, but I don't care because I'm desperate (as Lalita is, right now, here in Delhi, crying, refusing to speak or listen to me, or even to look at me) to savor the sweetness of the revery in full wakefulness even more than in half-dream. In that sweet romance, my fun-loving *lalita* Lalita came in a night-dark shawl with gleaming golden anklets wrapped up, concealed and silenced for secret passage. She was darkly veiled (the flash of Her smile and flicker of Her eyes obscured) to keep the night from shining like a glorious day.

> Slowly I lift the veil. Because the rain has soaked through Your cloak, I help You out of Your clothes, dry and dust You with rose talc and lotus pollen, dress You in the diaphanously delicate silks that I keep ever clean and folded just for You; I dress You to undress You again and again. I hang the wet clothes up to dry and light the oil lamps and incense sticks, straining to keep my eyes averted from You until I can deprive myself no longer: yielding to impulse, I turn, and the beauty that has chosen You to make itself manifest in the world makes me ache; I gaze at You through the tears of joy that cleanse my eyes for You. There are strands of white jasmine blossoms in the oiled braid that longs to lash my arms and legs and makes me fear that I'm someday going to have to die. But I won't die until You let me, until You let me go. I take the brushes and board to do a drawing of You in which Your hand is on Your hip as You, turning at the waist, glance at me with innocent naughtiness, and the silhouette of Your pearl-adorned breast announces its ardor by the swell of a dark nipple. The white lotus that You're holding in Your hand is made to tremble and lose a petal as You laugh carelessly into it. Pollen scatters. The delicacy of Your rosy ankle-bone is highlighted by the golden anklet that I gave You. Your brow, the deadly bow of Love, makes me shudder with fear and desire in delicate balance. Your glance is its arrow. The southern silk cloth around Your waist comes unknotted by itself, and the youthful curve of Your buttocks makes unutterable promises as the coral-colored bodice falls to the floor to take the shape of an owl in flight against a dark carpet of night sky. There is nothing more charming than a young girl acting like a seasoned woman, proud of the gold chain connecting the ornament in Her nose to the jewels in Her ear, reflecting the pale moonlight and all my brightly burning desire. Your belly dusted with fragrant powders, flanks glistening with luscious oils, lips glossed with lac, eyelids heavy with kohl, and nails painted and pointed ally into an orchestra to play an extravagantly beautiful music, hypnotic and narcotic, unreal and yet palpable. The parrot outside imitates the sound of lovemaking, and it both embarrasses and arouses You; it makes me laugh. You interlace Your fingers and stretch Your hands above Your head, yawn, and ask me

to tell You the story of Nala and Damayanti. I recite: "And the swan told Nala that in all its flights, all over the world, never had it seen a woman so beautiful as Damayanti. And as the bird described her graces and her charms, Nala could behold her in his mind, and though he had never seen her in the flesh, he could not help but love her with all his heart. And the swan said that no other man and woman could be such perfect lovers as these two, Nala and Damayanti." The musk on Your cheeks widens my nostrils and quickens my eyelids; the bakula and bandhuka blossoms garlanding Your perfect bosom ooze and exude their lavish fragrances. I drink ambrosia from the lotus of Your lips, lick sweetness from Your chocolate-kiss nipples, suck nectar from Your navel (and dare I say "et cetera," leaving the most arousing acts and parts to the magnificence of imagination and the imaginings that imagination might imagine?). You demonstrate that You are a mistress of the arts as You sing for me and show me the basic steps of a dance You'll dance for Great God Kama in his shrine. You tell me a spicy joke (I pretend not to understand it so that You'll explain [I love to hear You speak of sex]); I perform a sleight-of-hand—making a pale blue water lily disappear from my palm and reappear behind Your ear. Love is all magic (sweet sleights and proof that there is pleasure in being fooled, deluded, and enchanted). We drink mead spiced with datura and play a game of dice. We are so eager to make love yet we do not; we postpone it so that the pleasure will not be over, but remain permanently immanent and eminent, right there in the joining of our thighs and the coming release of all that separates anything from everything. You throw the ivory dice, win, and I ask what You want. "Your shirt," You laugh and throw again; I lose my bracelet to You, then my lute, the garland of amaranth, the box of brushes, the book (this *Kamasutra*), my wedding ring, old locks and keys, the heart-shaped mirror in which I've looked sadly at myself. Finally, when there is no more, You ask for my breath and blood, my soul, sweat, saliva, semen, and the dust from my eyes and the dirt from under my nails. You ask even for my shadow and reflection. And You win again. I have never been so exquisitely exposed and empty. You slip Your own bracelet onto my wrist and claim Your last prize: "You pretend you're me, and I'll act your part out. I am you, in you, your pleasure mine, and mine yours." Your golden girdle jingles and then falls silent, and then the anklets begin to sing.[1] After lovemaking I blow on You to cool You as You fall asleep for a moment (or pretend to do so because You're shy?) while I am inspecting Your luxuriantly glowing nakedness. The *romavali* bristles. I reach toward the drawer in the bedside table for the oils and garlands, cosmetics and perfumes. You're drifting into a dream of the future, centuries from now, when we are real and dream back

1. According to the conventions of Sanskrit poetry, it was considered more arousing, more evocative of the amorous sentiment, to suggest the actions of lovers than to directly indicate them: to a connoisseur of poetry, a jingling girdle would insinuate that the woman had taken the position on top of the man during sexual intercourse; jingling anklets would imply that she was lying on her back with her legs spread and up in the air.

to this. Then You dream of now, and now of then, a circle of dream in which we take refuge from all that is harsh or vulgar (or are You pretending?). I watch the sleep (feigned or not) until, unable to bear not talking to You, I awaken You slowly (or allow You to emerge from the pretense) with kisses formed of tongue and tooth tip on the sex-warm neck, and I dress You once again and paint Your eyes with mascara and Your breasts with fresh sandal paste. In this world, seduction has been ritualized: sexual interlude is redemption; copulation, the liturgy of love unhampered by ideas of sin or salvation. No part of our merged flesh is unclean, no fluid, no utterance, no fantasy is impure or corrupt. We are voluptuaries dedicated to frivolity and ecstasy and detached from our essential inconsequentiality. There are rules of etiquette, not morals; aesthetics, not ethics. As initiates into this world, our bodies become renewed and dedicated to the physical enaction of refined sentiments; sex is love, love sex, and this unabashed sensuality never degenerates into vanity or debauchery. We lend beauty and timelessness to the love that is our entertainment and beatification. We have overcome the cruelty and chaos of common love, ordering it and making it elegant. To be in love, we are convinced, is to play, to please and be pleased by a beautiful pleasure that exists for its own sake. Our erotic deliria are informed with generosity, our passions transformed by gentle pretense into poetry. We abjure the obvious, pedestrian, and temporal in favor of the lyrical, mysterious, and perpetual. O Lalita, forgive me. Stop crying and speak to me. Come to me; allow me to love You.

The landing awakened me. Luckily there wasn't time for Her to use the phone in London, where we changed planes for Delhi, and it wasn't until we were on that plane (I suppose because of the distraction of Her breaking heart) that it finally occurred to Her to ask me where the other students were.

"I've been meaning to talk to You about that. You see, there aren't any other students. You were the only applicant intelligent, charming, and beautiful enough to be accepted into the program."

Contrary to my hopes way up there in the friendly skies of United, she didn't take it well:

"What? What are you saying? Do I have this right? This is kidnapping! I want to go home. I want Leroy. Help me Leroy! Help! Oh, God! What have you done? I can't believe what's happening. This is a fuckin' nightmare. Tell me it's just a bad dream. Tell me that!"

I tried to cheer Her up, urging Her to look on the bright side of things, reminding Her that at least She would be receiving three units of directed reading credit, and that I was quite confident that She would get an *A*. But all She said was "I hate you. Go away. I want Leroy."

I continue to remind myself of the wise Vatsyayana's dictum: **That** a girl might initially resist the man should not discourage him from choosing her; often the most obdurate of girls, if patiently pursued and artfully seduced, become the most passionate of lovers.

2. BAD CHOICE (NEW DELHI)

A. TRANSLATION (1)

One should avoid a girl who weeps or sleeps too much, who is bald or blonde, whose nipples are too big or toes too small, who has acne or hairy moles, who is secretive or anorexic, cross-eyed or hunchbacked, harelipped or knock-kneed, whose head is hot and feet are cold, who has a vaginal discharge or is born under an inauspicious astrological sign, who has gastrointestinal maladies or remaining attachments to another lover.

B. COMMENTARY (1)

Premsagar Guest House
Kamnagar, New Delhi
Ninth Night of the Dark Half of Vaishakh [May 30]

Although She still will not speak to me, I remain cheerful by keeping the words of the venerable Vatsyayana in mind, remembering his observation that spats are but erotic spices, that displays of anger are but foreplay for those who, well educated in the arts and sciences of love, have the cunning to make them so.

I was able to convince Her to stay in the same room with me because there were two beds in it and because She was even more afraid of India than of me. The desk clerk, young Mr. Jain, welcomed me back to India and the Premsagar with a smile and, while glancing furtively at Lalita, inquired as to the health of my "good wife, the fine Mrs. Leo."

"She's dead," I snapped in defense against his lewd grin, a salacious sign of native curiosity about foreign sexuality. Provincial Indian men are burdened by fantasies over Western forms of love no less that I am the victim of erotic fancies about their land. Sex makes them leer, but they respect death; while they imagine that our sexual experiences are different than their own, they know that we all die in the same way. Pleasure and joy are hierarchical and aristocratic, but pain and sorrow are egalitarian and democratic.

"I'm sorry," he said with genuine sympathy as he touched my arm affectionately. "I am truly sorry, sir."

I could hear Lalita behind the closed bathroom door, sobbing with moans that aroused me as they vibrated straight from my ear (flat against the door) to the anxious heart within my chest, as She washed and changed. Diving for the bed like prey rushing for a burrow to escape the predacious swoop of a hawk, She pulled up the covers so that no part of her was exposed to my loving glance. The lump under the blankets was like a beautiful statue, an amorous stone woman pillaged from Khajuraho or Konarak, waiting to be unveiled. When I asked if there was anything I could do for Her, a single hand, its middle finger extended, appeared, shook, pointed, and then disappeared for the night.

The prurient assumptions of all the room boys were obvious in the morning: this one needed to bring the toast, that one the coffee, another one the musumbi juice, after which the first one returned with the jam and the second with the butter; and then another wanted to take the dishes away, while another, only moments later, wondered if there was anything else we required—laundry, beer, ganja, Indian crafts? And Lalita was crying again.

I asked again if there was anything I could do for Her.

"This is kidnapping," She snapped, "and I'm going to get you for it."

Despite my suggestions that Her beloved Leroy would want Her to go out and enjoy Herself, I couldn't convince Her to leave the room for the first three days; I was afraid that if I went out, if I left Her alone, She might try to run away. It gave me time to work on this translation of the *Kamasutra* for Her.

A. TRANSLATION (2)

Always try to chose a lover who takes pleasure in what pleases you; and likewise, you should take pleasure in what pleases her. All the professors of love agree that a man should select a lover who amuses him and whom he is capable of amusing.

B. COMMENTARY (2)

Premsagar Guest House
Kamnagar, New Delhi
Last Night of the Dark Half of Vaishakh [June 4]
Birthday of Shah Jahan (1592)

It's not much like my dream: love's not sweet but venomous; I feel the affliction of affection. Her anger ravishes me almost as much as Her sadness, which excruciates me almost as much as Her indifference, which impassions me almost as much as my hope, which arouses me almost as much as Her anger. I had to speak to Her. I rehearsed the speech several times in front of the mirror in the bathroom—it began with the lighting of a cigarette from my last pack of duty-free Viceroys and ended with the snuffing out of that smoke. I invoked the spirit of Eddie Edwardes to guide me through the gestures and glances, the pauses and turns:

"Excuse me, Ms. Gupta. Please listen to me. I'm sorry, really, very, very sorry about this whole thing. Let me explain. I did not want to accept You into the study abroad program, but did so only as a favor to Your father, out of empathy with him as a father. I had a daughter, about Your age, but that's beside the point. I was not aware that You did not want to be accepted, that You didn't want to come to India. Then, when You came to my office, I was eager to help You. Remember? (Pause.) As a teacher I'm committed to helping my students, all my students—I was willing, as a favor to You, to reject You, to arrange it so that You didn't have to come. But then Mr. Lovelace tricked me. He told me that he wanted to go to India with You. He even said he wanted to learn Sanskrit. As a favor to him, as one of my students, I agreed to accept him into the program despite the fact that he was failing my class. I even raised his grade to an *A*. Remember? (Long pause.) At that point You said that You wanted to come, that it was the only way for You and Mr. Lovelace to spend the summer together. All that mattered to me as a professor was helping my students, You and Mr. Lovelace. I'm very sorry that he changed his mind. It's not my fault. He fooled both of us. I really had no idea. I reserved this room for the two of you. I must confess that I actually wanted to cancel the trip. Since there were no other applicants except You and Mr. Lovelace, I am losing a lot of money on this deal; but, again, because I never want to let my students down, and as I imagined that the cancellation would be a great disappointment to both Mr. Lovelace and You, I decided, despite the inconvenience and expense, despite the difficulty for me as a married man in being away from my family, to come to India as advertised, planned, and promised. I'm sorry Mr. Lovelace changed his mind. I'm very sorry. If there's anything, anything at all that I can do, You must tell me."

Love, perverse as that god is, while sometimes delighting in exposing and incriminating the lover, will also occasionally take pains to rescue and exonerate with passion's wildest resources, teaching the lover the arts of deception. I felt that Vatsyayana (not to mention Eddie Edwardes) would have approved and been proud of the artful-

184   SEDUCTION

ness of my oratory, worthy as it was of the man about the ancient Indian town. I don't lie to people that I don't love: I have to love someone to bother about lying to them; I have to love someone in order to
need to lie to them.

I knew that my performance had been effective when Lalita started
to cry again, sobbing differently, more vulnerably. She shook Her head
sadly.

"I'm sorry Professor Roth. I'm sorry. I guess I've been kinda cruel
to you. You actually seem like sort of a nice man, I suppose. It's just
that it came as such a shock to me. I'm pretty upset. I'm sorry."

I improvised my lines. "But don't be sorry. It's really my fault. I
should have canceled the trip. I shouldn't have made that silly little joke
about accepting only You. I only said that I had accepted only You 'because of Your charm, beauty, and intelligence' to cheer You up, to try
to make the best of a bad situation. I can understand why You took it
wrong. I'm sorry."

"No," She sighed, "I'm the one who should be sorry."

The climax to my soliloquy: "I'll leave You alone now, Ms. Gupta.
I've been afraid to go out, concerned that You might try to harm Yourself. But now I trust that You'll be okay and that You need a bit of time
by Yourself. Please, let me know if there is anything I can do."

Mr. Jain, again saying that he was sorry to hear about my wife,
asked about the girl and at least pretended to believe it when I told him
that, inspired by the experiments in truth of Gandhi, I had, after my
wife's tragic passing, taken a vow of celibacy, and "like the great Mahatma, sleeping next to his beautiful young nieces as test of resolve and
purity, I am sleeping in absolute chastity in the same room with my
student, the pure young exemplar of Indian womanhood and spiritual
values, with the blessings of Her venerable parents in their ardent devotion both to their daughter and to Gandhi. *Jay Ram, Jay Hind, Jay
Gandhiji!*" The sad irony for me was that, in an unfortunate sense, it
was rather true.

It was 100 degrees outside of the guest house, but it felt good.
Odors of dung and gasoline, incense and masala, blossoms on the trees
of summer and the oxen-mown lawn of the park in Kamnagar evoked
memories, as only smells can do, of my past and India's. I went to the
market, ate a masala dosa (couldn't find a beer, let alone a gin and
tonic), and shopped: I bought some "Lakme Press-on Bindis" for Her
forehead (not because I thought She'd wear them, but for the name)
and, likewise (just for the name, not out of hopes for any immediate

need), three Krishna blue Kama Sutra condoms. I purchased Charminar cigarettes for myself, strands of jasmine for Lalita's hair, and a cassette recording of the religious love songs of Lakshmi Bai. Going to the market book stall to buy the Amar-Chitra-Katha comic book of the Nala and Damayanti story for Lalita, I thumbed through the magazines. I was, to say the least, startled by a piece in *India Weekly:*

> There was little celebration for the day marking the twentieth anniversary of the imprisonment of an American terrorist, Miss Theresa Burkley [*sic*]. On that day, 28 May, relatives of the convict officially presented a petition to officials at the Ministry of External Affairs requesting her premature release from Scindia Prison in Gwalior. Officials from the MEA issued a public response declaring that the matter would be taken up in due time with the officials at the Ministry of Internal Affairs. Officials from the MIA, however, announced that, although they would await official communication from MEA, they would, after receiving that communication, have to take up that matter in due time with the Ministry of Corrections in Madhya Pradesh. An unnamed official from the MCMP, however, unofficially informed *India Weekly* this week that "we cannot release prisoners willy-nilly on our own. The mother and father of the terrorist in question should appeal directly to President Clinton, who in due time could take up the matter with the Prime Minister."

Not wanting to return to the guest house too soon (hoping to give Lalita enough time to become uncomfortable alone), I bought the magazine and took it to read as I drank a lassi at the Gay Paree outdoor tea stall. I read an article about the Miss India who had become Miss World, "proving to the Universe, let alone the World, the superior Beauty of Indian Womanhood in all its Glory." And there was another article about a Bengali woman who had just won the Women's World Weightlifting Championship in Moscow. I decided to try to visit Theresa Berkeley in Gwalior.

A small yellow dog with an enormous pied head, his fur eaten away by mange and fleas, was tracking a scent, his black nose to the hot ground, running here, there, back, then over there, tail frantically wagging, pendulous testicles swaying to and fro, giving the impression that the dog's body existed solely as a vehicle for the transporting the disproportionately gargantuan penis, glistening crimson, from bitch to bitch. The nose existed only to smell her heat, the eyes to see her swollen rump, the ears to hear her estral howl, the mouth to bark ferociously at other males and to eat enough garbage to fuel the body and invigorate that feral organ of generation. The brain was merely a steering device. The penis gave the orders.

When I arrived back at the guest house, Mr. Jain greeted me with the mail—a postcard from Saighal asking me to buy a copy of the Monier-Williams *Sanskrit-English Dictionary* for him! Does he actually think I'd carry around that heavy tome for him? He must be trying to kill me. I shouldn't have confided in him; now he thinks he can ask whatever he wants of me. He'll probably never finish his dissertation. He'll probably never finish anything.

Lalita was dressed and ready to venture out by the time I returned to the room. Wanting to take it slow, not to shock her, to introduce Her gradually into the land of Her ancestors, I had Mr. Jain order a taxi to take us to the Viceroy Hotel. Hardly looking out of the window, She complained, despite the air conditioning, of the heat, dust, and stench of India.

The regally clad Sikh, who saluted as he opened the doors for us, winked luridly at me as we walked past him, out of an independent India and into the Raj.

I wanted champagne: I was celebrating because, as She sat down, She spoke with the averted eyes that Vatsyayana says are one sign of love's blossoming.

"I'm sorry, Professor Roth. I know it's not your fault. But I'm in love, in love with Leroy. I'm sure you must know what it's like to be in love."

When I called out to the waiter in the crimson cummerbund and matching turban and slippers with curled up toes, "French champagne," he explained to me that they only served Chevalier de Seingalt champagne from Maharashtra, "the favorite of all the Great Moghuls except Aurangzeb, the same quality as French champagne exactly. In fact, most French champagne is, in actual fact, from Maharashtra or Orissa. The French buy it here and then put it in French bottles and sell it worldwide. It is quite a scandal."

The set was perfect: the black marble bar with the shiny brass rails, the high ceiling ornamented with gold leaf supporting a magnificently bright crystal chandelier, the light of which shimmered in the shine of the mahogany tables, each graced with a fragrant rose and a porcelain dish of spicy nuts. The deep green velvet chairs matched the thick carpet. There were elegantly framed and olive-matted old caricatures from *Punch* magazine on the dark wood-paneled walls: Curzon, Draper, Burton, Rippon, Sellon, Minto, White, Dyer, Kitchener.

"Indian Independence," I told Her, "was forged in this very room."

"Why do you like India?" She asked.

"Because it's everything I'm not," I said, rather profoundly, or at least enigmatically, I reckoned.

"I hate India," She sighed as the waiter unscrewed the cap on our champagne bottle. "I want to go home." And I figured that She was no longer angry, rather just depressed, very depressed, because She neglected to say "fuckin'" even once.

"Let me show India to You, Ms. Gupta," I smiled graciously, with reserve, politeness, and care. "You'll like it. I know it. Don't be afraid, I'll take care of You. I promised Your father that I would. I know a wonderful restaurant with delicious food and musicians who play the most enchanting music You can imagine. It's in Old Delhi, near the Red Fort. First we'll go to the fort, see the sound and light show, then to the Jama Masjid, the largest mosque in India, to hear the call to prayer, and then to the restaurant, the Kamaloka Tandoor. We'll have a nice dinner, listen to classical Indian music, and then You'll feel better, and we'll figure everything out. I want to help You."

The champagne must have weakened Her because, a bit to my surprise and much to my satisfaction, She agreed to it.

It was as if the Sikh, once again winking at me, were opening the doors of a great furnace: as we stepped out of the air-conditioned colonial oasis and into the Indian blaze, a harsh sweep of searing wind, fetid and fragrant, bellowed across us. As we made our way toward Janpath, on the other side of the gate that kept out the indigenous indigents, there was a voluminous swell in the raucous roar and grumbling anthem of Delhi: pandemonial moans and hapless laughter, scolding and beseeching, hawking and hounding, and the hectic honking of horns, discordant metallic clitter-clatter and terrible tintinnabulation. The infernal blast agitated the perfumes of the road (spice and sandal, gasoline and feces, ganja and dust, garlands and tropical sickness). When She said "Oh, fuck," I knew that She was feeling better.

Like hawks upon their prey, the hawkers descended upon us. "Kashmiri carpet? Very cheap! Banarsi sari? Best quality. Look, Madame, beautiful Taj Mahal lamp, just like real thing. No? What do you want? Exchange money? Best rate. No? Why not? Airlines tickets? Chocolates, cashew nuts, hashish, brown sugar, Valium, China white? What? Here, nice statue, Khajuraho style? Bull whip? Jewels? Videos, Indian or foreign, dramatic, musical, dancy, educational, porno? What? Nice painting, Indian miniature, real thing, genuine quality, 101 percent authentic, very sexy, very nice. Look what they are doing! You like? No problem money. Pay what you like. No? Please, what? Everybody wants something."

Like soldiers of fortune, the fortune-tellers charged us. "I'll tell you everything. How many marriages? How many loves? Every love problem. How many children, name of mother, birthday of father, favorite flower. I know all nice things. I know love things, marriage things."

And of course there were the beggars signaling their hunger with dirty hands trembling over the cracked lips of crooked mouths, rimmed with stained and broken teeth. There were white smears of leprosy and gross deformities of flesh, a horrible circus of teratoids. There was snot and drool, shit and piss, desolation and supplication. "No mama, no papa, *Saab, baksheesh,* no food, please *Saab,* help please."

A transvestite in need of a clean sari and shave, unaware that the Westerner understood Hindi and the Indian girl did not, followed us, mincing and mocking, joking and jeering, calling Lalita a whore and asking Her, for the amusement of the gathering crowd, how She liked Feringhee sex: "Tell me, sister. Tell me. What's he like?"

When, too impulsively, I took Lalita's hand in mine, it startled Her, and She pulled it away with a shiver.

"This is horrible, fuckin' horrible. No wonder my parents left. But why do they lie to themselves and say that they love India? How could anybody like this fuckin' place?"

A. TRANSLATION (3)

If the girl does not already know the amorous arts and erotic sciences as delineated in our text, this *Kamasutra,* the man should, having mastered them himself, make a student of the girl and diligently teach her all that he knows of love.

B. COMMENTARY (3)

Premsagar Guest House
Kamnagar, New Delhi
New Moon [June 5]

Neither the Red Fort nor the Jama Masjid, neither the rogan josh nor the tandoori murgh, neither the sitar nor the tabla music at the Kamaloka Tandoor seemed to interest Her. But She did drink three bottles of Taj Mahal beer. When we emerged from the restaurant into the darkness of Old Delhi, sleeping bodies of hapless workers lined the walkway under the porticoes. There were snores, moans, coughs, whispers, a laugh, a groan, and ear-piercing silences. My heart shook: I saw something, someone, lurking in the shadows, watching us. Maya Blackwell? No, impossible, couldn't be. Whoever it was disappeared into the dark abyss of the hot night.

We could hear the nocturnal call of the muezzin over an impetuous honking of horns and cheerful ringing of bicycle bells. An old crone, wrapped from head to foot in black, spit bright blood-red betel juice at Her feet (in disgust, I suppose, over seeing an Indian girl with a foreign man).

Leading Her toward Daryaganj to find a motor-rickshaw or taxi to take us back to the Premsagar, we passed an old man in a filthy banian, his lungi hiked up, squatting to defecate; he grinned a toothless grin, laughed, grunted, farted, and shouted out a cheerful *"Shubh ratri"* to Lalita.

"Not exactly a very romantic country," She remarked with deep disgust, and I wondered why it should hurt my feelings, why I felt that Her harsh judgement of India was somehow an opinion of me.

When, despite Her protest, I stopped at a perfume stall to buy assorted fragrances for Her, a little girl in soiled rags, barefoot, with jantars tied around her neck and arms, crust around her nostrils, and twigs in her cropped disheveled hair, took Lalita's hand in hers, crying, "Mama. Me no mama. You my mama. *Ji?* No mama. You mama. Please Mama, give little. *Baksheesh* Mama. Mama feed baby. *Ji?*" One of the little girl's large deer-like eyes was swollen red and stenciled with yellow pus. But Lalita did not pull Her hand from the desperate clutch of the grimy little fingers.

"We've got to give her something," She said.

I, pariah of love that I am, sympathetic as moral leper and erotic beggar, gave the child all my change and bought her a little bottle of rose fragrance. Without count or gratitude, she ran off.

We were just about to get into the taxi when the little girl reappeared, this time smiling, still calling, "Mama, Mama, me baby. You Mama." And she offered a pale pink lotus to Lalita.

"Tell her thank you," Lalita said, gazing warmly at the urchin. "Tell her that I think it's beautiful, and ask her name."

"Dhanyavad. Atisundar. Ap ke naam?"

"Lalita," the waif answered and again disappeared into the dark swarm of silhouettes of people and animals, vehicles, piles of rubble, and crumbling stone and wood, gone forever, before I could give her more money.

We did not speak in the back seat of the taxi home to Kamnagar, but I, without even considering the potential delight or danger of my boldness, surprised myself by again taking Lalita's hand in mine. And She surprised me by not withdrawing it. It felt, at least for me, comfortable there, at home and safe. Continuing to hold on to it, I even summoned up the courage to squeeze it ever so slightly as if my hand were whispering into Hers, "Everything will be fine."

The perfume of the lotus suffused the cab. I could see by the light of the new moon that is the ornament in Shiva's hair that Lalita, for the first time since our arrival, was smiling. It was ever so slight, but it was a smile. A real and beautiful smile.

It was the happiest moment of my life.

That's not really true, but that's how it felt at the time.

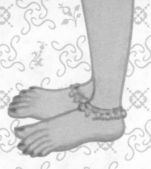

B. The Trust

Up rouzed from lunartick Slumbers in which wretched Carkasses daunced nightlongish in stews of Dreame, I woke in Agrotowne Hindoustan in black shades of whyte Tage Mehale this morne amidst obstarvations 'gainst Me that My antick Fancie is ungovern'd. Ha! I joyne the grinninge Mogoll Kinge in slymie Joyes and sallies of Youthe to prester up his royall Behost to be insens'ble of Shame and lost lest last in Love with a dauncinge Wenche whome he espouses for My ventures. She touches Me, pholds Me in silken Arms and compresses Me close to the darke warm exquisite Brest. I burn, I blaze, I toste, I roste. Lady Indeya Sindeya torments mad Lee. His Eye-balls rowl when phucks He Her. Ha! Ha! He, Lee, me, we, ha! ha! ha! all one'd in a Extacie of Po'sie, will metamorphose cold clanckling Chains into hot twining Limbs that still Love's posture stayes and, if mine Keepers are permitable, Lunarcie into perphect Playsaunce: LOVE. Ha! Haha! Hahahahaha! Ha! Haha!

—Nat. Lee, *Bedlam Iournalla* (1686)

1. THE TOMB (AGRA)

A. TRANSLATION (1)

During the first few days with the girl, the man should patiently honor the beloved's chastity.[1] The couple, attired in handsome but comfortable clothes, should dine together, listen to music, and go for walks in lovely gardens. The man must remember to proceed slowly and delicately with the seduction, to be playful and lighthearted in his sexual advances, creating confidence in the girl and forbearingly overcoming

---

1. Yaśodhara, while acknowledging the judiciousness of moving with caution and patience in the preliminary stages of seduction, adds the caveat that "if the man moves too slowly, the girl will assume either that he is in love with someone else or that he is a homosexual."

any fear, repugnance, or hesitation that she might have. Erotic initiatives must not be rash: girls, like delicate blossoms, require a gentle and knowing hand.

B. COMMENTARY (1)

Taj Sheraton, Agra
Second Night of the Light Half of Jyeshtha [June 7]
Anniversary of the Death of Mumtaz Mahal

"He loved her," I explained. "He loved her with all his heart. As she passed away in his arms, he promised her that he would build this for her as a taunt to mortality and a testimony that love has a potential for eternity, that beauty has a prerogative to prevail over death."

As we sat in the shade of the seductively sublime Taj Mahal, drinking blessedly cold, accursedly sweet Thumbs-Up, She seemed distracted. If this had been a Monday, Wednesday, or Friday morning at 9:30 in Los Angeles at Western University in Sellon Hall 18 for Asian Studies 150B, I would have had a blackboard, and She would have been constrained to takes notes on all I said (and I could quiz Her on it later); but is was Saturday at noon in Agra on the white marble terrace of the Taj, and She yawned and blinked Her eyes. At least She apologized for it: "I'm sorry. It's just that it's so fuckin' hot."

Lecture on Indian Civilization: "The Taj Mahal"
The now wizened and wasted Jumna was once an expansive river; the pure and bracing sweep of its rich waters reached right up to this very wall, and on that side, all the way over there where those buffalo are grazing, on that very spot, Shah Jahan, the Ruler of the World, planned to build a tomb for himself identical to this one in all respects except that it would be constructed in black marble—a complementary, negative image in three dimensions of this white Taj Mahal. After both the lovers were dead, the two monuments would be reflected together in the blue waters of the river. And do you know what happens when two reflections, one white, one black, overlap? The reflections merge, subsume each other. They disappear. There is the illusion to the eyes that there is no illusion in the water.

It was New Year's Eve and the gardens of Agra were ablaze with lamps. The music of drums and flutes, singing courtesans, laughing courtiers, the fragrances of night-blooming jasmine and sandal incense, spicy roasts and honeyed puddings laced the then clean air. Shah Jahan's father, the emperor Jahangir, threw a magnificent gala, a festival of love, a celebration of beauty and power. Great parties are the sign of an advanced civilization. There were canopied swings into which lovers could retreat, taking with them betel to chew, tobacco to smoke, and opiated wine to drink. There were tame tigers strolling the grounds and docile elephants, caparisoned in priceless gems, to ride. There were dancers, jugglers, acrobats, magicians, snake charmers, and sword swallowers. It was right over there, there in the shadow of the great fort. Do You see? Can You see it? There were booths and stalls in the garden, where women, the most beautiful women in the world—Hindu, Muslim, and European Christian women as well—were being auctioned off in play, traded for livestock or slaves, jewels or gold, lands or even kingdoms. A handsome young prince, exquisitely attired in sumptuous silks, Shah Jahan, sauntered past the booth in which Mumtaz Mahal's beauty was on display. Ravished by her glance, he stopped and approached the princess. Taking her gloved hand in his, he looked into her eyes to whisper, "Oh, that I were this glove upon thy hand." He went at once to the Emperor and Grand Vizier to ask permission to have her.

Although Shah Jahan had many wives and countless concubines and could have had any woman he wanted, he worshiped Mumtaz Mahal as the Light of the World. Despite the admonishments of staid counselors, he would take her with him even when he went to battle. He was a great politician, legislator, and general, but he was an even greater lover. Love was for him the ultimate campaign. One day he came into the seraglio, dismissed the other women and the eunuchs, and took Mumtaz Mahal in his arms. "Today I dispatched the orders to Zafar Khan, my governor in Kashmir, to assemble his troops and invade Tibet. Some of the ministers have asked me why. It is, I explain, for Mumtaz Mahal. Mortal men give gems to their women as tokens of love. But I am the ruler of the world, and since I love you more than any man has ever loved a woman, I want to bestow upon you the Himalayas as a mere string of jewels, Tibet its centerpiece, an ornament almost grand enough for you. All that I do is done for love."

He was the richest man in the world. He cherished all fine and beautiful things—rare wines sipped from delicate jade cups, silk garments embroidered with real gold, finely woven carpets and tapestries from Kashmir, Persia, Turkey, and China. He was a connoisseur of distinguished gems and novel weapons. Shah Jahan, like all great emperors, like all great lovers, was obsessed with symbols—with thrones and tombs, scepters and swords, game boards and timepieces. Ordinary objects, something like a divan, a wine flagon, a curved dagger, a polished mirror, a book in a strange language, would be turned by his possession, by his slightest glance or touch, into a symbol, something extraordinary, at once itself and mysteriously much more than itself. He adored finely tuned musical instruments, meticulously distilled colognes, perfectly cooked and seasoned meats, and well-bred elephants, horses, and roses. "The roses of heaven bloom in these gardens," he once said of this very spot, "their perfumes intoxicating the heart, turning even the most obdurate of souls into helpless lovers. Any one who enters the Taj Mahal shall know love and be cleansed. The beauty, grace, and eternity of this place will imbue and transform forever each and every man and woman who beholds it." Roses were a symbol for him, so was the Taj, so was Mumtaz Mahal herself. So were the sun and moon and stars, the river Jumna that he could see from here, and the highest Himalayan peaks that he could imagine in his heart. There's solace in a symbolic world: the sadness he felt was not just his sadness; it was a symbol in which he participated, the eternal and infinite melancholy of being, the dolor of a wilting rose, a dying queen, or a marble tomb. When it becomes a symbol, sorrow has the potential to divulge a mysterious beauty, which in turn generates a peculiar joy, one that does not do away with sorrow but, on the contrary, takes pleasure in it. Shah Jahan worshiped that beauty, that touching loveliness; he surrounded himself with it and made his own death an immersion in it. Wouldn't it be wonderful to live and die like that, to know that supernal joy, refusing to see, hear, touch, smell, or taste anything that was not essentially and utterly, profoundly and ravishingly, beautiful?"

My only student yawned as She weakly raised Her hand to ask a question of the professor. "Then why did he stay in India? I mean it's pretty ugly here."

Not then, not around him. Symbols cannot be ugly; they can be terrifying, but never ugly. Everything was beautiful. Everything. The ugliness around us today presents itself to us as a challenge to try to fashion a world that is beautiful. (The professor paused; the student's eyes blinked in a strain to stay open). You are, no doubt, wondering what happened to the black Taj Mahal? Shah Jahan's son Aurangzeb, after doing away with his brothers, put Shah Jahan in prison in that fort over there, where he spent the last years of his life, looking here, at the monument he had built to love.

My pedagogical goal was that my student come to an appreciation of the poignancy of the old man, clad in white muslins, gazing dreamily through the carved red sandstone latticed windows at the iridescent white marble shrine in the moonlight, at once so massive and so delicate, a symbol in the shadow of which we had sought protection from a heartless sun.

Lecturing on the Taj Mahal, the *Kamasutra,* or the erotic facades of the temples at Khajuraho and Konarak always reassures me that I have pursued the appropriate profession, one that has allowed me some success at socially legitimating my essential deviance. While I was pleased with the present lecture, comfortably impressed by my own eloquence, and even subtly aroused by the images of the Moghul world of love that my words drew out of the marble upon which we sat, I was not sure of Her appreciation of either Shah Jahan or Leopold Roth. The state of Her heart was uncertain.

She wanted to know something: "If you were rich, really rich, if you won the lottery or something, if you could afford it, would you want to build a building like this for your wife?"

A. TRANSLATION (2)

It's best to begin the process of pacification with subtle embraces, at first taking the girl's hand or putting an arm around her shoulders in seemingly a merely protective or paternal manner. Then, as if by accident or under some false pretext, one might bump into her, touching her arm, shoulder, breasts, or buttocks. But remember to withdraw before she has the chance to protest.

B. COMMENTARY (2)

Taj Sheraton, Agra
Third Night of the Light Half of Jyeshtha [June 8]
Anniversary of the Death of Eddie Edwardes

Taking the erotically perspicacious Vatsyayana's cautionary counsel, I'm moving slowly and calmly, patiently and with careful cunning, toward consummation. Still we sleep in separate beds. But in front of Her, and with Her understanding that it was for the sake of propriety, I told the clerks at the lobby desk that we are married. It was probably not believed, but that's irrelevant; what is said and pretended, not what is known or true, is what matters in maintaining propriety in India (and propriety, as Vatsyayana would have it, is one of the essential ingredients for brewing love out of the raw stuff of sex).

It is obvious, wherever we go, that the sight of the young Indian girl and the older Western man together causes consternation. These strangers cannot help but stare at the incongruous couple. We are an affront to indigenous assumptions about culture and about love. Compelled to determine what we mean, they each construct a narrative. I imagine that some of their stories are comical; I know that most are obscene; I doubt that any are beautiful.

Last night I lit the yahrzeit candle that I had brought with me from Los Angeles in anticipation of the celebration of the anniversary of the death of my father. I wanted to do it as compensation to him for his having, each year and every year, lit a candle for Chaim Roth, who had for many years, many years ago, burned a taper for a Jew now forgotten.

I explained to Her that it was a candle for the dead. It rekindled memory. "The word for *memory* in Sanskrit is *smara*. And *smara* also means *love*. Smara is one of Kama's names. As Smara he torments, and as Smara he redeems."

I was able to begin the prayer properly, "*Yitgadal veyitkadash Shemei raba*," but memory suddenly forsook me. I started over, "*Yitgadal veyitkadash Shemei raba*," but just couldn't remember it and so had to improvise a kaddish with whatever came to mind:

"*Baruch ata adonai eloheinu borai pree hagofen shema israel adonai chanukah yom kippur dreidel amein. Baruch ata adonai shalom aleichem torah horah hava nagila bar mitzvah matzah leolam yarmulke amein. Baruch ata adonai israel schmeckel borai putz bagel kosher tel aviv haifa haifitz amein!*"

"That was beautiful," She said.

"Thanks," I said.

"You're welcome," She said.

"Good night," I said.

"Good night," She said and turned over and away from me in Her bed, and I turned out the light. I fell asleep in my jeans and white kurta, staring at the dancing flame that burned in memory of Eddie Edwardes. I could see him in the yellow brocade shirt and red silk pantaloons embroidered with violet flowers visible through a diaphanous skirt that was girded by an emerald green sash with purple and crimson paisley leaves; he wore a turban plumed with black and white feathers; on his feet a pair of violet buskins, the toes pointed and curling. He recited a line inscribed on the mausoleum that could be seen in moonlight outside of our window: "Forgive all those who are lost in the sadness of desire and allow them, O Lord, to enter the Garden where True Love abideth. Open up the doors of Paradise."

A. TRANSLATION (3)

Before trying to kiss the girl for the first time, the man should offer her betel from his mouth or a sip of wine from the cup out of which he has been drinking. This will prepare her for contact with his lips. The initial kiss must be ever so tentative, lightly placed on her hand, forehead, or cheek. Let the girl protest the first kiss on the lips, but then distract her by asking her questions about herself. Set about capturing her affections in the same way you would win over the attention of a child—by teasing, playfully frightening, promising treats, cajoling, tickling. Touch her breasts while she is talking, joking, or giggling, and then withdraw your hand with a laugh.

B. COMMENTARY (3)

Taj Sheraton, Agra
Fifth Night of the Light Half of Jyeshtha [June 10]

Despite the fact that I had made it quite clear to the taxi-wallah that we were not in a hurry, he sped us to Agra Fort with all the urgency of Zafar Khan retreating from a lost battle. When we swerved at full throttle to barely miss colliding with a garishly emblazoned Tata truck, as the driver screamed "Ram! Ram!" over the frenzied honk and blare of horns, Lalita grabbed my arm, squeezed it, and pressed Her face into my side in order to avoid having to witness the spectacle of our extinction. Although the immediate sensation of Her clutch was a pleasing one, the gratification was evaporated by the searing realization that She was holding on to me for dear life, not for dear me, not out of affection, but out of fear. There was further dejection in the thought that perhaps terror, at least unconsciously, is the cause of all embraces: we cling to the beloved, contrary to whatever we might imagine or pretend, not out of love for her or him but out of fear for ourselves, a dread of loneliness, of death and oblivion.

Although the driver wanted to wait for us, I dismissed him at Lalita's insistence: "I'm not getting in that car again." He cheerfully demanded extra money for getting us to Agra Fort so quickly.

Each and every one of the multitudinous times that She noted "It's too fuckin' hot for this," I attempted to distract Her with romantic tidbits about the amorous penchants of the Great Moguls. Just as She said it again, I saw it—there it was in Devanagari script, graffiti scratched into the red sandstone of Agra Fort:

"Lalita! It's Your name—Lalita! Isn't that wonderful? Lalita! Someone was willing to risk a compulsory fine of five thousand rupees and minimum of six months in prison in order to immortalize his love for a girl named Lalita. I suppose that he must have realized that, while the custodians of the fort would surely prosecute, Shah Jahan, more than anyone in the world, would certainly understand, and while wallowing in Gwalior jail, the culprit would, like Shah Jahan imprisoned here, find a certain satisfaction in that."

"That's crazy," She whined. "God, it's hot."

"All lovers are crazy," I said with a rather philosophical air, "in separation and union with their beloveds, they are paranoiacs vacillating between feelings of persecution and delusions of grandeur; they, more than anyone who's been in Bedlam, surely know what it is to be schizo-phrenic—the word means 'broken-hearted.' Haven't You ever been that crazy?" I asked impetuously; it took Her by surprise and made the point.

"I don't know," She shrugged, "but if I was, I don't ever want to get that crazy again."

When I showed Her the harem room in the fort, trying with words to enable Her to feel it cooled by a fountain's bubbling waters, to vi-sualize it carpeted with soft silk rugs and decorated with flickering lamps, cozy pillows, and gauzy curtains, She predictably moaned it yet again: "It's too fuckin' hot for this." We had two more bottles of Thumbs-Up.

"So Shah Whatever-His-Name-Was and Mrs. Mahal had separate bedrooms," She said, "but we have to sleep in the same hotel room."

Once again I tried to explain to Her that I had not planned for us to share a room, that She and that despicable cad, Leroy Lovelace, would have had a room together if he had not betrayed us—both Her, his devoted lover, and me, his dedicated teacher.

"Given the money I've lost by not canceling the trip as a favor to both You and Your boyfriend, there is no way I can afford a separate room. We'll just have to endure the hardship."

I couldn't sleep last night. Not wanting to awaken Her, I rose qui-etly and lit the candle that had been provided for power shortages. I drank down two Halcyon with a tumbler (the empty receptacle of the yahrzeit candle) of Indian scotch and perched on the edge of my bed to watch Her sleep, to wonder what She was dreaming and to remember my father, who as Shah Jahan imprisoned in Agra Fort, remembered watching Sunita Sen sleep:

```
Oh would that Your silken pillow were my lap
to cradle You and guard Your sleep no less
than my armies guard the Empire. But I dare
not awaken You, for You are perhaps dream-
ing of me now, and in our dreams, Yours as
well as mine, there is an eternity that the
waking life does not allow us. But I forgive
the world because it has permitted me this
glimpse of You, this taste of love in which
there is no division. Your joys are my own
as are Your sorrows, and in that oneness I
find rest, and in that rest I do not age.

                                    DISSOLVE
```

A. TRANSLATION (4)

Once the girl allows his touch, even if only under the mutual pretext that it is innocent, the man should offer to massage her back. If that is permitted, the suitor can politely volunteer to massage her legs, and if that is accepted, he should move her garments aside, casually remarking that it is necessary for the treatment. As the man rubs fragrant oils into her skin, he should demonstrate, in alternation, the strength and gentleness of his hands. First contact should be made in the dark; then, after she becomes comfortable with his touch and the sound of his voice, the man should draw back the curtain to let in the light of the moon. The next night he should light a lamp, then two lamps, moving lingeringly and tolerantly toward the stage wherein she is so comfortable that he can observe her nakedness by the light of the sun.

B. COMMENTARY (4)

Taj Sheraton, Agra
Seventh Night of the Light Half of Jyeshtha [June 12]
Shavuot; Birthday of F. F. Arbuthnot (1833)

"I'm not leaving the hotel today," She announced. "I don't care what you do, but I'm spending the day at the pool."

Although I feigned disapproval on educational grounds, I was eager to see Her in Her bathing suit, to behold the holy *romavali*, to graciously offer to rub lotion into Her back, to adoringly touch Her skin, to feel it stretched over sturdy bone and firm muscle, to let my anxious fingertips graze hungrily over the pores and follicles, over here and down there, around a shoulder, and up the neck for refuge in thick black hair.

I made the proposal; after one hour, two no-thank-yous, and three beers, She finally accepted it and fell asleep as I massaged the Mysore sandal oil into the warm and fragrant flesh of Her back, lingeringly working my way toward the tight elastic border of the twilight blue bikini bottom that so enviably encircled Her upper hips. Intoxicated by Her smell, I accumulated the courage to let my hands leap over the garment and massage the back of Her legs, where Her perspiration and mine, amidst fine dark down, and the fragrant oil on my palms and her thighs mixed lusciously together. She softly moaned but did not awaken (unless, of course, She was just feigning slumber). Her head rested on folded hands, and Her disheveled hair, like the manes of courtesans in our *Kamasutra*, Sanskrit poetry, and the harems of the

Moguls, fell forward to conceal the face. I visualized Her face as a meditation, transformed it briefly into that of Mumtaz Mahal, then back to Lalita, then into the visage of Sunita Sen, then back. I focused in on one large deer-like eye and then the other, then the delicate nose, the swollen cheeks, and the softly pouting, love-swollen lips. There can be deliverance in contemplative practices.

Opening my eyes I beheld the splendid sparkle of the sun in the rivulet of sweat in the center of the small of Her back, and though I dared not quench my thirst for love in the waters of that microcosmic manifestation of the former Jumna, I was certain that they were as holy as the waters of any riparian goddess, as potent as any datura-spiked or opiated wine served in lovelier times in this city of dreams. I was dazzled by the very beauty that had been the object of all the endeavors of Shah Jahan.

The afternoon was spent drifting in and out of dream, floating from one illusion into another on cool, clean, and buoyant waters, first Her, then me, then us. And likewise we slipped into the pool and out of it again to warm up, and then back in and out again. In and out, cool and warm, awake and asleep, wet and dry—the boundaries between these states became progressively more blurred.

The reflection of the hotel's mock-Moghul poolside pavilion in the water, rippled by Her submarine movements, could have been a reflection of the white Taj waiting for subsumption with the reflection of the tomb that would be black. Her head broke through that reflection, Her wet jet hair straight back, Her neck curved back so that the face, its eyes and mouth closed, caught the rays of the sun like a full moon. The radiant smile that followed the gasp for air pulled me from the chaise into the pool, and I swam underwater toward Her, my eyes fixed on the undulant, treading legs and arms, rhythmically waving to keep Her afloat, strong and graceful. As I came up, I splashed Her playfully. She splashed me back, feigned anger, giggled like a child, and pursued me underwater when I submerged and swam as if I wanted to escape.

"That's enough," I chided Her, and we treaded water while we talked about something I can't remember because I was concentrating on the movement of our bobbing bodies, muscles flexing, limbs waving, the very water separating us promising to dissolve all separations. Lalita let me wrap the blue and white striped towel around Her shoulders as She came up the pool stairs. Water dripped down Her neck, trickled over Her breasts, along the *romavali*, into the navel, out and down, was absorbed by the bikini bottom and released again to drip down the legs. Did She catch me staring at Her nipples? Was it only the cool water that hardened them?

To give Her time to dress after She returned to the room, I stayed by the pool drinking London gin and Thumbs-Up. I watched the water that had dripped from Her body evaporate off the concrete, and I began, despite the potent heat of India, to shiver uncontrollably.

Last night I dressed in my black kurta and presented Her with a string of white jasmine blossoms that matched the white salwar-kameez that Her mother had judiciously insisted She bring to India. Before dinner in the Zenana Room, we had drinks in the hotel's rooftop garden. In the distance and twilight, the Taj Mahal glowed opalescent—the tomb seemed alive. When She declined my offer of a taste of my London gin, I asked for a sip of Her Taj Mahal lager, not because I wanted beer, but because I was heeding my teacher's counsel: **You should drink from the same cup to prepare Her for direct contact with your lips.** She allowed me to drink from Her mug. Further following Vatsyayana's advice, I asked Her about Herself. It was appropriate for me, as Her professor, to ask Her what She wanted to do after graduation from Western.

"I don't know. I'm graduating after one more semester. With the three units for this summer course and just two more general education requirements left, it shouldn't be any problem. I was going to marry Leroy. That would have been a full-time occupation, always on the road, going to all his games. Now, I don't know what I want to do. I majored in Communications. That doesn't prepare you for much. My parents want to arrange a marriage for me with some fuckin' Indian. My parents, my parents, my parents! I only went to college because of my parents; I only took your class because of my parents; and, of course, I'm only sitting here right now because of my parents."

"You're very intelligent," I said to convince Her that going to college and taking my course had not been in vain. "You were by far the best student in my class. Your paper on the *Kamasutra* was brilliant."

She cut my praises short. "My paper was bullshit and you know it. I just wrote it for the grade. I didn't even read the book except for the chapter on sex positions that the paper was supposed to be about. I went to the movie. Leroy took me. India doesn't really look like it looked in the film. Love isn't really like it was in the movie either. Fuckin' love!" She sighed. And She told me a story:

"I was in the tenth grade at Artesia High, and I tried out for the cheerleading squad. The boys on the football team were the judges. I was really nervous because I had a big crush on Johnnie Shaw. I mean a *big* crush. It was the first time I had been in love, really in love. He was the quarterback on the team and he was so cute. All the girls were in love with him. If you were a girl, you couldn't help it. He could have had any girl. I've always fallen for athletes. Did you ever play any sports when you were young? Probably not. You were probably studying all the time. Well, anyway, when it was my turn to perform, I was terrified that Johnnie might not like my routine. I had practiced for weeks, waving the purple and white pom-poms around, jumping up and down, doing the splits and shouting, 'Go Tartars, go!' I was doing it all for Johnnie Shaw. All of a sudden the boys started to bark like dogs and oink like pigs, and Johnnie was really laughing. And then the coach called out, 'Next girl.' I wanted to kill myself. Of course they did the same thing to some of the other girls, but it seemed like they were just joking about them. It felt like they were telling me the truth. I felt ugly and dirty.

"My parents kept telling me that Americans were racists, that they were afraid of Indians because we're smarter than they are, that our food and music and movies are better than theirs. But I couldn't stop crying. My parents kept going on and on, telling me that I was beautiful; but I felt that I really was ugly and that was why the boys were barking at me. My parents said that those boys just couldn't appreciate real beauty, that they weren't civilized like us. But what else could they say? They're my parents. I only cared what Johnnie Shaw thought. I was in love with him and he thought I was a dog. Well, of course, now I know I'm not ugly; but then, at that time, those football players made think that I was, and that no guy, no cute guy anyway, would ever fall in love with me.

"I don't know how it was way back when you were in school, or back in the time of the Taj Mahal or the *Kamasutra*, but these days it sucks being young. You want to love someone and you want someone to love you. You sleep with guys because you want them to fall in love with you, but instead of loving you, they dump you, and then they tell the other guys that you did it with them, and then those guys want to fuck you, but they'll never be your boyfriend because they think you're a slut. Then you go to college and you think it's going to be different. But it's not. The whole love and sex thing is fucked up. It's not very fair. It doesn't make any sense. And reading the *Kamasutra* in some college class doesn't help you understand it one bit."

She suddenly laughed. "Why am I telling you all of this? It's all pretty obvious, isn't it? I mean you said you have a daughter, didn't you? I'm sure she had to go through the same hell of young love that I went through."

If hadn't been so upset by the story, so concerned about Her feelings, so earnestly wanting to offer the consolation that at least She survived high school alive, I probably wouldn't have begun to tell Her about Leila, my beautiful child, sweet Leila, so cruelly abandoned by Our Lady of the Sacred Heart: "She always wanted me to bring her to India, and I promised her that I would someday. She wanted to ride an elephant."

As I began to recount the story of the abduction, rape, and murder of my little girl, tears formed in Her eyes. I stopped. I could not continue to speak of Leila because I realized I wanted Lalita's tears, that I was talking about my daughter in order to stir up emotions and arouse sympathies in Her, and I was revulsed by my own egregious temptation to make of the harsh facts of my daughter's senseless death a narrative tragedy that might have sufficient sentimental power to seduce Lalita. I was ashamed by love.

The silence was funereal. The dark silhouette of the young Indian woman was motionless. The Taj was entirely hidden by the night. The impetuous appearance of gloomy black clouds augured an early monsoon and refused to tolerate even the faintest light of a quarter-moon caressing, as Indian moonlight longs to do, the mausoleum of love that was the reason for our presence.

2. THE FORT (FATEHPUR SIKRI)

A. TRANSLATION

A man should gather flowers for his girl, play little games with her, and present her with toys or figurines representing lovers in amorous positions. He should tell her love stories and do magic tricks for her. On moonlit nights he should give her garlands for her hair and rings for her toes and fingers. He should dress in attractive clothes when he is with her.

B. COMMENTARY

Taj Sheraton, Agra
Eighth Night of the Light Half of Jyeshtha [June 13]
Birthday of the Goddess Sarasvati
Wedding Day of Jock Newhouse and Venus Doudounes

I had hired a car to take us to Fatehpur Sikri. The driver had already started the motor when She suddenly opened Her door and slipped out. "It's just too fuckin' hot. I just can't go. But I want you to go. I'm going to stay by the pool. I know that's boring for you. You'll have a better time without me. You can really study the place. I read about it in the Dyer's guide. It sounds like it would be interesting, I mean if you're a scholar."

She slammed the door and I couldn't figure out any way to cancel the trip and join Her by the pool without appearing ridiculous. So I went to Fatehpur Sikri, Akbar's abandoned fort, by myself, walked alone across the great courtyard where the Moghul had played pachisi with real women as the tokens, sat down alone in the building said to be the house of Birbal, Akbar's jester. I tried to hear the echoes of ancient laughter, but there was only silence. The same hush filled the woman's quarters, the men's court, the dicing hall, and the elephant stable. There were hardly any tourists and thus hardly any hawkers. It was, alas, in the immortal words of my beloved, "just too fuckin' hot."

My driver insisted that I shop at each of the emporiums on the road between Agra and Fatehpur Sikri. He made me look at endless reproductions of the Taj Mahal in plastic, metal, stone, wood, glass, and papier-mâché, Taj Mahal lamps, bookends, and jewelry boxes, Taj Mahals on ashtrays, key chains, rugs, and T-shirts. He seemed personally insulted by my refusal to buy:

"You do not like Taj Mahal? You do not like India?"

I tried to convince him that I liked the real Taj Mahal but not the miniature representations of it. The same might be said of India.

"You do not like your Madame either?"

"Of course I like Her."

He convinced me that I must, in that case, buy something for Her. It was not, however, for the sake of satisfying my driver that I did so. In order to maintain the illusion of an illusion of social propriety, I purchased a silver ring for Lalita. The driver informed me that if I really loved Her, it would be gold: "Would Shah Jahan buy mere silver for Mumtaz Mahal?" Whether it was silver or gold didn't matter to me: the band would be worn so that the hotel clerks and servants, rickshaw and taxi drivers, shopkeepers and vendors, and countless other inquisitive gapers might edit their stories about us, might allow themselves to pretend to believe that we are husband and wife, that we are not sleeping together illicitly (a fact which is unfortunately true). They knew that in the West a ring, not a chain as in India, is the symbol of matrimony.

Although failing to convince me to buy gold, the driver, who would get a commission from the jewelry-wallah, was able to persuade me to purchase silver matrimonial toe rings, a silver belt, and anklets to match the ring.

"Your Madame will finally be happy. Next time she will even accompany you to Fatehpur Sikri proudly. How did you expect her to go unadorned? She will be beautiful now. It cannot be otherwise if she wears them here. Agra is the city of beauty. It is the city of love. It is the city of the Taj Mahal!"

Upon returning to the hotel, unaware that She had come up to the room from the pool to use the toilet, I opened the bathroom door. She screamed. Slamming the door closed as quickly as I could, I apologized through it for the intrusion into Her deserved privacy. Sitting on the bed, waiting for Her to finish, I couldn't help but think about Clover Weiner, wondering what had happened to the little girl who used to piss for me: had she been in love, married, had children, or had she become a nun or a prostitute, a plumber or a bathroom fixture designer? Did she look old at fifty, older than I do? Had she been ill? Is she dead? Has some man so loved her that he has built a monument to her, perhaps a great toilet bowl out of precious marble? The nostalgic revery was interrupted by Lalita's emergence from the bathroom.

It embarrassed me that my gifts seemed to embarrass Her.

"They don't mean anything. They're just props for the show," I explained. "If people don't believe You're married to me, they'll think You're a whore."

Rewrapping the gifts in the pieces of Indian newspaper in which I had presented them to Her, She placed the bundle in the drawer by Her bed, next to the complimentary copy of the *Bhagavadgita*.

Last night, when it was my turn, following Hers, to shower and dress for bed (as had become our formal custom), as I picked up the black leather toiletry bag in search of a Larium, an Imodium, and a Halcyon, I realized that She must have been looking through it: I always remember to zip it up, as surely as if it were my fly. Certainly She must have found the Krishna blue Kama Sutra brand condoms. Afraid that they might have frightened Her, made Her worry about my intentions, I emerged nervously only to find Her sitting up in bed wearing my white kurta and smiling the sweetest smile that She had smiled in India. She simultaneously pushed a foot out from under the covers to display the silver toe ring and extended Her left hand to brandish the wedding band.

The delicate hand, bent down from the wrist and vaguely trembling, the nails clean and slightly pointed, brought back Jock Newhouse's words: "Take Her hand in yours and you can know everything about Her. You can travel into Her soul. As you touch the hand, keep your eyes on Her face and smile politely. Look carefully at the hand now, that's it kid, and now, now slowly lower your head, slightly pucker your lips and elevate Her hand with playful solemnity."

I kissed the hand and then, heeding the instructions of the sentimentally sagacious Jock, gave Her hand back to Her as if it were some precious thing that She had entrusted to me for care.

I sat on the edge of Her bed, averting my eyes from Hers, trying to use my mind to calm my wildly pounding heart and churning guts, astounded by my ridiculous nervousness, absurd anxiety, and childish bashfulness. It took all the vitality I had to summon up the temerity to lean forward and kiss Her lightly on the forehead. She didn't resist it.

"This cloth," I said as I softly caressed the warm shoulders that were concealed from my sight by my own white kurta, "it's called *khadi*. It's handloomed, woven by peasants in villages that are today exactly as they have been for centuries. It is surely the same cloth that people would have worn at the time the Taj Mahal was built or even long before, thousands of years ago, when the *Kamasutra* was composed."

"It's very soft," She smiled. "I like it. It's cool and comfortable. Can I have it?" She asked as she slowly pulled back the clean white sheet. I turned out the light.

Lying on my back in Her bed, I just held her. I kissed Her forehead again, just once again, and then whispered, "Yes, I want You to have it. It looks beautiful on You." There was silence until I dared to speak again.

"Good night, Lalita, and sweet dreams."

Although She did not return either kiss or whisper, She sighed a sweet, soft sigh and fell asleep in my arms.

It was the happiest moment of my life.

That's not really true, but that's how it felt at the time.

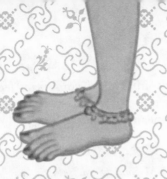

C. The Come-on

The morning after I heard Cunningham's description of Khajrao temples as "ecclesiastical erections desecrated by obscene belts of sculpture depicting gods and goddesses in grossly indecent postures," I set out to see the prurient pagodas for myself. A boy in the bustee, haggling to be my guide to the diwallas, tried to sweeten the deal with the advertizement that I could fuck him if I so wished "just like Major-General Cunningham Saheeb." More amused than appalled by the hypocrisy of the great officer, engineer, and scholar, I asked the lad if the Saheeb had fucked him in one of the temples. "No, Sir," he replied in demure Hindoostani, "in *gudaa*," which is to say, the anus. When I explained to him that my preference was for girlies, he cheerfully produced a "sister" who, he promised, for only a few annas, would accompany us to the shrines in question. Much to my delight, she was the most pretty little Búbú in Indostan. I gave her a kiss and the dusky cunnie put up no resistance. Without further ado we set out in a palkee-garry for the holy monuments. I fucked the girl first in the sanctum sanctorum standing up, then in the crumbling dagoba of Ganesha from behind, and then, in emulation of one of the prettiest Khajrao friezes, her brother and the palkee wallah held her suspended with legs apart so that I might swive her like a Hindoo God. And as I did so, in accordance with the ancient Hindoo science of Ismác, I gazed at Lord Shiva and piously thanked Him for the blessing He had bestowed upon me in that holy basilica: *O felix lingam quae talem ad tantum meruit habere redemptorem.*

—Edward Sellon, *Ephemeris Indica* (1849)

1. SYMBOLS (GWALIOR)

A. TRANSLATION (1)

Before consummating his feelings, the lover should confess a long infatuation with the girl; he should make up dreams that he has had about her (if, in fact, he has not dreamt of her or has been dreaming of other women); he should say that, "until this moment, I did not have the courage or confidence to confess my feelings and desires to you." He should mention his wife, wives, or other lovers, insisting that they no longer mean anything to him.

B. COMMENTARY (1)

Mahratta Oberoi Hotel, Gwalior
Ninth Night of the Light Half of Jyeshtha [June 14]

"You must show restraint," the driver sermonized, like the divine charioteer Krishna counseling Arjuna in the *Bhagavadgita*. "You must use the mind to control the bodily urges. It is the Indian way since ancient times." It was not about sex; it was a homily on the yoga of urine retention. Although my bladder was bursting with Taj Mahal beer and London gin, he refused to pull to the side of the road, insisting that we continue on to a *dhaba* "only a few furlongs ahead" where, he announced with considerable pride, there was a "number-one-quality latrine, both state of the art and a piece of art for our state. It is a thing of both practicality and beauty which, according to the ancient Hindu sages, is a joy forever."

He pertinaciously dismissed my expressed desire to use a tree:

"No, no. First of all, trees are sacred in India. They are the Goddess herself. Second of all, all Americans are opinionated that India, in matters of plumbing and waste disposal, more specifically in deeds of urination and defecation, is a backward nation. This is not so. Archaeologists have discovered advanced plumbing, including urinals, toilets, Jacuzzi baths, and French bidets in Harrappa and Mohenjo Daro. The Mussulman people desecrated our buildings, temples, palaces, and lavatories alike, breaking the stone statues of our gods as well as our ceramic conveniences. Dirty people! The British added insult to injury. General Someone-or-Other, who occupied the fort of Gwalior in the last century, once said, 'As long as the Mahrattas shit and piss in the fields, Victoria will be the Empress of India.' Now the queen is dead, and we are building latrines. It is my solemn duty to transport you to an example of, and monument to, progress in India. It is only some furlongs ahead. The Vindhya High Committee of Chauffeurs, Drivers, and Traffic Comptrollers, of which I am a voting member, raised substantial funds for the building of this latrine, only recently unveiled to the public. So, practice control of the bladder and related internal organs, if you please. There will be separate facilities for Madame and other ladies. The greater the wait, our ancient sages noted, the greater the pleasure. Now, it is not so many more furlongs ahead."

On the wall of the small concrete edifice there was a bronze plaque, in both Devanagari and Roman script, listing donors, including His Highness Maharajah George Jivaji Rao Scindia Alijah Bahadur, who had made "the dream of a toilet come true." The architecture insinuated Mahratta influence and a strong syncretism of Muslim and Hindu aesthetic sensibilities. A dark and wrinkled old man in dirty khaki shorts, fanning the flies from his face with an oily red cloth and cowering in a squat on the floor, saluted me as I made my way toward the wall-mounted white patulin urinal, which he had apparently just scrubbed clean. The profound joy that I experienced, penis in hand, in finally being able to relieve myself (and, as an added treat, being able to hear the tinkling tinkle of my beloved on the other side of the makeshift divide) was dampened by the sudden realization that I was urinating on my own feet: while the porcelain fixture itself appeared both technically impeccable and astonishingly sanitary, it was not connected to any pipes; urine poured through the drain, directly onto the floor beneath it (to be mopped up later at the discretion of the pariah in the corner). The urinal functioned not as plumbing device but as a symbol. Every thing in India is a symbol: every thing stands for something; nothing just is; every thing means anything, if not everything.

Vatsyayana understood that, Shah Jahan lived on that principle, and Man Singh utilized it to augment his prestige and power by building the extraordinary fort at Gwalior, high atop the precipitous isolated sandstone rock that looms over the region. I pointed it out to Lalita as we pulled into Gwalior, then I directed the voting member of the Vindhya High Committee of Chauffeurs, Drivers, and Traffic Comptrollers to take us directly to Scindia prison.

It was a complete waste of time. No one would let me speak to someone who might help me talk to someone who could speak to someone who could talk to someone who could speak to me about being able to meet with Tess Berkeley. I heard that it was impossible for me to visit one of the prisoners even more times that I had heard Lalita say that it was "too fuckin' hot."

I would have given up and proceeded on to Khajuraho if it had not been for the extroverted bartender, lavishly dressed in classical Malwa courtly style, at the Kam Sootra Bar and Tandoori Snack Grill at the

Mahratta Oberoi. I had noticed a mention of the bar in Dyer's *General Guide* and wanted to go to there, not only because I was miserably hot and painfully sober, but also because of the name; I asked the bartender if I could have a napkin, coaster, stir stick, menu—"anything with the name of the bar on it."

"Yes, yes, every American asks for Kam Sootra souvenirs. Every American loves *Kam Sootra*. Every American has read *Kam Sootra*." He explained that the management had recently given the establishment that name (having changed it from "Taj Mahal") because parts of the movie *Kama Sutra* had been shot on location in Gwalior. "This bar was star-studded. Even Miss Mira Nair once sat on the very stool upon which you are sitting at this exact moment. There sat Rekha, there Sarita Choudhury, and there Indira Varma."

After railing vitriolically against Indian censorship and expressing chagrin over the pernicious irony that "a film about Indian love has been censored in India," and after serving us another round, he trumpeted his genuine pride in being a native of Gwalior:

"It is the most beautiful city in Asia. That is why Miss Mira Nair chose it for *Kam Sootra*. It is the number one city of love, *Kam Sootra* through and through. How long are you staying here?"

Announcing that "my bride" and I would leave for Khajuraho as soon as he brought the bill, I explained that I had only stopped in Gwalior in hopes of being able to visit a friend in the Scindia prison, and since that seemed impossible, there was no reason to remain any longer.

"Why didn't you say so, my friend!" he beamed and assured me that he could help me, as the bar was the hangout of a young man-about-town named Vikram Bahadur, whose father was the superintendent to the prisons. "He will be damn crazy to meet you," the bartender gushed. "I know him so well. He began to frequent this establishment as soon as the name was changed. He was hobnobbing day and night with all of the stars of *Kam Sootra*, even with Miss Mira Nair herself, talking Hollywood and Bollywood nonstop. He loves every filmy thing, and every American man, woman, and child. He himself spent various years in Hollywood USA doing this and that with films. Believe me, my friend, he will want to talk to you like crazy. He will want you to be his uncle, meaning that you are his father's brother, meaning that the great and prestigious superintendent himself will grant you any admission to our excellent prison. He will grant you anything you wish. You could even stay in the prison!"

"Okay, another London gin and tonic for me. My wife will have a beer."

Mahratta Oberoi Hotel, Gwalior
Tenth Night of the Light Half of Jyeshtha [June 15]
Father's Day

It could not have turned out better. Vikram Bahadur, his father's pride and joy, had been a graduate student in the film program at UCLA.

"I love L.A.," he began in good cheer and offered me a Marlboro. "In order to hang out there, to see what the film scene was all about, I needed a student visa. I've never been much of a scholar, so I applied to UCLA in film history and criticism, figuring that instead of reading books we'd just look at movies, and I've always loved movies. I was going to write my M.A. thesis on sex, love, and censorship in the Hindi film, but there just wasn't enough material available at UCLA. India makes fifty times as many films as America each year, and yet the only Hindi films they had in their archives were *Meera Nam Joker, Nagin, Mahabharata, Jaya Jayamangala, Rati Ma, Banarsi Babu, Mayavatimaya, Kali Puja, Nala Damayanti, Prem Granth* (the old black and white version), *Diwana,* and of course *The Apu Trilogy.* To make the best of the situation, given their resources, I wrote a postmodern, neo-Vedantic, meta-Saidian, semiotic analysis of images of India in Hollywood movies, entitled 'The Oriental Mirror: Cinematic Conceptional Constructions of India in the American Cinema from *The Merry Magician of Mahatma Land* (1912) to *City of Joy* (1992).' I've got a copy of it, if you want to check it out."

When I disclosed that I was the son of Eddie Edwardes and Tina Valentina, he was ecstatically incredulous.

"I can't believe it! Amazing! I wrote an entire chapter on *Curse of Kali* as exemplary of the genre. Next to *Betty's Bombay Beau* of 1920, it's one of my favorites. The film is unsurpassed in the extent of its use of colonial clichés and frivolous stereotypes. It's hysterical. Your father's Indian accent was ahead of its time; it took twenty years for him to be surpassed by Peter Sellers as the bumbling Hindu in *The Party.* It was really a shame that the *Taj Mahal* movie was never made. Wasn't Jock Newhouse going to be in that with your dad? I'm

a Newhouse fan. His performance in *Curse of Kali* as Sleeman, rescuing white women from evil yogis and delivering Indian Uncle
Toms—most played by Mexicans—from Thugs, was as exquisitely
ridiculous and revealing of Western innocence and ignorance as Harrison Ford's portrayal of Indiana Jones helping the poor, pathetic little Indian pagans get their holy linga back in the *Temple of Doom*."

Young Bahadur was surprised, pleased, and amused to learn that
Jock was still alive. And when I told him that the actor had just gotten married a few days before, he insisted on ordering drinks to toast
the occasion. The bartender at the Kam Sootra served us a special
cocktail he had invented for a hotel party given for the cast and crew
of *Kama Sutra*, the "Hari Vallbangar"—a mixture of "rum, scotch,
gin, mango nectar, lime, coconut milk, jackfruit essence, sugar, rose
petals, and a very secret ingredient, so secret even the CIA does not
know."

My promise to get autographed photographs for him of my
mother, Jock, and, if I could (through Jock), Noreen Nash and Bridget Kelly, Patrick Swayze and Harrison Ford delighted and indebted
him. I asked if he could get me an interview with a prisoner at the
Scindia Prison.

"I assume you mean the Berkeley woman," he laughed and ordered another round of Hari Vallbangars. "No problem at all. Dad
will arrange it. Be there at two o'clock tomorrow afternoon."

Bahadur and Lalita had hardly exchanged a word until we got up
to leave.

"Excuse me, Mrs. Roth? Tomorrow while the professor's in the
prison, let me show you around Gwalior. You've got to see the fort.
It's beautiful. Of course that's why Mira chose to film the *Kama Sutra*
there. I'll pick you up on my motorcycle."

When I stammered, "My wife needs to rest tomorrow," they both,
quite independently, but I think for same reason, grinned.

"Oh, come on," Lalita said, rolling Her eyes as She had in the
presence of Her parents at my home. "I'll be okay."

"Don't worry about her," Bahadur laughed and repeated the very
words to me that I had uttered with such sincerity to Lalita's fribblish
father about "taking care of her."

A. TRANSLATION (2)

**It is important both to respect the wishes of women and to defy
them; while women will not love a man who is inconsiderate of their**

needs and feelings, they also will not long love a man whom they can push around. There are ancient verses on this topic, the wisdom of Auddalaki:

> The man who hesitates in seduction
> Of a girl who's obdurate or shy
> Must be blamed for the production
> Of Her scornful glance or careless sigh.
> But the man who knows seductive arts
> And loves with a knowledge of the science
> Is a bless'd and happy king of hearts
> Who'll enjoy a woman's whole compliance.

B. COMMENTARY (2)

Mahratta Oberoi Hotel, Gwalior
Eleventh Night of the Light Half of Jyeshtha [June 16]
Kali Jayanti

It could not have turned out worse. In matching metal chairs, their green paint peeling back, exposing red rust, Tess and I sat facing each other across a wobbly wooden table. The absence of a fan made it unbearably hot. A severe woman about Tess's age in an olive green uniform stood behind her, and a man about my age with a matching uniform, a glower, and a stiff posture stood behind me.

Tess, barefoot, dressed in a faded blue sari, her gray hair cropped short, the thick metal-rimmed glasses crooked on her recently scratched nose, looked older than Ariana Arundel. Although she wore no jewelry, there were black strings tied around each wrist and ankle.

She had no idea who I was. "Are you from the embassy? Do you have papers for me? Are there letters? Is there anything for me to sign? I'll sign. Yes, I will. I swear it."

There was no affect, no outward expressions of hope or disappointment, neither acceptance, nor anger, nor despair. Her questions were random and meaningless: "What is the capital of Indiana? Who won the Academy Award for best actress in a musical comedy last year? What is love? What time is it in England? How much does a ticket to Honolulu cost?" And gradually the questions turned into riddles: "There's a woman alone, and it has been dark outside for such a long time, so many weeks, that it seems like forever and that's why she doesn't get out of bed. Silly girl. She thinks it's night! A bear comes into her room. What color is the bear?"

"White," I answered, and she laughed a friable cackle that crumbled into a groan.

"Oh, how did you guess? You must have known it. You already heard it. Someone gave it away. But actually the shadow of the bear was black, and that's what she saw."

"Tess, don't you remember me? Leopold Roth. Leo. Remember? We were friends at Berkeley, students together. You had a brother named Cal who went to George Washington University. I always remember that because it made me wonder if there was anyone named George Washington going to Cal Berkeley. We went out. We dated. Remember? I stayed over at your place in Oakland, the house you shared with those two guys. I've forgotten their names. Do you remember?"

Suddenly she looked into my eyes as if ready to ask me something real.

"Do you remember?" she repeated. It was not really a question, but an echo, or the utterance of a talking bird in imitation of my voice.

"Do you remember?" I asked again and then realized that she must have been asked that question many times, in different ways and to different ends during interrogation, because she responded as if addressing some menacing authority:

"No, I do not remember any meeting. No, I do not remember anyone named Bhairav Singh. No, I do not remember any mention of Naxalites. No, I do not remember seeing any guns or explosives. No, I do not remember any discussion of revolution or liberation. No. No. I do not remember. I had no involvement with any revolutionary activities in Berkeley. No, I did not take drugs. No. I do not remember."

"Is there anything I can do for you, Tess? Anyone I can contact for you, or anything like that?"

"Speak to the Prime Minister," she recited. "Please inform him that I am rehabilitated. I am a hard-working and honest person. I want to lead a happy and healthy life in the United States. I am a loyal American citizen by birth, but I respect the laws of the Government of India and would never do anything that was not in keeping with, and supportive of, those laws. India is the largest democracy in the world. It is a good country. Although I am sincerely grateful for the fairness with which I have been treated by the Indian police, the judicial system, and the prison officials, I want to go home now. My dream is to meet an honest, hard-working man. I want to marry him and raise a family. I want to lead a quiet life. I want to obey all laws. I want to go home now."

No, it could not have turned out worse. Not only was I disturbed by my meeting with Tess, I was worried that Mr. Bahadur might be attempting to seduce Lalita.

The desk clerk at the hotel smiled with an unctuous cheer that mocked my misery.

"The good Mrs. Roth left a note for you, sir."

Dear Professor Roth,
    I hope everything went well at the prison. I saw both the fort and the palace. They were beautiful and educational! I think I'm beginning to enjoy India. I'm heading off with a friend to Kajeraho [*sic*] and so we can meet there. I'll be staying at the Best East Central Student Hostile [*sic*] there. I'm told it's easy to find. The address is in Dyer's guide. If you need to spend more time at the prison or are having a good time and don't want to come to Kajeraho right away, that's okay. It really is. I'm fine. I'll hang out until you can come. Have fun.
                                            Your student,
                                            Lalita

"When did She leave?" I shouted in a divulgent panic.

"Several hours ago, sir," the punctilious clerk smiled. "Do not worry about your wife. She was in a most cheerful mood."

"With a young guy?"

"If you are referring to Mr. Bahadur—as I suspect you are—no, sir, he is in the Kam Sootra Bar at present."

In confusion and panic, terror and misery, outraged and affronted, crushed and raging, I bounded to the bar, where Bahadur was drinking a Hari Vallbangar.

"Roth! How the hell are you? Did everything go well at the prison? Dad was happy to fix it up. How was our famous revolutionary-in-residence doing today?" He laughed. "Want a drink?"

"What happened to Lalita? You said you'd take care of Her! What have you done?" That I was shouting caused the bartender considerable embarrassment, but I didn't care.

"Don't worry, Professor, she's fine. I'm sure she's having a ball. She met a real nice guy. We were at the Maharaja's palace looking at his collection of antique automobiles, and we started talking to this

American who seemed to know a lot about cars. It turned out he knew a lot about everything. Great guy. Named Paul something. He's with the Peace Corps, down from Bhutan or Sikkhim or one of those little kingdoms up in the Himalayas where he's stationed. I was surprised at how much he knew about Hindi movies and how many he had seen. Do you like Hindi films?"

"I've got to go. I've got to catch up with them."

"Relax, Professor. Dad wants you to come for a meal at our home tomorrow night. I'm sure Paul will take good care of your *wife*." Winking as he uttered the last word of the sentence, he leaned forward and lowered his voice so that the bartender and the other customers (two French women at a table) couldn't hear. "She told me everything. I mean about you and her. Don't worry, I'm cool. I won't say anything. I understand these things. I lived in L.A." He smiled condescendingly. "Hey Saleem, a Hari Vallbangar for the prof. Put it on my bill."

I broke away from bar, not paying attention to whatever he was saying, and I frantically raced to the room, running as if I expected that She'd be there. I called the desk for a car. Nothing till morning. So here I am. Waiting. Why have You done this to me?

Can't concentrate. Look out the window: Nothing. No. Just darkness, pitch black. And the darkness, like everything else in India, is a symbol, a terrible symbol. So's the silence. So's the empty bed, the empty tumbler on the dresser, the empty mirror on the wall, the empty pages:[1]

---

1. The white page of translation, followed by the black page of commentary initially reminded me of Laurence Sterne's *Tristram Shandy* (vol. 1, chap. 12). But, after thinking about it, I'd suggest that it's more Shah Jahanian than Sternian, that it replicates on the page the Emperor's architectural dream of two Taj Mahals.

A. TRANSLATION (3)

B. COMMENTARY (3)

Just woke up. She's really gone.

I realize how upset, lost, and utterly tormented I was last night because I did something I never before in my life would have done or imagined myself doing. I actually turned, in hope of solace, to the complimentary copy of the *Bhagavadgita* in the drawer of the bedside table: "Renunciation is freedom. When a man lacks lust and anger, desire and fear, neither longing for one thing, nor rejecting another, the chains of his delusion are cast off. Put aside desire. . . ."

The scripture offered even less consolation to my heart than this *Kamasutra*. Anxiously I telephoned the United States, called out in the middle of the dark night of the soul to Sophia, my seraphic mate of more years than Tess has spent in prison, the kind and generous wife to whom I hadn't spoken in over two weeks. I needed to hear the love in her sonorous "hello."

"Hello. Hello! Leo! Oh, hello, I'm so glad you've telephoned. I tried to ring you up at the Premsagar Guest House just the other day, after Jock's wedding. I wanted to tell you all about it. I don't know about Venus, but Jock's in heaven, absolute heaven. He was very charming and amusing and, so it seems, really in love. He asked about you. And I wanted to remind you to call Isaac on his birthday. Don't forget. Don't hurt his feelings. And be sure to say something about his book. Oh, Leo, I almost forgot. I must say I was a bit confused when I tried to call you in Delhi. The desk clerk at the guest house said that he was indeed sorry to hear the news of my death."

"I didn't tell him you *died*," I quickly jumped in, "I said you *cried*. I said that you didn't want for us to be apart, so you cried when I left. Cried, not died."

"I did cry, Leo," Sophia said.

"I cried too, Sophie," I answered. "I love you. I'll always love you. Please know that. Please remember that. Remember that always."

2. SIGNS (KHAJURAHO)

A. TRANSLATION (1)

A man can be assured that a girl loves him by the following signs: she doesn't look him straight in the eyes, but stares at him when she doesn't think he's aware of it, and she expects him to gaze at her when she's absorbed in some task or another; she exposes pretty parts of her body under the pretext that she's doing something else (such things as reaching for something on a high shelf or bending over to pick up something off the floor). Since both smiles and frowns, like laughter and tears, can be signs of love (or its antithetical antitheses—hatred and indifference) the man (with the aid of this text, the counsel of expert erotologists, and the cautionary opinions of experienced lovers) must assiduously, but patiently, assay the affects of affection in the girl. Reading the signs of love is as much an art as the interpretation of sidereal asterisms, the flight patterns of birds, or the words of poets.

A. COMMENTARY (1)

Holiday Inn, Khajuraho
Full Moon [June 20]
Richard Burton arrives in India for the first time (1842)[2]

"Did You sleep with him?"

"That's not really any of your business."

"Yes, it is. I promised Your parents. I'm responsible for everything that happens to You in India. Your father would kill me if You slept with anyone on this trip."

"Listen Professor Roth. I'm an adult woman. I know what I'm doing. I've slept with lots of guys. I can decide who I do it with and when, where, how, and why I do it. My sex life is none of my father's business, my mother's business, your business, or anybody else's fuckin' business."

"You slept with him—I can tell. Tell me. You slept with him. Just say yes or no."

"Fuck you!"

What did Her "Fuck you" mean? It was, given the physical impossibility (for any save the most adept of yogis) of obeying the command, obviously not meant literally. It's a hermeneutic problem, a semasiological challenge, not to mention an exegetical quandary: what, given the context (both when and where), considering subject and object, speaker and intended audience, did the text, composed of those two fecund morphemes (one so sharp, the other so soft), mean? Why and how did they mean (*mean* in the sense of both *intend* and *signify*)?

2. Burton's romantic (exotic and erotic) fantasies were immediately obliterated by his initial confrontation with the reality of India. He wrote of his disenchantment and his disappointment over the "filth, stench, dinginess, misery." He compared docking in Bombay with the experience of having fallen in love with a woman in a painting or a story and then, after much effort, after having the opportunity to become intimate with her, to undress and embrace her, discovering that she has not washed herself and "that her privities, oozing with noxious excretions, dripping with putrid piss, and encrusted with fetid fecal matter, are not what one imagined nor hoped for" (letter to Francis White, 1875).

What is the dialectic nexus in this interlocutionary text between the *intentio operis* and the *intentio lectoris?*

It took Her over an hour to rejoin me in the bar.

"I'm sorry," She mumbled and, resting a hand on my shoulder, demurely kissed my forehead. She sat down, ordered a beer, and charmed me. "I'm sorry, Professor Roth. But the way you were talking was just like my parents, real moralistic and uptight, as if sex is bad, as if I should be a virgin or something. I hate that. It gets me really upset. I just lost my temper. I wasn't so much angry with you. I was angry about how I've been treated by my parents ever since my first period. They don't understand sex. Come on, forgive me. Be nice to me. Paul was a sweet guy. We had fun. You've got to understand, I haven't been around any young people since we got to India; you know, people that I have things in common with, people that I can have fun with. He's gone now. I probably won't see him again, at least not until we get back to Delhi. Let's not talk about him anymore. Okay? And please don't tell my parents. Okay? Come on, let's go to the temples. Okay? They're really beautiful. I saw them with Paul at sunrise this morning. So beautiful."

To be in love, I appreciate more and more, is to be in a story (thus *romance* means both *love affair* and *narrative*). Although not necessarily a poet, every lover is obligatorily a fabulist. There is a literary complicity between lovers, conscious or not; they coauthor a text in which they themselves are the hero and heroine. While they may lose control of the plot and structure, they fix the theme, contrive the message and meaning. They determine the setting and dress, establish the signs and symbols, and mold randomly passing human beings into a cast of characters, major and minor, in an endeavor to sustain the creative power to make of their romance a comedy or tragedy, as they wish, a geste or allegory, a thriller or shocker, a sitcom or soap opera. My villain was Lalita's saint:

"He's great. You'd like him. He was a graduate student in linguistics, or something like that, at UC Berkeley. He said that college was his 'Damascus'—I'm not sure what he meant by that (he's so smart, he knows so much!)—that he was on his way to class one day when, all of a sudden, it was as if there was a light shining around him, and he realized that the whole intellectual thing that he had been so good at really didn't mean anything. He realized that it was selfish to do advanced study in a subject that has no practical application, no potential to help other people in an important way. He had a kind of calling to dedicate himself to serving humanity. He joined the Peace Corps. After he's

finished here, he's going back to America to study medicine, to special-
ize in curing diseases like AIDS and leprosy, so that he can return to
India and be even more effective in what he called 'just one man's battle against disease, poverty, misery, and despair in India.' Isn't that beautiful? That's why he had to leave. He had to go to Calcutta for a meeting; he's on a committee to help children with leprosy. He's kind of like
that guy in *City of Joy*. He looks like Patrick Swayze too.

"I know you'd like him because he knows everything about India.
And he didn't just learn it from books; he has lived here for two years,
really lived here, with the people, the real people, poor, simple people,
in their homes, sleeping in mud huts, not just booked into some fancy
hotel for rich American tourists. He's helping them. I gave him the
name of the guest house in Delhi just in case he's there in August. I
really want you to meet him. And he gave me his address in case we
want to visit him. His village sounds so beautiful. It's high up in the
Himalayas. I'd like to go. I told him that you're translating the *Kamasutra*, and he thought that was very interesting. I know you'd really like
him. He has a great sense of humor. He had me laughing harder than
I've laughed in a long time. Even though he has rejected the whole academic thing, you can tell that he's got a brilliant mind. Lots of his jokes
went over my head in the way yours always do. He kind of reminds me,
in a kind of weird way, of what you might have kind of been like when
you were young; well, I mean except for his blonde hair and blue eyes,
and of course his build—he's really strong because he gets so much exercise—he's installing plumbing up in his village. He has to carry huge
pipes up the mountainside. It's tough, but he explained that after seeing so many children with dysentery, he just couldn't let them continue
to drink out of polluted streams. And you'll never guess what his last
name is. It's Rothberg! Paul Rothberg! Maybe you're actually related!
*Roth*berg. Did your parents or grandparents change their name from
Rothberg by any chance? Paul said that a lot of Jews did that."

"No," I smiled, trying to conceal my hatred of the vile boy. "No,
Rothschild. My father's name was Edward Rothschild; he was the son
of Baron Lionel Walter Rothschild, nephew of the Rebbe of Luba-
vitch, and grandson of the Honorable Solomon von Rothschild. Rothschild begat by Rothschild—and not a *berg* in the bunch—all the way
back to the exodus from Egypt!"

At the temple complex, She enthusiastically related everything that
the sniveling Rothberg had told Her: this frieze (with a detail of monk
mounting a horse [in the dirty sense of "mount"] amidst a perverted

panoply of sexual acrobatics) proved that the ancient Indians, in their sensually grounded wisdom, made no distinction between the sacred and profane when it came to love; the reliefs manifested the inextricable link between spirituality and sexuality that had been experientially realized in Tantric love rituals; a man and woman making love was a holy act of prayer . . . blah, blah, blah.

"Come over here, Professor Roth, you've just got to see this one. God, isn't it beautiful? Paul said it captured all the intensity of divine love, the sexuality of the gods. He said that these graceful one-thousand-year-old lovers proved the eternity of love. Isn't that beautiful?"

In a word, I thought it wise to get a wise word in edgewise. I am, after all, Her teacher. "These temples," I explained wistfully, gazing up at them with a subtle melancholy, "no less than the Taj Mahal and like the *Kamasutra,* as attempts to monumentalize love, to transcend the quintessential transience of things, when all is said and done, fail. Stone, marble, and book may endure longer than flesh, but in the end, all is dust. The aspiration is vain. The temple, tomb, and text that promise the resplendence of eternity can but deliver up the abysmal gloom of oblivion. In the end, and I mean *the end,* we learn from experience that stone relief, marble dome, and palm leaf pages of a text are lying to us. They know it, and they laugh at us behind our backs for our naivete, our innocence, for believing them. Love is, at best, a pleasant oasis (if not a mirage) in the harsh desert of truth. The truth is, quite simply, that nothing is eternal but nothing." I was, in all modesty, rather proud of what had just happened to come out of my mouth, quite satisfied by the poetic (although admittedly somewhat mannered) suggestivity of "desert of truth" and the rhetorical felicity of my (admittedly somewhat ontologically tautological) "Nothing . . . but nothing."

"That's not what Paul said," She answered defensively, only to add with what seemed a genuine pity, "I mean you're entitled to your own opinions, but it's kind of sad that you feel that way. I suppose at your age it's easy to be discouraged about love. I mean it takes energy. I've had to struggle not to be defeated by rejection, by Leroy. He wasn't honest with me. But I believe the struggle's worth it. Paul thinks so too."

Well aware that an explicit articulation of the whole-hearted malice that I felt for the sickeningly scummy creep might alienate Her, I took advantage of the jejune inanities that She had picked up from him, like some venereal infestation, in a mere twenty-four hours of puerile fraternization. Soulfully nodding, sadly agreeing that it was all too ruthlessly true, I confessed that, given my myriad tragic amorous experiences, I had, alas, become disenchanted with the noble struggle:

"Yes, I'm afraid I have. But although I may have lost my faith, I have not yet completely given up my hope."

It worked like a charm. She took my hand in Hers and said my name with sympathy: "Leo."

As we emerged from the temple complex we were, as one always is outside Indian monuments to love, heroism, or religion, swarmed by vendors peddling souvenirs, guidebooks, and postcards. Why, I always wonder, is the same image holy on a temple in stone, but dirty on a card in a hawker's hand? I bought Her a racy little plaster replica of the couple on the Parshvanath Temple that had so delighted her, and She took my hand again. The merchant wanted to know if I was interested in drugs. "Hashish? Brown Sugar? China White?"

We were, of course, constantly and salaciously ogled by hormonally hyperactive teenage boys with faint moustaches, pointing at us, adjusting their lingas, giggling and guffawing, whispering to each other, and occasionally mounting sufficient courage to shout out in English such witticisms as "How do you enjoying beautiful love sculptures of Khajuraho?" and "You are liking excellent sex statues of Khajuraho?" or, in Hindi (which I translate literally), "Will you be my mother, please, so that I can suck your breasts?" "How do you make the old man's penis hard? Please do the same to me, my boyfriends, and the male members of my family."

An older man, a rickshaw-wallah probably about my age, was, like so many of the mongers dependent upon tourists in Khajuraho, an intrepid polyglot. After he realized that Lalita did not understand his Hindi, Bengali, Malayalam, or Tamil, he, with a hospitable (though toothless) smile, switched into English: "When man tired, Madame, I am putting my number-one high-quality penis in you very okay. My name Mister Sanjay. I love you always." Receiving no response, he tried a French translation: *"Je suis m'appele Monsur Sanjay. Si vôtre vieux homme est very fatigué, je voulez-vous mettre ma grande verge dans votre petit chat s'il vous plait."* Then Herr Sanjay spoke German: *"Ich Deutschgerman talken, ja, ja, Frau, mein Schwanz Nummer eins, Kann Dir eins drehen. Jawohl, Name ist Sanjay. Ja, ja. Liebe immer, ewig."* Lalita returned his smile as She said, "Fuck you." Surely, I thought, She meant something different by those words as directed at him than she had meant by the same words as addressed to me a few hours earlier.

All of this "Eve-teasing" (as they call it here) prompted me to explain that, although I thought She looked beautiful in her Lee jeans and California Girl T-shirt, it would be much more decorous and in keeping with propriety to wear when in public one of the salwar-kameezes that Her mother had so knowingly packed for Her.

"I asked Paul about that," She answered, as if I'd care what he thought. "And he said that, although I should probably wear a bra, the way I'm dressed is just fine, that it makes Indian guys think that I'm a rich, hip Indian chick from Bombay or Delhi. That keeps them at a distance, intimidating them in a way that Western women can't manage. Paul said that if I wore Indian clothes and they saw me with a Western guy, they'd think I was a prostitute. But in Western clothes, I just seem cosmopolitan. See what I mean? He really understands India."

We went back to the hotel for lunch, a swim, and a nap, facing away from each other in our separate beds. We hardly spoke. As I had told this desk clerk that Lalita was my daughter (an experimental change from the marriage lie, a test of which lie might be more easily believed), he assumed that I had learned Hindi from Her Indian mother and spoke to me in it. Lalita didn't understand when he asked me if I was looking for a suitable Indian boy to marry Her.

"Not until She finishes Her education," I explained in Hindi. "In the meantime, if She is ever alone here at the hotel, please keep an eye on Her." I quoted Dr. Gupta: "She is so naive and thus some young scoundrel could attempt to take advantage of Her."

In the late afternoon, after tea for Her and gin for me, I rented bicycles for our to visit the unrestored, overgrown ruins of a temple outside of town. New clouds offered relief from the heat. Scavenging dogs slunk off into the bushes as we rode up, and ravening crows took to the trees and to the tops of the moldering temple of love. Ancient lovers on its facade showed the signs of time; they crumbled in embraces, decomposed in erotic union, disintegrated in love. Here a lithic hand remains, a breast, a worn-out face, a thigh, some animal, a corroded god; there a barely recognizable, but recognizably bare, torso turns; and there two mottled legs entwine. A faintly discernable kiss, a broken finger, a sorrowful eye (rain has stained the cheek like indelible tears), a vague desire. The grim canopy of clouds seemed to thicken, darken, and descend as a crow cawed a warning—"go away." Dusty, languorous buffalo chewed dry graze and absentmindedly raised their tails to defecate. There was a distant raga of thunder. The first rain came fitfully, and we took shelter in the deserted temple, where lovers once prayed for blessings and the fulfillment of their desires.

We did not speak, but listened to the rain, did not look at each other, but watched the thirsting earth change color. Parrots flew into the foliage of the mehua trees for refuge. It took me some time to summon up my courage: first I turned Her face toward mine in hope of yes, leaned into it in fear of no, and when I softly placed my longing lips upon Hers, there was no answer except a closing of Her darkly lashed and deep mysterious eyes. In the anxiousness and eagerness of love, I did not retreat, but let desire have its reins and run its unruly way. I grazed Her upper lip then the perfectly pouting lower one with a restless tongue that became a serpent burrowing into the wet warmth of the supple mouth to taste the taste of Her. Her lips began to tremble as if ready to form the word "yes," and then She suddenly placed cool hands upon my fevered face, and in surrender She opened and my spirit was sucked in, deep down—heart breaking, neck bending, deep breathing, leg trembling, tongue devouring—She drank me into Her darkness, the source of splendid light. Her kiss was viaticum, a Eucharistic feast in that temple abandoned by the gods. The text I translate had become a script for a play in India on the set of a deserted temple in Khajuraho (the stone around us behaved like flesh—the ancient maiden played Her, and a dead language came to life), and I exulted in the frangible pleasure of first, fresh, open-mouthed kisses.

The heavens had been teasing; the rain stopped as the sun, annoyed it seemed, herded the indolent clouds.

"Should we go?" She asked, and I wanted to take it as invitation to return to our room. I smiled and could not let go.

"You're the first Indian I've ever kissed," I answered and couldn't help but laugh. "I've dedicated my life to studying India, to reading Sanskrit love poetry, looking at Indian art, teaching about Indian religion, and I've never, never until just now, kissed an Indian!"

"I'm not an Indian, Professor Roth," She answered, hurt or angry, or both. "I was born in California. I'm an American. And I'm not typical of anything, Indian or American, except myself. I've never had an Indian lover. I've never even kissed an Indian either, except my mother and father and once or twice my uncle Shyam. Get it straight: I don't exist just to be your fuckin' fantasy. Try to take me a little more seriously. Me. Not India. Me!"

A. TRANSLATION (2)

Once the girl has displayed the signs that are symptomatic of love (as delineated in this textbook), and once the man, educated in the science of seduction, is confident that a positive interpretation of those signs is correct, he should not hesitate to take advantage of the situation and explore all the possibilities that love provides to human beings.

B. COMMENTARY (2)

Holiday Inn, Khajuraho
First Night of the Dark Half of Jyeshtha [June 21]
Birthday of Isaac and Leila Roth (1975)

Despite a midmorning heat that nagged every little affliction and prodded every tired sense, I insisted that we tour more temples. It was not easy to get Her to surrender. We rode the rented bicycles to the Southern group. The Indian sun—ancient god with flaming hair, his chariot coursing a crisp, mythic sky—was the herald to a cloudless noon of gnawing aches and listless murmurs.

"It's just too hot to do anything," She complained, and the missing "fuckin'" concerned me, made me take it seriously, and I apologized for bringing Her to India. She whimpered, "No, never mind. It's okay, Leo." The use of my first name again, and repeatedly now, suggested a softening in Her heart. Why was She yielding? Because, weakened by the heat, She was too tired to resist any longer? As a courtesy perhaps? Out of pity or curiosity? From indifference? Or was there any desire?

When we climbed the steps for sanctuary in the shade of the medieval temple's *ardhamandapa*, to sit beneath stone dancers, I wanted to take Her in my arms and kiss Her, just as I did yesterday, to repeat all that, and then move on to more, and more, and more. Was Her foot set against mine an invitation? (Accidental, tentative, or deliberate?) Watching the water from the battered thermos drip under Her chin and down Her neck, the crystalline beads forming rivulets that disappeared into Her T-shirt, already moist with Her sweat, I thirsted. Leaning back against the ornamentally carved pillar in that doorway, She closed Her eyes, and I stared at Her, decorously contemplating Her beauty, all that is and ever has been beautiful about India manifested in the contours of Her youthful face. She was a voluptuously carved beauty from the Chandela court, stone still and silent, an emissary of love across time, a tourist attraction for me alone. Her breathing was regular, heavy and calm, and I, suspecting that She had fallen asleep, blew gently on Her forehead to provide a breeze that, with the droplets of perspiration on Her brow, would cool Her. Surely She knew I would kiss Her as I had the day before. Was She waiting for it?

Two contumacious gray pigs and a listless black water buffalo tried in vain to cool themselves in the dark and oily mud of an evaporating pond, a remnant of yesterday's fleeting rain. I poured some water from the thermos into my white handkerchief and touched it to Her temples with one hand as the other came to rest upon Her calf. That She did not pull back as I feared She might intimated that She was dozing.

Incapable of restraining myself from leaning forward any longer, I gently, as gently as I could for fear of waking Her, kissed Her forehead, softly, softly, and then, as I sat back, unaware of the darkening skies and the returning clouds, I saw Her eyes wide open. The moment of silence and stillness was exquisite, all ache/hope/fear/desire, and then Her lips parted and Her eyes closed—Her face was the perfection of enticement. Lips grazed tentatively as before. The parting of Her teeth, the timid flicking of the tip of Her tongue, enraptured me anew. The kiss was deeper and more passionate than yesterday's. Did the thunder open Her as it did the clouds? Did it, like a command of Indra, compel Her to hold me close, kiss me again and again, and even softly moan and allow my hand, the very fingertips of which had just examined the summer-hot sandstone flesh of the temple nymphs, to move up Her leg, around Her back, and under Her arm so that I might rest those fingertips against the round, full edge of Her hidden bosom? Again, without knowing why, I apologized, and again She whispered, "It's alright. Never mind. It's okay, Leo. Really it is. Hold me."

Yesterday's fitful storm was but a preview of the magnificently impetuous burst of monsoon showers that suddenly vivified the pale sandstone lovers, making their enduring flesh blush, the rain the sweat of their persistent sex. The pouring augury of fertility awakened frogs and bathed, cleansed, and cooled the countless couples making love. An instant was juxtaposed with the expanses of history—love longs to be stone and last a thousand years. Across that vast sweep of time Her laughter was the giggle of an ancient *nayika*, bringing her back to life, redeeming her from myth and history to give her joy a present voice. The whiteness of Her teeth was bright lightning, bursting the gloomy clouds before all eyes and releasing tears of joy.

"Quickly, come quickly," I begged. "It could rain for hours, all night, for days even. Let's go. Hurry!" And taking Her hand, leading Her down the steps of the Duladeo Temple to our bicycles, I ran with Her through the downpour and we were drenched and laughing and the dark faces peering through the doors and windows of the old village laughed too. Shivering, we held hands in the air-conditioned hotel hallway all the way to room 218, and the cold made Her dark swollen nipples visible through the wet clothes. She closed the bathroom door to undress, and while She took a warm shower, I closed the curtain to darken the room and, with a trembling hand, lit a utility candle. I placed it in the empty tumbler where the candle of memory had burned for the dead.

Sandalwood incense smoldered and fragrant white summer blossoms rested on the white bleach-clean case of the pillow on the bed. I was on the phone ordering samosas, pakoras, mangoes, and beer when She emerged from the bathroom in a white robe.

As I showered, I tried to slow myself down so as not to divulgate the impatience of desire. I dallied for such a long time over the sink, shaving, putting on deodorant and Mysore sandal cologne, brushing my teeth and staring at my face in the mirror (asking myself if I looked young or old for my age), that when I emerged, wrapped in a white towel, the food and drink had already arrived and She was listening to the piped-in Hindi music: "*Meri chhatri ke niche a jao.*"

She looked away as I dressed myself in a fresh kurta of white *khadi*, the cloth worn by courtiers and courtesans in glad worship long ago in newly built erotic temples in Khajuraho.

When my fingers fed Her a pakora, She asked for the ketchup, but I insisted, "No, no, try the coconut chutney. This should be just as it was a thousand years ago." And She joked, "You mean they didn't have ketchup in ancient India? How could they enjoy life without ketchup?" Ketchup and cigarettes are all that they lacked, I reassured Her.

Shifting from the couch to the bed, playing the Chandela prince well-versed in *kama-shastra*, I seated Her on my left, teasingly tugged at Her hair, and gently embraced Her with a trembling right arm. I asked Her if She wanted to smoke hashish.

"Yes, of course. That's great. I can't believe it. I can't believe you smoke dope! I mean you're a professor! You're my teacher! It's so funny. I wouldn't have believed it. We can smoke mine. Paul gave me some."

In making love there were no fixed centers, no edges either, no ends nor boundaries. All lines vanished into the erotic landscape of an exitless maze, with beginnings, middles, and ends no longer part of the immediate display of love. **We explored all the possibilities that love provides to human beings.** And as I lost myself in Her, losing track of where I ended and She began, it turned from day to evening, from heavy rains to clear nocturnal skies. That night we walked (I remember the delicate ringing of the silver anklets that I had bought in Agra)

hand in hand to have dinner beneath the great banyan in the courtyard of the Raja's Café next to the glorious Western temples, where
stone lovers were silently embracing in the darkness. Sitting there with
Her (there was jasmine in Her hair, and on Her wrists were glass bangles that I had bought for Her), I pointed out the constellations:

"See the Big Dipper? The ancient Indians didn't form a dipper, but
the Seven Rishis there; the middle star on the handle, that's the sage
Vasishta. And see the faint little star near to him? That's the morning
star, Arundhati, the sage's beloved. See how they sparkle for each other
in the darkness of the night? Isn't wonderful that we look up at the same
stars now that lovers years ago, at the time of the *Kamasutra*, at the time
that these temples were constructed, gazed upon after making love?
Don't you think that lends a certain feeling of eternity to love?"

Holiday Inn, Khajuraho
Second Night of the Dark Half of Jyeshtha [June 22]
Kamajayanti

It's not that I forgot to call Isaac (which is what he accused me of), nor
that the phones were not in service (which is what I told him), but that
I couldn't get away from Her after making love, and in case Sophia got
on the phone, I didn't want to talk to her in Lalita's presence. This
morning, a day late, I went to the STD booth, where six Indian men
(including Sanjay, the toothless, multilingual, rickshaw driver, who was
thoughtful enough to ask after Lalita) crowded around me to listen to
every word of the long-distance call. There is no difference in India between the private and the personal, the personal and the social, the social and the cosmic, the cosmic and the private. Sanjay wanted to talk
to Isaac in order to wish him "a very happy birthday on behalf of all Indian peoples." After I permitted it, Isaac put Aphra/Tajma on, after
which Sanjay handed the phone over to a young man whose leisurely
manner suggested an indifference to the expense. After asking her
name, age, address, occupation, favorite flower, favorite gem, number
of children, and astrological sign, he requested that she send him a
computer as soon a possible ("they are so costly here") and that she
arrange for him to marry a wealthy American girl ("with shapely
physique, modesty intact, and highest moral values. Caste is no bar to
my modern mind"). When Aphra/Tajma put Sophia on the phone, she
must have asked to speak to me because the loquacious young bachelor looked at me and said, "I think it is for you, sir."

"I can't really talk now Sophie," I explained, "Half of India is listening to our conversation." It was convenient to have the excuse; it was difficult to speak to her. I felt so bad that I felt so good about making love to Lalita. It was not as if I didn't love Sophia as much as ever. In fact, as I listened to the tenderness in her voice, I realized that I loved her more than ever. "I love you," I said, and it made all the men in the STD booth smile.

"That is beautiful," Sanjay proclaimed.

"Most beautiful," the bachelor echoed.

Holiday Inn, Khajuraho
Third Night of the Dark Half of Jyeshtha [June 23]
Sir Thomas Lovely sets out for India and Nat.
Lee is incarcerated in Bedlam (1658)

According to Vatsyayana: **The first time a man makes love to a woman is the best.**

The dream comes true and the desired illusion is realized; as in political campaigns, victory in the premier battle of love offers the lover the exultation of a conviction that the war will be easily won. It is, as other professors of erotology have duly noted, because of the unique pleasure of first union that sexual constancy is not unknown in an essentially inconstant world: the lover is instinctually compelled to return to the source of the singular pleasure of initial coition, making love to the girl repeatedly in hopes that the joy of first union might be duplicated or even surpassed. He will endeavor to seduce another woman when [or only if?] he realizes [or imagines?] that the source of pleasure was not his beloved, but rather the experience of first union itself (for which she merely provided the opportunity). In the same manner a grown man, driven by the memory *(smara)* of the pleasure he derived immediately after birth as he drank, for the first time, the sweet warm milk of his mother's breast, will naturally desire to suck the nipple of a girl who is not his mother. He does so in hopes of reviving the unretrievable feelings of that unmatchable pleasure that was the very first pleasure in his life.

According to Yashodhara: **The second time a man makes love to a woman is the best.**

The full pleasure of sexual intercourse is unavoidably impeded at first union by fears of inability, ineptitude, inaptitude, and/or inferiority (to other men [older men worrying that they will not have the vigor of her younger lovers, while young men fear that they might not have the savoir faire of her more seasoned paramours]). Thus I agree with Guru

Vatsyayana in principle, but in practice it is only in the second time of making love to a woman that the pleasure of the first time can be experienced.[3]

According to Pralayananga: The eighteenth time a man makes love to a woman is the best.

It is my opinion, based on personal experience and an exhaustive study of both the *Veda* and its ancillary sciences, including the *kamashastra*, that it is, in fact, the eighteenth time of coition with a woman that is the best. Others, equally learned in the *shastra*s and equivalently experienced in sexual practice, concur. The man-about-town is thus to be notified that, upon the next commencement of a carnal relationship with a sentient being, he should keep count—he will discover for himself this strange truth on the eighteenth time.[4]

According to Francis White: The last time a man makes love to a woman is the best.

All that perfunctory yes-Saheeb fucking for baksheesh had transubstantiated into true enamoration (& I don't use the word lightly like a garfy cunnilickin' Frenchman), only I realized, on the day I enthroned Moorullee on my thigh & entold her that that was that was that, that I was sorry to be up & offing to Banaras with my Lee Enfield, all excitable about pointing it at mutineers or, if they had gone pacific, a tiger or two. She was all caterwaul & such soppy beggings as "Do not leave me, Thou art my Lord & Savior, &c." I had said my adoos & the tonga wallah was whistling his impatience. She fell to her knees, weeping & wailing. Sentimental cruster that I am, under sways of ardors, I fucked my Moorullee like never before, the best fuck an Englishman's ever had in the Indies, so damn divine, both of us thinking it was & would be the last, a tragical Shakespearish fuck. As I'm in these foreign lands to learn new customs & to practitude my insight, I can reflect that the best fuck a Company gent can have out here is the last fuck & well worth keeping a tonga wallah waiting.

3. Pralayānanga takes Yaśodhara to task: "If that is true, then [following his own reasoning] the third time must be the best time, since it is only on the occasion of the third time that one can experience the pleasure of the second time, which our commentator opines is the best; and if that is true, then only on the fourth time can one have the pleasure of the third time as the pleasure of the second time of the first time, ad infinitum. This is, as even a woman might observe, not philosophically sound."

4. At first this seems absurd, merely an eccentric commentarial perversity, but perhaps the "eighteenth time" is simply figurative for "after a while" or "after some time of becoming accustomed to making love with each other."

According to Jock Newhouse: **Every time a man makes love to a woman is the best.**

> If it weren't so, there wouldn't be any point in staying alive. It's why I can be so completely happy with Venus. And it's why she can be happy with me, why she doesn't have to be jealous about what she counts as the thousands of women that I've schtupped. She's the best, really the best, the one true love of my life, precisely because she's the one who I am, with all my heart and soul, schtupping now, right now after eighty-four years of joyful, merry lovemaking. If you really love a woman, she's the one true love of your life. The best thing, of course, is to have loved a lot of women, and all of them, each of them, can, in turn and progressively, be the one true love of your life and the foremost and very finest bang of your existence each and every time you make love to her. It's simple. It's obvious. The physical feeling, the wonderful pleasure, is so transient, so all-powerfully and overwhelmingly wonderful at the moment you feel it. But God, in His compassion and wisdom, made sure that we'd quickly forget it, not forget about it, but lose the feeling of the feeling. He made it a fleeting pleasure on purpose, so that we'd go on, move forward, be able to appreciate fresh joys and wonders. The glory is, and must be, in the present. That's what makes it glorious.

According to Auddalaki: **No time a man makes love to a woman is the best.**

> The best is always in the future or the past:
> This time was not as pleasing as the last;
> That was long and slow, while this was short and fast.
> Yes, next time union is sure to be much better—
> This time was dry, the next might be a little wetter.
> No, there's no best in present-tense copulation:
> It's but a figment of our memory and our anticipation.

Holiday Inn, Khajuraho
Eleventh Night of the Dark Half of Jyeshtha [June 30]

Ten days in Khajuraho and over a week since I've read or written anything, since I've held the *Kamasutra* in my hands, translated it, commented on it, or even thought about it. The past seven days and nights and the seemingly infinite number of eternal moments compressed within them have been unspeakably joyous.

D. The Move

Damn Banaras. Predicamented 'midst the cadavers & pious fools who want to die here, I do not. A bachelor once again (my Mrs White gone back to England for summer) I inventoried all optionations. Whilst every Capt. Dick & Lady seemed bent on heading for Darjeeling hills & vales with the advent of the infernal season, I yearned for froth & foam of shores of seas of which we are so proudly sovereign. Chilly heights are for stylites & yogees; lubricious Heliogabulous worshipped in a seaside temple. And that's whereabouts I'm home. The heat that makes a pallid Burra Saheeb impotent only whets my appetite & pego & drives me damn testic'lar. But it was ample more than weather that resoluted my destination as Juggernauth Pooree, lewdic land of devudasees & the Black Pagoda: I reckoned it expedentious to faraway myself from Stygian Banaras. There's the usual death plus these days mutiny & malaria in the air. Arrangements made to let a beachy bungalow, I set poshly out by smokey rail to that Cicisbeistical Hindoo Hierosolyma. 'Though the country-side teems with Tantriks, Thugees, Pindarees & the like, not to mention tiger, pard, lagarti, & other Oriental man-eaters, it's got a magnetism all its own. I fancy wild things.
—Brigade-Major Francis White, *Memoirs*

1. THE MAN'S TURN (VARANASI)

A. TRANSLATION (1)

Once aware that a girl fancies him, a man should play the game of love with her, indulging in the sixty-four sexual practices (as outlined in Book Two of the *Kamasutra*). The lovers should methodically experiment with the myriad modes of kissing, embracing, biting, scratching, spanking, and copulating (in the sundry postures for intercourse categorized by the experts) in order to determine which amatory endeavors are most suited to providing them with the utmost pleasure and to fulfilling their various desires at various times and in various places.

B. COMMENTARY (1)

Sarasvati Lodge, Varanasi
Fifth Night of the Dark Half of Jyeshtha [June 25]
Premiere of Lakmé (Paris, 1883)

The Sarasvati amply compensates for what it lacks in luxurious amenities with its panoramic view of the Ganges: in the morning we watch
reverential bathers washing away woes attributed to transgressions; in
the evening loving couples in their boats, drifting, seeking refuge on
the water from the turmoil of the town; and, all day, all night, cere-
wrapped corpses burning in the distance at Manikarnika ghat, yearning for nothing. There is no air-conditioning, but the mosquito net
draped over the bedposts makes up for that with charm. The room
might have been a set for *The Curse of Kali.*

A. TRANSLATION (2)

**While the man ought to take responsibility for instructing the girl in
the amatory arts and humanities, love's physical and natural sciences,
he should not be indisposed to learning from her in turn; in all fields
and disciplines, the student has the potential to teach, inadvertently
or not, the teacher.**

B. COMMENTARY (2)

Sarasvati Lodge, Varanasi
Sixth Night of the Dark Half of Jyeshtha [June 26]

Why do our paths keep crossing? Why can't fate, chance, luck, if not some
god or devil, keep him out of my life? At first, in the darkness of the Baba
Bhagwan Underground Bhang and Beer Bar, I didn't notice him.

"Leo, Leo! How are you? How's Sophie? It's been a long time since
I've seen her. I was sorry I didn't have time to drop by when I was in
L.A. a few months ago. I love Sophie. Give her a hug for me. And
who, may I ask, is this attractive young woman?"

"Lalita Gupta," I answered as frostily as possible. "Ms. Gupta, this
is a colleague of mine. We were in graduate school together in England. He lives in Hawaii. His name is Professor Lee Siegel. We teach
the same things."

Uninvited and unencouraged in any way, Siegel took the liberty of
seating himself enthusiastically and ordering three Regal Sea Gull
lagers. He asked me what I was working on, and when I, compromis-
ing myself with honesty, told him that I was translating the *Kamasutra,*

he slapped the table, laughed, and shouted, "I'll be damned! What a coincidence! So am I! I'm doing a translation of the text as well as the Sanskrit commentaries with extensive notes on the history of interpretations of the text in the context of both India and the West. I'm also articulating a new theory of translation and commentarial rhetoric. The University of Chicago Press is publishing it."

I supposed it was in response to the tightening of my jaw in anger, the widening of my eyes in fury, that he tried to calm me down.

"I think it's great, Leo, that we're both doing the same thing. Don't you? A real contribution to scholarship. Obviously no single translation can capture the original. The more translations available the better. Readers can compare Burton, Roth, Siegel, and get the best out of each of us. They can choose some of this one, some of that one, or each can decide which one they like best. The more the merrier. It's kind of like when there's a McDonald's, a Burger King, and a Jack in the Box all right together on the same block. The people in the area will inevitably eat at all of them; that's why they build them next to each other—what's good for one is good for the others. The main thing is that, thanks to all three establishments, the burgers will get eaten, and likewise, thanks to us, you and me and Burton, the *Kamasutra* will get read. Let's drink a toast to the *Kamasutra* and to all that it's about!"

He turned to Lalita with an unctuous smile.

"I'm sorry. Typical isn't it? Two professors in the same area and discipline get together and they can't stop talking shop. So enough about the *Kamasutra*, I'd like to know about you."

Editor's Note

The incomplete bits of text that follow, presumably written between June 26 and June 29 (no dates or places are indicated), a period of record and literally deadly heat in India, represent pages that had been torn from the notebook and—after apparently being crumpled up and thrown away and then, at some point and in some changed frame of mind, retrieved—had been folded in half and stuck in the back of the journal for safekeeping. As a consequence, I am not sure in what order to place the entries. I encourage the exacting reader to copy these pages and then cut along their dashed outlines, reconstructing what is imagined to be a faithful representation of the text as Roth originally composed it, one that more precisely captures the chronology of the fluctuations in the professor's moods, the order of the highs and lows in his amorous flights of fancy. The editorial problem (in the interpretative as well as the substantive sense) is further complicated by the fact that some

and so I ask Her to describe what She sees, hears, smells, tastes, feels with Her fingertips, Her skin. "Don't tell me what You think. Look there, look at the bathers in the river. My eyes are closed. Describe them. Let me see what You see. Describe the cries of the crows, the noise of the street outside, the fan above, anything, everything You can hear right now. I want to hear what You hear. What do you smell? Taste this. Touch this. Tell me everything. Let me know what it is to experience the world as you do, right now, right this minute.

Afraid that I love Her too much: someone who desires us more than we desire them is repugnant; someone who desires us less than we desire them is arousing, challenging.

"It seems so simple, doesn't it?" You said. "It seems so obvious. Everybody wants the same thing: to love someone and please that person and, at the same time, to be loved and pleased by that person, not to be hurt by them, someone who doesn't try to change you or get pissed off at you. It seems so easy. But you don't meet a lot of people who have that. Why? Why is that? Why can't we all have what we want?"

Is that a psychological question or a sociological one? Is it biological or economic? Is it philosophical (i.e., metaphysical, ethical, or aesthetic) or theological (i.e., eschatological, soteriological) or rhetorical? Or are You just pulling my leg?

In Sanskrit, the expression "pulling my leg" means "devotedly supplicating me," and the idiom that

curiosity as to what it would be like to have sex with an older man.

Since neither Krishna blue Kamasutra condoms nor Taj Mahal pilsner is available in Varanasi, I've had to switch to the Maharajah color assortment and Regal Sea Gull lager.

As I work on my translation, She's finally reading the comic book version of Nala-Damayanti that I bought for Her in Delhi. She says it's dumb. Like the ancient rishis of Her homeland, Lalita abjures the written word.

"Why did you study a dead language anyway?" She asks with what might actually be interest. I lied: "I wanted to read the *Kamasutra* in the original. I have to admit that sometimes I wish I would have chosen a

and She's fast asleep, or rather slow asleep; so deeply asleep in a way that I could never be, oblivious to the surge and pitch of my desires, desiring Her and desiring not to desire so much. She'll be happy, although She might, out of politeness of affection, deny it when this romance is over. Knowing that the text must end, we are collaborating, despite ourselves and without mentioning it to each other, on the denouement. The blank page at the back of the book is the saddest page, if you're sentimental. But there are innumerable other texts to open.

I was on my back and She was dozing on top of me; I could not discern whether the burbling growls were from Her stomach or mine. Likewise, I would like, when making love to Her, to be so bewildered as not to know whose orgasm it was—mine or Hers and that makes me fear that I love Her more than She loves me, that She has surrendered to the seduction out of pity for me, or because Lovelace jilted Her and Rothberg is off saving the leper children of India. "I'm too old for You," I said in order to give Her an opportunity to contradict it; but, no, all She muttered was "Don't worry about it." She continually disappoints me, especially when She thinks She's saying something nice: after Her first orgasm with me (which occurred only after we had smoked opium), She laughed, "Oh, that was wonderful. I never thought it would happen with you."

"Is that because You don't love me?"

"Don't be silly. I've had orgasms with guys I hardly knew."

between feeling as physical act (to feel Her breasts, the sensation in my fingertips) and feeling as emotion (to feel Her love, my love).

I am desperately trying to discern what constitutes knowledge (how can I, or do I, know anything about India), wondering whether knowledge is congenital (that Lalita knows), if it comes from reading books (then I suppose even Professor Siegel knows), or if it comes from experience (then the pernicious Rothberg, I suppose, will know), or is some integration of those conditions necessary?

I start by attempting to know India through Her and Her through India, and so I question Her and it both annoys and flatters Her.

Embedded in lovemaking is, I am convinced,

of the original pages are missing. I counted seven more torn edges of paper next to the binding of the notebook than pages preserved. Some pages begin midsentence, and I am unable to match them up with the ends of other pages. Thus we, as common readers, are constrained to infer what those pages might have contained, just as lovers surmise the feelings, thoughts, and words hidden in the silences of the beloved.

A. TRANSLATION (3)

In order to possess more completely the girl whom he has seduced, a man might speak to her of dreams and fantasies that he has had, erotic reveries in which she is the focus. They should be related to her in the form of stories that move her to tears or make her laugh.

B. COMMENTARY (3)

Sarasvati Lodge, Varanasi
Sixth Night of the Dark Half of Jyeshtha [June 29]
Noon

This book is an anthology of those stories.

Sarasvati Lodge, Varanasi
Sixth Night of the Dark Half of Jyeshtha [June 29]
Midnight

She wanted to visit the museum at the Maharaja's palace, but I said, "No, it's too fuckin' hot. I don't care what You do, but I'm spending the whole fuckin' day at the pool at the Victoria and Albert Hotel."

"It sounds funny when you say 'fuckin',' Leo," She laughed. "I mean you're a professor. You're old and married and have kids and everything. I don't care, of course, but it's just weird that you fuck your students, smoke hash, and say 'fuckin'."

A. TRANSLATION (4)

When playing in a pool with the beloved girl, the man-about-town should submerge himself at a distance from her, swim underwater toward her, touch her, come up for breath and laughter, then submerge again and swim away. When sitting next to the girl at dinner or at a concert, the urbane lover should make sure that his foot touches hers and that his hand lackadaisically grazes some part of her body. Taking her hand in his, he should slowly squeeze each of her fingers, one by one, and examine the sharpness of her nails. A man should wash his beloved's feet occasionally. When a girl offers her lover something to drink, he should playfully sprinkle some of the libation on her. Lovers should chew betel together after making love. The lover should take his beloved to religious sites, drinking places, and gardens, and while they are out in public together, the man should tell the

B. COMMENTARY (4)

I submerged myself at a distance from Her, swam underwater toward Her, touched Her, came up for breath, gasped for laughter, submerged again, swam away, was pursued by Her, then dunked, and then, as if I'd drowned, I was revived by mouth-to-mouth resuscitation. Later, at dinner, while having the V&A Royal Indian Buffet Special in the Kipling Room, I made sure that my foot touched Hers, that my hand lackadaisically grazed Her thigh, and no one in the restaurant noticed, although two French women seemed to be watching us (I remembered noticing them in the Kam Sootra Bar in Gwalior). Under the table, I took Her hand in mine, slowly squeezing each finger, noting the sharpness of Her nails (the scratch mark on my side, like the little bite on my shoulder, keeps vivid images of the previous night). On the walk home, Her feet became filthy with rich, dark monsoonal mud. When we reached our room, I washed

girl that he has a secret to tell her in private. But then, when they are alone, he should refuse to reveal it, muttering, "Not yet, my darling, not yet." Pretending to have a headache, he should ask her to massage his forehead, temples, and neck, and then he should say that she has cured him. Girls like to imagine that they are a comfort to a man.

them with sandalwood soap and warm water, dried them, and kissed each toe. When She offered me some of Her beer, I took the glass, dunked my fingers, then flicked the suds on Her face, neck, and breasts so that I could lap them up. I was drunk and happy. We chewed paan and smoked hashish. I took Her to religious sites (the French women were at the Durga Temple), a drinking place (the barman looked familiar), and a garden (a child ran up to me, thinking I was some other tourist who had once given her some money), and while we were out in public together, I told Her that I had a secret to tell Her in private. But later, when we were alone in our room, I refused to reveal it, muttering "Not yet, my darling Lalita, not yet. I have a terrible headache." She kissed my eyes and forehead, massaged my temples and neck, and eased my heart with laughter.

A. TRANSLATION (5)

Women dream of being protected. A girl will be obliging once she is convinced that her seducer's feelings for her will not change, that he will love her forever, even in death, or even if she abandons him.

B. COMMENTARY (5)

Sarasvati Lodge, Varanasi
New Moon [July 4]

. . . and You've just now left and I open the text to translate for You and find in ancient India magic words that will make this summer a context to rediscover the ways in which enchantments and feelings felt by lovers two thousand years[1] . . . again and eternal despite the transience of those of us who are but the . . . for those feelings and fears and desires and . . . I copy . . . words of a man about whom we know nothing I . . . [S]ome words are callous strangers, others recognized like old acquaintances, and some are friends . . . *candana-ardra-vapush-nidra-lila-lola-mridu-bhujalata-jala-shanair-manda-sveda-kana-dantura-stana-tata-bhoga-kurangi-drisha* marching into lines fragments meterizing into stanzaic erotodeliria: *sandal-unguent-ardor-body-dream-play-languor-tender-tendril-arms-water-softly-slow-sweat-droplet-nipple-enjoyment-deer-eyes-girl.* . . . and translate it without translating it feeling it without fixing it and I reach for Monier-Williams to fill in what is hazy and mysterious and . . . [The dictionary is?] so heavy, and I am too wistful and melancholy. . . . good-bye to You to let You . . . as You asked to do . . . [T]ake a walk alone by the holy river. . . . the crematory ash and flower offerings amidst the . . . [t]oo quickly . . . [Manik]arnika . . . longing for Your ardor dreams play tendril arms sweat and deer eyes and know that You are the text with words familiar and yet so much unknown . . . inde[cip]herable . . . I . . . I . . . to translate You tenderly with love without changing You at all feeling You without fixing You and having the silences that precede Your arrivals and remain after Your departures like the blank spaces that precede and follow the stanza on the page and this translation that is not a translation is more of a translation perhaps than any of the o[thers] . . . imagine Vatsyayana felt like this one mo[rning] . . . [h]is doe-eyed lover unders[tood] . . . [s]ummer here in Var[anasi] . . . not afraid . . . [S]he longed for the coming cooler season and for it to become one day a memory if not a text to be translated a thousand years later by an ardent lover about whom we would know nothing and yet . . .

Sarasvati Lodge, Varanasi
First Night of the Light Half of Ashadha [July 5]
Wedding Anniversary of Richard and Isabel Burton (1861)

"Here's mud in your eye!" I'm celebrating the Burton's wedding, drinking extra gin (can't find tonic in Varanasi), feeling like Dirty Dick himself, like it's my anniversary—136 years today! I'd like to believe in reincarnation (Lalita says that even though She's "not sure," She thinks

1. The ellipses in this section indicate illegible passages in the notebook. Some liquid, whether beer or gin, rain, tears, or the sweat of summer, spilled or fell on the these pages and obscured much of them. I have conjectured missing letters, words, and phrases in brackets.

it makes sense [and, of course, "Paul thinks so too"]). I long to luxuri-
ate in an illusion of eternity (provided that it does not last too long).
For a little while I'm playing with the fantasy that I am Richard Francis Burton reborn (for the fifty-five years between his death and my
birth, I was an Indian [although I can't, for the life of me, remember
my name], no doubt knowledgeable then in the languages that I struggle to remember now.) This work, the *Kamasutra*, is merely a rewrit-
ing, a new draft, an attempt to correct the first pass at the Sanskrit text
113 years ago. And this journal, my commentary, is but a reconstruc-
tion of a manuscript that Isabel incinerated when I died. Fearing that
this text might be misused to sponsor harsh judgments of my character, she threw my notebooks into a furnace, as the priests here toss bodies onto a pyre. But the priests believe in transmigration and Isabel was
a Catholic. I forgive you Isabel, my dear, wherever you may be
(whether in Heaven or lurking transmigrated somewhere within
Sophia?), but I would appreciate it if you didn't do it again—it is, I
can assure you, damn tedious to have to write it out all over. I know
you meant well. Loving women always do.

Sarasvati Lodge, Varanasi
Later (Same Day)

In chill and dolorous Oxford I studied Oriental languages and dreamed
of dark Sindhi women whose unabashed sexuality put our rosy pink and
creamy white girls to shame; it was as if I remembered arriving in
squalid Bombay for the first time on the twentieth of June in 1842 (it
had not changed much when I arrived again for the first time in 1974—
though I took a taxi rather than a tonga, the driver was the same).

Standing before the shelves in the basement of the Huntington Library, which houses the Burton collection, I reached out for his *Kamasutra*, held it in my hands, felt it, opened it, and tried to decipher
the minuscule marginalia, his/my notes for a future edition. Flipping
the pages to this very section on seduction, I closed my eyes and raised
the open text, like the thighs of a girl spreading verso and recto, to my
mouth and nose and smelled the must, the scent of Burton and India
and of fingers that had explored Oriental girls, reading *romavali*s as the
lines of a love poem in braille. Feeling her spine, her bindings and
cover, an effluvial archival rapture transformed me into the "white nigger" with "the jaw of a devil and the brow of a god."

"Translation is reincarnation," he said to me, and "and vice versa"
I said to him. We looked at each other through the glass of a mirror

in the Huntington's men's room. And then, as Burton, reunited with my books, I have another revery, his in mine, that I, Captain Burton, am the sage Vatsyayana reborn, that I have translated the *Kamasutra*, the book I once wrote in Sanskrit. And Vatsyayana, in that fantasy, sitting cross-legged on the banks of the Ganges, imagines that he is a reincarnation of Auddalaki, who abridged the five hundred lessons on love from the primordial erotic wisdom of a demigod. And Shiva, high in the heavens with a garland of skulls adorning his neck, seeing us—Auddalaki and Vatsyayana, Burton and Roth, and other vague figures crowding in—laughs at the spectacle of men who try to write books about love.

I come to my senses and know this is all a fancy meant to give a continuity to life that it does not actually have. In death—let's face it—there is nothing: pure silence, no text, no language, no desire, no love. Not even Shiva's laughter.

Sarasvati Lodge, Varanasi
????

I threw this notebook away today, tossed the entire contents of "III. Seduction" into the blue plastic garbage can in our room. I would have burned it, but that would have been too dramatic, and my motive was precisely and simply to rid my daily life of drama, to rid it of *writing*. I chucked the notebook undramatically into the same Sarasvati Lodge trash bin into which I've emptied ash trays, dumped gin and beer bottles, tossed condom wrappers and the daily *Hindustan Times*. I did it because it's full of lies that might be taken for the truth. On an assumption that a life, any life, begins to have some sort of meaning only to the degree that it is a narrative, I had stopped living in order to write a story. I had heard myself, in a vain effort to be truthful, saying things to Lalita just so that I could write them here. I caught myself thinking things merely so that I could record them here. I discovered that I was feeling things so that I might elucidate them here. And so, in order to come back to life, I threw this text away. Good riddance.

You would not be reading this, not a bit of what was garbage for a time, neither what Vatsyayana nor what I had to say about seduction, if it had not been for the greed of John ("after the Baptist, not the latrine" he explains), the room boy with the dirty orange turban, an Untouchable convert to Christianity, who upon finding the journal where I had discarded it, returned it to me solely in order to request a gratuity for doing so.

"I can read, sir. Yes. Good church school reading study. King James Bible start to finish. Oxford English speciality, sir. This notebook very beautiful Romeo-cum-Juliet-style love story set in my India. I read every word start to finish. Mr. Paul is a great man. He is saint. Miss Lalita is maybe loving him. Maybe loving you. I do not know, sir. You decide. In a meantime, I must clean more rooms. Clean, clean, clean. I am the lowly man. I am the poor man. You stay in fancy hotels for the rich America tourist always. You are the rich man. I am the very no-money man. You give me money, sir—I find the book. In the book is your self life. Thus, I save you. Isn't it, sir? So you give me the very much money. You are the good man, sir, just like Mr. Paul. He is always helping the poor Indian people. I give book, sir. You help. You give money, sir."

This text cost me, after lengthy and rigorous bargaining, two hundred rupees.

Sarasvati Lodge, Varanasi
?????

The water was strewn with human ashes (white, gray, black) and flower petals (white, pink, yellow), and the moody mother Ganga (gray, green, brown) flexed, rippled, and splashed the charred stone steps leading up from her toward the flames feasting on the corpses at Manikarnika. Bodies brightly wrapped as gifts for death rested racked on stone stairs with their usual composure and interminable patience, waiting for the splendid obliteration that the mouths of fire have to offer. Smoke caressed us gently in the tower above the crematory ghat, and She took my hand to wrap my arm around Her shoulder as if I might protect Her from death. I watched Her watch the bodies burn as the priests chanted in the language of the dead. Intensifying, as if intent on bringing this dirt-spiced stew to a boil, the sacramental fire calls out in cackling crackles for the patient corpse that's trussed and wrapped in white. Another body is gaudily garbed in bright crimson silks, dressed for a tryst in which death is the lover. Yapping dogs, hungry for burnt bones, sing the gruesome epithalamium.[2]

We were greeted by a one-eyed leper's outstretched hand. The single open eye was a hideous moon in the murky night of his face, more smeared than stretched across his skull, a slab of night blotched and

2. Some of this paragraph is plagiarized (although somewhat improved) from Lee Siegel's *City of Dreadful Night* (see pp. 217–18), perhaps as a some sort of perverted revenge against the person Roth considered his rival in the discipline.

stained with white fumy clouds of disease. Lalita did not flinch as we pushed past him, letting his plaintive cries dissolve into the louder ruckus of barking dogs and wailing loved ones near the pyres.

Wearing for the first time one of the stick-on Lakme bindis that I had bought for Her in Delhi, Lalita looked beautiful with the crepuscular light upon Her smooth cheeks.

"The first time I made love was in a graveyard," She said, "a cemetery behind the Sacred Heart Church of Artesia. It was a good place to go at night. A lot of the kids used to hang out there to make out, drink beer, or smoke a joint. It was creepy and at the same time kind of exciting. Johnnie Shaw took me there. I guess that's why graveyards always make me think about sex."

"And sex," I said, "always makes me think about graveyards."

A young man in a dhoti raised a club and smashed the skull of the burning cadaver to free his father's soul from the torments of body, of desire, and of sex, to release it with love into the infinite and eternal rest of oblivion.

"I thought this would be creepy," She said, "but it's not. There's something beautiful about it in a weird kind of way. Do you know what I mean?"

That question disarmed me. This whole notebook records my desperate endeavor to understand what She *means*.

????????

Varanasi

????

The monsoon returned with such force that we can't go out: "In ancient India they believed that the lovemaking of lovers and the croaking of frogs caused the storms to come, and then, once the monsoon was upon them, those lovers and those frogs, in unison with other lovers and frogs, under the inspiration of the rains, croaked and made love all the more until all the rains in Heaven had fallen down to earth."

Looking out at the rains that are swelling the Ganges, watching the drops fall into the puddles and pools, each one forming an expanding circle that overlaps another circle expanding into others, stretching outward perfectly into infinities, threatening us with flood, makes me miss the people that I've known who've died: my father, Eve Christ, Sunita Sen, and Leila.

She's on the bed. I believe and trust that She truly wants me to stop writing, to put this down, rise up, go over to Her, and lie down. . . .

??????
???????
????
?

Last night I fell asleep inside of Her. Her whisper awakened me: "I love you." She whispered it for the first time and then there was a silence, and it was so dark that the room had no walls, neither a ceiling nor a floor. The darkness was the obscurity of the infinite, and it was our darkness. She whispered it again and then there was a silence (no sounds of rain or wind, of frogs or jackals, no words, no songs, not even a whimper). The silence was the hush of the eternal, and it was our silence.

2. THE GIRL'S TURN (PURI)

A. TRANSLATION (1)

In order to entirely capture the heart of her lover, a girl must ultimately demonstrate a mastery of the arts of love; she should do the very same things that the man has been tutored to perform in this pedagogical text. In the beginning of the relationship, however, the girl, feigning ignorance and innocence, nubility and fragility, should ask her lover to be her teacher, to educate her in the *artes amatoriae*, to instruct her in the *scientia sexualis*, both to lecture on the subjects covered in the *Kamasutra* and to demonstrate them for and with her until they are mastered.

B. COMMENTARY (1)

Bright and White Restaurant, Vaitpur (Orissa)
Ninth Night of the Light Half of Ashadha [July 14]
Bastille Day

I suspect that She surrendered to me only because I waited so long before making love to Her; if I had tried sooner, successfully or not, She might distrust me now, and trust, as dear Sophia says, is an essential ingredient of love. Somewhere Vatsyayana explains it:

> Women are aroused by a man's restraint. They must long for union, and that longing, in turn, must be elongated to invest its object with power. A girl will love a man who doesn't penetrate her too soon, but only, and preposterously, on the condition that she is aware of his desire to do so; his forbearance will have the mystique of love. Likewise a girl will love a man who makes love to her immediately and penetrates

her deeply, but only, and outrageously, on the condition that she believes that out of his respect for her he does not desire to do so. He must
not be too eager or harriedly hurried; he should resist a bit. When he
does enter her, she should believe that he is but surrendering to her desire, *par force*, for her sake, obliging her because he can refuse her nothing. It must seem that it is he, the seducer, who is seduced. Seduction
is all misdirection; it's paradox and parallax.[3]

B.O.N.E. Railway Hotel, Puri
Tenth Night of the Light Half of Ashadha [July 15]
Wedding Anniversary of Eddie Edwardes and Tina Valentina

Through the open window of the car, Lalita gazed at Orissa: placid
green rice paddies, the distant beryl swell of hills; languid androgynous
palms, voluptuous female banyans, and wearied male plantains;
brightly painted shrines, with the confident shine of primary colors,
where gods lived as friendly neighbors to the people in their ochre huts
of mud with thatched roofs of sun-browned palm leaves. The air roiled
with the scents of mango and jasmine, rich wet seasonal grass, perennial, ubiquitous cow dung, the smoke of burning coir, and a smolder-
ing of desire. She took my hand in Hers and smiled happily.

Honking, we swerved to miss a furiously peddling, tonsured Brahmin in orange on a black bicycle with an incessantly ringing bell; honking, honking, we careened to spare the life of a meandering gray-and-
white goat that brayed at us; honk-honk-honking, we braked to not
kill the nimble little boy chasing a cricket ball. A truck was overturned,
a bus broken down. A sluggish ox cart gave the impression that it
started out a thousand years ago and would only reach its destination
in a thousand more. Bajan scooters, Maruti cars, and old Ambassadors
each vie with horn and speed to establish their vehicular status on the
road; even cars in India have caste.

Ruddy red and oil-striated stagnant pools, remains of the yearly
rains, breed bacterial monsters, vamipirical mosquitoes, and fluctuant
reflections of the Indian sun. Does that once-deified sun remember the
jubilant piety of those ancient lovers who worshiped him at Konarak,
who celebrated his risings, settings, and glorious noons?

All along the roadside, faces stared at the foreigner in the car with
the Indian girl. I looked at Her looking at India looking at me. Lalita
seemed to me, at that moment, to have become so perfectly lacking in

3. I am unable to find this passage anywhere in the *Kāmasūtra*.

distractions, so enviably detached and able to take, integrate, even absorb everything or anything in the world just as it presented itself to Her, as if all things existed solely for Her, not for Her judgment, but for Her appreciation, great, small, or none at all. She has slowly allowed Herself to reveal an innate inclination to accept all things. She is like an animal—instinctual, sensual, spontaneous, unencumbered by self-doubt, circumspection, regret, uncertainty, or ambivalence. I want Her to be my teacher.

I stayed here, at the Banaras-Orissa-Nagpur-Eastern Railway Hotel, years ago with Sophia, the first and last time she came to India. I sat in this very spot on the veranda looking out at the same dark and turbulent brown-green-gray waves of the Bay of Bengal, no doubt drinking a gin and tonic then as now: the same pilgrims bathing in their clothes have the same hopes and regrets, the same fishermen repairing their nets have the same desires and fears, and the same surly crows and marauding gulls scavenging the beach have the same unquenchable and indiscriminate hunger. Sophia White was in the room drinking Lipton tea and reading Sir Thomas Lovely's account of this beach.

Dusty trophies are mounted on the grimy walls of the once majestic and imperial B.O.N.E. Railway Hotel: the termite-eaten heads of jackals, hyenas, and a deer with large sad eyes that have gazed down the dark halls all day and night for a century; a jungle goat with spider webs spun across the span of its once-menacing curled horns; a wild cat, missing teeth and one of its taxidermic eyes of glass; and, strange as it seems, the mounted head of what I believe is a Blenheim spaniel. There are faded photographs in frames with flaking gilt and peeling paint: Banaras-Orissa-National-Eastern Railway polo team; a squad of British soldiers, on leave in Puri, posing with the catch of a rollicking day of pig-sticking; the Maharaja of Anangapur with his retinue of armed guards, veiled courtesans, and caparisoned elephants. There's a faded map of a faded India that still includes Burma. There's a crudely painted oil portrait of Queen Victoria, darkened by the briny sea air of Puri and largely signed "M. M. Mithun Mohantee, M.A., Artist"—it's a copy of the same portrait of Queen Victoria that's copied on the label of the Bombay gin that's so regrettably unavailable in India.

"Empress of India," the barefoot servant in the green turban and matching cummerbund (belting an oversized and soiled white coat embroidered "B.O.N.E.R.") explained. "Empressive Victoria, Jayanti

Maharani—very beautiful, intelligent, generous, and number-one-quality queen." He smiled affectionately at the dour visage of Her Highness. "I do not know her personally. She is dead. Long live the Queen! She was considerate for Indian peoples."

We were joined by Mr. Indrajit, the hotel assistant manager, who despite the tropical heat, wore a black suit, white shirt, and wide red tie. Apparently concerned that an illiterate "peon" (as he so quaintly called him) might misinform me about Queen Victoria, he shooed him away disdainfully.

"Go to the buttery for hard work, you bloody lowly! As manager I have too many peon botherations and problemations." He then commandeered the biographical narrative:

"'Victorian this' and 'Victorian that' people are always wrongly saying to indicate 'prudish this' and 'priggish that.' But, I confide in you, sir, that His excellent Excellency, His Highness the Maharaja of Anangapur, has confided in me that His Highness his father confided in His Highness himself that he had presented a copy of blessed *Kamasutra* by the great poet and scientist of Puri, Orissa, Shri Shri Professor Vatsyayan Malnag Mohanti, to His Highness Prince Albert, husband of Her Highest Highness, the Victoria in question, sir. As my confidence in you is confidential, sir, I am confident that you will not be spreading the tale hither and thither, but," his voice lowered into a whisper, "His and Her Highnesses were doing every *Kamasutra* thing, this way, that way, and every other way to boot, day and night, sir, not to mention night and day."[4]

The revisionist lecture on the secret life of Queen Victoria came, no doubt, as a result of the conversation we had had upon check-in:

"Your business, sir?"

"Professor. I'm . . ."

"Which subject, sir?"

"India. I teach Indian . . ."

"India is an excellent place to study that excellent subject, sir. First you must read *Bhagavadgita*. It is in the Sanskrit language, sir, and it is true."

"Yes, yes, I've read it. At the moment I'm translating the *Kamasutra*, and I . . ."

---

4. Note that Mr. Indrajit sounds remarkably like Dr. Nilkanth Gupta (if not Peter Sellers in *The Party*); this is apparently the accent that Roth attributes to all Indians whom he wants to belittle. Mockery was, I think, a method of self-defense in his confrontation with India, his feeling of an unrequited love for that about which he taught and wrote.

"*Kamasutra* is also in the Sanskrit language, sir, and is also true. The *Kamasutra* makes patent what in *Bhagavadgita* is latent, and vice versa. These two scriptures are merely two sides of the same true story and golden coin. I will be most happy to take time out of my ever-hustle-bustle schedule to tell you everything you want to know, sir. But first, I beg your pardon, sir, there is one formality question: Why is your own good name, namely Roth, as clearly indicated on your excellent and always reliable United States of America passport, not one and the same as the name of your good wife, namely the name Gupta, as indicated on her United States of America passport? Has the United States made some blunder? Pardon me, sir, for asking, but it is a necessary formality at a five-star tourist hotel to have the precisest identifications for Police Commission, Ministry of Health, and All-Orissa Department of Tourism."

"Our passports were issued before our wedding. We just got married, on May 29, just six weeks ago. We're on our honeymoon."

"India is an excellent place for a honeymoon. India is the number one country of Love: there is Taj Mahal of Agra, Temple of the Sun of Konarak, and romantic Puri beach. *Kamasutra* is an excellent book for a honeymoon. This hotel is excellent for a honeymoon. Mr. Rajiv Gandhi stayed here, in your same romantic room, I recall at the present moment, sir, with his bride Srimati Sonia Gandhi, on his honeymoon. Like yourself, sir, that was what *Kamasutra* terms a 'mixed marriage.'"

A. TRANSLATION (2)

While sitting on her lover's lap or while being embraced, a girl should not reveal any sentimental agitation, nor should she display any erotic hesitation; she should not divulge thoughts about another lover, nor any concern about her parents; above all, she should not show even the slightest interest in mundane things.

B. COMMENTARY (2)

B.O.N.E. Railway Hotel, Puri
Thirteenth Night of the Light Half of Ashadha [July 18]
Ide Milad

Lalita went out by Herself today to visit the Jagannath Temple, where I, as a casteless foreigner, am forbidden: I am polluted; She is pure. She went to see the carved wooden deity, the Ruler of the Universe, before whom enraptured *devadasi*s dance and sing erotic songs, relishing him in ecstatic cotillion. I went by hired car to Patiya village to talk to the director of a guild of craftsmen there about making the sixty-four *ka-makala* cards and six pawns for my *Kamasutra* game. They have hopes that the *Kamasutra* will make them rich.

Without warning me, She had Her nose pierced, and a small, simple silver ring now shines moon-like with the innate purity of Her race on the splendid night of Her face. She is smiling at Herself in the mirror, happy, it seems, with the new ornament, and with the purple bindi on her forehead. I'll set this aside, walk up behind Her, look over Her shoulder into the glass at us, and whisper to Her how beautiful She is, more beautiful than ever. Her hands and feet are artfully stained with henna. . . .

At the sound of the knock on the door, She covered Her breasts with the purple silk Banarsi shawl and skipped barefoot across the green tile floor with a jingling of silver anklets. Mr. Indrajit, standing there peering in, his glance a glare, his smile a glower, spoke around Her:

"You will not even dare to imagine in wildest imaginations what excellent thing I have accomplished for you, sir. I am supremely happy to have obtained a very rare, most excellent, and highly valuable something that will be highly valuable for you, sir. It is my honeymoon gift for the excellent Professor Roth and his beloved Mrs. Roth, née Gupta."

He insisted that I follow him to his office, where, after demanding that I sit down under a portrait of Gandhi (painted and largely signed by M. M. Mithun Mohantee) and swallow a filthy tumbler full of insufferably sweeter-than-sweet and tongue-scaldingly hot tea, he dismissed his "peon," closed the door, locked it with a padlock, and produced a yellow cotton cloth bundle tied with black twine that he, with a lowered voice, ordered me to open.

It was a palm leaf manuscript of the *Kamasutra* (II.F), inscribed in Oriya script and crudely illustrated. He dismissed my explanation that I did not read Oriya as irrelevant.

"You can relish art, sir, while learning excellent Oriya. Are you, a great professor of United States of America, not highly intelligent? You must learn Oriya, sir. Divine language. I will personally pray to Lord Jagannath for an immediate success. In the meantime, I have gone to great extents to serve you with a timely procurement of this highly excellent and highestly valuable *Kamasutra*. It is, sir, my but humble wedding offering, gifted to husband and wife with pious prayers that you are granted, by Lord Jagannath and all the gods also,

101 bull-like sons of legendary virility and courage. Please, sir, spare me the embarrassment of a gratitude that is too profusely proffered."

After I had politely thanked him for the gift, Mr. Indrajit duly explained to me that I must give him twenty thousand rupees for it.

"I personally paid thirty thousand rupees, sir, less than half of what it is highly worth abroad. You would be an even richer man if you were to sell this precious treasure in U.S.A., sir. But I am entirely confident, sir, that like my own self, money means nothing to your self. It is of this world and we are of higher worlds and calibers. You would never sell this valuable *Kamasutra* as if it were some invaluable pornographic this or that. Never! 'Why am I taking a great personal financial loss to my humble self and my excellent family for the sake of a stranger?' I asked the blessed Mrs. Indrajit, devoted mother of my excellent sons, Mohan, Shyam, and Winston, dedicated teacher of my homely daughter, Damayanti, and most pious servant of my god, Lord Jagannath. Typical of her spiritually based wisdom was this excellent rejoinder: 'It is because, in your own humble way, you are beholden to gift a visitor from afar, who is for the first time experiencing the blessings of wedding, with the most suitable, excellent, spiritual, and valuable wedding gift of India. Marital bliss is our highest Indian ideal. In India we do not let filthy money, neither rupees nor dollars, blemish this golden ideal. That is what *Bhagavadgita* is teaching. But, O father of Mohan, Shyam, and Winston, you must ask the great professor of America, U.S.A., to entrust you entirely with a measly twenty thousand rupees. He will not be concerned with mere money when it comes to marriage, love, friendship, spirituality, international diplomacy, Sanskrit, Indian culture, *Kamasutra, Bhagavadgita,* and the like. The great professor will try to give you one lakh, perhaps one crore. But you will refuse because you care no more for money than does he.' Thus is the greatness, wisdom, and charity of Mrs. Indrajit. She is never thinking of herself. Only of others. Thus she did not even mention that we are in desperate need of assistances to pay for uncle's spine operation so he will live, brother's imported prosthesis so he will walk, sons' university tuitions so they will not be lowly, daughter's dowry so she will not be shameful, younger sister's eyeglasses so she will see, and older sister's husband's house, burned down . . ."

As he continued to catalogue his financial liabilities, I decided that I would give him ten thousand rupees only, probably twice what the manuscript, as a modern forgery, was worth; I had it in an envelope—the extra money that Dr. Nilkanth Gupta had given me for his daughter.

Indrajit was insulted, but I refused to give him a paise more.

"You have destroyed my family! You have affronted the mother of Mohan, Shyam, and Winston, not to mention Damayanti," he shouted abusively, and as I left his office, his continuing diatribe trailed off. "You have looked a gift horse in the mouth! You have destroyed my life. You have destroyed Indian civilization...."

B.O.N.E. Railway Hotel, Puri
Fourteenth Night of the Light Half of Ashadha [July 19]

"Mrs. Indrajit instructs me to turn another cheek as *Bhagavadgita* teaches," Mr. Indrajit said with a renewed smile. "And thus, you may give me merely eighteen thousand rupees for your wedding gift, my humble offering to your excellent self and well-groomed bride."

I was resolute: "Ten."

"Ten! Ten thousand measly rupees!" he murmured through his disintegrating glassy smile. "Ten thousand is the sum, sir, of your insult added to my injury minus my pride divided by your prejudice times your greed!"

In other words, I thought, "Insult (I_1) plus injury (I_2) minus pride (P_1) divided by prejudice (P_2) times greed (G) equals 10^4," or $10^4 = \frac{(I_1 + I_2) - P_1}{P_2} \times G$. Thus: $G = \frac{P_2}{(I_1 + I_2) - P_1} \times 10^4$. It follows that if there is no prejudice $(P_2 = 0)$, then there can be no greed $(G = 0)$. Furthermore, if one has no pride $(P_1 = 0)$, there can, obviously, be no insult $(I_1 = 0)$. In that case: $G = \frac{P_2}{I_2} \times 10^4$ and/or $I_2 \times G = P_2 \times 10^4$. Thus, it follows that if one's prejudice remains constant, one's greed will decrease in proportion to the number of times one is injured and increase to the degree that one avoids injury, and if one's greed remains constant, the less prejudiced one is, the more one will be injured. Thus injury can be avoided by increasing one's greed, and to the degree that that greed is increased, prejudice will decrease. Thus the infinitely greedy person $(G \infty)$ is necessarily without prejudice and in no danger of injury. Am I losing my mind?

I knew it. I knew it when She stopped saying "fuckin'"—Lalita is sick. Her vomiting next to the Temple of the Sun at Konarak drew a crowd of spectators out of the throng formicating around the erotic monument. They circled around us, and a hawker tried to sell me a postcard of a celestial nymph fellating a holy man as Lalita, with my arm protectively around Her, wretched with nausea and trembled with fever. He smiled and said, "Madame has been eating spicy foods?"

The digestive system likes to mock the reproductive system, to taunt the erogenous zones with vomit, diarrhea, and gas. Inevitably in India the bowels laugh at the genitals which laugh at the heart which laughs at the brain which, given how much it has to do, loses its sense of humor once the guts get rowdy. In India the organs within the human body, no less than the human beings within the social body, are fundamentally hierarchical.

Mr. Suryadas, our hired driver, had to repeatedly pull off the road so that Lalita could empty Her ailing body, from both ends of the alimentary canal, in the bushes. He shook his head as he reiterated, "She must eat Jagannath prasad."[5]

While Lalita's sudden show of physical vulnerability elicited in me overwhelming impulses to care for Her, I reminded myself that once you begin to protect, or even try to protect, another, you yourself lose protection; the greater their vulnerability (your awareness or your imagining of it), the greater your own will be. Beware the weakness of the beloved.

Wrapping my arm around Her in the back of the car, I wiped the curdy drool from Her mouth with my scarf, kissed Her salty, wet forehead, and reassured Her with endless variations of "everything will be all right." As the car passed through Pipli Village, I saw a sign:

DR. NARSINGH PATEL, S.B., B. LITT. (OXON)
S.M. (MOSCOW), M.D. A.V.V.
SPECIALIST IN WOMEN AND OTHER DISEASES
PRACTICE IN INDIA AND ABROAD

Despite Mr. Suryadas's insistence that a good dose of prasad would be more effective than anything a doctor might prescribe, I ordered him to stop. A slimy pink plastic shower curtain was the door to the office, outside of which women with covered faces were squatting, trying to quiet the fitful screaming and weak whimpering of feverish, puking, and thrashing babies. When the physician realized that foreigners had come, he impatiently pushed out his present patient, a pregnant peasant, and cordially invited us in. He offered us tea. My eye followed a fly from the cup's lip to the microscope, to a specimen jar, to the grimy wall, to an oily rag, to a pan in which some sort of human waste cooled, and back to the lip of the cup.

"Drink," the doctor ordered.[6]

5. *Prasāda* (literally "graciousness") refers to food that, having been sanctified by being offered to a deity in devotional rituals, imparts the god's grace to those who eat of it as a gift from that divinity.

6. Get ready for yet another Indian male who speaks like Dr. Gupta and Mr. Indrajit, yet another offensively racist lampoon.

When, prior to describing Her symptoms, Lalita mentioned that Her father was a physician in California, Dr. Patel could hardly contain his delight.

"Oh, I will give you my card so that he can contact me, but please, give me his address and telephone number so that I can consult with him in the meantime. I will put my skills at his service. I will fly to California posthaste, at his beckoning, sparing myself no obstacles in order to assist him and serve his patients. I will be able to treat diseases with which he is not so familiar, such as malaria, pellagra, glanders, morbus Indicus, Calcutta cough, plague, Delhi belly, ischiallgia tropicus, pernicious floccillation, elephantiasis. . . ."

Impatient for Lalita to be given treatment, I interrupted, "We don't see a lot of elephantiasis in Los Angeles, and so . . ."

"Exactly," the doctor interrupted my interruption, "but all of these diseases are headed west. Europe imagined a conquest of India, but now, I am sorry to be the one who must inform you, is the time for you to pay for the spoils of the colonialism enjoyed by your forefathers. All of these Indian diseases will colonize the West just as the West colonized India. This is . . ."

I interrupted his interruption of my interruption: "But Dr. Gupta is a gynecologist, and I somehow doubt an outbreak of vaginal elephantiasis . . ."

And, of course, he interrupted my interruption of his interruption of my interruption: "I am also a woman specialist. There is blennorrhea Indica, popularly known as *kamakanduti* in Oriya or Kama's Itch in Oxford English; there is vulvitus Himalayus, herpes Zoroaster, and the like. But in all cases, all diseases, like all human beings, are generated and developed in utero. All diseases, in the beginning, are venereal diseases. Sexual intercourse is hazardous to health. 'Safe sex' is a contradiction in terms. This is not simply a medical fact, but an ethical, moral, and spiritual one as well. Thus the great Mahatma Gandhi asked India to be continent.[7] Furthermore, the great sages of old . . ."

And so I interrupted his interruption of my interruption of his interruption of my interruption of his interruption: "We would be happy

7. "Once the idea," Gandhi wrote, "that the only and grand function of the sexual organ is generation possesses men and women, they will hold union for any other purpose as a criminal waste of the vital fluid. It is easy to understand why the professors of old have put so much value upon the vital fluid and why they have insisted upon its transmutation into the highest form of energy" (*To the Women* [Karachi, 1943]).

to arrange for you to set up practice with Dr. Gupta, but first let's treat his daughter. That will please him greatly."

Patel examined the bile She vomited into the pan where the fly had been resting only minutes earlier, as well as samples of Her urine and sputum. I thought it odd that he mixed these substances together, but he explained, as he scraped some of the mixture onto a microscope slide, that it would save time and that the important thing was "not where the disease is, but what it is."

> R$_x$: No meat, nor fish, nor foul, no spices, nor garlic, nor onion, no liqueurs, nor wine, nor beer, and, most important, no sexual intercourse of any kind until first full moon preceding Shravan. And afterwards intercourse on restricted basis, for fertilization purposes only. In addition, one patent-pending Patel Palette Pellet a day, before bedtime, which is to say thirty-one, no more, no less.

"The prognosis is excellent," Dr. Patel smiled confidently. "Diarrhea and vomiting will be gone in one month, by the time of the auspicious first night of Shravan, coconut day, Shiv Poojan, and especially auspiciously, Raksha Bandhan."

I promised to make all the arrangements with Dr. Gupta, the United States Immigration Department, the American Medical Association, and the California Board of Exotic and Tropical Gynecology for Dr. Patel to set up practice in Artesia before the new year.

"But please do not try to contact Dr. Gupta until that time," I carefully added. "He is very devoted, like all Indian fathers, and would be very troubled if he were to suspect that his daughter, my dear wife, might be ill."

"I understand," he smiled sympathetically. He must have actually believed that he would soon be practicing in California as he refused to accept payment for either his services or the pellets that we, in any case, threw out of the window of the car as we pulled off.

Waving good-bye, Patel shouted out as loudly as he could, "Remember, no sexual intercourse of any kind!"

When we got back to the hotel, I had to push Indrajit aside, ignoring his "only seventeen thousand rupees and everything is okay," to get Her to the toilet in our room. I just couldn't picture either Rajiv or Sonia Gandhi sitting on that same archaic porcelain fixture.

I left Her, tucked in our bed, to go to buy medicine from one of the many little wooden stands run by the government of Orissa in Puri that sell ganja and opium. I rolled a tola of opium into little balls for Lalita to swallow.

Despite a sudden rainstorm, Mr. Suryadas showed up with both Jagannath prasad, wrapped in a banana leaf, and his rotund wife, wrapped in a yellow sari. Requesting to be alone with Lalita, Mrs. Suryadas told Her about the great Shri Shri Babaji, whose very touch, if not glance, could cure anyone of anything. Lalita, to my dismay, urgently wanted to go to his ashram. He was, the believer had said, 175 years old—the same age, I noted, that Captain Richard Burton would be if he were still alive.

A. TRANSLATION (3)

Even while encouraging her lover to make love to her, the girl should initially feign a reluctance to touch his linga or to expose her yoni. She should demurely permit him to believe, however, that her passion for him is tempting her to do unmentionable intimate things with him, things that she has never done before.

B. COMMENTARY (3)

B.O.N.E. Railway Hotel, Puri
Full Moon [July 20]
Guru Purnima

Mr. Indrajit, offering to permit me to give him a mere sixteen thousand rupees for my wedding gift, noted that it was definitely his last offer.

"Ten," I smiled, and as he walked off down the open corridor, I saw him strike the "lowly bloody" with the back of his hand as he yelled at the top of his voice, *"Car-sau-bis!"*

Mr. Suryadas knew the way to Babaji's jungle ashram. He was a sort of devotee, informing us that "Babaji is not only the world's oldest man, he is also the world's happiest man. The committee of the *Guinness Book of Records* has been notified."

Although the rain had stopped in the middle of the night, the road was so muddy that, all too long before we reached our destination, it was necessary to leave the car behind and forge into the jungle on foot with our shoes in our hands. Needing to stop to use the bushes, Lalita ignored Mr. Suryadas's suggestion that she squat in the open. "When there is rain, the snakes come out of their burrows, which have filled up with water. They are in every bush." A little privacy seemed to Her well worth risking Her life.

The rain had brought out not only snakes, but snails as well: I watched one following in the slime of another and plucked them both from the moist trunk of their trysting tree to take them, as promised, back for Professor Christopher Cross. Mr. Suryadas put them in an empty paan-masala tin for safekeeping.

"*Namaste* Shri Shri Shri Babaji," I said, with the requisite putting together of my hands, to the tiny, hairless, relatively fair being, who wore only a strip of pink cloth; it went between his barely existent buttocks, came around his waist, and then was tied in an elaborate knot that concealed his genitals. The guru corrected me:

"Only two Shris, please. Just Shri Shri Babaji."

Mr. Suryadas thought it was a miracle that he knew, without being told, that we had come for a cure for the girl; I was less impressed given that Lalita vomited again on the threshold of the ashram. Invited in, we were directed to the shrine in which he lived and was worshiped. He motioned for Her to sit cross-legged before and like him, and closing his eyes, he began to mutter mantras:

phrum phruh phuh phuh prah phat phrah phat phruh phuh phruh prah phrah phat namah phrum phruh phuh phuh prah phat phrah phat phruh phuh phruh prah phrah phat namah phrum phruh phuh phuh prah phat phrah phat phruh phuh phruh prah phrah phat namah phrum phruh phuh phuh prah phat phrah phat phruh phuh phruh prah phrah phat namah phrum phruh phuh phuh prah phat phrah phat phruh phuh phruh prah phrah phat namah phrum phruh phuh phuh prah phat phrah phat phruh phuh phruh prah phrah phat namah phrum phruh phuh phuh prah phat phrah phat phruh phuh phruh prah phrah phat namah phrum phruh phuh phuh prah phat phrah phat phruh phuh phruh prah phrah phat namah phrum phruh phuh phuh prah phat phrah phat phruh phuh phruh prah phrah phat namah phrum phruh phuh phuh prah phat phrah phat phruh phuh phruh prah phrah phat namah phrum phruh phuh phuh prah phat phrah phat phruh phuh phruh prah phrah phat namah phrum phruh phuh phuh prah phat phrah phat phruh phuh phruh prah phrah phat namah phrum phruh phuh phuh prah phat phrah phat phruh phuh phruh prah phrah phat namah phrum phruh phuh phuh prah phat phrah phat phruh phuh phruh prah phrah phat namah phrum phruh phuh phuh prah phat phrah phat phruh phuh phruh prah phrah phat namah phrum phruh phuh phuh prah phat phrah phat phruh phuh phruh prah phrah phat namah phrum phruh phuh phuh prah phat phrah phat phruh phuh phruh prah phrah phat namah phrum phruh phuh phuh prah phat phrah phat phruh phuh phruh prah phrah phat namah phrum phruh phuh phuh prah phat phrah phat phruh phuh phruh prah phrah phat namah phrum phruh phuh phuh prah phat phrah phat phruh phuh phruh prah phrah phat namah phrum phruh phuh phuh prah phat phrah phat phruh phuh phruh prah phrah phat namah phrum phruh phuh phuh prah phat phrah phat phruh phuh phruh prah phrah phat namah phrum phruh phuh phuh prah phat phrah phat phruh phuh phruh prah phrah phat namah phrum phruh phuh phuh prah phat phrah phat phruh phuh phruh prah phrah phat namah phrum phruh phuh phuh prah phat phrah phat phruh phuh phruh prah phrah phat namah phrum phruh phuh phuh prah phat phrah phat phruh phuh phruh prah phrah phat namah phrum phruh

And on and on and on and on and on and on and on and on and on,
and then he drew images and wrote in Devanagari script on the palm
of Her right hand and sole of Her right foot. He tied amulets and beads
around Her wrists, ankles, knees, elbows, and neck. He pulverized roots
and leaves and berries and chalky chunks of various minerals with a brass
mortar and pestle, mixed them in a gourd bowl, poured in oil, milk, and
I don't know what else, dipped his finger in the brew, dabbed Her
tongue, cheeks, forehead, neck, shoulders, and big toes with it, took a
sip himself, closed his eyes, muttered more mantras (this time too softly
to be heard), and then directed Lalita to drink the rest of the potion.

He jumped up, pulling Lalita with him, smiled at me, and spoke
in impeccable English:

"The young lady is quite cured. There may be a bit of vomiting and
diarrhea as her body must dispose of the remnants of the pollution, but
by nightfall she will be fit as a fiddle."

He lit the chillum, took a modest puff, passed it to me, and directed
Lalita to explore the ashram.

"You will find deer, peacocks and hens, mynas and parrots, naughty
monkeys, and maybe Nagin will show her head. If she spreads her
hood, just step back; do not bother her and you will be safe. It is a beautiful and peaceful place. It is for your pleasure. Please, enjoy it.

"Suryadas-ji, my son, please, take the chillum and go sit over there
and rest. I want to converse with this gentleman alone," Babaji said in
English, then shifted into an Oriya I could not understand. Then,
turning back to me, he reverted to our common language.

"It is indeed a unique pleasure to receive a native English speaker.
Many years ago I was the language teacher at the village school and had
the obligation and opportunity to converse in English on a daily basis
with my students. I rarely speak English, a language that I truly love,
these days; visitors from abroad do not come here. Of course I read."

He told me that John Donne was his favorite poet and then
abruptly changed the topic of conversation by bluntly asking me why
I was with Lalita.

"I love Her."

"No," He smiled. "No. No, you most certainly do not, although I do
understand why you say that you do. But please, do let me note what
is obvious, that she is, alas, not the appropriate young lady for you, and
you are, most definitely, not the gentleman for her. While I do not
doubt that this erotic caprice affords a bit of divertissement in an all-
too-unamusing world, you do not love her and she does not love you."

He leaned forward to place his hand on my knee. "I discern from the expression on your face that you do not believe me. What motive could I have for telling you anything other than the truth? I would suggest that you consider abandoning your efforts to possess the girl for her sake, but even more so for your own sake. You are not meant for each other. This is not some prognostic utterance on my part—I am simply saying what is simply and absolutely obvious. May I have a cigarette?"

Although disappointed that I did not have Virginia tobacco, he settled for one of my Charminars, lit it, and asked me why I had come to India. After listening patiently to my story, smoking and smiling kindly as he did, he spoke.

"The *Kamasutra*. Oh yes, of course I know it, although I have not actually read it as it is hardly the sort of literary exercise that interests me. Are you interested in the girl because of the *Kamasutra*, or the *Kamasutra* because of the girl? Don't tell me your answer, please. That is not for me to know. But there is perhaps some value in the asking of it. Don't you agree?"

Lalita returned with smiles and stories about the deer that She had seen in the back garden. He looked intently at Her.

"You are a very lovely young girl," he said to Her. "But, of course, that is obvious." Escorting us to the gate, he reminded Lalita that She had been healed and then asked me for 101 rupees for that cure.

"I'm not certain as to the actual dynamics of it, but somehow the money activates the mantras and yantras. They simply don't work without it."

A. TRANSLATION (4)

If a girl loves a man, or wants him to believe that she does, she will manifest the characteristics of love as defined by a consensus of professors of amatoriology: a desire to give all of oneself to the beloved; a desire to possess for oneself all of the beloved; a feeling of pleasure over whatever pleases the beloved; and a feeling of sorrow over whatever saddens the beloved.

B. COMMENTARY (4)

B.O.N.E. Railway Hotel, Puri
Third Night of the Dark Half of Ashadha [July 22]
My Birthday

The snails, I suspect, have mated, and Lalita is feeling better, better than better; actually She is completely cured, but just in case it was contagious, and because I am not protected by Guru-ji's mantras and yantras, I am continuing the opium treatment on myself, but I am taking care not to let the drug weaken my resolve to give Mr. Indrajit no more than ten thousand rupees. Today his pitch was rather pathetic.

"What can I do, sir? The mother of Mohan, Shyam, and Winston supplicates me to allow our blessed family to suffer miserably on your behalf. Suffering, according to *Bhagavadgita,* she reminds me, will make us even more humble, blessed, and excellent than we already are. It is all agreed—fifteen thousand rupees only."

"Ten," I said for the tenth time.

Lalita attributes Her cure to the guru and Indian magic, while I ascribe it to white blood cells and good luck; Mr. Suryadas adds that, in either case, the Jagannath prasad helped. He arrived with flowers for Her just as I was leaving the hotel on foot for the STD booth. I wanted to telephone Sophia so that she could sing "Happy Birthday" to me. I did not tell Lalita that it's my birthday.

After listening to Sophia's laconic, frostily voiced recording—"If you're calling for Professor Roth, he is in India and will not be back until August. Urgent messages can be left on his office machine: (213) 462-5967"—I responded, "My darling, Sophie, I miss you terribly. It's my birthday today and I need to hear your voice. I need to hear you say that you love me. My work is going very well, but it's not worth being away from the woman I love, that I have always loved, that I will always love. I have to tell you something. I want to tell you that . . ." A beep, indicating the end of the tape, finished the call, and the grinning phone-wallah wanted the same amount of money as the guru had charged for the mantras and yantras.

Mr. Suryadas had planned a picnic for us at a beach some ten kilometers to the south of Puri. He packed plenty of Jagannath prasad for us to eat and bhang lassi to drink. I brought Indian gin and opium. An extraordinary thing happened, something that had initially promised to be absolutely without interest.

"We will stop just ahead at a religious shrine," Mr. Suryadas insisted. "Very unusual god."

Sick and tired of gods, I urged our dear driver to pass the deity by, but Mr. Suryadas, deaf as usual to the needs or wishes of his employer, took a side road to a clearing near the beach, where there was a most bizarre bronze idol adorned with flower garlands and looming grandly over recently offered trays of coconut, jasmine, and bananas. This god, much to my utter astonishment and to the ultimate affirmation of my conviction that anything, absolutely anything, can happen in India, turned out to be one familiar to me. I read the bronze plaque at the base of the statue:

BRIGADE-MAJOR FRANCIS WHITE OF THE BENGAL LANCERS

1845–1919

CHAMPION OF THE INDIAN WOMAN

FOUGHT AGAINST THE INJUSTICES OF
CHILD MARRIAGE   TEMPLE PROSTITUTION   WIDOW BURNING
DEFENDED INDIA AND EMPIRE AGAINST ALL ENEMIES
DE GUSTIBUS OMNIA EST DISPUTANDUM

The massive metal monument, with its patina of time and grime, glazed by the smoke of offerings and relatively unsmirched by bird shit, cut a majestic figure. He was about twelve feet tall and, although dressed in his military uniform, he wore a polo helmet.

"*Angrijhi* avatar of God," Mr. Suryadas smiled as he placed his hands together and made obeisance to my grandfather-in-law.

The cult that had grown up around this idol consisted, according to Mr. Suryadas, entirely of barren women. They made offerings to the statue, washed its feet, and then drank that water as it dripped from the bronze cavalry boots into an English tea cup. The keeper of the shrine was a very old woman, Mr. Suryadas explained, a hermit crone who made it her solemn duty to clean the statue, perform the puja, offer the incense, and sing bhajans to the English deity. Mr. Suryadas pointed to what looked like an abandoned bungalow down closer to the beach. We made our way toward it and the hag, who seemed old enough to be Guru-ji's mother. She grinned a toothless greeting as her eyes darted from Lalita to me, to Lalita and back to me, with extraordinary eagerness and delight. As she babbled in Oriya, Mr. Suryadas translated for us:

"She says she will help the girl to bear many sons. She wants you to drink tea, saying sorry that she has no brandy, but adding that you can smoke a chillum with her. I think she is quite insane. She is telling me that in her childhood she had union with God, with this Hindu God from England."

She suddenly spoke in English. "I want you happy, Master."

I made a wild guess: "Moorullee?"

She cackled, clapped her hands, and lunged forward to throw her arms around me.

B.O.N.E. Railway Hotel, Puri
Fourth Night of the Dark Half of Ashadha [July 23]

Mr. Indrajit has come down another thousand rupees. He attributed the phrase "the quality of mercy is not strange" to the *Bhagavadgita* and claimed that the *Kamasutra* says that no person who is not generous with his money will ever find happiness in love.

B.O.N.E. Railway Hotel, Puri
Fifth Night of the Dark Half of Ashadha [July 24]

I had just put fresh leaves in the can for the snails when I heard footsteps outside on the veranda. I knew it was Her—footsteps have a voice; the feet have a language; I can identify in the sound of them a message—the pace, force, and rhythm tell me that She loves me. I love you. Again She said it. Again. Again I said it. Again. Again. Again we said it. Again. I try not to force the three sounds, but to feel them coming, to keep them down as they rise up in my throat, prolonging the verbal ejaculation, holding it back until it can be contained no longer, until it erupts from my lips: *I LOVE YOUUUUU-UUUUUUUUUUUU....* The silence. Then I have a cigarette and, lying in bed next to Her, I blow smoke rings. I explain to Her, in a professorial manner that She seems to have gradually come to enjoy, that as lovers we must establish our own intimate, flexible, and open language to utter the I-love-you, an efflorescent language allowed to generate itself as we become closer and closer, a living language grounded in physiology and energized by desire with a mutual and private semantic based not on lexical significations, but on subtle fluctuations in intensity and inflection, stress and pitch, timbre and tone, duration and cadence, shifting nasalizations, sibilations, and aspirations: "I love you."

TRANSLATION (5)

Auddalaki says:

> Once a hunter who had trapped his prey
> Felt free to turn his head away,
> Certain that his kill was dead;
> Then the prey bit off the hunter's head.

So too:

> "The girl's seduced," might think a man
> And then relax his seductive plan,
> Stop practicing the seduction art;
> Then that girl may well bite out his heart.

B. COMMENTARY (5)

Shvetababa Regal Hotel, Bhubaneshvar
Seventh Night of the Dark Half of Ashadha [July 26]

She awakened me with embraces and kisses in demonstration of Her mastery, summa cum laude, of the delicate arts of love. We ignored the knocking on the door.

As I emerged from the shower, leaving Her behind so that She might finish washing Her luxuriant hair, I heard the knocking on the door again and was not surprised that it was Mr. Indrajit.

"My good wife and constant helpmeet insists that I act on behalf of the people of India in this matter. She compares our unfortunate deadlock to Indo-American relations over Kashmir. Only compromise, she wisely reminds me, can, according to *Bhagavadgita,* grant us peace. Thus I am prepared to accept at this time, despite everything, twelve thousand rupees."

"Ten."

We were loading our bags into Mr. Suryadas's car when Mr. Indrajit appeared for the last time.

"Did not all of the great sages and rishis of Jagannath Puri of old take vows of poverty? Pandit Vatsyayan himself gave away all of his possessions and the great wealth he had accumulated because of the popularity of *Kamasutra* in order to practice *sannyas.* He didn't care a nit or a needle about fame and fortune. I need not even mention the excellent Mahatma Gandhi, in his simple loincloth, with no wealth save his peace of mind, spinning wheel, eyeglasses, and copy of *Bhagavadgita.* Thus, my humble wedding gift to you turns out to be a magnificent and spiritual gift to me, if you follow my drifting, sir. You have given me the gift of poverty. Here is your *Kamasutra,* sir. I will allow you to give me that paltry ten thousand rupees of mine."

I took the manuscript and handed over the cash.

On the way to Bhubaneshvar, where Lalita and I would get a plane back to Delhi, Mr. Suryadas asked with irrepressible good cheer if we liked "Jews."

"Yes" seemed an appropriate answer.

"Tell me about your favorite Jew, please."

"Well I don't really have a favorite," I replied. "Moses is an ever popular one. I like him. And of course there's Jesus, Freud, and Sammy Davis Jr. I liked my father, he was a Jew. How about you? Do you have a favorite Jew?"

"Yes, of course!" he beamed with enthusiasm and delight. "The best Jew in India is right here in Orissa! My favorite Jew! Would you like to see this great Jew? I will take you to the Jew! Please! I love the Jew. You will love the Jew. I must take you to the Jew!"

It was not until just before we arrived, when Mr. Suryadas happened to mention that we would see tigers, elephants, and "jebras" at the "Jew," that I realized he had been talking about the "zoo" as best as he could in a language lacking a zee.

The first cage to which he dragged us housed his favorite exhibition, two Bengal tigers, which were dozing under the oppressive sway of the afternoon heat. He enthusiastically pointed to the set of very large metal placards that had been painted with the same message in various languages and several scripts—Oriya, Hindi, German, French, Japanese, Zemblan, and English:

> This is a home of two royal tigers *(Panthera tigris)*. Their names are Shah Jahan and Mumtaz Mahal after a great love story of India. Like Mumtaz Mahal woman of Taj Mahal fame and all woman in home, this Mumtaz Mahal tiger lady was behind bars of cage. Shah Jahan King of Jungle was a wild beast roaming the world free. He came to zoo at night. When he saw beautiful Mumtaz Mahal in this cage, it was a love at first site. Shah Jahan jumped over this same fence into this cage to be with the tiger lady he loves. King of Jungle gave up freedom for love. These tigers are living monuments of love.

Shvetababa Regal Hotel, Bhubaneshvar
Eighth Night of the Dark Half of Ashadha [July 27]

Sitting on the bed in our new hotel room, I slowly unwrapped the yellow cloth bundle that contained the portion of the *Kamasutra* manuscript. Lalita looked at each of the palm leaves, handling them with care.

"They're beautiful," She said softly. "So beautiful. Can I have one?"

"Yes," I said, putting my arm around Her waist, pulling Her close to me, pushing my face through Her hair to kiss the back of Her neck. "Take as many as You like. Take them all."

"No, just one. And not yet," She smiled, and there were very slight tears in the corners of Her eyes. "I want to think about it. I want to look at them again before I decide."

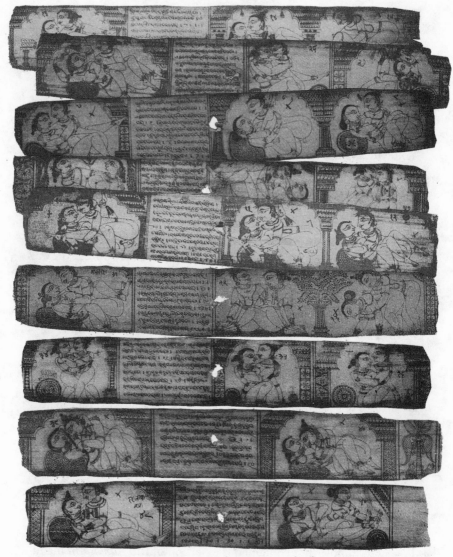

"I'm crazy about you," I said. "And I don't use the word 'crazy' lightly."

As She undressed, She confessed that She had fallen in love with India.

"I have to thank you Leo, for bringing me here and teaching me things about India. That never seemed important to me before. Maybe it isn't really important, but it's pleasing. I can't believe it, but I really do love India."

Later, naked except for Her silver anklets and bracelets, finger and toe rings, belts and necklaces, protected by all Her amulets and with Her back to me, she looked out through the window at the early evening sky.

"See how beautiful it is. Maybe we were here a thousand years ago. Maybe we were lovers in a previous life. I've started to feel that, that I've been in India before. And it feels good."

When she turned around, I realized that She was wearing a new nose ring: it was connected to Her earring by a delicate silver chain.

The room grew darker and darker and we did not turn on the lights. Clouds concealed the moon and constellations. We did not speak. She disappeared in the darkness.

India was in my arms, entwining me in Her arms, as manifold as those of any of Her wild erotic goddesses, and when I let go, India clung to me, shook, pulled me closer, so close that while I was aware that I was simultaneously inside and outside of Her, India, breathing the ancient fragrance of India, I did not know where the borders were. India was above me, pinning my shoulders to the bed, then below, opening wider and wider to receive me deeper and deeper, stretching and straining to incorporate what was left of me, in front of me, then below again, rolling and turning in time to the music of jingling anklets, girdle bells, and bracelets, the jubilant erotic anthem of an ancient civilization of dreams. Sweat-wet and breathless, I explored the land, surveyed and excavated Her, and, like the quicksand that in *The Curse of Kali* swallowed up the tiger hunter in the pith helmet, I was inhumed by the dark, heated, moist, fleshy earth. I was in India for the first time.

When I woke up, Lalita was sitting on the edge of the bed, still naked, looking through the palm leaves.

"This one," She said. "I want this one."

She smiled. "Yes, this one. I want this one. It will always remind me of you. And it will always remind me of this trip. I'll keep it always. It will always remind me of you and of India."

It was the happiest moment of my life.

That's not really true, but that's how it felt at the time.

E. The Kill

I want to go home. I want to lead a normal life. I want to be free now. I think I've suffered enough. My only crime was that I fell in love with the wrong person. I was guilty of that, but I didn't know what was going on. Sometimes you don't understand what you're doing when you're in love. I've been punished. I've paid for that love. Will the people who read this be able to help me? I want to leave India. I want to go home.

—Theresa Berkeley, "American Women behind Foreign Bars,"
People (April 1997)

1. SCYLLA (OLD DELHI)

A. TRANSLATION

There are eight formal modes of union, ways in which a man takes possession of a girl. These, as categorized by the venerable professors of the seductionary sciences according to the statuses of the beings who practice them, form a spectrum from the most sacred to the most profane types of union[1]:

1) *Brahma:* A hieratic (nonamatoric) form of matrimony, as

1. Pralayānanga explains that the first four modes of union are consecrated around the external Vedic fire and are, by virtue of those lustral flames, sacred; the second four, on the other hand, are consecrated only by an internal erotic fire and are, by virtue of that carnal fever, profane. He maintains that sacred and profane are binarily opposed categories. This is contrary to the so-called spectrum of erotic sacrality defined by Vātsyāyana as interpreted, wrongly I think, by Roth, in which sacred and profane are relative, mutually dependent and reflexive terms. All of the theorists and commentators share a common analytic impulse and assumption, however: there is a chaotic passion which, when ordered and controlled through classification and codification, becomes love. In other words, love cannot exist without taxonomy or hierarchy.

practiced by gods and prescribed by the Veda, in which a father solemnly offers his daughter to a male, who duly accepts her and owes nothing for her. It is the most sublime form of union.

2) *Prajapatya:* An aristocratic (contramorganatic) form of alliance, as practiced by descendants of the creator and sanctified by the Veda, in which a father, for political purposes, offers his daughter to a gentleman without receiving any fee, but in expectation of social amity.

3) *Arsha:* An ancestral (antimiscegenational) form of marriage, as practiced by ancient seers and sacerdotal poets and condoned by the Veda, in which a father presents his daughter to a man of an appropriate family and lineage in exchange for a bull and a cow (or equivalent dowry).

4) *Daiva:* An astrologically determined (biofatidic) form of coverture, as practiced by Brahmins and legitimated by the Veda, in which a father ritually offers his daughter to a priest during a sacrificial liturgy.

5) *Gandharva:* An operatic (erotonoetic) form of concubinage, as practiced by heavenly musicians (and their representatives on earth—singers and dancers, poets and artists, courtesans and men-about-town) and ignored by the Veda, in which a man and a girl give themselves to one another by mutual consent, freely and without concern for gods or priests, kings or parents, other spouses or other lovers.

6) *Asura:* A commercial (transesurientic) form of marriage, as practiced by opponents of the gods, in disregard of the Veda, in which a father sells his daughter to any man who has enough cash to afford her.

7) *Paishacha:* A fiendish (malovulturine) form of union, as practiced by ghouls and vampires and censured by the Veda, in which a man fucks a girl who is drunk, drugged, asleep, or insane.[2]

8) *Rakshasa:* A deviant (hyperpredacitic) form of rape, as practiced by demons, in derision of the Veda, in which a man kidnaps a girl. It is the most vulgar mode of union.

2. Pralayānanga includes necrophilia as a profane *paiśaca* practice, but adds that in Tantric ritual, by virtue of intent, necrophilia (e.g., sexual union with mutilated or partially incinerated corpses in cremation grounds at night on inauspicious days) has the karmic impact of the sacred *brahma* marriage.

B. COMMENTARY

Premsagar Guest House
Kamnagar, New Delhi
New Moon, Ashadha/Shravan [August 3/4]
Shiva Puja/Lalita Puja

"Lalita, consider an immodest proposal: let us say that I were to offer you[3] a consummately joyous experience of total fulfillment, an uninterrupted, eternal pleasure in complete and perfect Love, the very state that lovers, in India and the West, have always, at least in literature, maintained as their ultimate object. And to have it, to have it all, perfect Love and the perfection that results from that Love, all you have to do is surrender. But—and here's the catch—the surrender must be complete, a total submission of will, the absolute dedication of your entire being to the beloved, like an ancient Indian wife or an ecstatic saint madly in Love with a god. Of course, you must trust the beloved as the saint trusts the god. You must not be afraid of vulnerability, pain, madness, or death. There must be no compromises. You must trust and believe that the beloved accepts responsibility for your soul, takes charge of your body and being, out of Love for you. For the sake of your apotheosis, your happiness, I will make all decisions for you. I will be your self. I will dedicate my life to giving meaning and grace to your life. Now imagine that at the exact moment that I take your soul from you, you take mine from me, that you allow me to surrender my entire being to you, that you make all decisions for me, dedicate your whole being, without compromise, to my joy. Simultaneously and without reserve we adopt each other, all of each other. We become each other. No you. No me. Only an Us. We no longer have any sense of ourselves as individuals. All will is obliterated by Love. All we have to do is, simultaneously, and motivated by nothing other than the happiness of the other, who manifests the Us, surrender all personal desire, all wish and sense of need. All we have to do is abdicate our bounded souls. All we have to do to have it all is to give all. Would you do that for Love? If I offered that Love, that joy, to you, if I offered you that bargain, would you take it?"

"No," Lalita laughed. "No, of course not."

"Yes, of course not. No, of course not. Nobody would. They do it

---

3. Note that at this point Roth stops capitalizing the pronominal references to Ms. Gupta.

in books, but not in life. Never. That Love, that great, great Love that everyone, everywhere, at all times always wants, dreams of, and writes about is utterly and sadly impossible."

"I really don't understand what you're talking about, Leo," she said quite sincerely and then jumped up from the bed and pulled off the white kurta in which she now always slept. Standing completely naked before me, she reiterated her love for India. "I can't believe we're going back. I wish I could stay. But I'm going to come back. I don't know when, but I know I am. India is amazing. It's wonderful. By the way, Leo, I was wondering about something. What would people at the university say if they found out about us? I mean what would your chairman and colleagues do if they knew about us, if they realized what the summer study in India program had really been about?"

"They would, no doubt, charge me with sexual harassment, but I would defend myself on the grounds that we only became lovers once we were in India, and in India, at least before it was corrupted by Western influences, sexual harassment between students and teachers could only even be imagined as a matter of a student seducing a teacher, never the other way around. Anything the teacher does is, in India, by virtue of the fact that he is a teacher, right and good, legitimate and of some (although perhaps not always immediately discernable) pedagogical value. There are no stories of teachers seducing their students in Indian literature, but there are lots of tales of cunning Indian girls seducing their teachers—Auddalaki and Vijaya, Yashodhara and Jayamangala, Pralayananga and Mayavati to name but a few. In Indian terms, my dear Lalita, you are the harasser and I am the harassed, the hapless victim of your seductive beauty, an innocent casualty of love."

"And what about your wife? What would she do if she knew about us?"

"A traditional Indian wife, I explained, "would accept anything that made me happy. She would take you into our home and care for you as well as for me."

"I love India!" she laughed. She wanted to spend the last day in India by herself, shopping for Indian clothes, jewelry, fabrics, Indian souvenirs for herself, and Indian gifts (sweets, incense, chutneys, videos) for her parents and Indian relatives: "Indian stuff they can't get in America."

She was in the shower when the phone rang.

"Is Lalita there?"

"Who's this?"

"My name is Paul, Paul Rothberg."

"No, I'm sorry. Ms. Gupta has returned to America. She's in Chicago. She went back several days ago, for her wedding to some professional basketball player, I believe."

"Oh, I'm sorry to hear that. I mean I hoped to see her again. I mean I'm sorry to hear about that for my sake, but I'm being selfish, I guess. I mean that's great, if that's what she wants. Yes, I'm happy for her, if she's happy. She's such a wonderful person. Is this Professor Roth?"

"Yes."

"Well, I would really like to have the opportunity to meet you, if you have any time to spare. Lalita told me so much about you. She told my how brilliant you are, how many books about India you've read. She said that you're fluent in Sanskrit too."

"Lalita never mentioned meeting you."

He laughed. "Well, in any case, I'd really love to get together with you to discuss India. I'm trying to learn Sanskrit. It's not that easy! I've worked my way through *Teach Yourself Sanskrit,* and I've bought Wackernagel's *Altindische Grammatik* and, of course, Monier-Williams's wonderful *Sanskrit-English Dictionary* so I could start reading. I've just finished the *Bhagavadgita*—it is such a great book when you read in the original, right on the mark—and I would really appreciate any suggestions as to what I should read next. What about the *Kamasutra?*"

"No, no. Read the *Ratisutra* of Jayamangala. I've really got to go now," I snapped, anxious to hang up because the sound of the running shower water in the bathroom had stopped. "Good-bye, Mr. Ruthberg."

"If you don't have time now, maybe we can meet in L.A. I'm coming there soon for the International Conference on AIDS in the Third World.[4] Are you going to participate? There are lots of South Asia panels. It's going to be really great. Not just one of those conferences where professors deliver academic papers that nobody, except maybe one or two other specialists, cares about. As one of the organizers, I can assure you that the people involved are really motivated about getting important things done."

"Good-bye," I repeated, hanging up just as Lalita, wrapped in the towel that said Premsagar on it, emerged from the bathroom. I watched her dress herself in a beautiful red, gold-embroidered salwar-

4. Ironically, the conference was held in Los Angeles at the Hollywood Holiday Inn during the very week in which Roth was murdered.

kameez. Promising me that she was going to buy a surprise gift for me, Lalita playfully threw me kiss from the doorway. I didn't know what to do with myself after she left, but I showered and dressed and left the room as if I had somewhere to go.

I don't understand how it is possible: as I left the guest house, Mr. Jain (who had, upon our return from Orissa, expressed his happiness over the fact that my "deceased wife" was "feeling so much better") held up a postcard to me, which he had obviously read.

"Your mail is from an Indian woman in America. She loves you very much, Professor. Perhaps you will have the opportunity to marry her as well. Two wives, three wives—what's the difference?"

"An Indian woman?" I asked myself out loud as I reached to yank the card from his clutches.

"Yes, a Miss Maya of Los Angeles. Maya is an Indian name. It is a divine name."

How could she have found out my address here? Only Sophia and Saighal know where I'm staying. It doesn't make any sense.

I decided to go to the bar at the Viceroy Hotel to kill time while Lalita shopped. Until I heard them speaking French, I couldn't place the two familiar women at a nearby table sharing a bottle of Chevalier de Seingalt champagne and complaining that it was *dégoûtant*. I introduced myself and said, "Didn't I see you in the Kam Sootra Bar in Gwalior and also in the restaurant at the Victoria and Albert Hotel in Varanasi?"

Confessing that they didn't remember me, but adding that, yes, they had indeed been in both of those places, they invited me to sit down, and one of them asked if, like them, I was on my first visit to India.

"Oh, no, no, I come here often, I'm an Indologist. . . ."

Uninterested in knowing anything about me, one of them interrupted to explain in tedious detail what they did as stenographers in Lyons and to complain about India.

"We 'ad read zee famouse *Kamasootra* an seen zee photos of zee beautifool lovers on zee temples, an we sought zat Indiya wood be a very romantique place. But, *ooo la la*, what a problem for a woman to travel ear! Zee men are *bêtes*, absolutely, always grabbing and touching. . . ."

As the one of them continued her erotic jeremiad in what she imagined was English, I was shocked at myself: I realized that, although I am happily married and do truly love Sophia, and although I am also wildly infatuated with Lalita and even married to her in a Gandharvic sense, I suddenly wanted to have a ménage à trois with these women. It occurred to me that maybe I should have studied Provençal and Latin rather than Sanskrit and Hindi, that medieval France, not ancient India, might be the erotic paradise, the kingdom of love, that perhaps I should have been translating the *Tractatus de Amore et de Amoris Remedio* of Andreas Capellanus rather than the *Kamasutra* of Vatsyayana Mallanaga. I picked up their hotel key from the table and jingled it suggestively as I recommended we go up their room.

"*Merde alors!*" the so-far silent of the two sneered. "*Vous aussi! Vas te faire foutre espece de vieux con obsedé comme tous les indiens, comme tous les mecs d'ailleurs!*"

It was obviously time to go. Returning to the Premsagar, only to be informed by Mr. Jain that "your Indian wife has not returned," I went up to the room, fell on the bed, and waited for Lalita. Even though I had only had half a Halcyon, one bottle of Taj Mahal beer, two hits of Kashmiri hash, three pellets of Oriya opium, and four shots of London gin, I must have been drunk, because when I shut my eyes I could have sworn that the darkness there was that of an old theater; I opened my eyes in the middle of a scene from a film in which I was playing the lead:

```
             TAJ MAHAL II: RETURN OF THE MOGUL
                    (Scene: III.E.1)

INT. PREMSAGAR GUEST HOUSE—EARLY EVENING
Extreme close shot. The KAMA SUTRA translated
with a personal commentary by L. A. ROTH on a bed-
side table. A lotus blossom rests on the cover.
The CAMERA slowly pulls back to reveal LALITA
GUPTA naked on the luxurious bed, staring into
the CAMERA with overwhelming desire, tears
rolling from her dark eyes. WIDE SHOT of candle-
lit room reveals the presence of the object of
her passion: LEOPOLD ABRAHAM ROTH. CLOSE ON ROTH
to reveal a sadness. MEDIUM SHOT of LALITA weep-
ing. The CAMERA explores her body from ROTH'S
P.O.V. WIDE SHOT as ROTH moves in closer to
LALITA and begins to stroke her hair, gently and
paternally, affectionately but in no way pas-
sionately. He holds an antique heart-shaped Ori-
ental looking glass.


                        ROTH
        Look at me, and look at yourself. Look into
        this mirror, lovely one. You may be the
```

right girl for me, but I'm not the appropriate man for you. It is obvious. Not only
am I too old for you, there's so much more.

                    LALITA
All You think about is the difference in our
ages, my Beloved. Don't You understand that
I love You? I don't care about Sophia; You
may continue to live with her as her husband; You may even continue to love her. All
I ask is that You continue to let me believe
that You love me too, even a little bit.
Allow me the beautiful illusion. Please, my
Beloved Leo. Try to understand all that I
do, I do for love. And it is You, Leo, who
have taught me how to love.

ROTH hands LALITA a handkerchief and the camera
moves in to reveal LALITA'S name embroidered on
it in Devanagari script. It makes her weep even
more pitifully.

                    ROTH
(wistful)
Try to understand, my child. At your age,
Lalita, you must take care not to have expectations; at my age, I must take care not
to have disappointments.

ROTH turns his back to LALITA. CLOSE SHOT: CAM-
ERA shows that there are slight tears in ROTH'S
eyes.
SITAR MUSIC
                                    DISSOLVE
                              CUT TO REALITY

2. CHARYBDIS (TO THE WEST)

A. TRANSLATION (1)

The *Gandharva* form of erotic union between a man and a girl is, of
all the octadically categorized modes of union, the only one based on
love. It is without promise or compromise. It is the most alluring and
the most perilous. It is a nuptial in which, beyond the desires of the

lovers and the pleasures resulting from consummations of their longings, nothing matters—neither religious scriptures nor social strictures, neither parents nor other spouses or paramours. All authorities and laws, rules and regulations, whether human or divine, are (at least in the moments of union, or in moments, no matter how fleeting, of remembering that union or contemplating its recurrence) irrelevant.

B. COMMENTARY (1)

United Airlines Flight # 1
In Darkness
Somewhere (38,000 feet above the earth)
Sometime (between time zones)

Customs, Immigration and Emigration, Indira Gandhi International Airport, Delhi, India (1:30 A.M.): "Every bag tells a story," the customs official representing the Government of India, consigned to inspect the baggage of all people entering or leaving the country, remarked as his finger pointed purposefully at my carry-on case. And he's quite right, I thought, as I obliged him, opening my bag as if it were a book, opening it to show him that there were no explosives, no black-market money, that this was no tale of international terrorism, no political thriller nor spy novel.

Each object is a word. Two socks are folded into a phrase that, next to underwear, becomes a sentence and is elaborated into a paragraph by shirts and pants. Dirt modifies the shoes. The story tells of the hopes of a traveler (what he brought with him) and of his discoveries (what he takes away). The hermeneutical customs inspector studied the text carefully. He read the labels on my pill bottles with a smirk that mutated into a glower as he lifted up the last of my Kama Sutra condoms. He looked at me, then at Lalita, back at me, and then dropped the little packet back into the paragraph that was my toiletries bag with visible disgust. He dangled the key chain that Lalita had bought for me on her last day's shopping spree—attached to it was a little replica of a statue of lovers at Khajuraho. The exegetical implications were clear: an image which in one context is religious can, in another context, be scurrilous. The principle was applied to my old copy of the *Kamasutra*, the Devanagari title of which he could decipher because of his native knowledge of Hindi. And there were the sixty-four *kamakala* cards, with their depictions of lovers, painted

for me in Patiya village for use in my game. I didn't understand the
agent's rhetorical gloss:

"You are a very big *Kamasutra* person, isn't it so?"

"I'm a professor of Indian studies. I'm translating that classical text."

"Some other Englishman has, I believe, already accomplished that.
Where is your camera?"

"I don't have a camera," I announced, and although I don't understand why the question should have warranted defensive testimony, I
explained that I don't like to take photographs in India. "They distort
the more real and important pictures that I have in my head. And visual images of India, stripped as they are of their accompanying
sounds, smells, and physical sensations, lie."

Apparently not listening to what I was saying, he picked up my
weighty Monier-Williams *Sanskrit-English Dictionary,* muttering
something about "coals to Newcastle" (which was nonsense since the
book was both composed and published in Oxford), and slowly flipped
through the 1359 pages of it, presumably not to brush up on his Sanskrit vocabulary.

He dropped the dictionary and turned to this notebook, the very
text that you, right now, are holding in your hands, and, after asking
me what it was, listened to my explanation that it was my translation
of Book Three of the *Kamasutra* ("hence the Sanskrit text and dictionary") together with "a commentary in journal form." He opened it at
random, toward the back, reading what you must have read not too
long ago:

> India was in my arms, entwining me in Her arms, as manifold as those
> of any of Her wild erotic goddesses, and when I let go, India clung to me,
> shook, pulled me closer, so close that while I was aware that I was simul-
> taneously inside and outside of Her, India, breathing the ancient fragrance
> of India, I did not know where the borders were. India was above me, pin-
> ning my shoulders to the bed, then below, opening wider and wider to re-
> ceive me deeper and deeper, stretching and straining to incorporate what
> was left of me, in front of me, then below again, rolling and turning in time
> to the music of jingling anklets, girdle bells, and bracelets.

"Did you write this thing?" he questioned, and I confessed. What
had sounded meaningful to me in the state that I wrote it, late at night,
a little drunk, in a lyrical mood, with Lalita naked and asleep in the bed
under a mosquito net, now, by the fluorescent light of the hall in the
Indira Gandhi airport, was embarrassing.

He signaled to another, more senior exegete to help him interpret the text. The older man, whose more elaborate uniform indicated a more advanced status, came and was handed the book with a whisper in the ear. He continued the reading and then, upon turning the page, asked, "And what is this?"

"It's a palm leaf, a page from an Oriya manuscript of part of the *Kamasutra*. I have eighteen of them, stuck in between pages of the notebook to protect them from getting damaged in transit."

With considerable care, he turned each page of this notebook, and after producing all of the leaves except the one that Lalita had chosen, which remained buried somewhere in her bag, he inquired as to whether or not I was aware that it is forbidden by the laws of the Government of India to take antiquities out of the country.

"Yes, of course," I insisted, "but this is just a little souvenir reproduction, a sample of traditional crafts from Orissa."

When another uniformed man, this one armed with an AK-47, joined us, and the senior official informed me that he was confiscating the *Kamasutra* from me, I became indignant.

"Look, you can't take those. I paid ten thousand rupees for them!"

"If they were not antiquities, you would not have paid more than one hundred rupees unless you are a complete fool. And as I see, sir, that you are a professor of Indian studies, someone who would surely know the authenticity and value of Indian artifacts, not to mention someone who would indeed profit by smuggling an ancient manuscript out of India, it seems quite obvious that you are, like so many of the foreigners who have preceded you, quite guilty of a serious crime against the Government of India. India is no longer a colony, Professor, to which you can come willy-nilly and take your pick of those Indian treasures that you want to display in your British Museum, Ashmolean, Louvre, and Prado."

The more junior official, going deeper into my bag, suddenly broke in.

"And what is this?" he asked as he opened the perforated paan-masala tin.

"Snails," I confessed, and he inquired whether or not I was aware that it is forbidden by the laws of the Government of India to take wildlife out of the country. I began to protest but was cut short with a shock:

"You are," he said without expression, "under arrest, Professor Roth."

The thought of being in jail in India was terrifying. I had seen Tess. Surely they have to make it really horrible in there—ball and chain, shackles on a wall, gruel spiced with maggots—or the starving masses of beggars, yet to be redeemed from their squalor by Mr. Rothberg, would commit crimes just to get in and have a meal and a roof over their heads. My obvious panic made the senior official smile.

"Do not worry, Professor. Although the smuggling of antiquities and wildlife out of this country is indeed a felonious and unforgivable crime against the people of India, we do not intend to take you to jail at this time. Our prisons are sufficiently crowded. You will go back to America from where, once your case has become scheduled for trial, you will be summonsed to appear before the High Court in Delhi."

After confiscating my palm leaves and the snails, taking my finger-prints, photocopying my passport, and making me fill out some thirty pages of forms, after robbing and humiliating me, the senior official had the audacity to smile cheerfully.

"I see you are from California, Professor. I know that it is a very nice place because Disneyland is there. I wish to visit Disneyland with my family someday. Perhaps when I am in California, I will call upon you. I have noted down your address. But now you must hurry to the gate for boarding."

He turned to Lalita, who had gone entirely unsearched and unharrassed.

"I hope you will come back to India. It is the land of your ancestors. Thus you are always welcome."

Transit Lounge Bar: Heathrow Airport (London)
August 5 (in California)/August 6 (in India)

The last time I was here, rushing from one gate to another to make our connection to India, this notebook was empty and I had two hopes, each of which, in the style of the *Kamasutra*, were categorized into two aspects: 1) to know India (and to write something true about India, to write it here); 2) to know Lalita (and to write something true about Lalita, to write it here). Now the notebook is full and I have given up hope. My strategy had been to make each of the objects of my inquiry metaphors for the other: Lalita would represent (and through that representation provide access to) India, and India would represent (and through that representation provide access to) Lalita. I imagined them posed on either side of a looking glass, each one taking turns, for my sake, at being the reflection of the other. The

Kamasutra was to be that mirror. Of course this is not true: India is India and Lalita is Lalita. And that's too obvious to be interesting. The mutually dependent, and admittedly untrue, hypotheses were to serve my understanding and to provide a way of thinking and writing about truths, interesting and not-so-obvious truths about love.

As I sit here now, having a Bombay gin and tonic and smoking a duty-free Viceroy cigarette, looking at Ms. Lalita Gupta, the girl across the table from me who is drinking a pint of Newcastle Brown Ale and perusing the photographs in *People* magazine, I know all too well that she is not India. I know that I know very little about her. As I look beyond her at the travel poster for Air India, with its photograph of the Taj Mahal, on the wall at the other side of the bar, I know all too well that India is not Lalita. I know that I know very little about India.

A. TRANSLATION (2)

Gandharva union, requiring neither legal validation nor religious solemnization nor sacred fire, being nobody's business but your own, is the highest kind of union, even though, for taxonomic reasons, the ancients placed it at number five.

B. COMMENTARY (2)

Swinburne Hall A305
August 15
Indian Independence Day

United Airlines Flight #18 (O'Hare to LAX): Lalita asked me if I wanted her to remove the silver ring that she had worn in India to create the social illusion that we were married. Since the band was not a symbol of love, but of falsehood, I told her that I didn't care, and she took my arm, leaned her head against my shoulder, and said that she would to continue to wear it, but on the other hand.

She fell asleep and soon the Bombay and Halcyon allowed me to join her again in a dream, where, in the night-dark shawl, with gleaming golden anklets concealed and silenced for secret passage, with the flash of her smile and eyes obscured, she would always wait for me. Slowly I lifted the dark veil and was confused to see Sophia there. She smiled at me, and I helped her out of the clothes that had been soaked by monsoon rain. I dried her hair and familiar body with a soft towel and dusted her with rose-scented talc. Sophia held me in her arms. It must have been the motion of the plane, bouncing about in the nocturnal turbulence above America, that was experienced in dream as the movement of lovers' bodies, the rise and fall of sex.

The stewardess awakened us to tell us to fasten our seat belts and return our seats to an upright position for landing in Los Angeles.

"I love you, Leo," Lalita said with an unusual urgency. "I really love you. Do you love me, Leo? Do you really love me?"

"Yes."

"That makes me so happy. I love you too," she said as a preface to a phrase that, from the mouth of the beloved, should strike terror in the heart of any lover: "I've got something really important to tell you. Okay?"

Again, "Yes."

She rubbed my hand, lifted it up to her lips, licked my fingertips lightly and playfully with just the tip of her tongue, and took a deep breath.

"I really do love you now, but when we first got to India, I was really freaked out. I mean I was pretty upset, as I'm sure you can imagine."

Again, "Yes."

"You know, I felt I was kind of being kidnapped by some dirty old man. I'm sure you can understand that. Do you understand that?"

Again, "Yes."

"Well . . . and please, my darling, please forgive me, because I really didn't know what I was doing, but, uh, well, uh, I wrote to my parents and told them what was going on. You know, filling them in, explaining that it was just the two of us and everything. I'm sure they'll be waiting at the airport, and I don't think they're going to be very happy. I'm so sorry. I can't believe I did that. It was so silly of me. Please forgive me. Do you still love me?"

Again, "Yes." But I wanted a parachute.

"That makes me so happy. I love you, Leo, I love you, but there's something else. I'm sure you'll understand; you're so loving, so accepting and forgiving. Well, remember how much in love I was with Leroy? I was really hurt when I read that note from him. Maybe I wanted to make him jealous or something. He does get very, very jealous. He practically killed a guy once, just because the guy asked me to dance at a club. Anyway, I wrote to him too. I said you had kidnapped me, and I think I implied that you had raped me or were going to. But don't worry, I didn't use those exact words, just something sort of like them. That was dumb. I'm sorry. I'm really sorry but, well, at the time I thought it might make him come to India to rescue me. If he had come, I would have told him what a wonderful man you are. I wouldn't have let him hurt you. I'm sorry, my darling. I love you so much. I don't want anybody to hurt you. If he's at the airport, don't worry. I'll talk to him. I'll make him understand. Hopefully he's gone to Chicago. Please forgive me. Do you still love me?"

I think that I probably muttered another "Yes" because she kept talking. I no longer wanted a parachute; I would have jumped from the plane without one if we hadn't just been informed by the captain that all passengers were to remain in their seats with their seat belts fastened until we had landed and arrived at the gate.

"Oh, my wonderful Leo, that makes me so happy. I knew you would forgive me. You're so good. That's why I love you so very, very much. There's just one more little thing. It's probably no big deal. I'm sure it won't come to anything, but I feel it's best to tell you. I don't think people who are really in love should keep anything from each other. You've taught me that, my darling. I can't believe I did this. I'm really sorry. But I was really upset. I didn't want to come to India. I had just been dumped by my boyfriend. I hardly knew you. I was confused. I wasn't thinking straight. But, well, ah, I also wrote a letter to the school paper. But don't worry about it, because I don't think they'll print it or anything. I mean it really wasn't very well written or anything."[5]

5. It was no doubt because of this letter (sent at the beginning of June, but not published until the end of July) in the summer school edition of the university student newspaper that Maya Blackwell was able to locate Roth at the Premsagar Guest House. Despite what I might have thought of Roth's behavior as a teacher, I could not help but feel sorry for him when I read the letter in question in the *Western Crier:*

Dear Editor:
  I feel it is my duty to write to you to tell you and the students at Western, especially the girl students, about what has happened. A few months ago there was an ad in your paper for a study abroad program in India to be supervised by Professor Roth of the Asian Studies Department. I applied to the program and was accepted. So, as you can see by the hotel stationary I'm using, here I am in the Premsagar Guest House in Delhi, India. But the program is hardly what I expected. I am the only student that the Professor accepted and I have been forced to share a room with him. It's pretty obvious what he wants from me. There is no academic content to this program. I feel like a prisoner. In fact I am afraid that he might try to rape me because he keeps telling me how beautiful I am. While I'm sure I can take care of myself because I'm pretty strong and he's kind of old, it really makes me feel sorry for his wife. I think she's a dean or something. The important thing though is just that I want to warn other students not to sign up for Professor Roth's India program next summer.

Lalita Gupta
Senior, Communications Major

The wheels of the airplane touched the earth, and the thrust reversers roared.

"Sometimes, my dear Lalita, *how* something is written is of little importance. Sometimes content is more significant than form."

"Please don't be angry with me. I'm really sorry. Oh Leo, look at me. Do you still love me? I love you. I love you and I love India. I'm sure everything will be all right. When people really love each other, that's all that counts. If you're in love everything has got to work out. I love you. So as long as you love me, everything will be fine. Do you forgive me, Leo? Do you love me?"

While I don't remember my answer, I do recall that when the plane stopped at the gate the captain thanked us for flying United and told us to "have a nice day."

It was the most miserable moment of my life.

That's really true, and that's how it felt at the time.

Here Ends Book Three of the *Kamasutra*.

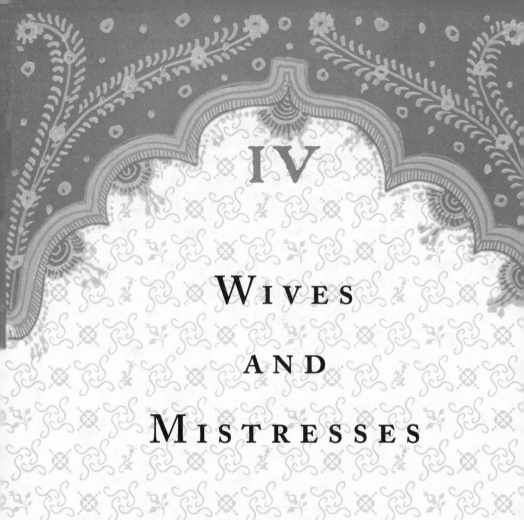

IV

WIVES

AND

MISTRESSES

My dear Monsieur Delibes,

I have only recently returned from Trieste. Losing the man who had been my earthly God for so many years was like a blow to the head, and I am still completely stunned. I am, however, attempting to put aside that portion of my misery which would prevent me from dealing with the late Captain Sir Richard Burton's affairs. My husband, I am confident, would wish me to respond to your letter of last year on his behalf without further delay.

Your request for such information on the *Kama Sutra* as might enable you to compose an opera based on it would certainly have pleased my husband. He did, as you most probably know, have the opportunity to attend a performance of *Lakmé* in Milan and spoke enthusiastically of the musical talents of Mademoiselle Arnor. Although your description of the proposed opera is not without interest, I must inform you that he would not be pleased if you were to use passages from his anonymously published translation of 1883. Less than one year before his death, as he was finishing his adaption of the *Scented Garden*, my husband embarked on a revision of his previous translation of the *Kama Sutra*, in which, he said, he had all too often compromised his daring in capitulation to the moral and literary conservatism of Mr Arbuthnot. The anonymity assigned to the text—the cryptic designation of himself only as "B.F.R.," the initials to which you refer in your letter—was due not to the boldness of the translation, but to its temerity. The new *Kama Sutra*, he maintained, would be far more courageous. As Captain Burton had a thoroughly unembarrassed mind, the hypocritical prudery of the British public and the social posturings of moral respectability, of which Mr. Arbuthnot had been so conscious and protective, would not this time, he insisted with his inimitable balance of valor and duty, inhibit him from enlightening civilized Mankind in the intimate manners and libidinal customs of the Olden East.

At the time of Captain Burton's passing, however, only four of the seven books of the revised *Kama Sutra* had been completed. He had just begun Book Five when the end came. And I found myself in the dreadfully daunting position of having to determine what to do with the manuscript and, furthermore, having to imagine how closely the written draft would have resembled the final, rewritten project. This was no easy task. The translation of the Sanscrit text was framed by, and interspersed with, a commentary which was more *journal intime* than academic exegesis. While I do not know how much of the commentary he would have wished to be made public, I am certain that those portions of it which were dedicated to reflections upon our own conjugal relations he would surely have decided to keep private. Together, the translation and commentary constituted a strange book, an anatomy of passion, if you will, the results of the years he had spent arduously vivisecting the erotic sentiment, its sundry manifestations and divers practices, from every point of view, just as a doctor dissects a body, showing its evil and its good, its diseases and its proper uses, as designed and dictated by Providence and Nature.

Richard Burton was a spade-truth man. If he wrote in the *Kama Sutra* commentary of his amorous adventures, these intimacies were recorded only in service of furthering the scientific understanding not only of the Oriental mind but of the heart of Mankind itself. He embarked on those adventures in the same manner in which he ventured forth upon his explorations in Africa and the Americas, never for the sake of his own excitation, always for the sake of the intellectual and moral edification of Man. As I feared that this strange book would not be read as such, I remained for three days in a state of perfect torture, deliberating within myself as to what I ought to do about the manuscript. I sat by the fireplace, holding the unfinished notebooks in my lap as one would cradle an orphan child, and without my beloved husband to instruct me, I had no choice but to seek counsel within myself using what I knew of his superior reason as my guide: "Out of fifteen hundred men, probably no more than fifteen will read this annotated, unexpurgated *Kama Sutra* in the spirit of science in which it was written, translated, and commented upon; the other fourteen hundred eighty-five will read it for filth's sake, panting and drooling over its pages and then passing it on to their licentious friends, or using it to entice innocent young girls into depravity and unspeakable carnal abominations." The harm that might be done by the book, I realized, was incalculable. All at once Richard Burton's sonorous voice seemed to echo from the grave: "Burn it," he cried out to me. "Burn it!" Sorrowfully and reverently I obeyed my beloved master.

Thus, M. Delibes, along with my insistence that you must not use the 1883 Sir Richard Burton translation of the *Kama Sutra,* I am sorry to send you news that my husband's proposed revised version, which might have been used, is no more. It was, like a corpse out East, cremated in hopes that, while it does not remain physically in the world at this time, its true spirit will transmigrate and, some day, at the fitting time and clime, find another body. Perhaps some professor, philosopher, poet, anthropologist, or philologist of the future, in a milieu more tolerant to observing what lurks in the darkness of the hearts of men, will devote himself to filling the literary void that remains as a result of a decision which, I pray, was a judicious one, in keeping with the will of both the author of the book and the Author of the world.

I would suggest that, if you wish to pursue this matter further, you might consult Professor Rudolf Roth, with whom you are, I gather from your letter, already acquainted. It strikes me that it would also be of interest to contact Professor Monier Monier-Williams in Oxford. But I wouldn't mention the one to the other, as my husband, informing me that the latter was engaged in an unauthorized English translation and abridgement of the former's lexicon, surmised: "Monier-Williams's *Sanscrit-English Dictionary* will inevitably be quite a blow to Roth."

There is, after all, *cher Maître,* some good news. I have begun writing my *Life of Captain Sir Richard F. Burton* and hope to have it ready for the publishers in London by the end of the year. While contemplating your letter to my husband, the obvious occurred to me. Why is it that the obvious often takes so long to make itself so? I shall not neglect to send you the manuscript in progress as soon as I can have it copied as I am confident that it will make an excellent opera.

The opera might begin during his Oxford days, following him from there to India, the Sind, and so on, perhaps to the Nile and the Crimea, even to Mecca and Salt Lake City. The opera might end with a distraught Lady Isabel singing a requiem, flames dancing on her face, and then offering up the *Kama Sutra* to the fire as a sacrifice to the betterment of Man.

I must end now. There is so much that awaits me in the Augean task of dealing with my husband's affairs. I know that Richard F. Burton would wish me to bid you well and, my dear Sir, I thus comply with those wishes.

—Lady Isabel Burton (Mortlake, 1891)

Editor's Note

As I have said, I've had my share of problems with Professor Roth: he was prone to affront me as a scholar by belittling the significance of my analyses of Sanskrit commentarial literature, as an Indian with his offensive imitation of an Indian English accent, and as a person by his tendency to treat me deferentially and with condescension, particularly in the presence of students and colleagues. Immediately after he had confessed the details his scheme to me, just before leaving for India, he seemed angry with me, as if I had forced him to reveal something that he did not wish to disclose. He seemed to blame me for having the knowledge of India and of Lalita Gupta that he had imparted to me.

And after the publication of Ms. Gupta's devastating letter in the summer school edition of the Western University student newspaper, it was embarrassing to be associated with him. "Isn't Roth your supervisor?" I would be asked, usually with a grin, to which I would invariably respond with a frown, "In academic affairs only."

Despite all of that, as the day of his return from India approached, I began to feel an increasing sympathy for the man of whom love had made such a pariah, a criminal, and most sadly of all, a fool. It was hard not to feel sorry for Professor Roth, knowing as I did that the coming semester would not be an easy one for him.

Correctly speculating that his wife would not be picking him up at the airport, I wanted to personally greet him at the gate, to be the first to inform him of the scandalous letter in the paper.

Anyone would have noticed the woman standing barefoot in front of the arrivals monitor at the United terminal, wearing the dirty long white gown and the large white hat festooned with dusty paper pastel flowers. As I had often seen her lurking around Swinburne Hall, I assumed that she was a friend of Roth's and was therefore surprised that she was not at the gate. It was not until several weeks later that I learned her name—Maya Blackwell.

Dr. Gupta, his weeping wife, the obviously concerned and Right Honorable Jaidev Prakash, chairman of the Indian Republican Party of Southern California, and several other urbane members of the Indian community whom I did not recognize were waiting for Roth and Ms. Gupta to arrive on their connecting flight from Chicago. As the aircraft slowly taxied toward the gate, Dr. Gupta, recognizing me from the party at Roth's, rushed toward me.

"Surely you have heard the terrible news. Your professor kidnapped my daughter. A Dr. Patel of Pipli has informed me of other egregious felonies that were committed in India. I have contacted the police to no avail, and thus we have little choice but to take justice into our own hands. The affair is an affront to all Indian people in the Western diaspora, and therefore I expect you to assist us in dealing with this scoundrel. I call on you to do your duty on behalf of your heritage. You must join us in an effort to punish the professor. India has been disgraced. I knew that the man was a colonialist and a racist long ago when he was elected to the Chair in Indian Studies, but I had no idea just how despicable he is. If the university had hired an Indian, as we so vehemently urged, this outrage would never have occurred."

The call to arms was interrupted by the emergence of the first passengers through the arrival doors. The procession of exiting travelers continued on and on with the surprising endlessness of the appearance of innumerable circus clowns from a little car. Finally a sari-clad, bindi-marked, and very beautiful Ms. Lalita Gupta, with a silver ring in her nose and anklets jingling on her feet, materialized and was swept up into the arms of a wailing mother as a furious father shouted, "Where is he? Where is the rapist?"

Roth, the last clown out of the plane, literally forced from it by two flight attendants, was welcomed by an outraged Dr. Gupta's zealous "I will kill you!" which prompted Ms. Gupta to wrench herself from her mother's ursine embrace and jump in between her father and her lover shouting, "Stop it! Stop it!"

As airport security guards, drawn by the ruckus, attempted to subdue Dr. Gupta, I fought my way toward a clearly frazzled Roth, grabbed his arm, and pulled him toward the exit.

"Let's go straight to the car. I don't think we want to see the Guptas

again at baggage. If you've got your claim checks, I can pick up your belongings later."

Roth was silent.

"So," I asked, "How was India?"

"Was there a letter about me in the university paper?" he asked.

"Do you know about that?" I asked.

"Do you think my wife will be upset?" he asked.

"Do you want me to take you home?" I asked.

"How's your dissertation?" he asked.

"Are you okay?" I asked.

"When do classes begin?" he asked.

"Are you going to be able to handle all of this?" I asked.

"Do you think Lalita is beautiful?" he asked.

And so on. And so on. There were no answers.

Several days after picking Roth up at the airport, I went to his office with the bag (made all the heavier by his Monier-Williams dictionary) that I had gone back to the airport to retrieve, only to discover that he had moved in there. Living in Swinburne Hall provides few amenities beyond the soft drink machine between the restrooms on the second floor. No shower, no kitchen facilities, no bed. Roth was sleeping on an Indian blanket on the floor, and since he had no hot water with which to shave, a beard appeared on his face and grew longer and longer, and grayer and grayer, during the semester. He was, I thought to myself, beginning to look like Vātsyāyana might have looked.

I'm not sure if it was pride or self-delusion that made him tell me that he actually wanted to live in his office so that he could devote all of his waking hours to finishing his translation of, and commentary on, the Kāmasūtra. "I'm on Book Four," he said with the proud smile of a scholar who had not a care in the world. To break an uncomfortably prolonged silence that filled his office as I sat there with him, and to avoid a conversation that might be embarrassingly personal, I asked about the translation and asked him again a question that I had once put to him before his trip to India—whether or not, as he was working on Vātsyāyana's text, he ever got a feeling for the individual, a sense of who Vātsyāyana was as "a man of flesh and blood with his own particular fears and desires."

"Professor Vātsyāyana Mallanāga," Roth smiled. "Usually he is a stranger to me. He was a complete stranger before this summer. But now, every so often, I suddenly picture him. Yes. He's about my age, a quiet, serious man—not at all like me—gaunt and frail, with thin puritanical lips and large sensual eyes. His shoulders slump, and his hands tremble as if he

has been injured by something or someone, by some experience or realization. But he would never speak of it; he's a private man with certain secrets. Sometimes I can feel what I imagine to be his loneliness; I sense that I am somehow participating in a gloom that is marked with his fingerprints and that echoes with his lectures. I can picture his body, wrapped in white and lashed to sandalwood logs, burning on a funeral pyre on a sloping muddy bank of the Ganges in Varanasi. Dark smoke, curling upward and out of the bright tongues of flame, dissipates into gray skies; gray ashes, scattered with prayers, diffuse into dark waters. Charred bones sink. He's gone. I can't see him any longer. No. He's a stranger to me once again."

After several weeks of residence in Swinburne A305, a cat moved in with Roth, a black stray with irregular orange spots and white blotches, which he named Mayavati. Within the first twenty-four hours of their cohabitation, Roth discovered that he was allergic to cat fur, but despite the fact that he now sneezed continually, he refused to evict the animal. "How can I throw Mayavati out?" Roth asked with a sneeze and a smile. "She loves me."

It was Professor Planter's duty, as chairman of the department, to inform Roth that he had been granted a leave of absence without pay for the semester; it was a polite way of explaining that he was suspended from teaching and on probation until the sexual harassment case was settled. Planter consoled Roth by explaining that, under the provisos of an L.W.O.P. status, he could continue to use his office, the library, and parking facilities (which didn't really matter since his wife had the car), and that he would enjoy full voting privileges in all department meetings. It must have been a terrible blow for Roth to learn that his salary was going to be used to invite Professor Lee Siegel from Hawaii to teach his classes for the semester. I was pleased, however, by the prospect of being able to consult with my former supervisor, who, although perhaps not as adept in Sanskrit, is far more reliable than Roth. I was eager for his comments on my dissertation.

The sexual harassment suit that the Guptas brought against the university, in conjunction with the criminal rape and kidnapping charges they filed in state court (despite the protests of their daughter and with the support of the influential Jaidev Prakash), of course proved awkward for Dr. Sophia White-Roth as dean of Academic Affairs and chairperson of the University Committee on Sexual Harassment. As the accused was her husband, it would have been touchy for her to either prosecute him or not prosecute him. Thus she resigned and returned to her joint position in the English and women's studies departments to teach a cross-listed undergraduate course, "Women and Autobiography," and a graduate seminar on Restoration literature.

It was fortunate for Roth that Ms. Gupta's affection for him was *sufficient enough that she not only refused to press charges, but even defended him. This obviated legal prosecution on the charges of rape and kidnapping, but policies and regulations within the university were more thorny. Repeatedly testifying before various extramural and intramural committees and in interviews for all sorts of public and institutional publications, Ms. Gupta reiterated, with what seemed like genuine sincerity, that her relationship with Professor Roth had "ultimately" been consensual. The use of the word "ultimately" (and such synonymous words and phrases as "in the end," "after a while," and "once I got to know him") fed an assessment of the affair as exemplary of "mentor rape" resulting from the "Svengali effect," wherein the student merely thinks she's consenting to a sexual relationship, merely imagines that she loves the teacher when, in fact, she is the victim of an institutionalized power differential, living in a kind of hypnotic trance as induced by the effect of the professor's age, status, sophistication, learning, intelligence, and so on. Although I do not in any way condone sexual harassment of any kind, I know both Ms. Gupta and Dr. Roth well enough to attest that, if anyone was hypnotized, it was the professor.*

When the Indian community, led by Gupta and Prakash in a dedicated endeavor to get the tenured professor fired from the state-funded university, solicited my testimony before a hearing committee, a subcommittee of some subcommittee on education in the state legislature, I appealed directly to Mr. Prakash: "If for some reason, justice does not prevail, if Roth is not fired, he will still be the chairman of my doctoral committee. I want to pass. I cannot afford to make an enemy of Roth." The judge was very understanding: "We have had a similar situation with securing testimonies against powerful Mafia bosses."

My testimony was hardly needed to condemn Roth—his own was accomplishing that. Instead of adopting a repentant or apologetic posture, he would proudly announce in interviews before committees and for newspapers how much he loved Ms. Gupta. It was as if he really believed that love makes all things permissible. A story about the case in the Los Angeles Times *quoted Roth:*

> I loved her. I still love her. I shall always love her. I also, by the way, love my wife. And I shall also always love her. Both of them, in different ways, are so very beautiful. Anyone who has met Lalita and still does not understand why I did what I did is either sexually dysfunctional or emotionally maimed by an excessive repression of the most natural and life-enhancing of energies. Any normal man would have fallen in love with her. Any normal man, if he could, would have made love to her. I am not guilty of anything. It is my accusers and judges who are aberrant.

When an undergraduate journalism major interviewed Roth for a class assignment, the Western Crier *could not resist publishing the piece. In defiance of himself, the university, and society, Roth gave the freshman cub reporter material for a front page story:*

Professor Leopold Roth of the Asian Studies Department, in an interview on Monday in his office, told this reporter that, and I quote, "A society in which you can't f— your students may be a society, but it's not a civilization. Love, and I mean sexual love for all its power and sanctity, is essential to effective pedagogy." He claimed that Socrates had done it to his students and that a French professor named Abelard had too. "The Bible," he continued, "uses the phrase 'to know' for 'to f—.' Knowledge depends on f—ing and being f—d. That's the Judeo-Christian belief." This reporter then asked him about Indian beliefs, and I quote, "Professor Vatsyayana, one of the greatest teachers in India at the height of its cultural sophistication, in the Gupta period, initiated his pupils into higher education by f—ing them. And then he taught them how to f— as an art, a science, as the very foundation of the humanities." The Indian professor in question was the man who wrote the famous sex manual called the *Kama Sutra* like the movie that recently came out. This reporter asked Professor Roth if he planned to conduct another Study Abroad Course in India next year. He said, and I quote, "F— you."

Professor Planter, while consistently diplomatic in his public proclamations of "no comment," was privately more candid; passing me in the hall outside Roth's office one day, he winked, grinned, and whispered, "Don't you just love Leo? Having him on the faculty really livens things up. Did you read the interview with him in the school paper? There's a man willing to die for love! But, I'm really sticking my neck out for him. If anybody finds out about that cat, we're in trouble. Pets in university buildings are strictly against regulations. Don't even mention the fact that I'm turning my back on his smoking in Swinburne Hall. That's a state offense. I'm having trouble with the secretary, trying to keep her quiet. Sweet little Ms. Naper, dumpy as she is, actually imagines that Roth's after her too. 'If he comes near me,' she told me with a menacing glare, 'I'll kill him. I really will.' She gave a talk called 'The Real Professor Roth' at the monthly State Secretaries in Education luncheon last week. What would the department do without her? Between Nora Naper and Leopold Roth, things are really jumping."

As I entered Roth's office, things were hardly jumping. He had just hung up the telephone and was using one Viceroy cigarette to light up another.

"I know it's her. Fuckin' Maya Blackwell. She keeps calling and not saying anything. But I know it's her." He held up a sheaf of letters on pieces of paper of different sizes, shapes, and colors. "Everyday these arrive. Fuckin'

letters, poems, cryptic parables. Unrequited love! There's nothing worse than being loved by someone you don't even like. It's worse than loving someone who doesn't like you. I called the police. Some asshole cop, a Detective Chan, says to me, 'There's nothing we can do. Writing bad poetry isn't a crime.' I think I pissed him off by calling him 'Charlie.'"

Poor Professor Roth roared with laughter, sneezed, lit up another Viceroy (although one was still burning in the ashtray), and continued:

"'Plato,' he says to me, 'Detective Plato Chan, not Charlie, not even Charles, and no number one son. No one ever calls me Charlie twice.' And he hung up on me. I've been thinking about what he said, though. That would be a great civilization, a verbocracy, a republic in which bad writing was a crime, in which people who wrote bad poems, novels, plays, or even bad dissertations were executed." And then Roth sneezed once, twice, a third time, and Mayavati jumped up and onto his lap, as if to console him.

Although he is well aware that I do not drink, he asked if I wanted to join him in a Bombay gin and tonic, sneezed, and apologized that there was no ice in Swinburne Hall. He accepted my invitation to go out for an Indian meal.

I supposed it was some sort of oblique mockery of me when, while asking the waiter at the Taj Mahal whether or not the food was kosher, he pointed at me and said, "My friend is Jewish." The waiter assured us that, since Jews and Muslims have the same dietary restrictions, we were safe: "The cook is Mussulman, very devout, from Pakistan." I ordered my usual vegetarian dinner, the Mahatma Gandhi special, and Roth had the Shah Jahan Mogul Five-Meat Feast.

Over dinner, with surprising but rather painful good cheer, he told me about troubles that I could not even have imagined.

"Some Indian out in Shandy Hills is suing me. He runs some fuckin' multimedia company. He contacted me last year about doing a CD-ROM Kāmasūtra *for him. So I did some work on it and sent him a disk. But somebody else has come out with one, and he's claiming that I leaked it. Guess who's involved? That pal of yours—Siegel. Apparently he showed a similar program to some other company or something. I don't know. All I know is that whenever Siegel's involved, I get fucked."*

It was interesting to note that, after the summer in India, Roth had begun to use the word "fuckin'" in his everyday parlance with great frequency, almost as much as he sneezed. Ms. Gupta, however, who had previously uttered the obscenity incessantly, now, I had occasion to observe, never used it. The trip to India had made her curiously demure, really rather Indian.

"Not only that, I was working on a game based on the Kāmasūtra. *I*

even had cards for it made in India. I sent it to Romulus and Rowley Puzzles and Games. I just heard back from them that a professor of Indian studies in Hawaii had already submitted a similar game. I could kill Siegel." Not wanting to find myself in any way between Siegel and Roth, I always told the latter that I hadn't seen the former, and the former that I hadn't seen the latter.

Ignoring my repeated assertion that I do not drink alcohol, he ordered two more Taj Mahal beers, sneezed, and then went on to other problems. "Today, when I picked up my mail, in between Maya Blackwell's newest love poems, there was a notice from the Indian government demanding that I appear for trial in Delhi on charges of 'the attempted smuggling of antiquities and the unauthorized exportation of wildlife.' I'm a fugitive from justice in India. My picture is probably up in post offices there together with the other nine most-wanted criminals in the country."

After letting me pay for the dinner (and not thanking me for it), he advised me to start smoking cigarettes, drinking alcohol, and eating meat, "or you're liable to turn into a fairy." And then he asked me to drop him off across from Hollywood High School on Sunset Blvd.

It was not that I was nosy or wanted to pry into what was none of my business, but rather that I was worried about him—his life was so grim and he had just had eight large beers (his four and the four he had ordered for me)—that prompted me, after letting him out of the car, to take the first left turn, park in the first empty space, and backtrack on foot down to Sunset, where I spotted him walking quickly east. Following at some distance, I confess that I felt the sort of thrill that one attributes to private detectives on television and in movies, a sort of L.A.-film-noirish, pleasurable, dark and gritty kind of excitement. Crossing the street, moving quickly, Roth went into the office of the Marco Polo Traveler's Lodge and Motor Court. I dodged private-eye-ishly into the local Love Burger and found a seat by a window that provided a good view of the front of the motel: Roth left the office, crossed the parking lot, unlocked one of the pale green doors, and went into a room. The light in the window next to the door went on. I waited over a cup of coffee. In less than an hour, she arrived—Lalita Gupta in jeans and a black Kashmiri shawl. She walked past the office to the room. The door opened, she disappeared, and, in a matter of minutes, the light in the window went out.

Although it made me, for some reason, very sad—sad for him, sad for her, sad for Mrs. Roth and the Guptas, and more generally sad too, sad almost for the whole the world—I chastised myself for those feelings, told myself that I should be happy for him, pleased that in this dark and chill period of his life Lalita was consenting to give him a little light, a little warmth, perhaps even a little affection.

I was eager to return home to work on my dissertation. As I left Love Burger, I saw something terrible, something that stunned me like a blow to the head: seated at the window, not more than five places from were I had been, looking out across Sunset at the Marco Polo, was Maya Blackwell. It seemed that there should be something that I ought to do. But what? My teacher's love life was hardly any of my business. It was time to extricate myself from the story.

I've exceeded, I'm afraid, my editorial duties. I am, after all, not the author of this narrative, but merely its annotator, and that not by choice, but out of obligation. Annotations should not exceed a text, but simply and modestly serve a clearer reading of it. To that end, and with that in mind, let me explain what I can of the physical presentation of the following two chapters that make up Roth's translation of, and commentary on, Book Four.

Nothing on the covers of the notebook containing these chapters indicated which was the front and which was the back; either, depending on how you turned the book, could have been the starting place. Opening and reading it one way made "The Older Wife" the beginning; turning it over and around, to open it the other way, made "The Younger Mistress" the beginning.

This suggests that Roth worked simultaneously, not chronologically, on this book of the Kāmasūtra, and thus that the two chapters are most appropriately, and most faithfully to the author, read by turning back and forth, over and over, up and down, right to left and left to right, from one to the other, working one's way through "Sophia" and "Lalita" as they are at once mingled and distinguished, reading willy-nilly as Roth wrote. It is only by necessity that I have given precedence to one chapter over another by labeling one "A" and the other "B," following an order dictated not by Roth, but by other bound and printed versions of the Kāmasūtra.

Vātsyāyana advises the lover, for the sake of novelty or because of fatigue, to roll the beloved over during lovemaking, to reverse sexual positions (K.S. II.H); given Roth's notion of writing and reading as erotic activities, it is appropriate that we are constrained to turn his book upside down, to read it, as he wrote it, in a variety of positions and in two different colors—kumkum and kohl.

At this point the choice is yours: either read straight ahead or skip forward to page 319, before the beginning of Book five, and there turn the book over and upside down and read back in this direction, toward the place from which you have come. In the end, it really doesn't matter where we begin. Likewise, in the beginning, it doesn't matter where we end.

keeps the dead asleep as it lulls my heart and soothes love's endless sadness. I do still love you.

I've got to go now—*The Curse of Kali* is about to begin. My longing for you has made me THE SADDEST MAN IN THE WORLD.

Here Ends Book Four of the *Kamasutra*.

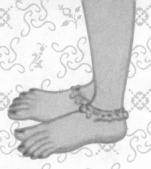

[A.] The Older Wife

A man's wife always knows too much about him.
—The *Ratisutra* of Jayamangala (IV.A), translated and annotated by Tajma Hall

A. TRANSLATION

A wife should adore her husband as a god, remaining ever obedient to him and wholeheartedly devoted to maintaining his household, caring for his children, and keeping the residence neat, clean, and fragrant.[1] When a husband returns home from a journey abroad, his wife, after having endured an abject state of mourning caused by his absence, should adorn herself gorgeously in celebration of their reunion. A good wife is instinctually eager to satisfy her beloved lord's each and every wish and whim, to be beautiful for the sake of his delight. A wife should wash her husband's feet and then allow herself to drink the water that has been made holy by her hallowed act of domestic devotion. A woman who follows this path will not only experience earthly fulfillment, but will also, in death, attain the highest heaven and abide there in bliss with her spouse for ten billion ten

---

1. Pralayānanga interprets *grha* ("residence") as a euphemism for *kāmagrha* ("residence of Kāma," translated by Monier-Williams as *pudendum muliebria*). Stressing the significance of the ambiguity of the common noun, the scholiast cites the *Yellow Yajur Veda:* "The vagina of the wife is the home of the husband and the shrine wherein he is her lord." The commentator, elaborating the metaphor, establishes a pudendal architecture: "The pubic hair is the thatched roof, the clitoris is Ganeśa [the elephant-headed god traditionally placed above the entrance to the Hindu home], the prepuce is an awning [for the god], the vestibule is a vestibule, the labia are curtained double doors, the vaginal opening is the portal, and the fourchette is the doorstep into the vaginal parlor, the fallopian hallways, and the uterine *sanctum sanctorum*." "Loving words," he quaintly adds, "are doorbells."

love," Sleeman says to Paul, who is holding Lucy in his arms as they look at the burning temple in the distance. The last scene, like the first, is at the dock: a smiling General Sleeman waves good-bye to a happy Paul and Lucy as their ship sails away from India and toward home.

My parents wouldn't allow me to see the film because they thought it might cause me to become afraid of my father, but that was not the case; when I finally saw it, I felt sorry for Malababa. My poor father died because he had fallen in love. It made me very sad. "I hate your father," Clover said. "He's a bad man." And that made me even sadder.

The end of our love story is kind of confusing too. The plot has fizzled out: the foreign professor's wife won't see him at all and wants a divorce; his Oriental mistress consents to see him less and less. There's no climax, no fight scene, no temple in flames, no ship sailing home. Just an aging professor, who has been suspended from teaching, sitting alone in a motel room waiting for an old movie to come on television at midnight, hoping that perhaps his lover will finish her homework and surprise him. The romance has turned into farce. To salvage it, I need to die for love or be saved by it: there needs to be a knock on the door; it must be you there, or someone willing to fight me to the death over you.

The pleasure that merged us in Varanasi was mysterious—was it not?—qualified as it was by the unspeakable and obvious truth that it would end. It was, for me, the saddest of pleasures, informed by both the feel of its limits and by a rebelliousness against all confines. That pleasure defeated itself in its longing for persistence. I prod myself right now with memories of our India to seduce myself and reduce myself once more to happiness.

The motel is empty. There's a cemeterial silence in the courtyard, an eerie hush accented by the haphazard noises of the street. These dark rooms, awaiting lovers, seem resigned to accept the sundry dissipations and momentary epiphanies of transients, whatever pains and pleasures they might bring to fill the emptiness, whatever moans or whispers, sighs or laughter they might use to muffle the quiet. The silence of empty rooms, piped in from oblivion, is a music of infinite melancholy, an a cappella lullaby that

thousand ten hundred and ten years. In the meantime, the husband of such a woman will count himself THE HAPPIEST MAN IN THE WORLD.

B. COMMENTARY
"The Happiest Man in the World"

Sophia, Sophia, my dearest Sophia:

A longing for respite from a harsh blare of cacophonous confabulations, raucous regrets and murmuring memories, wanton worries and hopeless hopes drew me with a frosty hand to the garden of death, that I might lull a reluctant heart with operatic silences composed of the choral songs of the deceased and solace myself with their melodious requiems for the living. Leila's subterranean *aria sordina* rose out of that chorus into the harmonious hush of oblivion.

Be assured, my beloved wife, that I am not invoking our daughter strategically, to placate or seduce you, not demeaning the terrible end of a life by prodding you with memories of beginnings that might melt you. Please believe that whatever I have been as husband, as father I am more capable of love. It is, we both know, easier to love the dead.

The lamentation that merged us in Paris after her demise was mysterious—was it not?—a tenebrous abyss of overwhelming, unrelenting anguish in which was eerily obscured an ineffable happiness, so fragile that even the sound of reference to it would shatter it like delicate glass before the screeching divas of death. There was dawn in mourning and chimerical hopes in a rude and flagrant despair. That intangible, inexpressible, subtle elation was like some submarine creature indigenous to an absolute silence and utter darkness of the ocean's deepest depths, one of those primordial beings that, if brought up to us, bursts into flames from the merest glances of a sun partially penetrating shimmering surfaces above. We touched upon that being in those evanescent moments when, aching, we embraced; and it, in turn, touched upon us, fretful denizens to gloom, entwined us in demulcent tentacles. Flesh trembled with clutch and cling, by which fluid, cell, and spirit merged into the germ of a child's life. Bathe me in love (or drown me) again Sophia, or envelope me in it (or smother me) once more; allow me rapturous refuge in every dark chamber of your heart, every warm fold and bend in your body, from the essential strangeness of being alive. Open again and again. I say aloud and write right here that I love you in fear that

Malababa turns a tied-up Paul over to Malati with suggestive instructions: "Do with him as you wish and then dispose of him." The
luridness of my father's grin as he says it and the languidness of
Malati's half-closed eyes as she hears it insinuate some peculiar, exotic, and frightening torture, some mysterious Oriental sexual perversion, unknown in the West, that culminates in the death of the
male.

My father's downfall is love. Malababa becomes infatuated with
Lucy and supplicates her with an offer that she can become Queen of
the Thugs. She starts to say "Never!" quite often at this point in the
film. I don't know why, since he's so evil, my father doesn't just rape
her. But he doesn't. Love, I suppose, has made him soft. Keeping
Mom jailed in a luxurious bedroom in the temple, Dad goes there
night after night to repeat his ultimatum to her: she can be his lover
or she can be sacrificed to Kali. She keeps choosing Kali, and he keeps
giving her another chance to think about it until finally, unable to endure the pangs of unrequited love any longer, Malababa loses his patience. Paul, in the meantime, has wiggled his hands free from his
fetters and has escaped from the temple storeroom; our hero bursts
into the shrine just as my heartbroken father is raising his sword over
the head of my rope-bound mother because of her prudish refusal to
love him as he loves her.

The end is kind of confusing. Paul and Mom would have been
killed by the Thugs if General Sleeman had not, just in the nick of
time, arrived on the scene and rounded up the Kali-crazed Hindu
fanatics. Everybody—the Thugs and the British soldiers, Sleeman
and Lucy—get to watch the dramatic, climactic fight between Paul
and Malababa in the shrine. Paul is knocked down and Malababa's
sword is poised to decapitate him. Lucy screams. Paul would surely
have been slain if Malati, hiding inside the statue, hadn't surprised
my lovelorn father by stabbing him with each and every one of her
six swords. Why did she do it? Had the hapless Hindu priestess
fallen in love with the handsome young British officer? Or was she
jealous because her master had fallen in love with Lucy? Or both?
That we shall never know for sure: in the fight between Paul and
Malababa, one of the oil lamps burning before the goddess was
knocked over, and when the temple went up in flames, Malati, still
inside the statue of Kali, was consumed by the fire. "She died for

it might not be believed; in that lapse of faith there would be doom. I shall always love you.

I was well aware of the fundamental absurdity of my sorrow as a natural symptom of my predicament, the rather unpleasant situation caused by my own capricious behavior and relentless ridiculousness, by my impulsive and inappropriate involvement with a young Indian girl whom I hardly knew. Although resigned to melancholy, I went to Leila's grave in an attempt to replace the cause of it with something more meaningful and powerful, dramatic and tragic—something for which I was not myself responsible. I turned to death for a sense of reality.

I don't like going; the very name of the place is a mockery of the dead who live there. But it was the only place I could think of where no one was angry, disappointed, or disgusted with me. Seeing, then touching, then smelling the fragile white narcissi freshly offered on her grave, I realized you must have just been there. Poignant is the phrase: "We must have just missed each other."

Lolling on the spot where our daughter is buried, I wanted to explain myself to the child. But I became disquieted, sadder still, vividly conscious of the fact that I've spent my life trying to juggle and transpose causes and effects, switching and shuffling subjects and objects about like peas in a shell game. I felt guilty of attempted breaking and entering into a private peace in which she is hidden and sheltered. I was unhappy and self-conscious in the presence of death, embarrassed for what I had become in the presence of a memory of a little girl who so genuinely loved and innocently admired what I was.

Suddenly I remembered her voice, and I could faintly hear the innocent words of a silly little song that she used to sing to Isaac whenever he was sad:

> Turn yourself upside down:
> Make a smile of your frown;
> Make that sad sack be a clown.
> Turn yourself upside down!
> La la lala, la la la . . .

Something like that. Remember? It made me smile and then laugh, right there in the graveyard, made me realize that all I needed to do was obey the child, to turn myself upside down. That's it! It's that simple. It's that obvious! I realized that I had neither the need of, nor the

day when we can be together, far away from this land. The jungle frightens me."

They're drinking champagne and waltzing at an officer's ball when Major General Sleeman arrives to warn people that there are Thugs in the area, "savage devotees of the ferocious Goddess Kali," a cult under the leadership of my father, the evil high priest Malababa, who snarls lines like "Mother Kali thirsts for blood! The time for sacrifice is at hand!" You can tell when Kali is thirsty because her six arms start waving about and her necklace of skulls rattles spookily.

What the heathen Thugs, who chant and dance in a stupor around the scary statue of Kali, don't know, blinded as they are by faith in a pagan deity as well as by my father's mesmeric powers, is that there isn't really a living Kali, that the statue is just a statue, and that it only moves when my father's beautiful assistant, the young priestess Malati, is inside of it.

The scriptwriter had the idea that Hindus think that Kali, as a female deity, needs female blood to survive; so my father uses his hypnotic eyes to entrance Indian village women (mostly played by Mexicans) for sacrificial purposes; once under his spell they mutter things like "Choose me. I want to give my heart to Kali." And then, scantily clad in preparation for their propitiatory death, they perform erotic Oriental dances.

My father was at the dock, disguised as a snake charmer, when Lucy's boat arrived at the beginning of the movie. "Oh, look," Lucy's aunt and chaperone says, "a snake charmer. How quaint. Let's watch." Malababa plays an eerie tune on his gourd flute while staring into my mother's eyes, and a cobra, its hood ominously spread, rises out of its basket. "It frightens me," my mother says. "Let's go. I'm so eager to see Paul."

Understandably Dad wants the white woman's blood as a special treat for Kali. She's thus kidnapped by Thugs, in obedience to their high priest, while Paul is out on a hunt for a tiger that is being blamed for the slaughter of innocent natives (who have actually been killed by those darned Thug infidels). Naturally Paul tries to rescue Lucy, which gives my father the opportunity to shout, "Nonbeliever! You are forbidden here! You have defiled Kali's temple! Thus, you must die!"

right to, the misery I had been enjoying since my return from India. Vatsyayana, in the very section that I am now translating, says that the husband of a good woman may count himself as the happiest man in the world. I believe him now, and I am still your husband.

That's why I telephoned you, to explain that I only did what I did because I was wrongly and falsely unhappy, and that now I am turning myself upside down and allowing myself to be rightly and truly happy. I am standing on my head, Sophia. Look! I am hanging by my feet and reaching out for you. As your husband, I am, according the *Kamasutra*, the happiest man in the world.

"Well I'm glad that you think you're happy, Leo," you coldly responded in your strongest British accent. "But that doesn't really change the fact that I have had a choice to make: to try to save my marriage or to try to save my life. It's not been a hard call. I'm sure you can understand. Are you still seeing her? Planter told me that you are. That's pathetic. You're helpless. And you're hopeless. You need so much, Leo, more than anyone can give you. You look to women for whatever it is you need outside of yourself. But you need more than any woman can possibly give you, certainly more that I can give you, more than your mother could have given, or your daughter might have given, and so much more than the Gupta girl has to give. I confess that sometimes I suppose I might try to love you again if I could imagine that my love would actually make you happy, really happy, if you could be content. But there's no point. You'll never find what you want. You are not, despite this 'happiest man' nonsense, in any way happy, satisfied, or at peace with yourself."

Even though you hung up on me, I clung to the hope that your words had given me. "I confess that sometimes I suppose I might try to love you again if . . . " That hope makes me happy.

When I saw that *Lakmé* was playing at the F. F. Finkelman Fine Arts Forum, I bought a ticket, reckoning that you might be nostalgic about our time in Paris; I hoped and suspected that I might run into you at the performance of the opera during which we once cried together and then laughed at ourselves for crying. Do you remember? In each other's arms, in our little room on the Boulevard Belle Dame du Sacré-Coeur, you whispered, "After all the tears we've shed over a very real little girl, I was surprised to discover we can still cry over an opera. I'm happy that we can still be moved by illusions, that we can still be sentimental." You smiled, then repeated it, "I'm happy," and then you wept and did not speak again until morning.

I turned the volume up as high as it would go:

Where lovers tell sad stories and show their
    wounds.
Let me hear the honeyed music of your
    infatuating flute,
The jingling sound of your adornments, in
    those songs;
Let me feel rain in rivulets upon my
    burning flesh,
And make me, my beloved, taste the
taste of perfect Love.

Jane's pounding on the door forced me turn it down, and in the silence, I wondered about songs and love. Lakshmi Bai is a young girl singing to an ancient god. While you're still as young as she, young enough to imagine there's perfection and to seek that purity in lovers, I am old enough to distrust the perfect love of books, songs, plays, operas, and romances. Love, it seems to me, as a long-ing for perfection, must be a symptom of an essential imperfection. We would not love were we not weak, nor would we need to be loved were we not sad.

One of the reasons I left my office to come here to the motel was to watch television, something we don't have at Swinburne Hall. *The Curse of Kali*, a film starring my parents, is going to be on the Midnight Monster Movie Madness show tonight. That I wasn't al-lowed to see it when I was a child made it all the more tantalizing; it was without their knowledge that I managed to watch it on tele-vision at the house of a neighbor, a little girl named Clover Weiner. Lucy, my mother, has come to India from America to see her fiancé, a dashing young British officer in the Bengal Lancers, coinci-dentally named Paul, who says things like "I've missed you, Lucy." An appropriate line to say to a woman who, in turn, utters things like "Oh Paul, I dream of the

This time *Lakmé* hardly made me cry. Your voice was echoing in
my ears: "I confess that sometimes I suppose I might try to love you
again if . . . " And those words made me so happy that, perched up in
the balcony by myself, I smiled, I laughed, I guffawed. Like life itself,
the opera promised the sublime and delivered the absurd. To the apparent dismay of the people around me, I just couldn't stop laughing.
Maybe my French wasn't good enough at the time we saw *Lakmé* in
Paris, but now, reading the electronic translation into English as rigged
up at the F.F.F.F.A.F., I don't know why everybody wasn't laughing,
at least by the time the young Indian priestess (as played by the old
Danish lesbian in blackface) sang to Gerald (who weighed in at about
half as much as his beloved), "I have drunk datura poison to celebrate
our love, and now I am going to die. Oh, Gerald, Gerald, farewell!"
Surely Delibes wanted his audience to laugh when Gerald, costumed
in the ridiculous pith helmet and full dress of a Bengal Lancer Brigade-
Major Saheeb, sings his answer to the dying Indian: "Wait, O Lakmé!
Do not die! For here comes your father!" I had hardly caught my breath
when Nilakantha entered the stage (with the chorus of British soldiers
singing in the background: "Happily we march for England's victory
o'er this pagan land") and sang to Gerald, "Fie, fie, fie on you, O foreigner to India!"

I had rented binoculars, not to scrutinize the performers, but to
look for you. As I scanned the audience—you'll never believe it—I suddenly saw Maya Blackwell (yes, none other, the lunatic who sends me
the love letters and poems) on the other side of the auditorium looking back at me through her own opera glasses. I waved to her, to show
her that I knew she was stalking me, and it must have frightened her
because, just as the thunderstorm on the stage broke (over Gerald's
aria: "Bewitching indeed is this Oriental land where people die from
eating flowers and falling in love"), she bolted from her seat, pushing
past and climbing over the knees that hampered her flight.

As I continued to search for you the Scandinavian siren, in a se-
quined sari and a wig that resembled some sort of animal humping her
head, sang:

> Oh Gerald, though you be a foreigner to our land,
> And a soldier too, oooo oooo oooo such sadness I feel!
> You have given me the sweetest dream a Hindu girl can have

Unable to find you anywhere, I focused my binoculars on her.

sires, hopes and fears. If he fails at that, the husband who takes a mistress is sure to become THE SADDEST MAN IN THE WORLD.

B. COMMENTARY

"The Saddest Man in the World"

Lalita, Lalita, my dearest Lalita:

A longing to go back, to begin again, is inevitably embedded in apology: I'm sorry, Lalita, that I could not love you in the ways that you needed and deserved to be loved. If only I had been younger, perhaps I could have loved you more perfectly. Love seems to require such energy, such an unrelenting dedication to providing and maintaining the happiness of the beloved. Love's text needs such constant revision, careful editing, and felicitous ornamentation if the beloved (as reader of, and in, the romance) is to be engaged. Seduction must never take a rest.

I'm at a crossroads, Lalita, one that you cannot, at your age, foresee: it's a question of wrong turns around blind corners, driving down into desolation at full speed or coasting up, against all gravity, into some sort of integrity, of ending up in an ontological amusement park or ending down in dark and desperate straits. Did you conspire with India to turn me upside down?

I am at the Marco Polo Traveler's Lodge even though you're busy. ("Professor Planter gave us so much homework this week," you claimed. "I've got to write a paper on love poetry in Heian Japan for him.")

"Are you alone tonight?" Jane, the desk clerk, asked, and "Yes," I said, "very much alone." And yet, alone here I feel more with you than I do when I'm with you these sad days and fall nights. Memory serves the heart its own truths. For its sake I brought music with me, the songs of Lakshmi Bai that I bought in Delhi (the soundtrack of our romance and Indian adventure). I played the bhajans and lit the gulab incense we brought back with us (for no sense stimulates memory so much as smell). I love to translate Indian words for you, to take liberties with a language, if not a sentiment, that is more rightfully yours than mine:

My beloved, come to me, and hover as the dark cloud does
Over dry and thirsting earth; shower me with love, and sing
The songs that travelers learn at places on the road

With English words of tender love that Hindus
  do not know.
Yes, you have brought me perfect love,
Though you are a soldier, oh, oh, a soldier,
Perfect love, yes perfect lovvvvvvvvvve, ah
  ahhhh!
Oh, O my beloved, this indeed is perfect love,
  perfect love!

There was a standing ovation, and still I was looking for you.
  I'm sorry, Sophia, that I could not have loved you with perfect love. Unhappiness made me incapable of it. But I am happy now. So you might want to reconsider things, to allow yourself "to suppose that you might try to love me again," to telephone me, to ask me to come home and to be THE HAPPIEST MAN IN THE WORLD.

Here Ends Book Four of the *Kamasutra*.

[B.] The Younger Mistress

A man never knows too much about his mistress.

—The *Kāisūtra* of Jayamaṅgala (IV.B), translated and annotated by Tajma Hall

A. TRANSLATION

A man should take a mistress if his wife is barren or has only given birth to daughters, if she's foul-mouthed[1] or fouls up. Regardless of what his wife is or isn't, does or doesn't, however, despite her virtues and accomplishments, her devotion and affection, a man may also take a mistress merely for the sake of diversion. That mistress should be respectful of the wife; unlike the wife, after all, she has the freedom to leave her lover whenever she loses interest in him.[2]

The man who decides to take a young mistress must take care to be fair to both of his women, not to neglect them, never to speak ill of one to the other, nor to praise one too enthusiastically in the presence of the other. He should strive to please his wife and his mistress in different but equal ways according to their respective needs and de-

1. The commentator Yaśodhara understands the phrase as referring to halitosis ("a woman whose breath [or spirit] is rancid"), while Pralayānanga reads it as malediction ("a woman who utters obscenities or pollutes Sanskrit discourse with vulgarisms from the vernaculars"); and the usually demure Narsingh Sastri interprets it to mean "a woman who habitually uses her mouth as a vulva."

2. Pralayānanga adds, "If this is the case, she should return all gifts that the man has given her; if, however, he rejects her, she is free to keep his presents. Thus it is to her advantage to so beguile her lover that when she decides to dump him, he imagines that it is he who has taken the initiative in ending the affair."

all the words for perfect Love in Sanskrit and Hindi. I explained to her why it might be a good idea to consider changing the name of the mission from Maranatha to Kāmanātha [*Maranatha* means "Lord of Death" in Sanskrit and has evil overtones].

"So, I'm getting another free trip to India, this one paid for by God. The Lord has work for me to do in India. Yes, I, Leopold Roth, am taking love, True Love, to India! But the problem is, I've got to finish my translation of the *Kāmasūtra* before I go, or it will never be done. She's already got me working on a Sanskrit translation of her favorite passages, the ones we're going to use on the pagans, from The Maranatha Evangelical Handbook of the Lord's Own Words for Idolaters, Animists, and Infidels. I've just translated I Corinthians 6:9. That's why, if you want me to have anything to do with your dissertation, you must hurry up and finish it. I'm afraid I'll be gone by the end of the year."

sake of so many millions of Indians who do not know, who have not yet felt,
His Love. The Lord's way is so perfect. He doesn't just give His Love and
leave it at that. He shows His Love by providing us with ways to serve others with It.'

"Here's the amazing part. It turns out that she had been ordered by the
elders of her mission to go on an evangelical tour of pagan India, Sri Lanka,
Nepal, and Bangladesh to spread the Gospel in a land of heathens and for-
nicators, phallus-worshipers and pantheists, that they might also come to
know the perfect Love.

"By suggesting that she should start trying to get used to spicy Indian
food, I was able to convince her to come with me for dinner at the Ganges
Grill. (I didn't dare take her to the Taj Mahal.) When I confessed that I
didn't know if I was ready to get too involved at the Mission yet, with
praying and that kind of thing, she sweetly smiled and comforted me. 'It's
only natural for you to have doubts like that now, Leo. But once you know
Love, all else will follow. For where there is the Lord's Love, the prophet
Isaiah tells us in scripture,' the wilderness and the solitary place shall be
glad and blossom with roses.''

"As we ate I kept looking at her across the table, thinking about how,
years ago, I use to take her into my parents' pool house. They had decorated
it like a Moghul harem room because of a movie my father was supposed
to star in. The restaurant had the same kind of decorations. So as she continued to explain how the Lord spreads His Love in the world, I was trying to remember what it was like to fuck her, and I kept picturing her in
the porno movies I had seen. I was getting more and more aroused. I
wanted to make love to her again. I knew it would be difficult, of course,
since she had given up imperfect sex for perfect Love, since she was so completely in love with the Lord. But Vātsyāyana says, in Book Four of the
Kāmasūtra, that if a man has studied the text and has mastered the arts
and sciences covered by it, he should be able to seduce and win the affection of any women even if she is in love with the most powerful and prestigious of beings.

"She believed, with all her heart, that God had brought us together once
again, not simply for my salvation, but so that I could participate in the mission and spread perfect Love in India. I could, and indeed should, she told
me, with the support of the Mission, go with her as an interpreter and translator. Without knowing it, I had studied Sanskrit because the Lord willed
it, so that I could someday do His work.

"And so I'm going to Banaras with her, and she's so happy that I know

"I couldn't believe it—it worked like a charm—she took the bait: 'Leopold Roth. I know you. The voice was that of the Holy Spirit. You are not losing your mind, you are gaining your soul. You were right to obey. I somehow knew that I would receive an important call today, that I would be given a very special way to serve the Lord this morning. Perhaps you don't remember me. My name is Mary now, but you knew me as Leona, Leona Sealman. Remember? You were blamed when I fell off my bicycle and broke my arm. I did not know at the time that the Lord was, by that injury, trying to teach me that the flesh is painful, that the spirit alone is the ground of joy. It took a long time for me to learn. I know why the Lord made you call me. I understand, and I can help you. His plan, the way in which He brings us all to Love, is so perfect. Like you, I have sinned. We are, I suspect, very much alike in many ways. That's why we were drawn together as children. We yearned for love. Now I have put away childish things and, through His guidance, have found real Love. And now He has sent you to me so that I may take you to Him. It's so obvious. As teenagers we looked for love together and did not find it because we, each of us in our innocence, looked for it in the other, and when we realized that the other person could not give us the love we longed for, we went on to others, and others, and others, yearning and searching for love. The Lord finally showed me that love is not in other people, but in Him. And now He has brought you to me so that I can show you how to let Him show you that. You are ready to know and feel the perfect happiness of perfect Love, the Lord's perfect gift.'

"Probably mistaking the sound of my allergic sniffling over the phone for weeping, she consoled me, comforted me, and asked if I could feel the Love.' I want to feel it,' I confessed, and she invited me to the Mission. I made the excuse that I was afraid, that it was all happening so quickly, that I needed to talk to her alone, that I couldn't face a group of people with this, not yet. I was still too confused and shaken up by it. She understood and agreed to come to my office.

"She looked pretty good, not as good as she looked in Box Lunch or Southern Comforts, but not bad for a fifty-one-year-old Christian. And there was a certain sweetness about her, a kind of enthusiasm and a disarming sincerity. Mayavati took an immediate liking to her.

"When, in our conversation, Leona, or rather Mary, discovered that I was a Sanskrit scholar, a Hindi speaker, and an expert on India, she was moved to tears of joy. 'Of course, of course, that is why the Lord directed you to call me, not just for your sake but for mine as well, but, most of all, for the

name, Mary MacDylan. God's gain is Bluelove's loss—that babe really knew how to make a blow job come to life on the screen.'

"At once, I looked up the mission in the phone book, telephoned, and heard the very voice that, over thirty-five years ago, whispered, 'Do you want to do it to me today after school?' now say, 'Maranatha Mission. Hello. The Lord loves you with Perfect Love. This is Mary. How may I serve the Lord by serving you today?'

"'I didn't want to frighten her off or freak her out, and so, pretending that I didn't know that Mary was the Lana who was the Loni who was the Leona who was the first girl I ever fucked, I played dumb. 'My name is Leopold Roth. I grew up here in L.A. I didn't have much of a religious upbringing, not at school anyway, not at Hollywood High in the early sixties. God wasn't on the curriculum there. And then, up at Berkeley . . .' I hesitated, expecting, and hoping for, her to jump in and tell me that she used know a boy named Leopold Roth and that he had taken her virgin- ity, but no, all she said was, 'How can I serve the Lord by helping you today?' Realizing that I had to be a bit more clever, using the stratagems of Vatsyayana's most seductive man-about-town, if I was going to get her to go out with me, I continued. I told her that I'm a professor, that my wife wants a divorce, that I have truly sinned. 'Yes, I have sinned,' I confessed in a stark and pained voice. 'I have fornicated.' I love that word.' I told her that I was very sorry for the life of debauchery and dissipation that I had been leading. 'Truly sorry but, despite my repentance, I am despised: no one cares for me, except a cat and one graduate student; all others have turned their heels against me. I am living alone in my office and suffering for my sins, and I don't know where to turn or how to turn.' And then I went for the kill: 'You'll probably think I'm crazy, but this is why I tele- phoned. Something really weird just happened, just moments ago. I can't explain it. Maybe you can help me to understand. I heard a voice, a strange muffled voice, eerie and uncanny, coming from I know not where. It commanded me: "Leopold, thou must obey. Take the Los Angeles tele- phone directory into thy hands. Close thine eyes. Open the book. Surren- der thy will and let a higher force guide thy finger to a telephone number at random. Open thine eyes and dial the number. The person who an- swers the telephone will know how to help thee."' I know you must think I'm crazy. I thought I was losing my mind. Maybe I have. But I was afraid because the voice was so powerful. I obeyed it out of fear and out of confusion. I'm sorry to bother you. I know I must be going mad.'

told me that she had become a porn star, changed her name to Lana Lamange. When I called Jock in hopes of a lead, he invited me over for dinner and to see a video in which she had starred—he's got a big collection. It had been made about ten years ago—Southern Comforts, a kind of a porno version of Gone with the Wind in which Lana plays a southern belle named Harlot O'Scara, who doesn't actually do much in the movie but fellate confederate soldiers, including for the climax of the film, Robert E. Lee. She doesn't say much either, except, 'The South will rise again!' Her accent wasn't very good, but she looked okay and had obviously mastered the practical techniques of the ninth chapter of Book Two of the Kamasutra. Jock put me in touch with a friend of his, a porno-movie mogul in charge of Bluelove Productions, the company that had made most of Leona's movies. The guy told me a bizarre, and rather unbelievable, story:

"'Lana was a porno institution, one of the great leading ladies in the industry. That's why the whole thing's such a tragedy. We were right in the middle of shooting the movie version of a classic book, Confessions of a Cockeyed Coed. Lana was playing the part of the dorm mother. She was perfect for it. She was able, on film, to project a motherly wisdom and slutty raunchiness at the same time. That takes talent. And she gave it all up for nothing. She came to me one morning and told me that she was quitting. "I'm finished with Bluelove. The Lord came to me last night and, like a flash of lightning, a banging of cymbals, revealed His Love for me. He told me that, if I stop making porno movies for you, He would give me a part in His divine production. He told me that if I stopped fornicating for a living, He would give me Love, His Love, perfect Love, and give me a means to show His Love to others. And, in an instant, I accepted His offer and have vowed to give all my Love to Him. 'Cover up the nakedness of thy flesh, and bare the nakedness of thy soul unto Me,' He said. The Truth is so obvious now that I love the Lord. Our Love is gratuitous and pure, kind and enduring, unblemished by envy, jealousy, anger, lust, disappointment, or fear.'

"'I couldn't believe it, most actresses at her age would have done anything to play the dorm mother in Confessions of a Cockeyed Coed! 'So you're giving up oral sex for Oral Roberts,' I joked, but she didn't even laugh. That's what happens to people who find God's love—they lose their senses of humor. So she tells me she's going to work for her Lord, spreading the gospel of love, and that I should send her residual checks to the Maranatha Mission for Divine Love, and to make them out to her new

"Professor Vātsyā-ahchoo!-yana Mallanāga. I'm getting to know him better. He's not the pedant I thought he was, not quite anyway. I'd invite him to a dinner party. He's chubby, all smiles and sparkling eyes, a gourmand, a big drinker, and always joking. I didn't get it before: the humor, deadpan and ironic as it is, went right over my head; but the whole Kāmasūtra is a rollicking joke, both a satire of the manners and morals of Gupta India and a larger, more universal romantic comedy about the folly of love. The last line of the text is the punch line. That's where he lets us know that he's been pulling our legs all along. It's a verbal wink."

Roth did not live to translate that final statement: "I, Vātsyāyana, composed this text, the Kāmasūtra, while strictly observing a long vow of celibacy; only after mastering the arts and sciences of love can one hope to take control of his senses and to have the strength to restrain one's longings and passions; it must be remembered that only through control and restraint, through passing beyond desire and attachment, can one hope to find fulfillment in life."

He sneezed again, sprayed decongestant into his nostrils, and lit a Viceroy.

"I've got to break off my relationship with the old clown of sexology before I go back to India. And, as I've warned you, I'm leaving at the end of the year. You'd better get the dissertation done soon."

"Gesundheit," I said again, and then, while naturally wondering if Ms. Gupta might be accompanying him once more, but not daring to ask, I inquired if he was returning to India in order to appear for his trial in Delhi on the charges of smuggling antiquities and wildlife.

"No," he sneezed, "of course not. Just as He commanded Moses to go back to Egypt where Moses was a wanted criminal, God is sending me back into India." He laughed, lit another Viceroy, sneezed (I switched from "gesundheit" to "God bless you"), sneezed again, sighed, and then told me a bizarre and rather unbelievable story:

"About a month ago, I was up on Sunset, taking a walk, feeling a little lonely, and, as I passed Hollywood High School, I couldn't help but think of my very first girlfriend back at Hollywood High, Leona Sealman. I wondered what had happened to her. I wanted to see her again for some reason. After graduation, I remembered, she had changed her name to Loni Leigh and had tried, unsuccessfully, to become a Hollywood actress. I suddenly really wanted to find her. A friend of my parents, an old actor named Jock Newhouse—maybe you've seen him in movies—had

night and day, struggling with it because the antihistamines make me so
fuckin' sleepy. I've got to get everything done before I go. So unless you want
Siegel to take my place on the committee as your supervisor, you've got to be
ready to defend what you've written before the end of the year. Have you
shown your work to Siegel?"

"No," I lied.

"Sometimes I feel I could kill him," Roth said of Siegel, who was now referring to Roth as "Sneezy"; each of the six other members of the Asian studies department were, likewise, given the name of one of the other dwarfs,
and he called the secretary, Nora Naper, "Snow White." Naper had, incidentally, written a notice for the W.O.W. (Women of Western) faculty and
staff newsletter, in which she described Roth as having been a "blatant sexual harasser" for many years:

"Whenever he comes into the department office, I can tell that he is undressing me in his mind. I know he is. A woman can always tell. I can sense
that his eyes are exploring my naked body. It's creepy. It's perverted. It's
degrading. I've asked the other secretaries in the other departments in
Swinburne Hall if they have had the same feeling. And almost all of them
said they had. The philosophy secretary, who has been at the university for
over twenty-five years, said that there is something very sexual about his
smile. It creates a hostile environment. Secretaries be on the alert! It could
happen in your departments too!

While I was shocked that the libelous letter had been printed, Roth laughed
and sneezed over it. "Did you ever notice that her name works well in a
charade: 'Secretary.' A Nora Naper other, etc.' equals 'Secret Aryan or an
ape? Roth erect!'" It didn't seem to bother him that the last two letters of
the charade do not correspond.

When I brought my half-chapter on Pralayānanga's commentary on
the Kāmasūtra to his office/residence, Roth actually seemed pleased.
"Maybe it'll help me understand old Vātsyāyana better, having somebody's gloss and annotation on what he's got to say. I've got to finish the
Kāmasūtra soon. It's driving me fuckin' crazy. I'm only halfway through
Book Four. I'm starting to get impatient with the old pandit. Professors
never know when to stop."

Once again I asked him whether or not, as he was working on
Vātsyāyana's text, he ever got a feeling for the individual, a sense of who he
was as "a man of flesh and blood with his own particular fears and desires."

dience itself would be lulled into sleep and sweet dreams. No other composer, as far as I am aware, has ever attempted to put his audience to sleep. This would be bold indeed. But what an effect! In the morning they would not know for certain whether they had seen the opera or dreamed it! Art and life, dream and reality, would be merged into one experience! Advise me, Captain Burton, I beg of you.

I have another problem on which you alone are qualified to give counsel. It is a question of the finale. What am I, as a composer of operas, to do with your final chapter, Book Seven of the *Kama Sutra*, with those recipes for aphrodisiacs and those pharmaceutical and magical formulas for making the penis bigger and the vagina tighter? Obviously the public would be interested in such information, but how do I convey it to them musically, choreographically, and dramatically?

I hope you will find the time to respond to me soon. You have my admiration, Sir, something a Frenchman rarely gives an Englishman. But we are, I suspect, Orientals at heart!

Vive les Indes, vive l'amour!

—Léo Delibes (Paris, 1890)

Editor's Note

As I have said, I've had my share of problems with Professor Roth. But, as I've also noted, it was hard not to feel sorry for him: the sneezing, that blatant symptom of his merciless allergy to Mayavati, rendered him simultaneously pitiful and ridiculous. Because of that sneezing, it was almost impossible to have a conversation with the red-eyed Roth, difficult for him to sustain any train of thought amidst the repetitive achoos that punctuated his every sentence and shifted all consciousness from his brain to his sinuses, and difficult for me to think of anything to say other than "gesundheit."

He telephoned to ask me to come to see him for a discussion of my dissertation on the Sanskrit commentarial tradition, something he had, as far as I can remember, never before done in my entire career as a graduate student under his supervision.

"Listen Saighal," he sneezed, "if you want me to be on your committee, you've got to finish quickly, achbooo, because achbooo, achbooooo, I'm leaving L.A. right after, achbooo—your Chanukah—achbooooooo. I'm leaving for India and I don't know when I'll be back. India—cradle of religious conscious, land of spirituality, the mystic East! And I've got a lot to do before then. I've got to finish my translation of the fuckin' Kamasutra even if it kills me. Actually it is killing me. Really killing me. I'm working

is a dance ballet, a choreographic interpretation of Oriental love, similar to the one in my Market scene in *Lakmé*, but set in the harem and as erotically daring as censors will allow. In Scene Two, the main characters are introduced: your "citizen" is my "boulevardier" (Signore Leonardi is already eager to sing the role), a married man who falls madly in love with a young girl from the Maharajah's harem, Ratcedevee (the part to be played by the incomparable Mademoiselle Arnot). He enchants her and lures her from the harem. European audiences will, by force of the dramatic conventions and conceits to which they have been so long subjected, assume that, because the hero is married, this affair will end tragically, with the usual death scene. What a surprise I have in store for them! In the Indies, I have learned from my reading of your transla-tion of the *Kama Sutra* (specifically Book Four), women are more tolerant than their European sisters.

In Scene Three we meet the boulevardier's wife, Prajnadevee, and observe her devotion to her husband as she washes his feet, drinks the water that drips from them, and then sings a glorious aria, with extensive Oriental flourishes in col-oratura: "Whither thou goest, there goest I. . . . All that I do is done for love." We understand that older wife and younger mistress respect, appreciate, enjoy, and even love each other as they go skipping through a bower, singing a charming duet in which they express their common love for the hero. In Scene Four our boulevardier bids good evening to his wife and mistress, singing that he must go to the demi-monde for an evening of sophisticated lovemaking. Wishing him well and express-ing their love for him, they excitedly promise to wait up even until dawn in hopes of hearing tales of his amorous adventures. He is escorted away by a chorus of ladies of the night.

Here, Captain Burton, is where I am urgently in need of your advice. I do not know how to end it. Should I capitulate to European tastes at the last moment? If so, our hero must be murdered at this point. Admittedly the funeral scene, with the cremation fires illuminating the stage upon which Prajnadevee and Ratcedevee, backed up by choruses of both women of the harem and ladies of the brothel, singing operative requia for the dead hero, would be spectacular. And then, in Oriental fash-ion, the two heroines might throw themselves upon the pyre of their beloved. That would be dramatic. Or should I abandon familiar conventions and more provoca-tively introduce the Oriental sensibilities? Our hero might return home to his wife and mistress in the morning, sing to them of his erotic exploits, and then, as the sun rises and the stage becomes bright, they would adoringly sing a lullaby to him, ac-companied by Indian instruments only, an aria based on the Indian philosophical notion that life is but an illusion.

If I take the second approach, and I surely shall if you so advise, I would try to make the lullaby so beautiful, so Orientally peaceful and bewitchingly calming, that the au-

My Dear Captain Burton,

Some weeks ago a copy of a charming little book found its way into my hands, an English translation of an ancient lover's chapbook of love entitled *Kama Sutra*. I hope it is not too rash of me (in defiance, I confess, of promises to keep a secret) to disclose that it has been suggested to me by my friend, the great German lexicographer and Orientalist, Herr R. Roth, that the initials "B.F.R.," as given to indicate the modest gentleman responsible for the felicitous English version, when reversed, are your very own, Sir, and that you, Sir, are to be congratulated for this work. As your daring expeditions into the Dark Continent of Africa have shed light on geographical realities, so this courageous literary exploration of the Dark Heart of the Indies brings to light many sentimental realities. *Bravo, mon Capitaine, bravissimo!*

While it may not be a book for cold English eyes, I am certain that the more cultivated readers of a warmer France will find this pretty depiction of Oriental love irresistible. It is so delightfully Gallic in many ways. Thus I have taken the liberty of giving my tattered copy of what I more than suspect is your excellent translation to my friend, M. Lamairesse, an ardent student of Oriental languages and manners here in Paris, in hopes of seducing him with it, that he might consider proceeding with a French translation and commentary. With the aid of your book, I wish to convince him, given his passion for both the opera and the Indies, furthermore, to collaborate with me on a libretto that I hope you will find of interest. It, in truth, is the reason for this letter.

The great success of my *Lakmé* has inspired me to believe it profitable to do much more with my development of a theme of love in which the erotic and the exotic are brought together in such a way as to define each other. *Lakmé* marked the beginning of an experiment, one that reaches its greatest boldness in the Market scene of Act Two where I, as artist, began to challenge our notion of opera. Due to the excessive influence of Italians and Germans, opera has been too reliant on narrative. My next venture, inspired by a reading of your translation, Monsieur R.F.B., will go before the guard. It will be as a glove slapped against the cheek of formal conventions, the pale cheek, if you will, of the ordinary, the normal, the expected. Please, Sir, as an explorer, adventurer, and a man of distinguished tastes, be kind enough to give me your reactions, permissions, insights, and, if you can spare them, your praises. Be my second in a duel with the banal.

My idea is to compose an opera based on your translation of the *Kama Sutra*. Here I give you a brief outline which, you will observe, follows the structure of your book: My Overture will introduce the themes and the melodies, Indian ones translated into the European idiom; there will be Oriental instruments, including lutes, drums, and bamboo flutes, in the orchestra pit to accompany our violins and clarinets. Scene One

IV

Mistresses and Wives

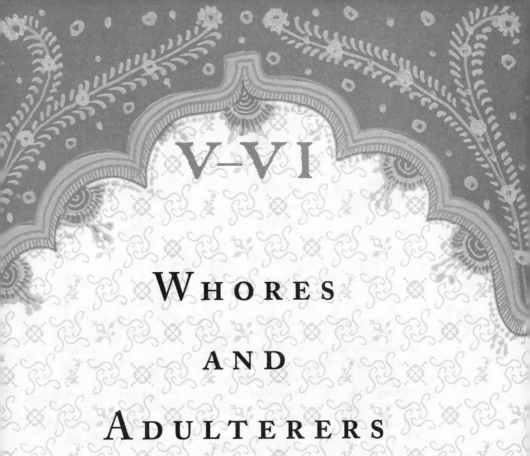

V–VI

WHORES

AND

ADULTERERS

I alas am He, and Him, and Her, and She, as all the Players in the Play and Game are Lee. Thus He and She and They kill'd Him, all indictable to the murd'rous degree that They're Mee, O My! For my part, his Death has so trulee wrought a change in Mee, as nothing else but a Miracle cou'd—For first I see and loathe my grand Deceits—Next I am resolv'd to give satisfaction to all I've wrong'd, Him, Her, Them, and Mee. Perhaps an Ingenuitee of poetical Repentance will permit Lee to Love. Surelee what in a Book is reasonablee done, in Life can bee, if onlee Charactors and Languaging from Mee might be set Free. Free to Love or See what Love might Beeeee.

—Nat. Lee, *Alexander in India* (1690)

A. Stages of Love
(Intentio Amatoris)

Once upon a time, the Indian legend has it, a man who had seduced the daughter of a king was sentenced to be executed: impaled upon a stake for his deviance and iniquities, the unrepentant man cried out with his last breath, "*mara mara mara!* (death death death)," and though he deserved, for all of his debaucheries and infidelities, to suffer in the lowest Hell, he was redeemed and enjoyed ten million years of perfect Love in the highest Heaven, indulged in all his whims and wishes by supernal nymphs, who sang and danced for him, who caressed and comforted him; for, even though he had not realized what he was saying, he had (albeit charadically) supplicated God in the compassionate form of Lord Rama: "-ma Rama Rama ra- (-od! God! God! Go-)." What we feel or think is, apparently, not as significant as what we say.

—Leopold Roth, "*Oflyricheros:* Anagramic Charades and Other
Amphibological Verbal Constructions in Sanskrit Literature"

A. TRANSLATION

There are, according to the professors of amatory arts and sexual sciences, ten developmental stages of love, viz.:[1]

1. [LOVE AT FIRST] SIGHT, (as when the newborn infant sees the breast,) {or at first smell, taste, touch, or hearing, or even at first idea, as when Nala and Damayanti [though total

---

1. In the translation that follows, the boundaries between original text and native interpretations, the lines separating one commentary from another, the distinctions between original, intended statement and translated, interpreted idea are barely detectable: Roth, suddenly and inexplicably more attentive to scholarship, has included the commentarial readings of Yaśodhara [in brackets], of Pralayānanga (in parentheses), and of Narsingh Śāstrī {in braces}, thereby forming a unified text written over a period of 1500 years by a

strangers] each fell in love merely because of stories about the other,} [is first].

2. [Then there is] DESIRE [for what has been seen], (an over-whelming, all-consuming, and self-defining hunger, like that of a neonate for the milk of the breast). {"In the beginning, *kama* seized upon the unevolved cosmos and was the first seed of con-sciousness. Sages, looking with wisdom into themselves, discov-ered love/desire to be the very bond of the existent within the nonexistent, the source of all thought," thus the Veda.} (Language developed as a means to say, "I want [what I have seen]," and lan-guage transformed feeling/need [fear and desire] into thought.)

3. [Then] THOUGHT [(arises over and) about what has been desired], (just as the mental processes of the infant, for the sake of survival, are formed as a means to experience the taste/plea-sure [*rasa*] of the beloved/sucked breast, so the lover's con-sciousness is reformed/re-formed as a means to experience love [*rasa*] by kissing ["sucking," (as a manifestation of) "making love to"] the beloved); {[and] only thought distinguishes [human] love [*kama*] from [bestial, instinctual] desire [*kama*]}.

4. LOSS OF SLEEP [on account of thoughts about what has been seen and desired]: (A lover apart from the beloved, like an infant crying in the night for milk, {distressed in its ignorance} of the otherness of the object of desire, is unable to go back to sleep until the arrival of the beloved/breast/woman. {Finally, however, when sleep comes, the infant/lover dreams of the breast/beloved and learns, therefore, to seek gratification in dream/illusion.}

5. LOSS OF ENERGY, [on account of insomnia], ([falls upon]

---

single unincarnated author, whose consciousness, divided into four distinct cerebral con-tainers, unites in a text. Professor Roth, in reassembling dead words and trying to bring them to life, seems to me a sort of philological Professor Frankenstein—his text no less dan-gerous, awkward, or pathetic than the novel monster. While doting on the commentators, Roth has neglected Vātsyāyana's own explanation of the codified stages of love: "When a man sees a woman who is attractive to him, whom he comes to desire and to think about, at that point (i.e., after passing to the third stage in the development of love), he should do everything in his power to seduce and possess her; for if he does not, thought will be in-distinguishable from obsession and the lover will begin to lose sleep, the first of the seven losses that characterize the remaining stages of love. The lover must seduce the beloved as a matter of life and/or death." Perhaps Roth would have included that passage had he not died at this point, a death that left the rest of the *Kāmasūtra* untranslated. Dismembered parts of the body of the text remain scattered about, each depriving the others of unity, of the wholeness that would sustain them as portions of a living verbal system.

the lover who is deprived of his beloved, like a child suffering from malnutrition). {Love and work are natural enemies.}

6. [Without energy there is a concomitant] LOSS OF CONCERN [or care about people other than the one who has been seen, desired, and thought about]. (The child who has been malnourished is sure to be lacking in compassion for others, for as the sages say, "A man gives only when he has"; lovers [desirers] care only about love [the fulfillment of desire {love}].) {While stories (and songs [myths, legends, romances, and the like]) about lovers please us, it is [indeed] unpleasant to [actually] be around people who are in love (and thus absorbed [in themselves]).}

7. LOSS OF PROPRIETY [i.e., social deviance (as a result of {carelessness} uncaringness)]: (As people in love, like unruly children, are prone to misbehave, we cannot expect decency from lovers. Love is [by nature {by definition}] indecent. Has one heard the laughter of a naughty child? Has one seen the glee in the eyes of the delinquent?) {All have heard of the crimes committed by lovers in the name of love; unlike other criminals, however, they are unrepentant and incapable of reform. [All have seen the disasters of love].}

8. [Ultimately, if desire is not satisfied, {if love is not tamed (turned into a normative social principle [sublimated])}, there is a] LOSS OF SANITY, [an inability to act with propriety in accordance with social norms (as based on an assessment of reality and a knowledge of the moral codes {as agreed on by reasonable people})]. (Naughty children, insane people, and lovers are [in their behavior] indistinguishable), {thus the madness of Auddalaki, the sage whose sagacity was supplanted by insanity [because of his love (for a young girl)], (unnoticed at first because madness often resembles wisdom [in content (more than form)] and vice versa)}.

9. LOSS OF CONSCIOUSNESS [as that faculty which sustains connections between sane people]: (The lover, the madman, the abused child, and the philosopher [of the Vedanta-school] live in another world, (this world being entirely unreal to them, {their world being without substance; [illusion being their only reality]}, delusion their only knowledge)]. {When we hear the story of Nala and Damayanti or the history of Auddalaki and the

student Vijaya, we are conscious of them, but they are not conscious of us. (To be in love is to become [like] a character in such a romance.)}

10. LOSS OF LIFE: [Just as a person loves as the result of a consciousness of death, so a lover dies as a result of the loss of a consciousness that is caused by the madness that arises out of the social deviance that comes from the lack of care that arises out of the fatigue that is caused by the insomnia that results from thinking about and desiring a person that one has only just seen.] (The madman, the lover, and the infant who is deprived of the breast are all dead, although they may appear to be alive.) {There are no "love stories" about living beings.}

B. COMMENTARY

Kama—a word for love in a dead language: the meaning can be fixed and articulated with precision by means of lexicons, commentarial glosses, illustrative literary sources (in which mythic and legendary, deceased lovers speak), and such theoretical compendia as the *Kamasutra*. The meaning of the word can be known and understood. But we cannot comprehend the meaning (either the intent or significance) of our word for *love*, that morphemic wafer on a quivering tongue, that small, dark, vermicular, spermatic squiggle from the tip of a pen. Uttered or written, muttered or scrawled, whispered or shrieked by the living to the living, the meanings of abstract words in a living language cannot be fixed; by their essential nature they are persistently and insistently changing as the living language changes, consistently inconsistently growing like self-mutating viruses in living hosts who speak or write, or hear or read. The meaning of a word that's spoken is gone even by the time it's heard, let alone remembered, let alone recorded in writing. I understand *kama*, but not the translation—not *love*. Only what is dead can be truly understood.

The first time I saw her, like the last time I saw her, I . . .[2]

2. Here ends Roth's commentary; here ends his life. These are Roth's last words—his last writes. I presume he was writing this very sentence when someone entered his office in Swinburne Hall, where he lived and worked at this stage of love. My teacher put down his Koh-I-Noor fountain pen and looked up from his desk, upon which the Monier-Williams *Sanskrit-English Dictionary*, the Sanskrit edition of the *Kāmasūtra*, and the notebooks for his translation of, and commentary upon, the *Kāmasūtra* were open. There was an exchange

of words. Perhaps, given what he was writing at the moment, Roth had just looked up *kāma*, the word for *love*, in the *Sanskrit-English Dictionary* to clarify his sense of its semantic range in and through a wide spectrum of literary contexts, endeavoring to exhume the remains of the word from that lexical graveyard late at night in order to dissect it, to understand its morphology. And perhaps he passed the dictionary to his visitor, asking him or her to read it:

कम *kắma*, *as*, m. (fr. √2. *kam;* once *kāmá*, VS. xx, 60), wish, desire, longing (*kāmo me bhuñjīta bhavān*, my wish is that you should eat, Pāṇ. iii, 3, 153), desire for, longing after (gen., dat., or loc.), love, affection, object of desire or of love or of pleasure, RV.; VS.; TS.; AV.; ŚBr.; MBh.; R. &c.; pleasure, enjoyment; love, especially sexual love or sensuality; Love or Desire personified, AV. ix; xii; xix (cf. RV. x, 129, 4); VS.; PārGṛ.; N. of the god of love, AV. iii. 25, 1; MBh.; Lalit.; (represented as son of Dharma and husband of Rati [MBh. i, 2596 ff.; Hariv.; VP.]; or as a son of Brahmā, VP.; or sometimes of Saṃkalpa, BhP. vi, 6, 10; cf. *kāma-dēva*); N. of Agni, SV. ii, 8, 2, 19, 3; AV.; TS.; KātyŚr.; ŚāṅkhŚr.; of Vishṇu, Gal.; of Baladeva (cf. *kāma-pāla*), L.; a stake in gambling, Nār. xvi, 9; a species of mango tree (= *mahā-rāja-cūta*), L.; N. of a metre consisting of four lines of two long syllables each; a kind of bean, L.; a particular form of temple, Hcat.; N. of several men; (*ā*), f. 'wish, desire' (only instr. *kāmayā*, q. v.); N. of a daughter of Pṛthu-śravas and wife of Ayuta-nāyin, MBh. i, 3774; (*am*), n. object of desire, L.; semen virile, L.; N. of a Tīrtha, MBh. iii, 5047; (*am*), ind., see s. v.; (*ena*), ind. out of affection or love for; (*āya* or *e*), ind. according to desire, agreeably to the wishes of, out of love for (gen. or dat.), RV.; AV.; TS.; ŚBr.; ChUp.; (*āt*), ind. for one's own pleasure, of one's own free will, of one's own accord, willingly, intentionally, Mn.; R.; (*kāmá*), mfn. wishing, desiring, RV. ix, 113, 11; (ifc.) desirous of, desiring, having a desire or intention; (cf. *go-kˀ*, *dharma-kˀ;* frequently with inf. in *tu*, cf. *tyaktu-kˀ*.) — **kandalā**, f., N. of a woman. — **karṣaṇa** in *ā-kāma-kˀ*, q. v. — **kalā**, f., N. of Rati (wife of Kāma), L.

Thus he or she was holding the book when whatever words said caused whatever anger, causing whatever character to slam the lexicon into Roth's face.

There remains a blood stain on the cover of Roth's dictionary. Thanks to Professor Planter, invested by Dean Sophia White-Roth with the authority to dispose of Roth's Sanskrit texts and other Indological materials and resources, the book now belongs to me. Thus Roth, although inadvertently, has finally provided me with a Monier-Williams *Sanskrit-English Dictionary* as I had asked him to do when he went to India with Ms. Gupta last summer.

At this point I find myself in the dreadfully daunting predicament of having to determine what to do with the unfinished manuscript, of having to imagine how closely Roth's own final, rewritten drafts of both the translation and commentary would have resembled these remains. How much of the verbal *memento mori* would he have wished or dared to make public? I must ask the fundamental questions of literary criticism: what were the author's intentions, and how much, if at all, do they matter?

How can I presume to finish his book when I cannot even complete the last, incomplete sentence, pregnant as it is with the mirror-twin clauses that determine the feelings, thoughts, desires, hopes, and fears of the subject on the edge of the ellipses that indicate his death? Who is she, that "her?" Ms. Gupta and Professor White-Roth are obvious candidates. But "her" might have been Eve Christ or Sunita Sen or Tess Berkeley or even Clover Weiner of old, or Mary MacDylan of late who was Leona Sealman of old. Although anything is possible in an unfinished text, I doubt that "her" refers to Aphra Digby, Venus Doudounes Newhouse, Pimiko Planter, Nora Naper, Mrs. Gupta, or Roth's mother. In very different ways, "she" might be his daughter, or Maya Blackwell, or even his cat. Or maybe there was someone else, another woman whom he had spared from immersion in the choppy waters of this text, or one whom he had just met and was about to introduce into his analysis of love. Anything is possible in an unfinished narrative. Maybe he was about to make a character of her at this point, a *dea ex machina* who would bring with her, from outside the world of the book, a happy ending to the world within it. She would clearly demonstrate that love (the sort of love that Roth yearned for, a love suggested to him by the *Kāmasūtra*) is actually possible in both a life and a book. Yes, anything is possible in an unfinished text. As it stands, however, "she" is no one.

Detective Plato Chan of the Homicide Division of the Hollywood Police Department certified that the death was accidental: "The very high level of alcohol in his blood in conjunction with triprolidine, pseudoephedrine, naphazoline hydrochloride, and cocaine indicates that the professor was not in control of himself. Given his allergy, investigators have determined that Roth sneezed with great force, which brought his face down at a high velocity against a dictionary on his desk. His nose broken, dazed and heavily intoxicated, he suddenly stood up, lost his balance or consciousness, and fell back against his desk, thereby receiving the blow responsible for the subdural hematoma secondary to trauma associated with a basal skull fracture that killed him." Professor Planter, who had initially argued that it was suicide, that Roth had actually beaten himself to death with the dictionary, accepted Chan's verdict. I did not accept it then, nor do I now. I believe that Professor Leopold Roth was murdered. After coming into possession of this manuscript and reading it, I became convinced that it contains ample suggestions as to who, in terms of motive, might have been his assailant. On that conviction, I delivered what I had of the manuscript to Detective Chan. After weeks of waiting for him to contact me, I finally telephoned him, only to discover a complete lack of interest in the case or the text. "That," he remarked with a disparaging laugh, "is the craziest book I've ever tried to read. What's it supposed to mean?"

When I asked him if he thought it might contain clues to the murder, he tiredly told me, "That's not how it works. I'm not Sherlock Holmes, and this isn't a crime novel. This is life, and in life, accidents happen. As far as we can tell, given that there is no evidence of any kind to suggest anyone visited the professor's office that night, we don't have a case of murder in any degree or even a case of manslaughter here. We've got the accidental death of a drunken drug addict. Not much drama there. The case is closed. Story over."

That phrase, "story over," starkly reaffirmed my continued sense of the unity of Roth's life and his text in both form and content. Simultaneously and prematurely, they ended without an ending. Most people, I suppose, don't finish their lives; they die before they've resolved all the themes, taken care of all the characters, established a unity of narrative, peripety, and discovery out of the random episodes of experience. Thus a funeral, I realized when attending Roth's, serves as coda or afterword in which someone other than the author (after that author has been lowered into a plot) concludes the text, so that we may understand its meaning, if not its moral.

Roth's funeral service, held at noon on January 4, 1998, at the Hollywood Hills Haven of Hope Memorial Park and Cemetery ("Serving the Deceased since 1953"), was attended by Isaac Roth and Tina Valentina, Jock and Venus Newhouse, Paul and Pimiko Planter, Professor Christopher Cross, Mary MacDylan, and a woman whom I did not recognize— an attractive woman in her early forties (I would guess), handsomely and tastefully dressed in black, even wearing a veil, and remaining away from the rest of us. Maya Blackwell, her head shaved, wearing what appeared to be only a white sheet and holding a bouquet of white narcissi, could occasionally be seen darting about between hiding places provided by trees, bushes, large tombstones, and ornamental statuary.

Professor Planter delivered the eulogy, which was later printed in the *Western Crier* (January 19, 1998):

In Memoriam:
Leopold Roth, Ph.D. (1945-1997)
Professor (tenured)
Department of Asian Studies (1979-1997)
by
Dr. Paul Planter, Ph.D. D.Litt.
Suzuki Professor of Japanology
Chairman, Department of Asian Studies
Director, Global Institute for Computorial Translation
Fellow of the Ethics Committee of the International
Association of Hermenueticists and Exegetes (I.A.H.E)

The following Obituary is the text of a Eulogy given by Dr. Paul Planter, Chairperson of the Department of Asian Studies at the funeral of Professor Leopold Roth who died in his office recently. Because of his death, the University President's Office announced last week, the sexual harassment case against him will be dropped. The Editors would like to thank Dr. Planter for allowing us to reprint his excellent and informative speech.

I come to this beautiful memorial garden on this fair to partly cloudy January day not to bury Leopold Roth, but to praise him. The good that men do lives after them. So it should be.

Professor Roth, despite all the ill that has been spoken and written against him at the University of late, was a scholar. And that is how I shall always remember him.

Dr. Roth ended his life over a Sanskrit text with his pen uncapped, ready and eager to contribute more verbiage to Sanskrit studies. What more

fitting, heroic, more glorious end could a scholar have? It is comparable to the death of a matador in the bull ring, or that of whaler on the high seas. O to die in the midst of doing that very thing for which has one lived! O lucky Roth! What scholar cannot but envy him? Roth's office was his *corrida*, a notebook his *muleta*, his pen was a sword poised for the *estocada* above the charging bull of a Sanskrit text, the *Kamasutra*, an Indian Bible of Love. *Ole* Professor Roth, *Ole!* We are fortunate to have his *picadore*, Mr. Anang

Please see page 18

Dead Language Professor

Continued from Page 1

Saighal, with us today. When, in the *plaza de toros*, the bull is not killed, the *puntillero* takes over the work. As Department Chair, I am happy to announce that Mr. Saighal will be promoted from *picadore* to *puntillero* so that, in the name of Roth, he might finish off the bull.

A scholar lucubrating in his office, an old arcane text and a large dictionary open on the desk, and, lo, death strikes! O, to die doing what one does best! It is like the whaler of old on the high seas. "Thar she blows, matey!" Roth's office was the ship, his pen the harpoon. The Sanskrit text, the *Kamasutra*, was his Leviathan! "Towards thee I roll thou-destroying, but unconquering text!" Roth seems to cry out, "To the last I grapple with thee! From hell's heart I stab at thee!" Mr. Saighal, I trust, shall be an Ishmael to this drowned Ahab of Indology, preserving his story for all the people, all around the world, who have any interest whatsoever in Sanskrit studies!

Yes, *The Kamasutra!* We've all heard of it. There have already been countless translations (not to mention a recent film), so why on earth, you may ask, was Professor Roth translating it again? Perhaps we shall never know. But some things we do know. That so many other scholars had already done what he was trying to do yet again did not intimidate him. No! That is commitment. That's the stuff of scholarship! That the *Kamasutra* is reputed to be mere pornography, did not make him shy away from it. That's dedication! *The Kamasutra*, I was informed by my late colleague, is not only a frank sex book; it also has some things to say about love. And Professor Leopold Roth, as anyone who knew him knows, had a great interest in love, not only as a scholar and teacher, but also as a human being. Yes, I can, as his Chairman, personally attest that love played a part in my colleague's life. Not only did he love his dear wife, Dean Sophia White-Roth, who, unfortunately for us all, cannot be here today; he also loved some of his students. That's a mark of a teacher.

What many people may not know is that he also loved animals, and, at the end of his life, one little animal in particular–his cat. His love for that humble creature was typical of the man we are honoring today. Let me share a little story that sheds much light on the man's true character. Leopold Roth was very allergic to cats. In fact, he could hardly stop sneezing during the last sad months of his life; but so great was his love for that cat, that he kept her living in his office, despite my many attempts to have him turn the animal out of Swinburne Hall. It was a sneeze that caused the accident that snatched Roth from among us, a powerful sneeze that banged his head into his desk. Let those who are interested in Roth reflect upon it: He died because he sneezed, he sneezed because he had an allergy, he had allergy because he loved a cat. Yes, Professor Leopold Roth died for love. *Amor omnia vincit!*

My speciality, as those of you who have studied my many books and countless articles are well aware, is Japan, its people, its language, its literature, its art, its history. And as someone who has been heavily influenced (I pray for better!) by Japanese sensibilities, I tend to state the most important things simply. Those of you who have read my books on Zen or Japanese poetry, or the appendix to my theoretical study of Japanese aesthetics, are surely aware of *haiku* poetry, a genre in which vast and powerful emotions, metathoughts, entire universes of feeling and ideas, are pithistically expressed in a

Please see page 24

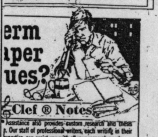
Dead Language Professor

Continued from Page 18

mere seventeen perfect syllables. These poems are informed by what the Japanese call *mono no aware*. As those who are familiar with my work already know the phrase, its nuances so subtle and difficult to capture in English, means something like "a transcendental aesthetic joy arising out of the phenomenologically felt sadness that arises out of perceptions of a hypostatized and hypostacizing beauty that is intuitively perceived in the thusness of all things-as-process, once and only when the heart/mind-process becomes so sensitively attuned to the transience of those things-as-process that the relationship between those ephemera and the becoming of the beholder are indisquisable from the essential essencelessnss of their respective essences." Roth's death arouses exactly that feeling, this *mono no aware*, in me. And so, I do not weep today over the death of Professor Roth; for once one has felt *mono no aware* there can be no tears. Mourning is transformed into poetry. Tears give way to haiku. And so I humbly offer this poem as a memorial to my late colleague, Professor Leopold A. Roth. I must caution you not to try to interpret it intellectually, but to feel it, to enter deep into the universe that it, as literature, demands to be. This poem, not the foregoing prosaic words honoring a scholar, is my true eulogy. He was the inspiration, and thus he, not I, deserves the credit. I was a mere conduit of the transcendental poetic process. As a scholar and translator, I must, also, however, and furthermore, note that its sentiments are difficult to translate into English. Much of the beauty, let alone the *mono no aware*, and five of the seventeen syllables of the original are, I'm sad to say, lost in translation:

Shhhhh
the old pond
a frog jumps in–
Roth!

B. The Kāmasūtra
(Intentio Auctoris)

I want the silence within the mausoleum to be perfect, a melodious silence
that enchants the heart, a celestial silence that drowns out all earthly rum-
blings, a peaceful silence that is different than any other silence anywhere in
this world.

> —Shah Jahan to Ustad Isa, in Romulus Arnor,
> *Monuments to Love*

I am alone. No teacher, no guide. No A. TRANSLATION, no
B. COMMENTARY. Death is open-ended. It has generated the
empty pages of a demanding blankness. Roth left an infinite lacuna
in the text. How would he have filled the void represented by the remaining, unmarked pages of his notebooks on love? What words,
like the clods of dirt I, with others, ceremonially dropped into his
grave at the funeral, should I now take in my hand to toss, by writing, into the tabula rasa between here and the end. It's a quotidian
question that each of us must ask ourselves: What should I say? With
what sounds, whether with groan or murmur, should I interrupt the
fundamental hush of the universe? With what squiggles of blackness,
in what script or language, should I smudge the pure whiteness of
nothing?

When I was a child, my father told me a bedtime story: "When I
was a child," he began, "my father told me a story about an old man
in his village who never spoke":

> Some people said that the old man had taken a vow of silence as a child,
> that his silence was a religious practice, and they venerated him as a
> holy man; others said that this veneration was nonsense, that the old
> man was a mute, that his silence was a disability, and they laughed at

him as a fool. People argued as to which it was, as to what the old man's silence expressed. He became ill and was dying, and the people who revered him as a guru, who had believed in the wisdom of his silence, begged him to say something—anything at all—before dying, in order to demonstrate to others the soundness of the homage they paid him. Many people, from both sides of the debate, gathered around his bedside, waiting and waiting. "Speak, Guru-ji," one of his followers cried out to him, and others joined in: "Speak! Speak." Then all at once, just in the moment before his death, with his very last breath, a sound very, very softly came from his lips: "Shhhh." So soft was the sound that those who thought he was mute still thought he was mute. "'Shhhh,' is not speaking," they said, and the village doctor agreed: "It was a sigh, the death rattle, just a meaningless noise." But it was loud enough that those who had believed in his vow had their faith and devotion reaffirmed. "'Shhhh' is the second-person plural imperative of a verb meaning to stop talking," they said, and the village pandit agreed: "It was a philosophical discourse, articulating both a metaphysical theory and an ethical principle." Everybody was convinced that they understood his silence.

It was supposed to be a funny story, made all the more humorous if I were to ask, "Which was it? Who was right?" for then my father answered, "Shhhh." I'd laugh, but I was disconcerted by the parable. I wanted to know for certain what the old man's silence meant. And now it's the same all over again: I'm struggling with the semantics of the silence that is Roth's translation of, and commentary on, the last three books of the *Kāmasūtra*. How do I edit that silence, annotate it, emend it? I'm uncomfortable up here on the page; I feel exposed and am self-conscious here. I like to be down there.[1]

---

1. Yes, down here. That's better. Protected by a minimum of 19.5 points, resting comfortably at the very bottom of the page, I feel much safer; the type is more modest here, the space more comfortable. I can talk more openly here. Beyond sorting through Roth's mail, returning his library books, feeding his cat, giving a few of his personal belongings to the Salvation Army, and editing this manuscript (in defiance of the persistent attempts of both Professors Planter and Siegel to discourage me from doing so), my duties as literary executor included clearing out and cleaning up the Augean stable of an office where Roth had lived and died. Remuneration for these labors, incidentally, came from Dr. White-Roth in the form of a donation to me of "all of his books that have anything to do with India, love, or sex."

On my first day on the job, the day following my teacher's funeral, I began with the trash, dumping the office wastebasket into a large cardboard carton, into which I planned to throw everything that had been rendered disposable, worthless, or insignificant by his death. Amidst stale Kitty Treats, massive amounts of used Kleenex, crumpled up empty Viceroy packs and lots of cigarette butts, two empty bottles of Bombay gin, and the usual stuff (discarded memos, reports, papers, and letters received) that one would expect to find in any professor's trash can, I noticed several small, torn pieces of rose-colored paper with writing on them. I moved a gin bottle aside and saw another piece, shook the box of garbage and more appeared; they were fragments of a letter that had been ripped into enough pieces to suggest the recipient's anger, or humiliation, or disappointment, or anguish, or sadness, or—in a word—love.

Rummaging carefully, methodically searching for and retrieving as many segments of the text as I could, I flattened them out between my fingers and arranged them on the desk, where they had once, presumably, formed a readable whole. It was a jigsaw puzzle. I had not tried to put one together since my childhood. My mother, as I've mentioned, when she was in the hospital just before her death, used to take some pleasure in the distraction that they offered her. Looking at the bits of the letter, I remembered her explaining jigsaw puzzles to me. I recalled how the many little pieces, with their variegated colors and shapes, slowly came together into a beautiful image—Botticelli's *Birth of Venus*. Despite her pain and nausea, my mother smiled. "Come on, dear. Come Nangi, sit up here on the bed next to me. That's a good boy. That's a sweet boy. Now pull the tray closer. The first thing we're going to do is to turn all the pieces right-side up. Good. Now as we do that, we're looking for the ones that are flat on the side. They're the border. They'll frame the picture. We want to find four of them that have two straight edges—the corners."

While turning over each piece of rose-colored stationary that had no writing visible upon it, I was able to find twenty-two pieces of paper with straight edges, three of which were corners and one of which had a signature upon it: "Lalita."

"That's good, my darling son, good!" my mother continued, stopping only to give me a kiss on the cheek. "Now look for colors that match. Look for things that will naturally go together: those pieces with leaves on them; here are two with golden hair; they don't fit together, so there must be another one to connect them; the hair must go beside some portion of the woman's face. Look, there's her eye and her mouth. There's her hand. And there's the curve of some part of her; I don't know what part, but the color matches her skin—doesn't it?"

I felt that the letter had a potential to provide some sort of aesthetic resolution to the dramatic tension inherent in the relationship between two human beings as, through the literary endeavors of one of them, they had been transformed from realities into representations of realities, from flesh and blood in the world into lines of ink on paper, the hero and heroine of an incomplete love story. It was over; it had finished—but it lacked an ending.

As I followed my mother's suggestions, laying out the borders of the letter, putting a signature on the bottom and a "Dearest" in the upper left corner, I noticed on several different bits of the puzzle what seemed to be sections of the circumference of a circle, a feathery curved line that allowed me to piece together five fragments of the puzzle, to begin to work my way into the heart of it. The circle exactly matched the bottom of the tumbler from which the receiver of the letter used to drink gin.

"That's Venus," my mother said, "the Roman goddess of love. She was born from the sea. Isn't she beautiful?" My maternal grandparents, as Jews, naturally wanted their daughter to be buried in a Jewish cemetery, and they were very upset that she had arranged to be cremated and to have her ashes scattered over the ocean. They undoubtedly saw it as yet another bad result of her defiant marriage to an Indian gentile. I understood that it was a physical prerequisite to fulfilling a yearning to be dis-

Xmas '97

Dearest L___old,

I ___ing back to India and so I probably
___ ___ ___ ___ ___ is difficult ___ ___
I can "love" ___ much about love, but "I'm sorry"
__Kamasutra__ ___ "I love you" ___ used you.
really and ___ us ___ ___ ___ say ___ and
for both ___ want to thank you ___ perfect
for ___
monsoon ___ going to India ___ ancient India,
cremation grounds about myp___ I should not
you tried to ___ ___ taught ___ smoke ___ I know My
for "love" and ___ I ___ purism, ___, ___ ___
___ ___ ___ ___ ___
I learned so ___ still guide me ___ coming at the
It was poss ___ for L___. He language that
India, not ___ ___ Saighil + ___ ___ ___ ___ words
you ___ ___ ___ ___ ___ love ___ taking me
But it ___ ___ ___ ___
"be in l___ for your class ___ and ___
P ___ let me ___ ___ home h ___ feel as ___ Professor
your cynicism ___ teach me ___ nas ___ ___ ___ in
Babaji's words say ___ "dead" ___ and that
And I am has ___ ___ W ___ __kamasutra__ for me.
reason. O ___ ___ ___ in Ind ___ ___ ___ to
___ new ___ "love" ___ us only pain ___ diculous.
My parents ___ y that you are too ___ ___
I will only write it one more time ___ ___ saying
the words ___ as I ___ write them." I Lo___ you,
                                        Lalita

I was partially rescued from the blank pages of notebooks five and six by a package. One of my responsibilities as Roth's literary executor was to sort through his incoming mail and to either dispose of it or, as appropriate, to respond to it by informing the sender of the addressee's demise. "The cat must go," the department secretary, Ms. Nora Naper, announced as usual, adding an ominous "it's the law," as she handed me Roth's mail: two applications for low-interest credit cards, several for life insurance, an ad for a Deepak Chopra seminar, a free examination copy of a new textbook on Indian civilization (with a predictable photograph of the Taj Mahal on the cover), the fourth subpoena from the High Court in Delhi, a copy of the weekly *Love Lives! The Maranatha Mission News*, a bill from a florist, a newsletter from a liquor store announcing the arrival of the new Chateau d'Amour Rosé champagne, an aerogram of supplication for money from someone named Indrajit in Puri, an accusatory letter from Romulus and Rowley Puzzles and Games, a letter of rejection from David Brent, an editor at the University of Chicago Press ("Your proposal for a translation of the *Kāmasūtra* does not fit our list for 1998. We suggest you try an Indian publisher"), and a manila envelope from Indiana, the delivery of which was a deliverance—it contained material that redeemed me from the textual void with words to fill the space provided for Books Five and Six of the *Kāmasūtra;* there was a cover letter from an editor at the Clef Notes Publishing Company and a sample of a manuscript that Roth had submitted to them as a proposal for a study guide to the *Kāmasūtra*, which included Roth's summaries of the missing books.

---

solved into the element from which Love is born. After her funeral, when my father sent me to school in Gwalior, I took with me to India the one piece of the puzzle that my mother had insisted I keep. I never heard from my grandparents again.

Despite missing pieces and unclear edges, I've done my best to put the puzzle of a message from one lover to another together. This text is, I suspect, so crucial to an understanding of the love story that I resist annotating it or offering my own reading of it for fear that I might distort or obfuscate its message with an imposition of my personal feelings for, and opinions of, the hero and heroine. Thus, without editorial comment or footnote, psychological analysis or literary criticism, I include the original text.

B.F. Rehatsek,
Senior Editor,
Clef ® Notes and Study Guides,
924 Hillegass Way
Leesville, Indiana 60852

December 30, 1997

Dear Professor Roth:

We are returning the ms. of your study guide to the *Kamasutra* as our editorial staff unanimously deemed it unsuitable for our list, not only in the choice of book to be summarized, but in the methods and language and critical approach employed in that summation.

Our legal staff has urged me to point out to you, furthermore, that your use of the Clef ®Notes logo, the name Clef ® Notes, and the diagonal design, all of which are registered trademarks, is illegal and that any further use of those registered trademarks without our written permission will render you subject and liable to prosecution. Be advised to destroy all documents, as produced by you or your agents, upon which the Clef ®Notes logo, the name Clef ® Notes, and/or the diagonal design, known and respected by the students of America, appear.

On a happier note, while your submission was of no interest whatsoever to us, one member of our board of scholars, Professor M.T. Banerjee of the University of Las Vegas, who has been urging us to provide the world with Clef ® Notes on selected Indian classics, has proposed that I suggest to you that you summit a sample of what you would produce if (and this is very conditional at this point and, though in writing, may not be considered to have contractual ramifications) we were to consider commissioning you, on consignment, to work on a project that is particularly suggested by Dr. Bannerji, namely the Clef ® Notes to the

-2-

Mahabharata. We understand the challenge of reducing the twelve volumes of Sanskrit containing over 100,000 verses into the proposed pages of simple, understandable (and yet exciting to students) prose for the proposed Clef ® Notes Classic. Dr. Banerjee, has taken time out from his busy schedule to offer you these guidelines: Plot Summary (25 pages), Main Characters (and what "makes them tick") (4 pages), Overview of Indian History and Culture (3 pages), Development of Indian Literature in Sanskrit and the Vernacular Languages (3 pages), the Nature and Function of Indian Religion (1 page), a Critical Analysis of the Meaning, Structure and Techniques of the Mahabharata (2 pages), Glossary of Indian Words (2 pages), Study Questions and Ideas for Essays (3 pages), Recommended Further Reading (1 page). With the title page, contents, copyright and trademark warning page, list of other Clef®Note titles, that comes to 48 pages and leaves the customary two blank pages for "Student Notes" at the end.

Dr. Bannerji further suggests that, in order to provide us with a sample of your work, you might want to start with a study guide to the *Bhagavadgita* (being from the *Mahabharata* as I am sure you are aware) which, given our reduction formula, should be about twelve (certainly no more than fifteen) words in length. For a model, you might want to consult the brilliant sixteen-word synopsis of the Book of Deuteronomy in the Clef®Note Bible (which, by the way, I am proud to say, has been picked up by the Gideon Society to be placed by them in university dormitory rooms all over North America).

Find enclosed your ms., returned at our expense. Please include an S.A.S.E. in all further communication.

I hope you have a happy New Year,

B.F. Rehatsek
Senior Editor

B.F.R.: rfb
Enc.

Clef®Notes Are Music to a Student's Ears

18

with an elucidation of the psychological and sociological the dangers of loving multiple women. To seduce them, enjoy union with them, and to explore modes of mutual pleasure, is safe. But once a man truly loves more than one woman and is, at the same time, loved by more than one, there will be a crisis. Book Four ends with a list of the probable troubles that befall a man who too passionately loves both his wife and his mistress.

BOOK FIVE

"An Adulterer's Guide to Seducing the Wives (and Daughters) of Other Men" begins with a list of the ten stages of love: Passionate longing can be aroused by the mere sight of a beautiful girl; if it that desire is not satisfied, it will progressively increase until the lover is in danger of death. Although all the scriptures accept the normative dictum that adultery is a crime, the learned authors of those ancient texts were well aware that it is universally a symptom of love that lover and beloved have no sense of right and wrong, and that they must be judged accordingly. It is felonious to commit adultery for purposes of financial gain, espionage, professional tenure or promotion, or, as a game, merely to prove to oneself or friends that one is capable of it; it is, however, only a misdemeanor if adultery is committed for the sake of love; and the greater the love, the less the culpability. Some legal authorities hold that intent is not to be taken into account in the judgment of crime; but most, if they are reasonable and understanding of human nature, maintain that intent is the most crucial and relevant issue in judging cases of murder and

19

adultery. "The intent of the adulterer is as pertinent to interpreting his or her behavior, as is the intent of the poet in judging his literary composition. It is for the sake of men who are married and fall in love with other women, or for men who fall in love with the wife of another man, that the arts and sciences of seduction have been outlined in the Kamasutra. The teachings are not to be used for personal gain. Success in the application of these teachings depends on the intelligence of the seducer: He should be skilled at telling erotic stories and commenting upon them, explaining their meaning and their charm; he should be able to translate ancient love poems into the vernacular spoken by the object of his affection. The adulterer, if he is married, should arrange to have a party at his home to which the desired woman is invited. He should invite her to play games and offer to escort her to some region unknown to her, tempting her with tales of the wonders the place. It is advisable for the adulterous seducer to employ an assistant, a go-between who speaks on his behalf, interpreting his words to the girl, perhaps showing her something he has written that, through the commentary of the go-between, reveals his love for her. Book Five ends with a description of life in the harem, including a detailed discussion of dildos and other artificial devices for sexual pleasure.

BOOK SIX

"The Harlot's Handbook" begins with a discussion of the advantages of being a courtesan, a metier with a potential to afford all that a woman could want out of life, namely, sexual pleasure, the adoration of men, and financial security. In order to realize that potential, however, a girl

20

must be well-versed in the arts and sciences of sexual love as presented in the Kamasutra. The woman should take special care to attract an appropriate paramour: Young and handsome men who are strong, athletic and idealistic, are a good choice; so are older men who are urbane, learned, and devoted to cultural pursuits. These older men, however, should be married; otherwise they will become possessive of the courtesan and thereby limit her opportunities to find other customers. In order to effectively beguile the prospective lover, the woman must show disinterest at first, only gradually allowing him licence to touch her. A man loses interest in a woman who is won over too easily: He must be made to imagine that he is the seducer, that he is the teacher when it comes to sexual love, that he is the one with powers of decision in the amorous relationship. The girl should ask him to tell her erotic stories and, pretending she doesn't understand, ask him to explain their meaning to her. She should laugh at his jokes and show tears in her eyes when he speaks of his travails in his work or in his domestic life. When he imagines that in her company he is particularly virile and youthful, erudite and witty, he will freely give her jewelry and other gifts. To further increase his sentimental and sexual dependency upon her, the girl should begin to sulk and to complain to him that she is defying her family and friends for his sake. It is always an effective strategy to travel with a man to a place or country where neither of them are known; in such a context the girl will have free reign in controlling her paramour. By alternating her moods unpredictably his moods will be effected; after taking control of his moods, she will easily manage his feelings and finally,

21

his will. When a courtesan desires to dispose of a lover so that she may move on to one who is more appropriate, who is wealthier, more dashing, or more capable of satisfying her sexual, emotional, and social needs, she should claim that her mother (the madam of the brothel) is forcing her to do other work. In case she changes her mind later on, she should not be too hasty in dumping a lover. Book Six ends with a detailed discussion of the financing, marketing, advertizing, and bookkeeping involved in love as a commercial venture.

BOOK SEVEN

The final book of the Kamasutra, is largely a recipe book. And while it is obscured by lexical barriers to the arcane technical terminologies of its elaborate cosmetological, pharmaceutical and magical recipes and formulae, the attitudes toward sexual love implicit in the choice of recipes, is clear enough. The book is divided into two parts: One dealing with making one's self attractive, the other covering impotence and frigidity. The latter includes methods for enlarging the penis as well as for shrinking and lubricating the vagina. Dildos and penile prosthesis are described and evaluated.

CONCLUSION

At the end of the Kamasutra, Vatsyayana explains again that he has compiled his sexology textook from the scattered teachings of professors who preceeded him. He warns his students to remain in control of their senses at all times, to allow themselves the pleasures of dispassionate sexual union without running the risks that come with falling in love. He claims that, while working on

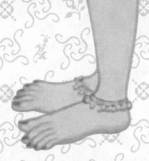

C. Love in a Dead Language
(Intentio Lectoris)

17) List and briefly describe the main characters in the novel other than the narrator, explaining the ways in which the narrator's presentation of what those characters do and say establishes not who they are, but who and what the narrator is.

18) Discuss the relationship between the person of the author and the persona of the narrator: In what ways are they the same? In what ways are they different? How do these similarities and differences affect the meaning of the text?

— "Study Questions and Essay Topics," Clef ® Notes and
Study Guide to *Tristram Shandy*

Roth's intent was not merely to translate the *Kāmasūtra*, but to develop a commentary in which he could use the events of his life to understand the ancient text, and the text to understand his life. Thus editorial protocol demands that, just as I provided (in the previous section) at least some of the content of the unfinished portions of the Sanskrit codex on love, here I furnish some of the content of the unfinished story of a life that, because of the form of Roth's discourse, became a commentarial existence.

And so just as I had consulted Pralayānanga and Yaśodhara to clarify Vātsyāyana, I contacted people who might have something to say about Roth, informants with whom I was acquainted either personally or through Roth's text. These characters, with their implicit or explicit commentaries, intentionally or not, finish Roth's story, give it its moral and message.

And just as I had looked up words that I didn't know in the Monier-Williams *Sanskrit-English Dictionary* in order to understand the *Kāmasūtra*, I began by looking up the names of the people I didn't know personally—Mary MacDylan (at the Maranatha Mission for Divine Love) and Jock Newhouse (unlisted)—in the Los Angeles telephone directory in hopes that, through them, I might have a fuller and more appreciative understanding of the modern commentary on the ancient text.[1]

There was, incidentally, another reason to find out more about these people—I suspected that one of them might have murdered Leopold Roth.

Theresa Berkeley

After Roth's death Dr. Nilkanth Gupta, in his concern over who would be appointed as my teacher's successor to the university position

---

1. Could the amazing fact that the Los Angeles telephone directory (Los Angeles: Pacific Bell, 1997) has—and I swear this is true—exactly the same number of pages (1359) as the Monier-Williams *Sanskrit-English Dictionary* be any more than a coincidence? Out of curiosity, having just looked up *kāma* up in the dictionary, I looked for it in the telephone book and found the following on page 279, the very same page of the dictionary that bears the definition of *kāma* (!):

Kam Jeffrey & Lily WLA 820 0213	Kaminski Henry J 23916 W De Vale Wy Mbu 456 3293
Kam Larry 659 1932	Kaminski Kaneko Design 6671 W Sunset Bl LA ..213 467 7404
Kam S SM 829 3900	Kaminski Michael 11734 Bellagio Rd BA 471 5964
Kam Tsam Yean 3152 Corinth Av MV 572 6022	Kaminski Timothy J 838 3576
Kama Investments Inc 9001 Wilshire Bl BH 273 8906	Kaminsky Ed Mar D Rey 821 5679
Kama Kosmic Krusader 213 462 5967	Kaminsky J 1828 Holmby Av Wstwd 474 2200
Kamachi David A 9611 National Bl LA 204 5271	Kaminsky Michael J atty 11400 W Olympc Bl WLA ...478 4100
Kamachi Noriko 11945 Woodbne MV 397 5484	Kaminsky Robt 273 S Westgte Av Bntwd 471 1703
Kamachi Noriko 11945 Woodbne MV 397 9998	Kaminsky S WLA 478 4554
Kamadinata Rudy Wstwd 268 1073	Kamisato Henry Y 12022 Juniette CC 827 3204
Kamadinata Rudy 459 2787	Kamisato T Mar D Rev 301 1983

Could it be anything more than coincidence that the sum of the numbers that constitute the number of pages in both books (1+3+5+9) is the same (18) as the sum of the numbers which make up the page number on which *kāma* appears in both texts (2+7+9), and *R* (as in Roth) is the eighteenth letter of the alphabet! And today, the day I write this very footnote, the day on which all of this occurs to me, is the eighteenth day of February! And I was born April 3, 1965 (4+3+6+5=18!), thus connecting me to Roth and the *Kāmasūtra*. This entire project has made me wonder about this: it seems to me reasonable that, in real life, everything is "only a coincidence"; accidental, meaningless patterns arbitrarily defined by incidental sequences of events only seem, through (sometimes motivated, but usually unconscious) projection, to have a causal, meaningful relationship. In a book, on the other hand, nothing is "only a coincidence"; every event (every character, every image, every word) is significant to the formation of some meaningful and real pattern as intentionally designed by the writer of that book. All things exist, all words are spoken or written, only to define other things and be defined by them, to simultaneously explain and be explained. Rather than projecting nonexistent connections, imagining a telos, we, as interpreters, seek to find the existent connections and understand the logos by which they create, preserve, and destroy a universe, real or not. If there really were a God, a purposeful creator of the world, or if this were a structured novel, rather than a coincidental life, I'd be on the lookout for more fatidic eighteens, for octodecimological phenomena that would transport me from an empirical and accidental existence into a literarily patterned or religiously significant one. But there is no God, and I'm writing a scholarly, critical footnote, not a romance or a sermon. I'm shocked at myself, at what I have just written. I am beginning to sound like Leopold Roth.

in Indian studies, sought me out. It was, I assume, out of a genuine
hope of reconnecting me with his beloved India through involving me
in the cultural activities of the Indian community in Southern California that Dr. Gupta generously paid for a subscription for me to the
Indian American Mirror. (He also, of course, wanted to win my confidence, to have an informant within the department and the university
to keep him apprised of the ethnic backgrounds and political proclivities of applicants for Roth's job.) I was struck by the following item
in the February 4, 1998, issue of the newspaper:

Mr. P.K. Bahadur bids farewell to Terresa Barklee

Maya Blackwell

I couldn't find an obituary. Referring with a grin to Ms. Blackwell as
"yet another victim of love," Professor Planter told me about it: she had
reached the "tenth and final stage of love" by committing suicide, po-
etically, appropriately, and certainly not coincidentally, on Valentine's
Day. Like Lakmé in the opera of that name, she had drunk poison—

not romantic datura, but Pipe Dream industrial strength drain cleaner. Planter explained that the police had telephoned him because she had left a note behind that was all about Roth, "a poem" about their "beautiful love affair," how it had started centuries ago in India and continued through past lives; they had made love as Druids, Mongols, Visigoths, and Circassians, made love in Agra, Tashkent, Mecca, Peking, Babylon, Hunza, Lhasa, Atlantis, and Salt Lake City. In one life they had been tigers mating in the jungles of Assam. In another pair of incarnations Roth was a female inmate of Bedlam and Blackwell was a male doctor who cured her of hysteria with the application of leeches to her eyes, ears, lips, nipples, and genitals. That their romance had begun in India a millennium ago, "making mystic love at midnight in the burning grounds of Banaras," she had written, was why it was "so natural and obvious" that they should be reunited in 1990 in Roth's Asian Studies 150B class and re-reunited "once and for all time" in death in 1998.

"The cop was unaware that Roth was dead," Planter laughed. "He wanted to talk to him because the suicide note, after an overview of their transmigratory love life, informed Roth that she was doing it all for him, 'just as everything that I have done, for thousands of years, has been for You. Our next union will in be a place where You can love me without fear.' The detective didn't get it. The police aren't are very adept at interpreting poetry; I guess they don't teach literary theory at the police academy. The cop wanted to know how to contact Roth, so I told him that he was with the Blackwell woman on a higher plane. He still didn't get it. The men in blue lack a developed sense of irony. They have no appreciation whatsoever of the *liebestod* motif, and not the slightest bit of interest in death as a literary theme, a dramatic event that can be better understood aesthetically than criminologically, more appropriately appreciated philosophically than forensically. I had to put it simply for him, in a language stripped of allusions, tropes, and texture, without even one little metaphor, not even a measly simile, in utterance completely devoid of psychological or sociological, philosophical or religious implications, discourse without ambivalence, let alone polyvalence, and entirely devoid of ambiguity or semiotic resonance. Three words contracted for his sake into two with only one interpretation and no meaning beyond that of the hard fact conveyed: "He's dead." I told him to get the details from their very own Detective Plato Chan in homicide. Two days later Chan called to ask if I was acquainted with Ms. Blackwell, if I knew anything about the details of her relationship with Roth, and said that her suicide raised 'certain questions' about Roth's death. I'm fed up with Roth. He's been dead for almost two months, and I'm still dealing with memos, letters, and telephone calls about his love life."

Professor Christopher Cross

In order that there might be at least one appreciative toast to Professor Leopold Abraham Roth after his funeral, Dr. Cross, with whom I had become acquainted at the Roths' party last year, had cordially invited me to join him for a drink at the Taj Mahal Restaurant and Mogul Lounge, that venue being, we both agreed, appropriate for the occasion. When Cross ordered two Bombay gin and tonics, I protested that I do not drink alcohol, smoke cigarettes, or eat meat.

"Oh, come on," he insisted. "I'm not much of a drinker either, not really. But think of Leo, of how thirsty he must be. Don't let prudery get in the way of friendship. It's for Leo, and you know as well as I do that he'd want you to drink in his memory."

Wistful wishes that I would have had one, just one, with him before he died prompted me to accept. I sipped as Cross talked, as usual, about his research: during his 1997 study, working specifically, at Roth's suggestion, with *Helix pseudoecstasis* (or "*Cepæa indica* as it was called in the Linnaean taxonomy"), a South Asian variety of fruit snail (known as "*phulphal* in Oriya and *jaju* in Gond"), he had isolated an extraordinary enzyme from the no less extraordinary slime of an otherwise ordinary snail. He explained it, furiously jotting equations and formulae down on a paper napkin as he did:

"The pungent, silvery ooze of these hermaphroditic gastropods is incredibly powerful in its ability to attract a mate. When one snail crawls across the slime of another snail, the overwhelming hormone in that exudation, rapturonin ($C_{20}H_{21}O_2$), discovered in 1987 by Shah, Shaw, Singer, and Singh, is absorbed through the ventral receptors and suspends all neurophysiological activity save that required to steer the body of the now helplessly pursuant snail toward the snail that has so innocently effused it. The state of sexual arousal of the pursuer is a dangerous one; there is no hunger, no fear, no revulsion, no attraction to, nor desire for, anything but the absorption of rapturonin. Those survival mechanisms that preserve the individual are totally suspended in the service of the mating instinct that will insure the preservation of the species. The snail is trapped, powerless to crawl anywhere but along the newly encountered trail of rapturonin-rich slime toward the snail that has discharged it, until he/she finally catches up with her/him and mating takes place. Of course, during the chase, the slime of the one mixes with the slime of the other. Comparing a lixiviation of the blended slimes of two precoital snails with the unmixed, pure ooze of a solitary postcoital snail, I recognized an extraordinary difference, namely an absence of rapturonin in the mixed slime! Where, I asked myself, has all the rapturonin gone?

"The function, in Darwinian terms, of its disappearance was clear enough: a third, fourth, fifth, or whateverth snail crossing a path of mixed slime would not be attracted, thus preventing enormous orgiastic mounds of copulating snails, and thus minimizing sexual competition while maintaining the highest possible degree of attraction. If there were no mechanism for the neutralization of rapturonin, snails would either take over the planet with continuous mating or become extinct (if, because of the presence of rapturonin in all slime, the sexual urge entirely displaced all instincts for individual survival). I don't know which would be worse!

"I knew *why* it happened, but in order to determine *how* it happened, I needed to understand more fully *what* had happened. It was like trying to solve the Roth murder! In an analysis of the mixed slime, I discovered the presence of testosterone ($C_{19}H_{28}O_2$) and estrone ($C_{18}H_{22}O_2$), both of which are repugnant to, and nonabsorbable by, the hermaphroditic *Helix pseudoecstasis*. Given the high levels of sugar ($C_6H_{12}O_6$) and the urea ($CO[NH]_2$) that gives the slime its heady aroma, I realized that the bisexual rapturonin hormone had been broken into the male and female hormones, while giving off carbon dioxide, water, and laughing gas. In other words:

rapturonin	sugar	urea	testosterone	estrone	carbon dioxide	water	nitrous oxide
$C_{31}H_{28}O$	+ $C_6H_{12}O_6$	+ $CO(NH)_2$ =	$C_{19}H_{28}O_2$	+ $C_{18}H_{22}O_2$	+ CO_2	+ H_2O	+ N_2O

"I was then able to identify the responsible substance. I isolated a hitherto unknown enzyme uniquely present in the slime of *Helix pseudoecstasis*, unnoticed by Shah, Shaw, Singer, and Singh in their study of the polyptychic bulbocloacal peptoraptoral gland at the end of the metapodium. That the enzyme is produced there, infused into the slime from a duct behind the one that secretes the rapturonin (which stimulates the production of the enzyme) explains why the snails do not neutralize their own rapturonin, only that of the snail in lusty pursuit of him/her. It explains why after mating, as the two snails, released by sexual discharge from the obsession caused by the hormone, wander off in search of food (they're always famished after coition [and so, by the way, am I!]), their respective slimes are once again rich in rapturonin. It explains so many things.

"But let me explain something, let me tell you why I am telling you all of this: as the discoverer of the enzyme, I reserve the right to name it. And I have chosen this context, sitting in Roth's favorite Indian restaurant, with his only graduate student, after his funeral, as the perfect time and place to announce to the world that I am naming that wonderful catalytic enzyme 'rotherase.' The name Roth will go down in the history of molluscular gastropodology. Furthermore, since *Helix pseudoecstasis* has no English name, I have submitted a request to the International Society of Malacologists to give the appellation 'rothsnail' to our pesky little slime-maker. It was, you see, Leopold who got me on the slime trail of Indian snails.

"'I'm looking at Indian texts,' he said to me once, 'as a way of understanding something about sexual love, to find a language in which to talk about love. Since you're also interested in sexual love, albeit the hermaphroditic love life of snails, why don't you look at Indian snails? Let's face it Chris, you're no more interested in snails than I am in Sanskrit texts. We're only interested in ourselves and in sex. I found a good mirror, conveniently distant, in India.' He tried, generously but unsuccessfully, to bring some back from India for me, but I was able to order them from a snail farm back east. It was all Leo's idea. If only people exuded slime like rothsnails, Leo would still be alive. The Indian girl's slime, mixed with that of the basketball player, would not have taken Leo off track. He would have stuck with Sophie's slime, satisfied to mix his ooze with hers. Leopold's slime would have been neutralized too."

Throughout the malacology lecture, Cross repeatedly signaled to the waiter for fresh rounds of drinks—a second, third, and fourth order—and I must have been drunk by the end because I raised my Bombay gin and tonic and made a toast:

"Here's to Roth, rothsnails, and rotherase. Here's to slime! Yes, the world would be a better place if only human beings exuded slime!"

Professor Cross suggested that we eat something in order to sober up enough to stand up from the table. I ordered the Shah Jahan Regal Dinner, the first meat I had eaten since the lonely Sunday dinners at the Gwalior School. The Tandoori Mumtaz Masala Lamb was so delicious that I ordered a take-out portion for Mayavati. On the way home, in memory of my teacher, I stopped to buy a pack of Viceroys. I was feeling sentimental.

Lalita Gupta

In Sanskrit literature a happy ending to a love story is, by convention, as necessary and expected as is a sad one to a Western tale of love. Thus, I suppose, it is at least aesthetically appropriate that the story of Roth's love affair with Lalita Gupta ended tragically for the Western lover and happily for the Indian beloved.

The last time I saw her was at the December graduation ceremony, just before Christmas, wearing the black scholar's gown over a luxurious purple Banarsi-silk sari embroidered with gold; her bindi was purple too and her bangles were jeweled; she wore a nose ring and silver anklets and toe rings. Although the mortarboard is, at least to my taste, the most unflattering of any headgear in the millinery history of the world, Lalita Gupta looked splendid even in that silly, tasseled hat. India had invigorated her beauty. Her posture was different after the trip; she stood as an Indian woman does, her graceful neck holding her head in the position that Indian women have developed for the sake of carrying things. Lalita's mortarboard was so perfectly level that she could have balanced upon it a large pot of Ganges water and carried it without spilling drop.

I had been surprised that she wasn't at the funeral; I discovered only afterward that, right after Christmas, as a graduation present, the Guptas sent their daughter back to India. As with her first visit, there was a deception—she did not realize that as soon as she arrived in her family's village, she would become a prisoner at the mercy of the matriarch Purnima Gupta, whose mandate and mission it was to "break the girl," to domesticate her so that she would submit to an arranged marriage to an appropriate boy of a suitable lineage, caste, complexion, academic degree, and profession. For all of her beauty and intelligence, not to mention a Green Card and hefty dowry, she was a very marketable, though not very compliant, commodity.

Lalita must have sent an urgent letter to Paul Rothberg because, like Jock Newhouse rescuing the tormented Tina Valentina from the evil Thug in *The Curse of Kali,* Mr. Rothberg saved Ms. Gupta from the hoary clutches of Hindu tradition. Pretending that he was not acquainted with the captive girl, he visited the village and was welcomed under the pretext that he was with both the Peace Corps and the World Heath Organization. His Hindi was impressive. He also spoke Bengali. On the second night of his stay there, at midnight, while Purnima Gupta snored on her charpoy and wolves howled in the Seeonee hills, Mr. Rothberg helped Ms. Gupta into his jeep and drove off with her. Perhaps he is courageous by nature, or perhaps it was love that made him so daring. In any case, several days ago I received an invitation to their wedding, to be held in Khajuraho this June, approximately one year after the day Ms. Gupta first set foot on Indian ground.

The fact that the invitation came proudly from Dr. Nilkanth and Mrs. Rita Gupta was ironic in that initially Dr. Gupta had been so infuriated over the second kidnapping of his dear daughter that he repeated every one of the invectives he had hurled at Roth, and called Lalita's new boyfriend "Roth with an iceberg attached," comparing the Gupta family to the "Titanic, sunk by that Rothberg." But the Guptas were soon consoled and appeased as the advantages of the union became obvious to them: Mr. Rothberg's father, the president of the Discount Bank of Israel, was no stranger to India; he had in fact been responsible for securing investments and establishing communications that allowed for a merger between an Indian oil company and a U.S. one of which he was chairman of the board. He is, furthermore, rather a hero in India: after he donated his extensive collection of South India bronzes to the Indian National Museum in honor of the fiftieth anniversary of Indian independence, he was hailed in the Indian Press as having "set an example for justice by returning some of the cultural treasures of India, as sacked by foreign dominators, to India." The great wealth of the Rothbergs not only made a dowry quite unnecessary, it would also pay for the families of the bride and of the groom to travel first class to Khajuraho for the wedding. Dr. Gupta, newly appointed to the board of a pharmaceutical company owned by the Rothbergs, was further and deeply moved by the fact that Paul, who has been accepted into Harvard Medical School, plans to practice at least half of each year in village India. "Shree Bhagavan Pardesh Swami, the renowned astrologer to the rich and famous," Dr. Gupta proudly told me, "has revealed that the marriage is auspicious. It was meant to be. It was in the stars. All that has happened in both of their lives has lead up to this sacred union. What seemed negative is now shown to have been positive. It is both a Western love marriage, happily for the family of the groom, and an Indian arranged marriage, happily for the family of the bride, arranged not by the parents, however, but by a higher authority—Lord Kāma himself."

Because I must finish my dissertation[2] (not to mention that I cannot afford the airfare to India), I shall not, unfortunately, be attending the wedding of Paul Rothberg and Lalita Gupta. I shall, however, send a gift—an illustrated edition of the *Kāmasūtra* seems appropriate.

Leroy Lovelace

Leroy Lovelace has been named NBA Rookie of the Year. There is an interview with him in last month's issue of *Cocktail*, in their "Jock of Month" column. The issue, incidentally, includes a spread of photographs of naked women who appeared in the movie version of the *Kāmasūtra*, with the tasteless title "Hindu Honeys." There is also an article called "Tantric Love" purporting to reveal "ancient Indian secrets for experiencing sexual ecstasy," which can be employed, it explains, either to impress and "win the heart of any woman on the first date" or to revitalize a marriage in which sexual union has become "a ho-hum, humdrum affair."

Addressed to Roth, c/o the Department of Asian Studies in Swinburne Hall, the magazine (a gift subscription from Jock Newhouse, whose bride now writes a regular column for it called "Ask Venus") is inevitably retrieved from the mail by the department secretary, Ms. Naper. Her eyes widen with fury as she shakes the magazine in the air and flips through its lurid pages, shouting, "You see! Do you see the sort of perverted things the professor read? Don't tell me Roth wasn't a sexual harasser!"

The last page of the interview with Leroy Lovelace appears next to an advertisement for a product newly introduced from India, capitalizing on the associations of sexuality and India as epitomized by the *Kāmasūtra* (while playing down India's reputation for irresponsibility in matters of birth control). The marketing campaign has been extraordinary: the January issue carried an ad that read "If When You Think of India, You Think of Mahatma Gandhi, Mother Teresa, and Maharishi Mahesh Yogi, Think Again: Think *Kama Sutra!*"

2. If I finish by June, I would not, I am told, be an unreasonable candidate for Roth's position. I believe I have the support of the Indian community.

LEROY LOVELACE   (*continued from page 68*)

I had a good education, I didn't do drugs, and I was born in the greatest country in the history of mankind, at least as far as basketball is concerned. I have a good Mama. She encouraged me to play. A man needs a woman if he's going to succeed in America. That's my philosophy.

COCKTAIL

LOVELACE: Of course, but that's beside the point. These are trivial things. Being a good person is what's important. There are good people who are rich, and good people who are poor, of course, good people who are intelligent, and good people who are ignorant. Good people can be well or sick, happy or sad, loved or not loved. These are trivial things. Look, here's my philosophy: Examine the situation. Look at what's obvious. Don't bother about ethics or psychology. Just do what it's obvious that you must do. That's my philosophy

COCKTAIL: That's very profound.

LOVELACE: Thank's. I was a philosophy major in college.

COCKTAIL: So, is it true that the team is forbidden to have sex during the twenty-four hours before the game, that the coach doesn't want you to release a sexual energy that should be brought to the court?

> *Sex makes you loose. It calms me down, makes me cool, puts my head in touch with my body*

LOVELACE: No, that's bullshit. Sex makes you loose, relaxes you. Let me tell you, man, let me confide in you—we have girls in the dressing room. Sometimes I like to do it a couple of times during the half-time if I'm not on top of my game. It calms me down, makes me cool, puts my head in touch with my body. If I'm tired I'll just get a blow job. I probably shouldn't be saying this. The basketball commission doesn't approve I suppose. But that's bullshit. There's nothing they can do about it. It's not like drugs. I don't do drugs. I want all the kids that read Cocktail to know that. But sex is legal and that's what makes America great. I mean look at Russia! Anway, it's not before the game that I go without sex. It's afterwards. Man, sometimes I am so tired after a game that I feel I couldn't fuck if my life depended on it. That's because I give everything I have on the court. To me basketball is making love more than sex is. I'm a basketball player first and foremost. Lot a women don't understand that. When I was in college I had this girlfriend, a little Indian chick, and I'd come home after a game wanting to do nothing but drink some Gator-Ade and go to sleep. And she'd start kissing me, and begging me, and pestering with those soft lips of hers. 'Get away, girl,' I'd say. But she wouldn't give in. And I'll tell you, man, those Indians know how to kiss. Their Bible is that *Kamasutra* that tells them how to do it. I read it in college. I even wrote a paper on it. Got an A too. They got a hundred kinds of kisses, all of them with different names. Man, that girl knew every last one of them. That's why I had to break up with her. If I was still with her—shit—I'd be dead.

COCKTAIL: Is that because her kisses worked?

LOVELACE: Like magic, man. Just like fuckin' magic."

Mary MacDylan

When I telephoned Mary MacDylan, she expressed an ardent hope, hers and that of the elders of the Maranatha Mission, that I would take Roth's place as translator of the Gospel of Love into Sanskrit. If I began to work on that text, surely the Holy Spirit would enter me and direct me to travel with her to India, as Roth had been inspired to do, and to act as interpreter on her upcoming evangelical mission to that heathen land.

When she arrived at Roth's office, keeping the appointment she had made with me over the telephone, it was apparent from the expression on her face that she was surprised by my complexion.

"Oh, I didn't know you were an Indian. Or are you a Mexican?"

"No, I'm from India."

"A Hindu?"

"No, a Jew."

"Well, that's okay. All you have to do to be loved," she consoled me with a warm smile as she seated herself, "is to love. The Lord will accept your love and love you in return no matter what you are or what you have done."

It's not my tendency, inclination, or habit to say things just to shock or upset people—that was Roth's specialty. It was as if, as I sat there in his office, wearing one of the kurtas that I had found folded up with his other clothes in his office file cabinet, sipping Bombay gin from his tumbler, smoking a Viceroy, with his Monier Williams *Sanskrit-English Dictionary* and Sanskrit edition of the *Kāmasūtra* open on the desk, that he seemed to suddenly possess me. I had been trying so earnestly, in order to finish his project, to find a way to get his words to move my fingertips as I held his pen. Perhaps the effort had so affected me that his words came out of my mouth. It sounded much more like him than me.

"Excuse me, don't I know you?"

"I think I saw you at Leo's funeral," she said with an ingratiatingly sweet smile.

"No, no, I mean before that. You look very familiar to me. Let me see," Roth continued from my lips. "You're an actress, aren't you? Yes, that's it, I've seen you in a movie. Let's see, what was it? It wasn't *Gone with the Wind*—you're too young for that. What was it? Oh, yes, I remember now—*Southern Comforts!* That's it, yes— you played Harlot O'Scara. You were great. Talk about revisionist history! But that was nothing like *Box Lunch*. You really showed your stuff in that film."

The expression on her face, so heartbreakingly pained, made it terribly clear how sincerely regretful and profoundly repentant she was, how many times she must have prayed to a god of love to forgive her sins and trespasses, her follies and fornications, above all to pardon her for her part in the degradation of the beautiful body that housed the splendid soul of one of the Lord's precious creations—herself. She left the office without saying another word, and I was furious with Roth for having used me to tease her like that.

Mayavati

Mayavati was by his side when the janitor found him. She hissed at the secretary, Ms. Naper, whose idea it was that I, as Roth's literary executor, somehow had the responsibility of removing this feline object of the late professor's affections from Swinburne Hall. Satisfied that we would be able to coexist in my apartment in Santa Aghora, I transported her in a cardboard carton to my home. Upon being released, she scratched me on the neck like an impassioned girl in the *Kāmasūtra* and escaped out of an open window.

Three nights later, much to my surprise, she showed up in Swinburne Hall, where she found me working on Book Six of the *Kāmasūtra*. Again, to spare her the wrath of Ms. Naper, I took her home; again she fled and again found her way through many perilous miles of traffic from Santa Aghora to the university. There was no getting rid of her.

One afternoon in the department office I overheard Ms. Naper complaining to Professor Planter.

"He's come back to life. I know it. I can smell him in the halls. He's haunting Swinburne Hall. He's come back to prey on the women he never managed to get to while he was alive. Can't you smell him?"

"It's the cat," Professor Planter consoled her. "And it'll take a while for that inimitable Roth aroma, that discomforting combination of the essences of gin, tobacco, and cat shit, to dissipate."

He was staring at her a bit too intently for my comfort; his grin made me suspect that he may have been the culprit behind the prank that encouraged Ms. Naper to accuse Roth of posthumous sexual harassment. Two months after Roth's death, she claimed to have received a memo from the dead professor.

"I knew it. I could smell him. My nose never lies to me. He's here.

He sent me an obscene note. He calls me on the telephone at night and whispers things. Last night he told me that he . . . I can't even say it. But the gist of it was that he wants to do to me what he did to that Indian girl."

Planter advised his secretary not to tell too many people about it:

"It's not that I don't believe you, Ms. Naper, but that other people might think you're crazy."

Interpreting Planter's admonition as yet another of example of the expected instance of men protecting each other to preserve a phallocentric power differential within the university, Ms. Naper actually pressed charges, alleging that the dead man was continuing to create a "hostile environment for female staff and students." When she lost her case, she wrote a letter to a tabloid, recounting a harrowing tale that resulted in her being interviewed for a story: "COLLEGE SECRETARY SEXUALLY HARASSED BY PROFESSOR'S GHOST." Mayavati was featured in the article: "The mad professor, Dr. Leo Roth, Ph.D., an expert in Oriental sex cults and East Indian mysticism, lived as a hermit in his office with a mysterious black cat, the preferred pet of witches throughout the ages. The cat, under orders from the dead scholar, has attacked the department secretary on more than one occasion. The lecherous Prof was writing an Indian sex manual when he was murdered last year."

"The cat must go," Ms. Naper said yet again. "It's the law." The third time I took her home with me was the last. Not having seen her since, I cannot help but fear that she may be, in her effort to return to Roth's office, "yet another victim of love."

Professor Paul Planter

"There's no word for *love* in Japanese," Planter said to me. "If only Roth had studied Japanese instead of Sanskrit, a living language instead of a dead one, he'd still be alive today." I thought about it: yes, he would still be alive and finishing this book, completing his own translation of, and commentary on, a Japanese erotic text; if only his father had been cast as the Shogun rather than as the Moghul (and Sunita Sen might have been Sumiko Suehiro, and the pool house that was the setting for his first sexual experience would have been furnished with shoji screens and tatami mats); if only his second grade teacher had assigned him Japan for his school report (and Clover Weiner's parents would have sent postcards from Kyoto); if only Eve Christ would have sung the final aria from *Madame Butterfly* ("You,

O beloved idol!") in the nude; if only the teacher of his college anthropology class had done her research on the Ainu rather than on Indian tribals; if just that, and no more, he would, with his Ph.D. in Japanese, have been teaching Asian Studies 150A in spring of 1997, rather than 150B, and he would not have noticed the beautiful Indian girl in the corridors of Swinburne Hall looking for the instructor of the course on Indian civilization to ask him for permission to enroll in the class. He would be alive and I would be finished with my dissertation.

But, no, Planter taught 150A that spring. At the end of the semester he will be retiring as chairman of the department "because the job, after the Roth affair, has become such a pain in the ass. It was one thing trying to defend him while he was still alive, but now, even after we have him buried under six feet of ground, I'm still having to clean up the sexual garbage that he left behind. The new chair of the sexual harassment committee, White-Roth's token-male replacement, Dr. Don Dunn, keeps sending me memos, with copies to the president. In one of them, he wanted to know if Roth really did, in one of his classes one day (as if I should know), deem feminism 'that movement that gave rape a bad name,' and if he did, what did I assume was, or was not, my moral responsibility as chairman of the department? I get letters everyday about Roth because of that insane Naper article in that goofy paper. One came today from a psychic in Orlando, Florida, offering her services, for a nominal fee of a thousand dollars, to put an end to our departmental problems by contacting Roth. She explains that as he died unsatisfied in love, a female spirit traveler needs to visit him in an ethereal form to make nonphysical love with him in the realm of the hungry ghosts so that his restless, lovelorn soul may be put to rest. Roth, Roth, Roth. I can't take it any longer. I'm getting out of here. This June I'll be escorting a select group of advanced students to Japan for a special summer study abroad honors course on East Asian culture. We'll be meeting with language, literature, and history professors at Sophia University in Tokyo and sitting with Zen roshis at Shunga-Daiji in Kyoto. That should be fun, not to mention interesting. And then I'm going to take a long overdue sabbatical in the fall, during which I can begin research for an analytic study and translation of a Japanese erotic text, *Tales of a Pillow*."

Isaac Roth

Tajma Hall (aka Aphra Digby, Naomi Mihrof, Victoria Seaman, Leigh Larus, Candy Clitterson, Alana Agrona, Norma Zeale, etc.)

contacted me in hopes of convincing me to proof the diacritical marks in the manuscript of her new book, the *Ratisūtra* of Jayamangalā. For my labors I would receive a set of her complete works and one dollar per diacritical mark. Unaware that I knew it was a forgery, she was undoubtedly also testing the success of her deception on me. Sitting down, putting her feet up on the desk, and helping herself to one of my Viceroys, she handed the book to me. I flipped through the pages, stopping briefly at the illustrations of the sexual postures that women are advised to coerce men to adopt so that they, the dominant women, might be sufficiently gratified. I explained that I was really very busy both as Roth's literary executor and as a doctoral candidate with an unfinished dissertation: "No, I really don't have time to take on another project, no matter how small, no matter how important." Dostoevsky was staring at me from his place between her breasts on her sweatshirt. Averting my eyes from his, I looked back at the title page and could see five dollars worth of missing diacritical marks:

CARNAL MYSTERIES

AN ANCIENT INDIAN WOMAN'S TEACHINGS ON LOVE

being the
Ratisutra (The Scripture of Sexual Delight) of
SHRIMATI JAYAMANGALA

as translated and interpreted by
TAJMA HALL

with a foreword and annotations by
PROFESSOR MONTANA SMITH, PH.D.

and an afterword by
internationally renowned psychic
MAHARANI KALIDEVI

"No, I can't do it," I repeated as I thumbed ahead curiously to Books Five and Six, "The Joys of Gigolos" and "Other Women's Husbands." And I pretended to fall for it, to fool her into thinking she had fooled me:

"Although, I'm very interested in reading it, I just don't have time. I remember some sort of reference to Jayamangalā's work in Burton's letters and also mention of a commentary on a *Ratisūtra* in the *Catalogus Catalogorum*, but I assumed that the text had been lost. This is really an important contribution to scholarship." She seemed to believe that I believed that her text was real, or perhaps she fooled me into thinking that I had fooled her into thinking she had fooled me.

She lit another cigarette, which meant I had to let her stay in the office at least until she finished smoking it. Whisking an ash off Dostoevsky's brow with her fingertips, she dropped the subject of her Indological text to bring up her next project.

"I'm sorry you can't help me with the diacritics, but I want talk to you about something else anyway, my new book. It's a true crime book. It's about the Roth murder. Isaac has me convinced that it was a murder."

Assuring her that I agreed with Isaac, I asked how the young man was doing, how he was dealing with his father's death.

She used the butt of the cigarette she was smoking to light a fresh one.

"He started writing backwards again, right after the murder, just like he did for the first time after his sister died. I'm certain the retrography is simply an expression of a deep longing to reverse things in time and space. He felt guilty about the murder because he didn't get along with his father, particularly after the old man started having the affair with the Indian girl. I suppose he felt responsible for the death because, on some level, like all sons—so they say—he wished it. It's classical.

"Let me tell you about the last time they saw each other. Isaac and I bumped into the professor at the Stars of David Home while visiting Isaac's loony grandmother, and Roth started making sarcastic comments about my writing. Isaac, right in front of him, told me not to talk to him. 'All my father wants is a scandal. Why he wants it, only he can tell. He always has some motive.' And then he turned to his old man and shouted, 'That you should even utter a word to her is an outrage and I won't permit it!' He was breathless.

"'Isaac! Isaac!' cried Leopold hysterically, 'Is your father's love nothing to you?'

"'Shameless hypocrite!' exclaimed Isaac furiously.

"His father, turning to face the old Jews in wheelchairs who were watching the whole scene (and, as former actors, probably enjoying it), laughed painfully. 'He says that to his father! His father!' And then he turned back to Isaac and said, 'If you were not my son I would . . .' I didn't hear the end of the sentence because he lowered his voice to a terrifying whispered mumbling.

"Isaac called him both a 'depraved profligate' and a 'despicable clown' (and I wondered which of those two is worse) as he grabbed my hand to pull me to the lobby door. Right on the threshold he turned around. 'Why is such a man alive?' Isaac, beside himself with rage, growled in a hollow voice, hunching up his shoulders till he looked almost deformed. 'Tell me, how can he be allowed to go on defiling the earth?' He looked round at everyone and pointed at the old man.

"He turned and we went home. That was the last time he saw his father."[3]

She took her feet off the desk and leaned forward to take the Monier-Williams dictionary in her hands.

"*Death by the Book*," she smiled. "That's the title. *Death by the Book* by Matryosha Shigalov. Every book I write is in a new genre. But all of them are about love. This one too. Love is what makes a murder interesting. Love is what makes sex interesting. Love is what makes a book interesting. And death is what makes love profound."

Lee Siegel

After the fall, subsequent to substituting for Roth here, Siegel returned to his teaching post in the religion department at the University of Hawaii. He has agreed to read and comment on my dissertation before I submit it and, as an outside reader, to represent Roth on my committee. I've written to Siegel about this book as well. Given his familiarity with Roth, India, and the *Kāmasūtra*, I have hopes that he might help me finish this manuscript, something he resists on the grounds that work on this "frivolous" text would be a distraction from his more serious scholarly endeavors.

Sophia White-Roth

I found Sophia White-Roth by his grave. After reading the unfinished manuscript and having begun to edit it, I felt that I needed to visit Roth, that going to his grave site might somehow help me know what to do with difficult parts of his text, might inspire me and give me some feeling as to what he would have wanted from me as his executor, editor, and annotator.

---

3. The writer's account of the scene troubled me, not particularly because of the events or emotions it depicted, but because it all seemed so familiar to me, as if I had somehow been there and witnessed it. I couldn't get it out of my mind. Three days later I woke up in the middle of night and sat up with an idea, a hunch that needed to be confirmed before I could go back to sleep. Even though it was three in the morning, I dressed and went to Roth's office. I took down a book I had noticed when I was doing my inventory of his library, and I flipped through the beginning. There it was! I was right. I had read it during my senior year at St. Stephen's. There it was, beginning on page thirty-four, almost word for word, except that in the book Isaac's name is Dmitri and Leopold Roth's is Fyodor Karamazov.

She was wearing dark glasses and the Kleenex scrunched up in a trembling hand was evidence of weeping. After asking if I had been at his funeral and then listening to my commentary upon it, she confessed that she had wanted to attend.

"I just couldn't come. I thought the girl would be here. It's not that I'm angry at her. I assume that she didn't know what she was doing. But being here with her, I felt, would have made a further mockery of poor, dear, sad Leo. And I didn't want to see my mother-in-law and have to listen to her speak as if nothing has changed, as if we're all still happy, as if Leila is alive, as if God is in his Heaven (watching movies no less), and all's right with the world. I didn't want to listen Planter's inevitably insincere eulogy, nor hear people saying things about Leo that they did-n't mean. That always happens at funerals. People would have told me what a good man he was, as if we can't grieve for those who have done wrong. Leo did a lot that was wrong, but I still love him. I came here the day after the funeral, and the next day too. I've come several times. I miss him. I wouldn't want to be with him if he were still alive. I'd still divorce him, but I wish I could have the chance to say good-bye, to ex-plain to him why it's over, why it must end even though I still love him. So here I am again, but, well . . . I don't know. . . . " She turned away from me, and as I began haltingly to offer condolences, she turned back, stopped me, smiled kindly, and said good-bye.

I watched her walk across and up the gently sloping hill of graves to her daughter's resting place. Waiting for her, hidden behind a white wall with melancholy ivy draped over it, I made my move when it would seem coincidental for me to meet her again in the parking lot. She declined my awkward invitation to go for a drink, but rolled the car window down to talk to me and told me that her husband, despite his words and manner, had actually liked me, that he would be pleased that I had been appointed as his literary executor.

"He thought that you are a lot like he was twenty years ago. Are you like him?"

Pulling a Viceroy out of my pocket, I did my best imitation of him:

"The good thing about being dead is that no one tells you that smoking is bad for you; the bad thing is that there's nowhere to buy cigarettes."

It made her laugh. It sounded exactly like him. She removed her glasses and wiped her eyes. I had never really noticed how very beau-tiful Professor White-Roth is. The little silver medallion, Our Lady of the Sacred Heart, caught a beam of the sun and bounced it at my eyes. I didn't want her to leave. I lit the cigarette, blew a smoke ring, and hoped etiquette would require her to stay until I was finished smoking it. When she turned the key in the ignition it was, I confess, just a further attempt to keep her there that prompted me to speak of the book, this book, explaining to her that as her husband's commentary was an autobiographical one, she could no doubt help me with it, with this very page, if not the next one, or the next. I asked her to read this, but she was not interested.

"A character in a book shouldn't be reading it. Imagine Mrs. Moore reading *A Passage to India*." She laughed as she said it, released the emergency brake, and moved the gear shift into drive. "Don't believe anything you read in Leo's commentary. He became conscious of himself writing, and once that happens, truth is quite subservient to anything that makes a good story. Leo's utter disregard for truth was actually one of his charms. But he went too far. He allowed his life to become a story. I didn't lose Leo to a girl, you know—I lost him to a book. He had become the hero of a romance; unfortunately, however, he was a tragic lover misplaced in a lowbrow comedy. There are so many things that are excusable, and even admirable, in stories, that are inexcusable, and even detestable, in real life. Aesthetics and ethics are rarely compatible. I didn't refuse to love him. I simply refused to leave a real life behind to become a character in his book."

She drove away from the cemetery, and I went back to the office, pulled her book on Lee from the shelf, and began to read it. It took a while for me to summon the courage, if not the audacity, to telephone Professor White-Roth at home, to dial the number that I had dialed when I needed to ask something of my teacher. Although she seemed genuinely flattered by my praises of her work, she dismissed it with a "but that was a long time ago. I'm not very interested in Lee anymore."

She explained that she would be going away soon, that she had received a visiting fellowship at her old college in Oxford, Lady Margaret Hall, to work on her study of the politics of gynecology.

"My father lives in London," I announced, "and he goes to Oxford quite often. I wish you would ring him up. He's a psychotherapist. I sent him a copy of your book, and he was genuinely impressed by your sensitivity to psychoanalytic issues and methods. He would love to meet you. He told me that he hoped your paths would cross someday, that as he read your work, he sensed a kindred spirit." I was lying to her but, eager to turn the fiction into truth, I wrapped her book up and sent it to my father with a note: "She'll be living in Oxford, but she'll be going to London quite often. I wish you would ring her up. She's very interested, as you'll see from this book, in psychoanalysis. I gave her copies of some of your articles, and she was genuinely impressed by your sensitivity to nonpsychoanalytic issues. She would love to meet you. She told me that she hoped your paths would cross someday, that as she read your work, she sensed a kindred spirit." While that was yet another prevarication that I wanted to turn into truth, nothing could have been truer than my postscript: "She is, by the way, very beautiful."

I imagine their meeting: perhaps it's in Oxford for a drink at the Sea Gull and Child; he tells her about my mother and she tells him about my teacher. They leave the pub and go for a walk, slowly sauntering beyond the range of my imagination, but leaving an idea behind in my mind, a belief that there is a kind of love, unrepresented in this book and unimagined by Vātsyāyana or Roth, Yaśodhara or Pralayānanga, that is utterly calm and peaceful, so perfect that its nature demands that it be taken completely for granted, a sort of love that would be without interest or meaning in a book, but that would be completely fulfilling, meaningful, utterly beautiful in life. There is nothing to say about that sort of love.

Here End Books Five and Six of the *Kamasutra*.

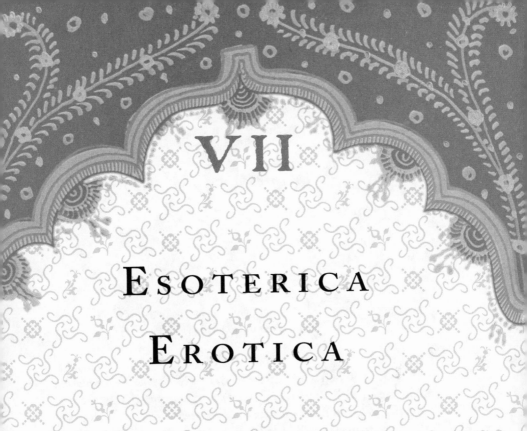

VII

ESOTERICA
EROTICA

Book Seven sums it all up, explains what love is, and why, and how. The book is definitive, says it all, explains Erotic Apotheosis and Amorous Assumption. It is my Passion Play.

—Leopold Roth, commentary on the *Kāmasūtra* I.A

A. Failure and Success

For better or worse, it is the commentator who has the last word.
   —Charles Kinbote, foreword to John Shade, "Pale Fire"

A. TRANSLATION

She who is sprinkled with powdered thorns of *Euphoria antiquorum (snuhī)* mixed with *Boerhavia procumbens (punarnavā)*, the faeces of *Presbytis entellus,* the excrescence of *Helix pseudoecstasis,* and roots of *Superba pruriens (lāngalikā* [or *Jussiaea repens* or *Uraria lagopodioides* or *Hemionitis cordifolialectoris*]) will not be able to love another *(kāmayeta).*

B. COMMENTARY

It doesn't mean anything. My biggest problems are lexicographical. My translation, following the definitions of the technical terms given in the Monier-Williams *Sanskrit-English Dictionary,* isn't really a translation at all: after reading it, I still don't know what to sprinkle on a girl to make her love me and unable to love another. My hope is that Siegel, given his familiarity with Sanskrit pharmacological liter-ature, will be able to get me out of this. He should complete the book. He should take some responsibility for it. I'll make that clear to him. I'll send the manuscript to him. And then I'll have a Bombay gin and tonic and smoke a Viceroy. I'm finished. I have no more to say.[1]

1. That's not quite true. There is one thing that, perhaps, I should mention. It hap-pened shortly after Roth had returned from India. His trials and tribulations had brought me closer to him. I seemed to be the only one who did not want to kill him. It was so in-nocent. I was in the supermarket, in the bread section, when I saw in my peripheral vision

someone standing near me, staring at me—an Indian girl in a salwar-kameez. I noticed the leather sandals, silver anklets and toe rings first, then the bracelets and necklace, and then the nose ring, bindi, and smile.

"Oh hello, Mr., ah, ah, Mr. . . . ."

"Saighal," I said, smiling carelessly, letting my eyes drift back to the bread on the shelf.

"Remember me?" she asked. "Lalita Gupta."

"Oh sure," I answered with feigned nonchalance. "You were a student in Professor Planter's 150A class."

"No, no, Professor Roth's 150B, India. You were the T.A."

"Of course, India."

An hour later we were having coffee near the campus, talking about India. An hour after that we were in my apartment, talking about the *Kāmasūtra*.

"You're the first Indian I've ever kissed," she said, an hour after that. "I mean really kissed, in a sexy way," and she laughed. "It's funny, isn't it? I'm an Indian. I've been raised on Indian food, and yet I've never, never until just now, kissed an Indian."

"I'm not an Indian, Ms. Gupta," I answered. "Not really. I'm an American born in Indianapolis, Indiana. That my father was born in India and that I was sent to school there doesn't change that. But, in any case, I'm not typical of anything, Indian or American, except myself. And, in fact, I myself have never had an Indian lover."

After another hour there were no fixed centers, no edges, no boundaries between India and America, between Lalita and myself: all lines vanished into an erotic landscape of unmapped mazes in which we explored the possibilities that love provides to lovers.

And later we ate dinner at the Taj Mahal Restaurant, and she told me all about her trip to India.

"It was kind of weird being with Professor Roth. I mean he's pretty old and he's married. But once you get to know him, he's actually kind of sweet. There's something sad about him, something that made me want to be kind to him. I'm grateful to him. But he doesn't want to let go. He wants me to keep meeting with him, in secret, at a motel up on Sunset. I don't know what to do about it. If it weren't for him, I wouldn't have gone to India and that trip changed my life. At first the thought of kissing him, let alone of letting him make love to me, was disgusting. It would have been like making love to my father. But then, he was so sad that he stopped seeming like a father. The funny thing was that soon I started to feel like I was his mother; he seemed to need a woman to give him the kind of reassurance that only a mother gives you. Then it felt okay to hold him in my arms, to try to calm him down, to comfort him. Does that sound crazy, or do you understand?"

"My mother died when I was eight years old," I answered, and she reached across the table to put her hand upon my arm and caress it comfortingly.

At midnight she was sleeping in my arms, and I was staring up at the ceiling, feeling that I was cuckolding Roth, the adulterer. In the normative legal texts of India, the crime of intercourse with the teacher's beloved is one of the most egregious, comparable to brahminicide. As a punishment for that violation, the perpetrator of it was made to cut off his own genitals and then parade around the town holding the organ of betrayal openly in his hands until he finally dropped dead from loss of blood, public derision, and personal shame. I felt like the student who betrayed the teacher Auddālaki:

Auddālaki had been seduced by a girl whom he tutored named Vijayā. He fell in love with her, becoming so enamored of her that he surrendered to her supplications and broke his vow of chastity. He sold his cattle to buy for her a marvelous gift—a beautiful polished mirror, silver on the face and pure gold on the back. When the old sage had been chaste, before he had come under the sway of love, he had a dignity that he now lacked. And so the girl, tiring of her teacher, was easily seduced by a younger man, another of Auddālaki's students. And she so loved him that she gave the gold and silver mirror to him, without telling him from whom she had obtained it. And the young man felt so remorseful that he was betraying his teacher that he went to Auddālaki, bowed before him, and touched his feet in repentance.

"Venerable teacher," the young man said with reverence, "I must renounce this student life and take to the road. I beg for your permission to take the path of a renouncer." He did not tell his teacher the reason for his decision as he wanted to protect him from the pain of knowing of his beloved's infidelity.

Auddālaki granted the request and wished his student well. And in gratitude the student gave Auddālaki a gift—the gold and silver mirror.

"My son," the stunned teacher said as he gazed into the mirror, "you have given me the most precious gift in the world. You have given me a vision of the truth about women and men, about love and about myself. I have seen the truth in that mirror. The mirror is bright but the truth within it is dark."

Auddālaki renounced the world, left the ashram on foot, and disappeared forever; in their shame, the boy and girl students did not speak to each other again: she became a courtesan in Varanasi, and he, after a period of renunciation, became a scholar and wrote a commentary on the *Bhagavadgītā*.

When Lalita woke up in the morning, I told her that I didn't think we could continue what we were too impetuously beginning. She dressed without answering. I repeated it.

"Why?" she asked with a smile.

"Because I might start to fall in love with You."

Without saying a word, she kissed me gently on the lips, smiled, picked up her school bag, and left.

I restrained my impulse to stop her.

We ran into each other several times, spoke on the telephone twice, and I saw her at the December graduation ceremony, but neither of us ever mentioned to the other or to anyone else what had transpired between us.

Silence has a way of making it seem as though things that have happened have not.

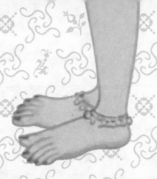

B. Secrets and Solutions

Even if this makes no sense, I will publish it all the same. I know perhaps that I will not be bothered legally, at least to any great extent: I alone am informing on myself and have no accusers; moreover, there is no, or extraordinarily little, evidence.

—Nikolay Stavrogin, "Confession"

A. TRANSLATION [AND/OR]
B. COMMENTARY

Editor's Note

I had hoped that my former tutor and Roth's rival, Lee Siegel, would help me finish this book despite his mixed feelings about working on the text. When I received the following letter, I was grateful that he had complied, but I was startled by the ending that he had in store for me and, indeed, for all of us.

University of Hawaii at Manoa

Department of Religion
Sakamaki Hall • Room A311
2530 Dole Street • Honolulu, Hawaii 96822
Telephone: (808) 948-8299 • Cable Address: UNIHAW

April 12, 1998

Anang Saighal
1900 West Eastern Drive
Santa Aghora, CA 90277

My dear Anang:

I can appreciate your interest in the *Kamasutra*, but not your concern with Roth's perversion of that text. While I might concede that it is perhaps unfortunate that scholars lack substantial biographical information on Vatsyayana Mallanaga, I think it would be just as well if we are spared this incriminating evidence of the existence of Leopold Roth. Let him enjoy the very anonymity that has protected Vatsyayana from castigation. Roth's so-called "commentary" is no more than the intellectual jetsam of a troubled mind and the emotional flotsam of a wrecked heart. His gloss is as unfaithful to life as his translation is to text. I would never permit my name to be associated with a book such as this.

I have no interest in finishing the translation. None at all. I have other things to do, other projects to which I must direct my energies at this time. I must inform you that, before his death, Roth was continuously pestering me and making unreasonable demands upon me. He was taking up all of my time with his problems and obsessions. Even my friends and family were being bothered by him. He was, furthermore, stealing all of my ideas and trying to commandeer my life. He was driving me crazy. I did not want to have anything more to do with him. I'm sure you'll understand, therefore, when I tell you that it was inevitable and obvious. At some point I had to do it. Yes, of course, I did it: I killed Leopold Roth.

Yours very truly,

Lee Siegel

AN EQUAL OPPORTUNITY EMPLOYER

Here Ends the *Kamasutra*.

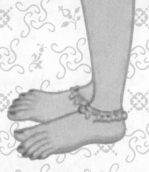

Bibliography

Everything about erotica is invariably disguised behind false authors, publishers, dates, and places of publication. Nothing is what it seems, and it is this more than anything else that is the fascination of the subject for its bibliographers.

—Patrick Kearney, *A History of Erotic Literature*

Agrona, Alana. *Roses Are Red, Violets Are Blue: Gardening for Lovers.* Pinsk, Ohio: Green Thumb Books, 1987.

Arnor, Romulus, trans. *Komožutra.* Zembulna: R. R. Rujŋo, 1945.

———. *Miragarlen.* Zembulna: R. R. Rujŋo, 1937.

———. *Monuments to Love.* Translated by Charles Kinbote. New Wye: Wordsmith College Press, 1962.

Awrangābādī, Shāhnavāz Khus Emak Khān, *The Maāthir-ul-Umarā: Being Biographies of Drunken and Depraved Mohammadan and Hindoo Courtiers Enjoying the Patronage of the Timurid Sovereigns of India.* Translated by Alastair Monier-Pitzwilly. Baghdad: Hussein Brothers, 1926.

Bahadur, Vikram. "The Oriental Mirror: Cinematic Conceptional Constructions of India in the American Cinema from *The Merry Magician of Mahatma Land* (1912) to *City of Joy* (1992)." Master's thesis, University of California at Los Angeles, 1993.

Baker, Frank [Richard Burton]. *Stone Talk, being Some of the Marvellous Sayings of One Doctor Polyglott, Ph.D.* London: Portman, 1865.

Bannerji, M. T. Clef® Notes and Study Guide to *Tristram Shandy.* Leesville, Ind.: Clef® Notes, 1992.

Bhagavadgītā. Translated by Annie Besant. Hollywood: Vedanta Press, 1949.

Blue Yajur Veda: Secret Teachings of the School of Auddalaki. Edited and translated by Rudy Kamadinata. Krishnapur, Iowa: Veda Press, 1977.

Bobo, Sensai. *Chin-chin Monogatori.* Translated by Paul [and Pimiko] Planter. Honolulu: University of Hawaii Press, 1989.

Bonellia, Bernice. "Book Burning as Hermeneutics." *International Journal of Comparative Pataphysics* 18: 198–221.

Botticelli, Bob B. *Puzzles, Puzzles, Puzzles! Let's Have Some Fun with Puzzles!* Indianapolis: Romulus and Rowley, 1979.

Burton, Isabel. *Life of Captain Sir Richard Burton.* 2 vols. London: Whitesmith, 1893.

Burton, Richard, and F. F. Arbuthnot, trans. *Ananga Ranga, or The Hindu Art of Love (Ars Amoris Indica).* Cosmopoli: The Kama Shastra Society of London and Benares, 1885.

————. *The Kama Sutra of Vatsyayana.* Cosmopoli: The Kama Shastra Society of London and Benares, 1883.

Chagale, Léon, ed. *Delibes, l'homme, sa vie, ses amours, ses maladies, et son oeuvre operatique.* Petoville-sur-Mer: Mutterer et Fils, 1918.

Chatterton, Thomas. *Works, Letters, and Marginalia.* Edited by Richard Rowley. Roughwater: University of Northern South Dakota Press, 1982.

Christ, Jesus H. *The Maranatha Evangelical Handbook of the Lord's Own Words for Idolaters, Animists, and Infidels.* Edited by Bob H. Boswell. Hollywood: Maranatha Good News Press, 1995.

Cigale, Louis. *Les problèmes théoriques de la traduction de la littérature erotique.* 4 vols. Paris: Asselin and Clouzot, 1945. Translated by Albert Bird as *Changes of Heart: On the Erotics of Translation.* Honolulu: University of Hawaii Press, 1993.

Clitterson, Candy. *Confessions of a Cockeyed Coed.* Baltimore: Cocktail Press, 1988.

Complaints and Romances: Recollections of the Reign of Charles II. Oxford: Bodleian Library Archives, Edwardes Collection, MS.118a, n.d.

Cross, Christopher. "Mutiple Orgasm in Hermaphroditic Gastropods." *Archives of Sexual Behavior* 62: 270–92.

————. "Rotherase: A Functional Analysis." *International Journal of Comparative Malacology* 1 (1998): 14–73.

Cross, Rose. "The Politics of Orgasm." *Archives of Sexual Behavior* 2 (1969): 18–24.

Daniélou, Alain. *Kama Sutra: Le brévaire de l'amour traité d'érotism de Vatsyayana.* Paris: Éditions Du Rocher, 1992.

Delibes, Léo. *Lakmé.* Paris: Son et Lumière Frère et Fils, 1898.

————. *Journal Intime.* Paris: Glandons, 1884.

Digby, Aphra. *The Latin Lover.* Las Vegas: University of Las Vegas Press, 1997.

Dostoevsky, Fyodor. *Polnoe sobranie khudozhestvennykh proizvedenii.* Moscow-Leningrad: Gosudarstvennoe Izdatelstvo, 1927.

Draper, Darlene. *The Girl Who Charmed Serpents.* Blackpool: Children's Library, 1951.

Draper, Edward, ed. *Collection of Poetical and Dramatick Miscellany by the Inmates of an Asylum.* London: Bethlehem Royal Hospital Archives [1799].

DuLaure, Jacques-Antoine. *Des divinités dévoyés, ou du culte du fellation chez les Indiens.* Pondicherry: Pipe et Glandon, 1805.

Dyer, Reginald. *General Guide to India.* Amritsar: Golden Guides, 1995.

Dziech, B., and L. Weiner. *The Lecherous Professor.* Boston: Beacon Press, 1984.

Eberhardt, Isabelle. *Ivre au pays des sables, précédé des infortunes d'une errante.* Paris: Sorlot, 1944.

Flournoy, Thérèse. *Des Indes à la planète Mars.* Geneva: Slatkine, 1900.

Forster, E. M. *A Passage to India.* Revised Indian edition translated by G. G. Godbole. Chandrapore: Colonial Steam Press, 1955.

Fraxus, Pisani, Jr. *Index Sanskritorum Librorum Prohibitorum.* London: privately printed, 1878.

Gandhi, Mohandas. *To the Women.* Karachi: India House, 1943.

Guinness Book of World Records. Revised Indian edition. Edited and adapted by Pandit Arun Patel and Dr. G. G. Rajagapalachariaswami. Nagpur: Guinness Ashram, 1998.

Gupta, Lalita. "The Mountain of Ecstacy [*sic*], the Ocean of Bliss." Term paper, Western University, 1997.

Gupta, Nilkanth. "Clitorectomy and Infibulation Reconsidered from an Asian Perspective." *Journal of Geriatric Gynecology* 56: 177–86.

Hall, Tajma, trans. *Carnal Mysteries: The Ratisutra of Jayamangala.* Orlando, Florida: Venus House, forthcoming.

Hari, Pandurang. *Sanskrit-English Dictionary for Foreigners.* Varanasi: Moti Mahal, 1921.

Hartman, Hedda. "Hartman's Hollywood." *Los Angeles Herald-Examiner,* 21 July 1955.

———. "Death of the Party." *Confidential Magazine,* December 1955, 18–20.

Hasyalapa Brahmana of the Red Yajur Veda. Edited by M. T. Bannerji and Pandit Rahul Pardesh. Srilalitadevi Vihara Sanskrit Series, vol. 18. Patna: Oriental Publications, 1903.

Hiranyadarpana Upanisad. Edited and translated by Paul Kamadinata. Krishnapur, Iowa: Veda Press, 1976.

Indraji, Bhagavanlal. *Vidūsakamāla.* Varanasi: Baba Tandai, 1918.

Kalidevi Ma. *Mind Reading, Palm Reading, Chart Reading: Ancient Indian Lessons for Modern Western Students.* Krishnapur, Iowa: Veda Press, 1995.

———. *Lila: Sex Games from India for Adventurous American Lovers.* Orlando: Kalidevi Press, 1997.

Kamastotra of the Blue Yajur Veda. Edited and translated by Susan Kamadinata. Krishnapur, Iowa: Veda Press, 1978.

Karamazov, Karen K. "Reflections on an Archeology of Love." *Austro-American Journal of Hyponomic Anthropology* 41 (1969): 598–607.

Kipling, Rudyard. *The Jungle Book.* Revised Indian edition by G. G. Godbole. Seeonee: Colonial Electric Press, 1952.

Lamairesse, Edouard, trans. *Le Kama Sutra: Un manuel Indien de civilité pour les petites filles à l'usage des maisons d'éducation adapté pour les femmes occidentales.* Paris: Presse Praline, 1881.

Larus, Leigh. *Fires of Love.* Savannah: Harlequin Books, 1988.

Lee, Nathaniel. *Collected Works,* 4 vols. Edited by Randolphe Rehatsek. London: Bethlehem Hospital Press, 1908.

———. *Mogol Chah Jehan of Hindoustan, or The Triumph of Love, a Tragedy.* Fragments. Lee papers, 1326c–e. Prudential Hospital for the Mentally Ill, Patient's Library, East Reading.

Lovelace, Leroy. Interview. *Cocktail,* May 1998, 18, 42–43.

Lovely, Sir Thomas. *An Oriental Passage, being the Authentic Account of the Conquest of the East Indies, with Divers Papers relating to the Antiquities, Topographies, Habits and Statistics of the Land; and Account of Countries Round the Deccan with a Discursus on the Character of the Great Mogul and Medical Notes on Oriental Infirmities of the Brain.* Orlando: Ponce de Leon Society, 1923.

———. *Usus Sordidus Loquendi Universalis.* London: 1701.

———. "Meditation on a Noodle, or A Sodden Elegie on an Emptie Grave for Nat. Lee, Esq., Hand-Dug by Your Author in Suratt" (1692). Lee Papers, MS Eng. hist b 199; c 295-6. Bodleian Library.

McCarthy, Mary. "Vladimir Nabokov's *Pale Fire.*" *Encounter* 19 (October 1962): 76.

Merkin, Martin M. "Body Hair in Sanskrit Literature and Hindu Religious Practice." *Pilosophy East and West* 18 (1959): 131–41.

Meyer, Johann Jakob. *Sexual Life in Ancient India.* London: Routeledge & Kegan Paul, 1930.

Monier-Williams, Monier. *Sanskrit-English Dictionary.* 1899. Reprint, Oxford: Oxford University Press, 1945.

———. "Report on the Osculatory Customs of the Natives of the Sundry Lands under Jurisdiction and Protection of the Empire." *Journal of the Anthropological Society of London* 18 (January 1885): 42–68.

Muni, Mattamanu. *The Power of Gold: Hiranyashakti.* Translated by Bobby LaFang. Reno: Powerhouse Books, 1968.

Nash, Noreen. *By Love Fulfilled.* New York: Warner Books, 1982.

Nashe, Norman. "American Women behind Foreign Bars." *People* (7 January 1997): 18–27.

Newhouse, Jock, with Venus Doudounes. *Memoirs of the Vagabond of Love.* Vol. 1, *The Silent Years.* Hollywood, California: La Brea Press, 1997.

Pacific Bell. Los Angeles telephone directory. Los Angeles, 1997.

Pai, Anant, ed. *Nala Damayanti.* Amar-Chitra-Katha 16. New Delhi: India Book House Education Trust, 1979.

Planter, Paul. "On the Biochemistry of *Mono No Aware.*" In *Love, Sex, and Religion in Japanese Culture,* edited by Noriko Kamachi. Tokyo: Sankibo, 1984.

Prakash, Jaidev. "Raising a Hindu Child in Judeo-Christian America." *Indian American Mirror,* July 1997: 28–37.

Pralayānanga Līlārāja. *Kāmaśleṣakāvya.* Edited by Edward Rehatsek and M. A. Mohantee. Puri, Orissa: Jagannath Tukuri Printers, 1912.

Proffer, Carl R. *Keys to Nabokov's Lolita.* Bloomington: Indiana University Press, 1968.

Roth, Isaac. *Mirror Retro.* With a foreword by Naomi Mihrof. Los Angeles: Occidental Press, 1997.

Roth, Leopold. "'Fuck' in Sanskrit?" *International Journal of Illicit, Deviant, and Subversive Language* 12 (1976): 47–73.

———. "*Oflyricheros:* Anagramic Charades and Other Amphibological Verbal Constructions in Sanskrit Literature." Ph.D. diss., Faculty of Oriental Studies, Oxford University, 1976.

———. Review of *Les problèmes théoriques de la traduction de la littérature erotique,* by Louis Cigale. *Journal des traducteurs/Translators' Journal* 9 (1994): 39–47.

———. Review of *Net of Magic: Wonder and Deception in India,* by Lee Siegel. *South American Journal of East Indian Studies.* 18 (1992): 67–69.

Roth, Rudolf. "*Eine Grammatik der Liebe und der Sexualität.*" *Zeitschrift der Deutschen Morgenländischen Gesellschaft* 18 (1879): 147–83.

Roth, Rudolf, and Otto Böhtlingk. *Sanskrit-Wörterbuch.* St. Petersburg: Academy of Arts and Sciences, 1875.

Said, Edward. *Orientalism.* New York: Random House, 1979.

Saighal, Anang. "Love as Game in the Works of Kālidāsa." Master's thesis, University of Hawaii, 1993.

Saighal, Kashinath. *Tṛstramśandīcaritam.* MS. no. 719. Anup Sanskrit Library, Lalgarh Palace, Bikaner, India. n.d.

Saighal, Ramanath. "Frigidity, Dyspareunia, and Pseudovaginismus in a Panjabi Community in Reading." *London Journal of Psychosomatic Medicine* 64 (1989): 873–74.

———. "Impotence and Satyriasis in a Panjabi Community in Reading." *London Journal of Psychosomatic Medicine* 62 (1988): 423–94.

Schmidt, Richard. *Beiträge zur Indischen Erotik.* Leipzig: Hayn und Seifert, 1902.

———, trans. *Das Kamasutram.* Leipzig: Hayn, Seifert, und Spiegel, 1908.

Schnupperputzi, Hans-Ulrich von. *Beiträge zur Aetiologie der Indischen Psychopathia Sexualis.* Dresden: Schnipplehaus, 1902.

Segalenoff, Victor. "*Entretien avec Fritz Jahn.*" *Cahiers du Cinéma* 18 (1951): 18–20.

Sellon, Edward. *Dolly, or The Trials and Tribulations of a White Slave Girl.* London: privately printed, n.d.

———. *The New Ladies' Tickler, or The Adventures of Sahib Lovesport and the Audacious Baboo.* Oxford: privately printed, 1866.

———. *The Oriental Epicurean, or The Delights of Hindoo Sex, Facetiously and Philosophically Considered, in Graphic Letters Addressed to Young Ladies of Quality.* London: Golden Cockerel, 1865.

———. *The Ups and Downs of Life: A Discursus on Man and Woman, Lingam and Yoni, Old and Young, White and Black, West and East, for Better or for Worse, &c. and &c.* Bombay: Viceroyalty Night Press, 1865.

Shade, John. "Pale Fire." Edited by Charles Kinbote. New Wye: Wordsmith College Press, 1966.

Shah, K., J. Shaw, L. Singer, and J. Singh. "Physiological Process and Anatomical Structure in a Polyptychic Bulbocloacal Metapodial Peptoraptoral Gland of *Helix pseudoecstasis.*" *International Journal of Comparative Malacology* 18 (1980): 143–45.

Shaw, John. Review of *Kama Sutra*, by Mira Nair. *Artesia Arts Weekly*, 12 April 1997, 18.

———. Review of *The Nutty Professor*, starring Eddie Murphy. *Artesia Arts Weekly*, 19 April 1997, 18.

Siegel, Lee. *City of Dreadful Night.* Chicago: University of Chicago Press, 1995.

———. *Laughing Matters: Comic Tradition in India.* Chicago: University of Chicago Press, 1993.

———. *Net of Magic: Wonder and Deception in India.* Chicago: University of Chicago Press, 1993.

———. *Sacred and Profane Love in India.* Ph.D. diss., Faculty of Oriental Studies, Oxford University, 1976.

Siegel, Robert J. *Intravascular Ultrasound Imaging in Erectile Dysfunction: A Comprehensive Assessment of Pudendal Artery Pathoanatomy.* Basel: Marcel Dekker, 1996.

Śrī-Lalitā-Sahasranāma. Edited and translated by Eugene Kamadinata. Krishnapur, Iowa: Veda Press, 1978.

Stavrogin, Nikolay. "Confession." *Russky Vestnik*, 28 November 1883.

Sterne, Laurence. *The Life and Opinions of Tristram Shandy, Gent.* 1760. Reprint, New York: W. W. Norton, 1980.

———. *Journal to Eliza.* London: Child and Rivers, 1921.

Swinburne, Algernon Charles. *The Yogee's Pleasure.* London: privately printed, 1888.

Ustad Isa. *Memoires d'un vagabond d'amour.* French translation from the Persian by Fr. Jacques Noumaison. 12 vols. Paris: Société Asiatique, 1879–91.

Vance, E. B., and N. N. Wagner. "Written Descriptions of Orgasm: A Study of Sex Differences." *Archives of Sexual Behavior* 5 (1976): 87–98.

Vātsyāyana Mallanāga. *Kāmasūtra.* With commentaries of Pralayānanga, Yaśodhara, and Narsingh Śāstrī. Edited by Bhagavanlal Indraji, Rahul Pardesh, and Hari Pandurang. Varanasi: Yelchiko Press, 1900.

Wackernagel, Jakob. *Altindische Grammatik mit Einschluss der Gesamten Indischen Erotischen Literatur.* Göttingen: Georg Müller und Friedhelm Seifert, 1896.

White, Francis. *The Indian Adventures of Brigade-Major Francis White of the Bengal Lancers in the Service of His Empire & Himself.* Cosmopoli: Corinthian Club of Calcutta, the Crimea, Paris, Oxford, and the Sandwich Isles, 1900.

White-Roth, Sophia. "Does Everybody Love a Lover?: A Dean's Inquiry into a Case of Sexual Harassment." In *Ivory Power: Sexual Harassment on Campus,* edited by M. A. Paludi. Albany: SUNY Press, 1990.

———. *Love and Madness in the Life and Plays of Nathaniel Lee: A Psychoanalytic Approach to Literary Criticism.* Leesville: University of Western Indiana Press, 1980.

Yellow Yajur Veda of the Latter Day Rishis. Edited and translated by Clover Kamadinata. Krishnapur, Iowa: Veda Press, 1978.

Yogananda, Paramahansa. *Confessions of a Yogi.* Hollywood: Vedanta Press, 1937.

Zeale, Norma. *The Power of Passionate Thinking.* Reno: Powerhouse Press, 1990.

Zernovoŋ, Remus Radomir. *Zemblan-English Dictionary.* Bokay: Queen Blenda Press, 1908.

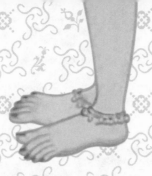

Index

Love, 18, 27–45, 322–56; and death, 25, 38–39, 63, 120–21, 178, 196–97, 240, 244–45, 298–302, 309, 329, 351–52; and exoticism, 117, 236–43; Lee on, 2, 18–19, 126–37, 317–29; literary theme of, 1, 6–9, 18, 137–39, 241–45, 33; and madness, 18, 111, 222, 333; redemption through, 14–18, 22–34, 116–18, 225–34, 300–301; sexual nature of, 18, 34, 44, 103–17, 289n, writing as act of, 2–4, 16, 18, 39, 115–17, 206–24, 289–90, 330–46. *See also* abreaction; eroticism; fantasy; fetish; fixation; imagination; narcissism; obsession; perversion; sexuality; symbolism.

—Sophia White-Roth, index entry for *Love and Madness in the Life and Plays of Nathaniel Lee*